MIND'S EYE

Douglas E. Richards

Paragon Press

Copyright © 2013 by Douglas E. Richards
Published by Paragon Press, 2014
ParagonPressSF@gmail.com
E-mail the author at doug@san.rr.com
Friend him on Facebook at Douglas E. Richards Author, or visit his website at www.douglaserichards.com

First Edition

ALSO BY DOUGLAS E RICHARDS

WIRED

AMPED (The *WIRED* Sequel)

THE CURE

Middle Grade/YA (Enjoyed by kids and adults alike, ages 9 to 99)

The Prometheus Project: Trapped (Book 1)

The Prometheus Project: Captured (Book 2)

The Prometheus Project: Stranded (Book 3)

The Devil's Sword

Ethan Pritcher, Body Switcher

Out of This World

To my daughter, Regan, the first to read my every novel. Thanks for your enthusiasm and sharp eye. You are an extraordinary young woman: bright, funny, determined, and endearing. The joy you have brought this proud father over the past seventeen years is truly immeasurable.

PART ONE

"The paradox of reality is that no image is as compelling as the one which exists only in the mind's eye."

—Shana Alexander

1

The stench was so utterly horrid that it seemed to be attacking him. It was the putrid stink of rot and of food gone bad. It was an unholy soup of dozens of odors that each would have been bad enough alone, but which seemed to clash in revolting and impossible ways when forced together.

Panic squeezed his heart to near bursting as he realized he was *drowning* in this noxious cloud. He fought desperately to take a breath, but this act was somehow impossible. It was as though he had forgotten how, as if the mental wiring that triggered his breathing response had been neatly snipped. His burning lungs screamed at him for air, and he knew he had but seconds to live.

Suddenly, from the depths of his panic, an epiphany burst forth. He wasn't drowning. Instead, he was in the middle of a terrible nightmare, and his breathing reflex was only failing in the vivid dream world his mind had constructed. His physical body was asleep and paralyzed.

He threw all of his will into tearing off the crushingly heavy cloak of unconsciousness, and an instant later his full mind exploded to the surface, like a swimmer held down too long in the depths of a cold and murky ocean, and escaping just in time.

Now fully conscious, albeit groggy, he felt the weight of eyelids that were shuttering his vision. He heard whispers in his mind; dozens of them. He could catch words and phrases; images. A kaleidoscope of activity just below the surface, blending together into a white noise; incessant chatter from hundreds of non-stop talkers all speaking at once. He shook his head to try to stop the maddening whispers in his mind, but without success.

He anxiously opened his eyes.

And was greeted by an absolute, impenetrable darkness.

Fighting off the panic that now returned with a vengeance, he carefully extended his right arm and was rewarded when his hand made contact with a smooth surface that felt like steel. He continued to probe his surroundings, and seconds later, his hand came into contact with yet another surface over his head. A roof. One made of steel, like the wall he had found.

The roof was heavy, but by raising both hands above his shoulders, he was able to push it upward, flooding his prison with blinding light. He continued pushing until he hit a literal tipping point, and the roof fell downward as if on a hinge, slamming into the side of the metal container noisily.

Even before his eyes fully adjusted to the light, he could see he was in a living sea of garbage that filled about half of the large container, which was painted a familiar shade of green.

He was inside a dumpster.

The sight of the nasty garbage along with the smell forced him to do what his unconscious body had managed to avoid until this point: he leaned over and vomited, although his stomach must have been nearly empty, because it was more of a dry heave than anything else.

He peeked his head over the top of the industrial-sized container, his eyes now fully adjusted to the light. He was in the back of what appeared to be a strip mall, and judging from the garbage he had been sitting in, one whose retail tenants included grocery stores, butcher shops, restaurants, and most unholy of all, diaper-changing stations.

He climbed out of the container and inspected himself. He had sneakers on his feet and was wearing a black T-shirt and faded jeans. He was painted head to toe with stains and fluids of unknown kinds, including one that may well have been blood.

What had he been doing in a dumpster? He searched his memory. And found nothing.

How drunk did one have to be to not remember spending a night in a garbage-filled coffin?

He gasped as a deeper truth penetrated his mind: he couldn't remember *anything*. Not only didn't he know how he had come to be in a dumpster, he didn't know how he had come to be on this *earth*.

He strained to at least remember his own name, but it wouldn't come.

He checked his pockets but found no wallet or other identification. What was going on?

His heart rate leaped to well over a hundred beats per minute and he felt dizzy from the shock and adrenaline rush. He had to calm down. He had to *think*.

But he found it hard to concentrate. The whispers and images in his mind continued unabated, and he couldn't imagine anything being more disconcerting or inimical to organized thought. He couldn't seem to get them to stop, although he was at least able to suppress them somewhat, willing them into a deeper and less obtrusive place in his consciousness. Still, he wondered how much more of this he could take and retain his sanity.

Or was he insane already?

No. It couldn't be. He *felt* totally rational. And totally sane.

He laughed out loud. *Sure*, he thought. *I'm as sane and rational as any other guy without a memory who wakes up in a dumpster and hears voices in his head.*

Off in the distance, across a field of dirt and scrub, he spotted a Shell gas station. It was far more isolated than his current location, and he was sure to find a bathroom there he could use to clean himself up, something he desperately needed to do. He couldn't take his own pungent stench much longer.

He had walked toward the station for about five minutes when he came to a narrow side-street, and waited for a lone car to go by, its windows open and music blaring.

He recognized the song immediately. It figured. He had instant recall of the lyrics to a random song, but didn't have the faintest idea of where he lived, or who he was.

The driver was a kid of seventeen or eighteen. "Wow, what's with this guy?" he heard the driver say clearly as the car passed him. "Ever hear of something called a *shower*?" the teen added, and then the tone of his voice changed, now conveying discomfort and confusion. "Is that *blood* on his neck?"

But the man without a past knew that he couldn't have heard this. He had been looking at the driver at the time—*and the teen's lips hadn't moved.* Besides, the car radio was putting out far too many decibels for him to have heard the words as clearly as he did.

What he *thought* he had heard was just another voice among the many in his head. He shook his head vigorously, like a dog after a bath, but the voices remained.

He arrived at the Shell only minutes later, entered the men's room, a small, one-man facility behind the main station, and locked the door carefully behind him.

He looked into the small mirror but didn't recognize the face that stared back at him. But he did recognize one thing immediately. He had a trail of caked blood on his neck, running down from his hairline, and more dried blood on his head.

His eyes widened as he recalled the words of the teen driver of the car that had passed. The words he had hallucinated. The kid had said he had blood on his neck. Pretty accurate for a hallucination. He felt around his scalp and found a tender spot that his fingers sensed as being dried blood and a newly forming scab, and then quickly removed his hand so he wouldn't inadvertently reopen it.

He stared back into the mirror and continued his self-assessment. He was clean-cut, with a head of jet black hair, brushed back, and a day or two's growth of stubble. His teeth were perfectly straight, although he had the feeling that several years of braces sponsored by loving parents whom he could not remember had played a big role in this perfection. He wasn't classically handsome, but he suspected his face was symmetrical and rugged enough to attract women. He guessed that he was just under six feet in height.

He removed the horrid shirt he was wearing, wet in many places where it had sopped up stains and distilled odor, and dropped it in a small trash container in the corner. His body was lean and well-muscled, his chest hairless.

He stared at himself for several long seconds, willing his memory to come back. But it would not.

Luckily, the bathroom had plenty of liquid soap and paper towels, and he scrubbed every last inch of his face, neck, and torso, and washed grime and blood from his hair, remembering to be exceedingly gentle near his wound. He shoved his head as near the small faucet as he could and splashed water on his hair until it was clear of soap. He then dropped his jeans and scrubbed his legs. While he could exit the bathroom without a shirt, he knew he needed to put his pants back on, which he did with great reluctance.

An image separated itself from the multitude of whispers and scenes buzzing around in his brain. He jerked his head around as the image pierced the dense thicket of internal chatter and stabbed at his consciousness. It was a view of the door to the bathroom he was now in. But a view from *outside* of the bathroom.

He focused on this now-isolated thread, not knowing why his subconscious had decided this particular hallucination was in such urgent need of attention. The bathroom door was being viewed through the windshield of a car that had just pulled into the Shell lot. He saw a finger pressing a cell phone touch screen to dial a number, and then the phone disappeared from view.

"I found our boy, Hall," said a voice in his head with perfect clarity, and for just an instant, an image of the face he had been staring at in the mirror only moments before flashed into existence. *His* face.

Only he wasn't looking into the mirror now. He sensed that he must *be* this Hall. But the name didn't trigger a *this-feels-right* emotion, or a cascade of memories.

"Let the others know they can pack it in," the voice continued. "My post was the lucky winner."

Once again, the man in the bathroom, the man who decided to temporarily adopt the name Hall until he learned otherwise, knew that he had not *heard* any of these words. At least not with his ears. But they had registered with utter clarity, nonetheless.

He was reading these people's minds.

It was impossible, yes. But it was also becoming undeniable. He might not remember anything about himself, but he was quite sure he believed in science. And that he *didn't* believe in conspiracy theories, or ghosts, or aliens, or ESP.

But ESP was the only explanation. What was crazier, hearing voices in your head, or thinking you could read minds?

Probably a toss-up, he decided.

You gave us quite a chase, Hall, he picked up with perfect clarity, and he realized this last had been an internal thought of the man he was monitoring, and had not been spoken aloud. Exactly *how* he knew this wasn't clear. *But you're done running now, you little prick.*

A moment later, the man spoke aloud into his phone once again. "I have no idea," he said, no doubt in answer to a question. "He holed up like we thought. Who gives a shit where? The prick must have thought he lost us, too. He was on foot, not seeming to care he could be seen for miles. He's at a gas station with nothing but scrub brush surrounding it." The man paused. "And just when I was beginning to think this guy was clever."

He lowered the phone and prepared to end the connection. "I'll call you back when he's a corpse," he finished calmly.

2

Hall decided instantly that he had to proceed as if he wasn't delusional, and the voices in his head were completely accurate. Given that the man outside the door wanted him dead, he had no other choice.

He could clearly read the growing impatience in the man's mind. His quarry had been in the bathroom a long time, the man was thinking. And while he had originally planned to follow him from there, waiting to shoot him until he was isolated, the assassin had noticed that no one was around now, and was coming to the conclusion that a silenced shot to the head as Hall began to emerge from the bathroom, or even two or three shots at chest height through the closed door, would do the trick nicely.

Hall guessed he had forty-five seconds at most to come up with a way out of this. His mind raced, despite the continued presence of the myriad of voices in his head. If his ESP *was* real, the second he opened the door he was dead—and possibly even before. There was nothing in the bathroom or in his possession he could use as a weapon. No tire irons or lighters or knives. Nothing but water, a small plastic wastebasket, a towel dispenser, and bargain brand toilet paper.

He could try to kick through the wall of the small bathroom opposite the door, hoping that it shared a wall with the main station, where he suddenly realized he could easily read the thoughts of the attendant, somehow isolating them from the rest of the babble. Even if he was unable to crash through, the attempt should cause enough noise that the attendant would come to investigate.

But just as he tightened his leg muscles to make the attempt, he realized he was too late. He caught the decision and resolve in his stalker's mind and knew the man was even now crossing the ten yards between his position and the door, holding a silenced gun under his gray windbreaker.

A desperate plan materialized in Hall's mind. He quietly disengaged the small silver button in the middle of the door handle, unlocking it.

The man continued approaching, with practiced quiet. Hall's five senses couldn't have possibly detected that he was outside and approaching, let alone his precise position, but the sixth sense Hall now possessed could see from his attacker's eyes, so he could judge with uncanny accuracy when to launch his attack.

He whipped open the door with all of the speed and strength at his command, just as the man in his mind's eye began to raise his gun, and was rewarded when the door handle slammed into the man's outstretched hand, sending his gun flying.

The assassin stifled a scream, and reflexively brought his now bloodied paw to eye level to assess the damage, discovering that at least two of his fingers were now broken. Hall dived for the man's gun, having no time to ponder this verification that his ESP was real, after all, and highly accurate.

Hall snatched the gun from the pavement and rolled to one knee, extending it in front of him. "Freeze!" he said, his voice guttural and commanding, but low enough not to be heard by the attendant. He knew without looking that the hundreds of voices inside his head were still coming from the strip mall across the way, and he and his attacker were out of sight of the attendant and the two customers currently filling their tanks.

"Hands behind your head!" ordered Hall, rising from the pavement and taking a few steps backwards.

Shit! raged the would-be-assassin, a single, visceral thought emerging from a sea of pain and shock that Hall picked up as though it had been screamed aloud. *What the fuck?* the man demanded of the universe. *There's no way this little prick could have heard me coming.*

"Turn around!" said Hall.

The man turned, and his mind sorted through possible counterattacks. He considered the backup gun holstered to his ankle, calculating if he could pretend to double over and reach it in time. He decided against it. Not only was it risky, his draw would be slowed by his broken fingers.

"Who *are* you?" demanded Hall.

"*Fuck you*," spat the man bitterly, but in the time he uttered these words, a flood of impressions and information entered Hall's mind from his. The man was Frank Baldino. He had been a mob enforcer, but he'd had a falling out with the boss. So given that he had a talent for killing, and enjoyed it, he had undergone cosmetic surgery to disguise himself and had taken up a career as a high-priced mercenary.

When Baldino had delivered this two-word response, Hall had heard it with a subtle but unmistakable vibrato. He wondered if it was an echo caused by a timing difference between receiving the *thought* of the words, and hearing the actual words with his ears. An offset of mere milliseconds. This might be due to telepathy traveling faster than sound—which would make sense if it was an electromagnetic or other exotic phenomenon—or it could all be due to a slight delay between thinking a word and vocalizing it. Hall decided that for this analysis to have spontaneously sprung to his mind, he must be fairly well-educated.

"Who are you working for?" asked Hall, and when it was clear he wouldn't be getting an answer, he drove deeper into Baldino's mind and fished out the answer for himself.

Frank Baldino didn't *know* who he was working for. There was a middleman who set up his jobs and took a percentage. Baldino had been sent a photo of Hall, and given his name and last location, and that had been about all. The mercenary had no idea why someone wanted Nick Hall dead, and couldn't have cared any less.

Hall absorbed the fact that his first name must be Nick, which he decided he didn't particularly care for.

What fascinated Hall was his growing realization that he could access Baldino's thoughts and memories as easily as Baldino could. He couldn't help but appreciate the ultimate irony of being able to instantly recall every aspect of Baldino's past he cared to know, but none of his own.

Once again, out of the endless swirl of thoughts flooding his mind, one rose up and pierced through the rest. One of the customers had finished pumping gas and would be driving away in less than a minute. And Hall would then be in full view, wearing filthy jeans, no shirt, and training a gun on Baldino.

His time was up.

"March into the bathroom," ordered Hall, continuing to monitor Baldino's every thought. Frank Baldino did as he was told, at least outwardly. But Hall read that he had reached a decision. Once he entered the bathroom, he would launch a counterattack, regardless of the risk. Hall looked clumsy and unsure of himself.

Baldino never got the chance. Just as he crossed the threshold of the door, Hall slammed the hard butt of the gun into the back of Baldino's skull with all the adrenaline-boosted strength he could muster.

Baldino fell forward into the small bathroom like a puppet whose strings had been cut, and Hall had no doubt he was no longer conscious. He bent Baldino's legs at the knee, joined him inside the bathroom, and then closed and locked the door.

He reached down and pressed his fingers into Baldino's neck, feeling for his carotid artery and a pulse. Nothing. He tried Baldino's wrist and put his ear to his mouth. No pulse. No breathing.

Shit! he thought, almost hysterically. *He was dead!*

Hall clutched at the small sink for support, reeling. *He had killed a man.* Hall didn't remember who he was, but he was certain he had never killed before. Bile rose in his throat as he pondered taking a life. Even though the man had been intent on taking *his*, Hall suspected he would have puked if his stomach wasn't totally empty.

How many movies and TV shows had he seen where a man was knocked out by getting hit by the butt of a gun? Dozens? Hundreds?

But never in any of them that he could remember—he was long past considering the frustrating irony that he could remember everything about the world except when it pertained to himself—had such a blow been fatal. But then again, he knew that a single hard, bare-fisted strike to the face would knock out just about anyone—cold—but

Hollywood often showed fights in which the combatants barely slowed down after trading dozens of insanely forceful blows.

Hall blew out a long breath. He knew what he had to do next. As distasteful as it was, he had to become a grave robber. Baldino was slightly taller and thicker than he was, but any clothing that hadn't spent the night in a dumpster was a *godsend*. Hall stripped him with great difficulty, given the confines of the bathroom, but was soon wearing tan khaki slacks and a light-green polo shirt, both of them a size too large, leaving the gray windbreaker behind.

Baldino's wallet contained no identification or credit cards, but Hall confiscated the thick sheaf of twenties he found inside. He pocketed Baldino's gun and silencer and took the smaller gun from the man's ankle holster as well. Not that he had any idea how to use either one of them.

He removed the keys to Baldino's silver Acura parked outside, and took an extra minute to apply a soapy paper towel to his sneakers, since he had worn them in the dumpster.

Finally, sensing no one was within eyeshot, he locked the door from the inside and stepped out of the bathroom, hoping the locked door would prevent Baldino's body from being discovered for at least an hour or two.

Nick Hall took a deep breath and walked calmly toward Baldino's Acura. Nearby was a wire rack with several stacks of free publications, one selling used cars and one entitled, "Homes for sale in Bakersfield, California. Your free guide."

So he was in Bakersfield, California. Good to know. But this knowledge didn't evoke an avalanche of memories, just as his own name had failed to do. A long list of California cities came to mind: LA, San Diego, Palm Springs, San Francisco, Oakland, and others, but as far as he could tell, he had never even known Bakersfield existed.

Hall started the car, and despite his blood being so alive with adrenaline he felt as if a marauding colony of ants were marching under his skin, he forced himself to pull calmly out onto the street and away from the station.

3

Nick Hall drove for several miles as voices continued to ricochet around his head. Knowing that he had somehow acquired ESP didn't make the voices any less grating or less capable of eroding his sanity. He was shocked to read the time on the car's digital clock. For some reason he had assumed it was morning, but he had regained consciousness in mid-afternoon.

The air was still cool, probably in the high sixties, so it must be fall or winter in Bakersfield. Good thing. Had it been summer, he would have been roasted alive in a steel barbecue pit of garbage—not exactly the way he hoped to die, which he decided should involve the Dallas Cowboy cheerleaders and his heart giving out from exhaustion.

Hall had no choice but to assume he wasn't stark raving mad. His senses told him he could now read minds and that the world around him was behaving consistently with this new world order. But this was the age-old conundrum of the philosophers. What was reality? Was *anything* real? Didn't every schizophrenic convince themselves that their reality was self-consistent and rational?

So what did he know? He knew that a large group of dangerous men had been after him, and no doubt still were. Apparently, he had eluded them by taking a dive into a dumpster. One would have to be awfully desperate to take that kind of action, but given Baldino's orders to kill him in cold blood, this level of desperation wasn't at all surprising.

So why did they want him dead? This had to be about his mind reading. What else could it be? Memory loss or not, he knew this was something recent; a mental ability he had never had before. Even in its untamed form—in a form that could drive one to madness because, while there seemed to be a dimmer switch, there didn't seem to be an off switch—this ability conferred incredible advantages on him. Without it he would by lying dead on the floor of the Shell bathroom instead of Baldino.

And if the ability was this useful when untamed, even wielded by a man without memory who had only begun to learn to use it, how useful could it be when tamed and wielded by someone with knowledge and experience? It would be the ultimate advantage. Anyone who was power mad in any walk of life: criminal, business, politics, government, military—what would they give to have such a power? And what would they do to *get it?*

But then why kill him? It would make far more sense to capture him and use him as a guinea pig. Try to find out why he had this power and duplicate it. Or force him to use it for their ends.

He considered. The only reason they would be so desperate to kill him would be if . . .

What if he had read something in someone's mind? Something big. In this case, he would need to be terminated at all costs.

He pulled up to a red light. As more and more cars came up on all sides, the intensity of the voices in his head increased. "Stop it!" he shrieked at the top of his lungs, covering his ears with his hands, which of course did nothing to lessen the clamor.

He forced himself to take several deep breaths. Getting worked up about his predicament wasn't going to help him. If he couldn't find a way to turn it off, he would have to find a way to get used to it. To ignore it; tune it out. But easier said than done.

If it wasn't bad enough to have to live with incessant chatter in his brain, or have a hit squad intent on snuffing him out, he also didn't have any idea of who he was or what it was he knew. This knowledge could at least give him a *chance*. But as it was, he was the ultimate deer in headlights; without his memories, helpless and disoriented. His newfound ability had kept him alive so far, but he was under no illusion that this power alone could hold off the posse that was now on his tail. If the men's room door of the Shell station had swung *inward* instead of *outward*, he would be dead now; ESP or no ESP.

He had to find his bearings. Somehow.

His memory was perfect when it came to some things. He knew lyrics to songs. And he realized he could recall countless movies as well. He might not be able to remember anything about the circumstances of the viewing, but an intimate knowledge of a movie at least indicated he had seen it many times—like the first *Terminator* movie. He could quote Kyle Reese's lines as though he had played the role himself: *You still don't get it, do you? He'll find her! That's what he does! That's ALL he does! You can't stop him! He'll wade through you, reach down her throat, and pull her fucking heart out!*

Hall couldn't help but shake his head that the one movie that had sprung to mind involved a relentless assassin pursuing a helpless victim who had no idea why she was being hunted. Just perfect.

He supposed locations would work the same as movies and song lyrics. If he thought about nearby locales and one of them evoked a high level of familiarity, this might at least tell him *something* about himself.

Hall scrolled through his memory of California localities. When he came to La Jolla, he realized it had more of a familiarity to him than the others he had recited. He could visualize a high cement walkway cut into the ocean, overlooking a small beach on which seals liked to come ashore and lounge in the sun. He recalled restaurants and a hang glider park above cliffs. He knew that La Jolla was an upscale beachfront community in San Diego with a strong scientific presence, particularly in biotechnology.

When he thought of science his mind instantly held a picture of the Scripps Institute of Oceanography. He felt certain he must have been there on many occasions. He didn't seem to know it well enough to believe he had *worked* there, but perhaps he was friends with someone who did.

There was only one way to find out. He needed to make a visit in person. If he was very lucky someone there would recognize him. Someone who could tell him who he was. Give him a past.

He switched on the car's built-in mapping program. "Give me directions to The Scripps Institute of Oceanography," he said.

The street in front of him disappeared!

He gasped in terror. His entire field of view had been totally eclipsed by a 3-D image of California from space, which had materialized in front of his face from out of nowhere, with a route drawn in red from his current location to La Jolla. The image had become his entire world. The road, traffic, and pedestrians were *gone*.

He was now driving totally blind.

4

Hall slammed on the brakes, surprising the car trailing behind him, which had to swerve blindly into the next lane to avoid a collision, narrowly missing an oncoming car in that lane. In both lanes tires screeched and horns honked, and it was only by blind luck that his action hadn't resulted in a multi-car pileup.

"What the fuck is your problem, asshole!"

"What happened over there?"

"Damn," thought a teenage boy pulling out of a McDonald's on the corner with a bag full of food. *"Just missed. A crash would have been so cool."*

Hall picked up dozens of other thoughts related to his reckless maneuver, but he paid them no attention. He was too busy panicking. And struggling to see something other than a massive three-dimensional map that hovered directly in front of his face.

Suddenly the road came back into view. His mind had made some kind of adjustment. The map was still present in his visual field, but now, so was the road. And he could choose which one to look at. Like having side by side televisions, each with a different football game. He could concentrate on either one to the total exclusion of the other if he wished. Or like bifocals. When one wanted to see something far away, one looked through the top half; close by, the bottom.

He tilted his head back and blew out a long sigh of relief toward the ceiling, ignoring the horns that continued to honk at the idiot who had decided to take a sabbatical in the middle of a busy street, and a myriad of other choice words he was able to read that were far less charitable than *idiot*.

Hall chose to ignore the map and it shrank from his view. He carefully resumed driving. A few minutes later he pulled into the parking lot of a mini-mart. The map was now gone. He guessed that by not focusing on it at all for a period of time, the software behind it had told it to vanish.

He studied the car's GPS. It was also displaying directions to La Jolla, but they were standard, not floating far larger than life in front of his face in ultra-high-definition 3-D clarity. He reached over and turned the device off, as well as the car.

"Give me directions to the Scripps Institute of Oceanography?" he said aloud, and instantly a map sprang into sight once again, hanging in front of his face. He studied it for several long seconds in disbelief. It was a standard Google Map. It even had the Google logo on it, and the directions looked to be accurate. And it hadn't been generated by the car's GPS device either, since this device was still off.

Hall thought about the map disappearing and it promptly complied.

Coincidence? Or did it somehow respond to his thoughts? Companies had made great strides with game controllers and artificial limbs that could be operated by thoughts alone, so it wasn't out of the question. He thought about the map reappearing, and there it was.

So could he do this trick only with maps?

Show me the Wikipedia entry for Bakersfield, California, he thought, and immediately, like the map, the Wikipedia entry was before his eyes, overlaid with his real vision. Again, he could focus on both views at once, although, like watching two different movies, he could only do so at a very superficial level. But as before, if he focused on one, the other would recede completely until he decided to focus on it again.

He tried several other searches in rapid succession, each of them appearing instantly. There was no way around it, he was tapping into the Internet. He could surf the web using thoughts alone, and the text or graphics or video would magically be projected in front of his face in ultra-high definition.

But projected by what? And how?

He thought about how this might be working for several minutes, coming up blank, when it occurred to him to use the Internet itself to understand what was happening. *Search 'accessing the Internet using thoughts alone,'* he instructed to whatever it was that was responsible for this miracle of technology.

A results page popped up. It wasn't Google or any of the other search engines he recognized, so perhaps it was a proprietary one just for this purpose.

He scanned down the page and chose the earliest article, calendar-year-wise. It was from *ComputerworldUS*, published on November 20, 2009. It began by quoting Intel researchers who predicted that someday, "you won't need a keyboard and mouse to control your computer. Instead," he continued reading from the page that was always centered, regardless of how he turned his head, "users will open documents and surf the web using nothing more than their brain waves."

Hall paused and let this sink in. He was sure he hadn't heard about this technology before, even though it had clearly been discussed as far back as 2009. He continued reading:

Scientists at Intel's research lab in Pittsburgh are working to find ways to read and harness human brain waves so they can be used to operate computers, television sets, and cell phones. The brain waves would be harnessed with Intel-developed sensors implanted in people's brains.

The scientists say the plan is not a scene from a sci-fi movie. . . . Researchers expect that consumers will want the freedom they will gain by using the implant.

"I think human beings are remarkably adaptive," said Andrew Chien, vice president of research and director of future technologies research at Intel Labs. "If you told people twenty years ago that they would be carrying computers all the time, they would have said, 'I don't want that. I don't need that.' Now you can't get them to stop. There are a lot of things that have to be done first, but I think [implanting chips into human brains] is well within the scope of possibility."

Intel research scientist Dean Pomerleau said that users will soon tire of depending on a computer interface, and having to fish a device out of their pocket or bag to access it. He also predicted that users will tire of having to manipulate an interface with their fingers.

Instead, they'll simply manipulate their various devices with their brains.

"We're trying to prove you can do interesting things with brain waves," said Pomerleau. "Eventually people may be willing to be more committed . . . to brain implants. Imagine being able to surf the web with the power of your thoughts."

Hall read several more articles, but it was clear that only five or six years later, all efforts toward this goal, by Intel and others, had been largely abandoned, leaving only a few scattered pockets of activity. The challenges had been greater than first appreciated, and the payoff much farther down the road. And animal models, while surprisingly useful, still couldn't yield enough data to fully translate into the human experience.

But, apparently, this technology hadn't been as abandoned as everyone had been led to believe. He was living proof. He had no doubt he was the beneficiary of the implants spoken of in the article.

Which meant that it wasn't projecting the images in *front* of him. Instead, his further reading made it abundantly clear that his implants were somehow tied into his visual cortex, *from the inside*, or else were sending information directly to the region of his brain responsible for interpreting the steady stream of visual input from his eyes.

The implants were converting the Internet images into a complex, multi-pronged binary code that was tied directly to his visual centers. His mind, only having experience receiving these signals through his eyes, from sources external to himself, insisted on interpreting the images as hovering in front of him, rather than coming from within.

A woman named Sheila Nireberg had been a pioneer in this arena, in her effort to treat blindness. He watched a video of a presentation she had given to an organization called TED in October of 2011, in which she discussed the complex patterns of electrical pulses that were produced by the retina, processing the information delivered by over a hundred million photoreceptors. Hall was somehow able to "hear" Nireberg's presentation, indicating the system was also capable of sending signals to the hearing centers of his brain.

He searched for Nick Hall, but the attempt to find himself was sheer folly. A quick search revealed that Nicholas throughout the nineties had been one of the top ten most popular baby names, and according to the US Census, over half a million people had the last name of Hall.

His access of the Internet was almost instantaneous. Web pages flashed up with no discernible loading times. He knew that the 6G WiFi technology that had only recently come to blanket the country was orders of magnitude faster, and with a far more penetrating signal than any previous WiFi generation, but having web pages appear on a desktop or tablet when conjured by a mouse or a finger was one thing; having them pop up with the speed of thought was quite another.

The software was spectacular. More than spectacular. Whatever search and presentation algorithm was being used was stunningly advanced. And it seemed to be capable of learning. Even after the few searches he had done, the system became more and more seamless. More intuitive. Even from the start it had somehow known when he wanted to access external information, and when he was just thinking or speaking a question, with no intent to invoke the system. It had only erred when he had spoken a question to the car's GPS, having incorrectly interpreted this as being a direct query to the system, and responding accordingly—and nearly getting him killed in a car crash in the process.

But now, after only ten minutes of working with him, the system had already evolved, improved, and any content of interest to him appeared magically almost before he was fully aware that he wanted it. And the algorithm read his interest with uncanny accuracy, rivaling even the most recent iteration of Google.

Hall also found himself becoming more and more facile with viewing and digesting information while maintaining his vision. He became more adept at ignoring and manipulating the second, internal stream of data going to the visual centers of his brain, seamlessly shifting his glance to see through the top half or bottom half of his metaphorical bifocals.

He wondered just how complex the surgery on his brain had been, and his internal Internet provided the answer before he had finished the thought. An article from the *Wall Street Journal*, from June of 2012, hung in the air before him.

Neural implants, also called brain implants, are medical devices designed to be placed under the skull, on the surface of the brain. Often as small as an aspirin, implants use thin metal electrodes to "listen" to brain activity and in some cases to stimulate activity in the brain. Attuned to the activity between neurons, a neural implant can essentially "listen" to your brain activity and then "talk" directly to your brain.

If that prospect makes you queasy, you may be surprised to learn that the installation of a neural implant is relatively simple and fast. Under anesthesia, an incision is made in the scalp, a hole is drilled in the skull, and the device is placed on the surface of the brain. Diagnostic communication with the device can take place wirelessly. While it is not an outpatient procedure, patients typically require only an overnight stay at the hospital.

Hall examined his skull with the tips of two fingers, feeling a number of small imperfections that might have been scars, but he had recently undergone trauma so he couldn't be sure.

He had been sitting in the small lot of the mini-mart now for twenty-five minutes. Pangs of hunger from his empty stomach now competed for his attention with the random thoughts of hundreds of minds. This small store would not have been his first choice for dining, but since he was here, he could get some food and be on his way to La Jolla in minutes.

He entered the store and walked through several aisles, eying candy bars, trays of doughnuts that looked as though they had been abandoned there during World War II, and frozen, microwavable burritos.

When he saw an enclosed container with heated steel rollers in the back of the store, cooking plump, all-beef *Hebrew National* hotdogs, he had an almost Pavlovian response. He decided he either loved all-beef dogs beyond all else, or his body knew what it needed, and saw these as providing a quick, easily digestible injection of both carbohydrates and protein.

A pair of long tongs was stationed nearby and he quickly began removing three dogs and placing them on buns. A few quarts of water and he'd be on his way.

A thought broke through the noise in his head, from outside of the mini-mart, and it was clear as a bell.

He was about to have company. He had loitered in the lot for too long.

Someone had just pulled into the store. Someone who knew he was inside. A man named Cody Radich.

A man who was already mentally counting the bonus money he would receive for ending Hall's life, which he planned to do shortly, and with a ruthless efficiency.

5

Radich was approaching the door slowly, and Hall's psi ability told him that the man was concentrating on appearing as casual and unthreatening as possible. He would wait until Hall was checking out, and then stealthily appear behind him, possibly even holding the door open for him. Following only inches behind, he would put a silenced bullet through Hall's heart. When Hall collapsed in front of him, Radich would kneel down to check on the poor man, shouting for someone to call 9-1-1 as he did, as though he were a good Samaritan who just happened to be standing nearby when Hall collapsed.

Hall couldn't help but admire the plan, which Radich continued to examine from several angles to ensure he hadn't missed anything. He hadn't. And neither had Hall.

Hall abandoned his hotdogs, wandering up and down the aisles while Radich kept his distance, pretending to read a magazine out of sight and watching him in a large, rounded security mirror that was wedged in the back upper corner of the store, and which gave a distorted but clear view of the vast majority of real estate within.

Hall did some quick research on his internal Internet, continuing to be amazed by how quickly he could get to useful information. He waited until a short black woman with a baby stroller left the aisle Radich was in, took a deep breath, and rounded the aisle to join him.

Radich didn't glance up from the magazine as Hall approached, and looked for all the world to be oblivious. But Hall was deep inside the killer's head, monitoring his every thought, and knew that Radich was as keenly attuned to his every move as a lion stalking its prey.

Hall raised Frank Baldino's Glock in a smooth motion and pointed it at the man.

Radich's eyes widened and his mind exploded in surprise. *How the fuck was I made?* he thought, dropping the magazine to the floor. *That's impossible!*

"Turn around," whispered Hall. "Hands in your back pockets."

Radich hesitated. He had been told very little about Hall. His quarry was supposed to be bright, but completely untrained. A civilian all of his life. Athletic, but probably hadn't been in a fight since he was in third grade. And probably hadn't held a gun in his life. Until now.

"You're out of your league, Hall," said Radich, and once again Hall was aware of the slightest echo from receiving these words both audibly and mentally. "You really gonna shoot me with Baldino's gun? Don't you think you should remove the safety first?" he said, sneering. And while he continued to affect a casual air, his mind remained superbly alert and primed, waiting for Hall to glance down at the gun in his hand, looking for the safety, so he could lash out and disarm him.

Hall's gaze never wavered from Radich's eyes. "Nice try," he said, keeping his voice low. The web page he had accessed, with instructions for how to operate the gun in his hand, was still up in his visual cortex. "But we both know Glocks don't have traditional safeties, *do they?* As long as you depress both the main trigger and the tiny secondary trigger when you fire, it's good to go." He shot Radich a withering glare. "This gun has a five-pound trigger pull, *asshole*, and I'm guessing I'm squeezing at four and a half right now. So turn around. I *won't* ask again."

What the fuck! thought Radich, turning around and putting his hands in his back pockets. He had been told his target was an untrained civilian, not a man who was clearly comfortable handling a gun, and who had obviously done so often. The intelligence he had received had been *shit*.

Radich had severely underestimated his prey. He decided he had to act soon or he was a dead man. He glanced at the round, convex security mirror in the upper corner of the store and tensed his leg muscles to launch his body backwards in an act of desperation.

Hall danced back several steps, an act Radich caught in the mirror, just an instant before he would have launched himself. He was just able to stop what would now be a fruitless attempt.

"I won't hurt you if you cooperate," said Hall, trying to appear as calm as possible and ignore his racing heart and pounding temples.

Hall knew that Radich had been right. He *was* out of his league. *Far* out of his league. And he knew he'd be lucky if someone didn't enter this aisle within the next thirty seconds. His psi ability told him that two people were at the counter checking out, and one other was choosing a candy bar two aisles over. But two more customers had just entered the store and his luck was about to end.

"What do you want?" said Radich.

"Your car keys and gun. First the keys. If I have them in the next ten seconds you survive unscathed. If not, I put a bullet in your head and take my chances. Nine. Eight. Seven. . ."

The assassin turned, showed his hands palm up, and then slowly reached toward his right pocket.

"I said *keys* first," hissed Hall, extending his gun. "Which are in your *other* pocket. Four. Three. . . ."

Radich's hand dove into his left pocket and pulled out a set of keys, tossing them to Hall before he finished his countdown. Hall snatched them from the air.

"*Now* your gun. Pull it out with two fingers and place it on the ground."

Radich complied.

"Now move!" commanded Hall in a loud whisper, gesturing with his head toward the back corner of the store, where two doors were marked *men* and *women*. This would be a close call. An elderly woman would be entering the aisle in seconds.

Radich walked to the back corner while Hall followed, scooping up Radich's gun from the floor as he passed it. The woman cut into the aisle behind him, but Hall's body blocked the gun he was pointing from her view until they were once again out of sight.

"Into the women's room," snapped Hall, still being mindful not to raise his voice.

He had reached into both rooms with his mind and knew the men's room was occupied, even though it would not have been apparent without checking the door otherwise.

"Now!" he demanded, knowing that Radich was busy wondering what twisted logic had caused Hall to insist on the women's room rather than the men's. Some feeble attempt at humiliation, Radich finally decided.

Hall suspected his life continued to depend on how convincingly he could act like a bad-ass, even though, from the sickness he felt in his stomach and his pounding heart, he was pretty sure he was anything but. "I have some things I need to take care of in this store," lied Hall. "But I'll be watching this door in the mirrors while I do. Open it in the next five minutes and my promise not to hurt you goes away, replaced by a promise to blow your fucking head off."

The instant the door closed, Hall marched purposefully to the exit, glancing at the security mirror on his way out to be sure Radich hadn't attempted to follow.

Hall started Radich's black sedan and peeled into the street. Hundreds of voices swirled in his head, but at a lower level than before, thankfully. He wondered . . .

He reached out with his mind, trying to send it into the bathroom stall in the mini-mart that was receding into the distance behind him. He recognized the thoughts of Radich instantly. He had had no idea if this was going to prove possible, or how he was pulling it off, but it was working. Radich had only waited a minute before he had left the bathroom, calling Hall's bluff, but without a car he had no way to follow. Instead, he was on the phone, reporting Hall's position.

I'm such an idiot! thought Hall, fuming. How could he have been so *stupid* as to have left Radich with his cell phone?

"Fuck you!" hissed Radich into the phone, his thoughts as he voiced this sentiment perfectly clear to Hall a half mile away. "*I earned my reputation. The problem wasn't me, it was shitty intel. Powder-puff, my ass. This Hall knows his shit, and he has some major brass balls. And he made me somehow. How the fuck is that possible? I didn't even know I was going to be part of the hunt until an hour ago. I swear I did nothing to tip him off. You better spread the word to stay frosty with this guy, or you'll have more dead bodies than just Baldino's."*

Hall almost slammed into the car in front of him, a white Honda, as it slowed for a red light, and decided to return his full concentration to the road and his current predicament. The light changed to green and the line of cars once again picked up speed.

He needed to ditch Radich's car as soon as possible. But then what?

An alarm went off in his head. Something was wrong.

He scanned through the hundreds of voices in his mind and found the reason for the alarm in seconds. Another mercenary was approaching in the oncoming lanes and had spotted him and the car.

Hall yanked the wheel to the right, cutting across two lanes like a maniac before screeching into a hairpin right turn, an SUV two lanes over having to swerve halfway onto the sidewalk to avoid a collision. He could read the dismay in the mind of the merc in the oncoming car, who realized he couldn't weave his way through a dense stream of traffic to make a left turn and follow.

Without further hesitation, the driver sent a high caliber slug through Hall's side window as he was completing the turn, narrowly missing his torso but taking a chunk of flesh from his upper left arm. Because of the shock and the adrenaline rush from the sound of the window being shot—the safety glass now heavily veined with a spiderweb of cracks and a huge hole in its center—Hall didn't even realize he had been hit until blood started running down his arm, tickling it.

Hall wiped the familiar red liquid away to inspect the wound, relieved to find the bullet had cut only a shallow groove and his blood loss would be limited, despite appearances. He popped open the glove compartment as he drove and found a small first-aid kit, which wasn't entirely surprising given Radich's line of work. He covered the groove in his arm with an industrial-sized bandage and wrapped gauze around it to hold it tight.

He had been driving aimlessly and now found himself on an industrial road. He needed to ditch the car. He had no doubt he could find a tutorial in cyberspace on how to steal a replacement, but he didn't want to go that route. Radich had called in his position, and his colleagues would be descending on the area like locusts.

Holing up had saved him before. Maybe it could again. If they couldn't find him in four or five hours, they might have to assume he had slipped the net, in which case he could be almost anywhere, and they would have to extend the boundaries of their search perimeter over a hundredfold.

A gleaming glass office complex, with hundreds of cars parked all around it, appeared on his right. It covered quite a lot of territory but was only two or three stories high. He pulled off and parked the car behind the building, out of sight of the road. He took a deep breath and entered the office building's first floor.

Hall found himself in a main atrium with fake foliage and a small stream. Very tranquil. Wide glass doors appeared on each of the four sides of the atrium rectangle, beckoning visitors into the lobbies of four different companies in the complex.

The doors on his left had a familiar hand-painted bright red sign, *WeOfficeU*. He had seen their ads. It was an office co-op. With more and more people working freelance these days, there was a greater and greater need for office space and support. Individuals and very small businesses rented out offices by the month, and shared a receptionist, phone systems, parking, and conference room facilities. This allowed sole proprietors and consultants to meet with clients in a state-of-the-art office building, giving them a far more professional and accomplished aura.

WeOfficeU might be ideal, Hall realized. The inhabitants of these offices didn't all work for the same company, and there was likely a high turnover among tenants, so a stranger in their midst would almost certainly go unnoticed.

He found a nook near some heavy foliage and crouched low, trying to disappear. The arm of the oversized shirt he had taken from Baldino was now soaked in blood, but the flow had largely stopped.

What a sight he must be. Wearing bloodstained clothes that didn't fit, a two-day growth of stubble, a hair style that could only be achieved by washing your hair in a sink with hand soap and then letting it dry haphazardly while you ran for your life, and various small cuts and bruises. At least he no longer carried an odor that would be offensive to a skunk.

He smiled. You had to look for the silver lining.

He thought he might have to wait until five o'clock, thirty minutes away, when the official business hours of the office were ending, but after only a few minutes of reading the vapid and relentlessly selfish thoughts of the WeOfficeU receptionist, she left her desk to make copies of some paperwork on an expensive copier in an adjoining room.

Hall practically flew through the lobby door, detecting no one else around the reception desk. He walked quietly past the desk and through another door into the main floor. Large office spaces were often filled with impersonal cubicles in the center and offices along the walls for upper management, but the entire point of this business was to provide private offices for individuals, so there were enclosed offices throughout.

Several tenants had their office doors open, but the majority didn't. Perfect. He avoided the open doors and paced briskly along one wall. He ducked down as one man returned from the bathroom and entered his office, closing the door behind him. It was clear WeOfficeU was thriving and the space was at full capacity.

Hall passed maybe twelve more offices, feeling with his mind for occupants in each case, until he finally found one that was empty; a corner office with a neighbor on one side of it and a tiny kitchen alcove on the other. Hopefully, whoever was renting this office was gone for the day.

Hall thrust open the door, backed into the office, and closed it gently behind him.

He heard a loud intake of air, as though he had just startled someone half senseless, and spun around to face a petite young woman sitting at a desk.

She opened her mouth and prepared to scream.

6

"Don't scream!" said Hall in desperation. "I'm a friend."

It was a ridiculous thing to say, but it was all he could think of. How had he failed to read her presence here?

The woman at the desk was taken aback by the sheer audacity and incongruity of the statement, which had the desired effect. She held her scream as surprise and panic gave way to rationality, and she reflexively tried to make sense of what Hall had just said.

She was about five foot five and very petite, with raven hair, cut short, a flawless complexion, and an alertness and energy that seemed to gush out of her. Hall judged her to be in her mid to late twenties. She could best be described as cute, but not beautiful. The type who could end up being appealing to a man, or not so much at all, depending on if her personality enhanced her appearance or detracted from it.

And he was still unable to read her, despite the considerable effort he was now making. Thoughts from hundreds of minds in the building were swirling in his head, but hers failed to register in any way.

"A friend?" she repeated in confusion, taking in Hall's sordid appearance and being far from reassured by it. "I've never seen you before in my *life*."

Hall's eyes widened. He couldn't read her mind while she was silent, but when she had spoken he had "heard" the familiar, just-discernible echo of her words. This indicated that he *could* read words from her mind, but only when she focused them enough for imminent speech.

"Well, yeah . . ." replied Hall. "What I meant was that I'm, um . . . *friendly*. You know. Not a danger. That sort of thing. Wrong office. I'll just leave now."

She nodded, a visible look of relief on her face. He didn't doubt she was relieved. It wasn't every day that a man who looked like he had been through a war barged into her office. Who could blame her for being happy to see him go?

And then her hopeful look changed to one of horror, as if she had seen a ghost, but only for an instant. She quickly flashed him an awkward smile to cover up her reaction, but he had caught the movement of her eyes just before her expression had changed.

She had seen the handle of the Glock sticking out of his waistband.

What incredibly bad luck! Not only had this freaked her out—and rightly so—it also ensured she would call the police the second he left her office.

"You saw my gun, didn't you?" he said with a sigh, and this had the effect of ratcheting up the girl's fear even higher. She shook her head no, looking as though she was certain she was about to be killed by a psychopath.

"Look, I promise you that you won't get hurt. Really. I'll leave, and it'll be like I was never here. But before I do, I need *you* to promise not to try to make my life more difficult after I'm gone." He rolled his eyes. *As if it's even possible for my life to get more difficult*, he thought.

"I won't," she assured him. "I promise. Absolutely!" she added emphatically.

Hall decided he needed to level with her. It was the only way. He reached over and locked the door. He could no longer rely a hundred percent on his psi ability to warn him of approaching minds. The woman in front of him was living proof of that. She shrank back in ill-disguised terror. Hall shook his head. Locking the door *before* he tried to win her over wasn't exactly putting her at ease.

"Let me explain what's going on. And then I'll leave. Okay?"

She nodded.

He took a deep breath, knowing that honesty in this case would only make things worse, since no more ridiculous story had ever been told. If he was fast enough on his feet to think of a plausible lie that could win her trust, he would have tried it, although he suspected the entire point about winning trust was actually *telling the truth*. Besides, his mind reading, limited though it was in her case, should be able to turn skepticism into belief in a hurry.

"I woke up about two hours ago in a . . ." He paused for several seconds. Finally, wincing, he came out with it. "Okay. I woke up in a dumpster. Which doesn't exactly make me James Bond, I guess."

She tried to keep her face impassive, but a hint of disbelief and disgust flashed over her features.

"Wait," he continued, as though even he was having trouble believing what he was saying, "it gets worse. I returned to consciousness without any memory of how I came to be there." He sighed heavily. "Actually, without any memory of who I am at all. Total amnesia."

She studied him closely, as though if she stared at him intensely enough, she could somehow peel back any deceit.

"I managed to wash myself pretty well and get a change of clothes," he continued, nodding toward his outfit. "Which obviously don't fit all that well." He smiled. "But trust me, anything beats clothing that has spent time in a dumpster."

She faked a smile back at him as he continued. "And somebody— who hired a *group* of somebodies—wants me dead. They don't want to rob me, or talk to me. They simply want to kill me. And as soon as possible. I took the gun you saw from one of the people after me. I came in here to lie low, since I stupidly forgot to take the cell phone from the last guy I stopped from killing me, and he called in my position."

"That's *terrible*," said the girl, trying to sound sincere but failing miserably. Hall wasn't sure of her occupation, but it wasn't acting. "I can't even imagine what you must be going through."

Hall shook his head. "Look, I know you don't believe me. How could you? You're sure to think I'm insane. Believe me, I thought the same thing. I want an open exchange. I promise not to hurt you, but I want you to be skeptical until I can convince you. I won't hold it against you. So let's have a dialogue. Ask questions so I can satisfy you that I'm being honest."

"Okay," she said guardedly, trying to figure out how best to play this invitation. "Any idea *why* they're trying to kill you? And how is it that you've been able to survive against trained killers?"

"The answer is the same to both of these questions. I discovered when I came to in the dumpster that I can . . . well, I can read minds. I'm sure it's something I couldn't do before."

"Uh-huh. So you're reading my mind right now?"

Hall frowned. "Actually, no. You're the exception to the rule. The one person out of hundreds whose mind is closed to me. I don't know why."

She tried to keep her expression neutral, but failed.

"I don't need to be a mind reader to know you're thinking something like, *that's convenient.* I claim to be able to read minds and you just happen to be the one I can't read. So I can't prove it to you. But the fact that you're the rare person I can't read is *why* I'm in your office in the first place. I could tell that every other office was occupied. Since I couldn't read you, I chose this one, thinking it was empty. I was just as surprised as you were when I barged in here."

She opened her mouth to reply when he rushed ahead. "But I think I can still prove it to you. I have no idea how this ESP, or psionic power, or whatever you want to call it, works. But I think I can read you. But only when you're formulating words in your mind and just on the cusp of speaking. I don't know why. So do this. I'll ask you a question, and you *think* the answer to me in words. Projecting them as firmly as you can. As if you're speaking them—just don't move your lips. Okay?"

She nodded.

"What is your name?"

She tilted her head and stared at him.

He grinned. As expected, he had heard her name clearly. "Megan," he said triumphantly. "Megan Emerson."

Her eyes widened, but then her shock seemed to fade and she glanced down at her desk, at a business card holder next to a picture of her and several girlfriends in parkas on a ski lift. The outermost business card of the stack was clearly visible, with her name prominently displayed.

"Yeah, I didn't see the business cards when I asked the question, so yeah, I could have cheated on that one . . . Megan. So let's try again. Think anything you want, but again, project it to me as though it were speech."

"Okay, psycho, do I pretend your guess is right?" she thought, words Hall picked up as clearly as though she had spoken them. *"Will humoring you keep me alive or get me killed?"*

"You won't have to pretend," said Hall calmly. "Because my guess *will* be right. I may be crazy," he added as an aside. "I can't entirely rule it out. But no matter what, I have no interest in hurting you— whether you *humor* me or not," he finished, raising his eyebrows.

Megan gasped. This time, an intrigued look spread over her face, and he guessed she was about to think at him again. *"That was uncanny,"* she thought. *"But maybe you've just got some kind of psycho gift for reading body language. The question is, can you read my words when I project at you and you're not prepared?"*

"Apparently, yes," he replied smoothly. "And I'm not just reading body language. Like I said, I can read everyone else's words and thoughts and . . . everything . . . all of the time, projected or not. To be honest, it's like having a hornet buzzing around your ear all the time."

He paused. "I have no idea what makes you different." He thought the words, *Do you have an unusually weak mind?* but decided not to voice them, since the question was a bit insulting.

Megan's jaw dropped open. "Did you just think, 'Do you have an unusually weak mind?'"

7

This time it was Hall's turn to startle.

He could *send* words as well as receive? Or was it only just with her?

"I didn't know I could send until just now," he thought at her. *"Very, very cool,"* he added. *"Do you mind if I sit?"*

"Not at all," she said with a giddy smile. "Un-*fricking*-believable," she added. "That came through loud and clear."

She gestured to the one chair facing her as she sat behind her desk, surrounded by an expensive computer and two large monitors. The fear that had hung over her like a cloud since he had entered vanished, to be replaced by utter fascination.

"I take it my ridiculous story is becoming a little less ridiculous?"

"Yeah. Or your insanity is infectious," she replied.

Hall laughed. The way things had been going, he hadn't been sure if he would ever laugh again. "Do you get some kind of echo when I speak out loud?" he asked, serious once again. "Like a millisecond after each word starts it's repeated again?"

She shook her head slowly. "I have no idea what you're talking about."

Hall tilted his head in thought. This effect may have been slight, but it was also unmistakable. The fact that she wasn't experiencing it meant that when he was speaking aloud, she couldn't read his words. Only when he was concentrating on amplifying pure thought in her direction did her ability to receive his words kick in. Which wasn't the case going the other direction. But since he was the epicenter of the effect, he wasn't surprised it wasn't symmetrical.

The vast majority of people he could read at all times—in fact, could not *stop* reading. As simply and thoroughly as if their minds were his own. They didn't know they were being read, and they couldn't read him.

As for this Megan, her thoughts were completely unreadable. But he could read *words* from her mind. As long as she was either speaking them out loud, or consciously broadcasting them to him. And *he* could transmit words to *her* as well, telepathically. But only when he amplified them somehow through pure thought, which didn't happen forcefully enough for her to pick up when he was merely speaking.

He wondered what other categories of people might exist. Could he transmit words telepathically to *anyone*? Or was she special in this regard as well? If he stayed alive long enough, perhaps he'd find out.

"So you really did wake up in a dumpster a few hours ago, didn't you?" said Megan.

Hall smiled sheepishly. "Believe me, it's not something I'd make up. It wasn't my proudest moment." He paused, and then out of the blue added, "Do you have any food in here?"

She opened a drawer and removed a Kit Kat, handing it to him. He tore it open gratefully and devoured it in seconds.

"Not much of a meal," she commented.

He smiled. "Well, when the last thing you've seen that resembled food was in a dumpster, this is heaven."

Megan returned his smile. Even though they had discovered they could communicate telepathically, they had both fallen back into life-long patterns of speaking aloud. "So you don't have any idea who you are? None?"

"I think my name is Nick Hall. At least that's what the guys trying to kill me think it is." He paused. "I hesitate to bring this up, but there's more."

"More?"

"I seem to be able to access the Internet inside my brain, using my thoughts alone." He explained to her how the visual and auditory aspect worked.

Megan shrugged. "Why not? Just as plausible as reading minds, I guess. *More* plausible, actually."

"Hold on a few seconds," said Hall. "I want to try something."

He used his internal Internet connection to call up G-mail and establish an account. The username and password information he needed to fill text boxes was typed in magically as soon as he thought the words. "What's your e-mail address?" he asked.

She told him.

"Check it now," he said.

"Cassidy," she said, addressing the Personal Digital Assistant, or PDA, function of her computer using the name she had given it. "Any new messages?"

"One new message from Nick Hall," replied the soothing feminine voice.

"Read it."

"*Nice to meet you, Megan,*" said the PDA. "*Sorry for dragging you into this.*"

"Awesome," said Hall excitedly. "Do me a favor and reply."

This time she ignored her PDA and typed in the message herself. Seconds later Hall scanned the inbox to his new account and her reply was there.

Got any other tricks? she had written

Hall read this back to her to confirm he had received it, and then, just to satisfy his curiosity, he went on her Facebook page. He found it instantly. He focused his thoughts on her name and Bakersfield, and quickly found her from among the twelve results Facebook returned.

Megan Emerson was twenty-seven and had been born in Keokuk, Iowa. She had graduated from UCLA, and now worked as a graphic designer. Hall may have been fighting for his life, and his psi ability was a nuisance as well as a blessing, but instant access to trillions of pages of information was intoxicating. He decided not to tell Megan he was scanning her public-access information on Facebook. He wouldn't blame her for finding that a bit creepy.

"How's your arm?" she asked, nodding toward his blood-soaked shirt. "We should probably get that looked at."

He raised his eyebrows. "*We?*"

"Yes. *We,*" she repeated. "Maybe it's the Florence Nightingale syndrome. Or maybe it's just the joy of being alive when I was sure you were going to kill me. Or maybe meeting someone with ESP is the coolest thing that's ever happened to me. But I want to help. You need to figure out who you are. Two minds are better than one. Even if one of them is, um, apparently so weak you can't even read it."

Hall winced. "It was a stupid hypothesis. You're obviously very bright. I was just trying to figure out why you're different. No offense."

"None taken."

"I can't tell you how appealing your offer is to me. How disorienting and terrible it is not to know who you are. It's a state of aloneness that's unimaginable. I don't have any friends in the world, at least none that I'm aware of, and I don't even have a sense of self to anchor me." He sighed. "But as much as I would love your help, I have to refuse. Trust me when I say that my odds of living out the day aren't all that great. I won't put you in that kind of danger."

Megan considered, and he could tell she was struggling with how much she wanted to persist. The most exciting and intriguing thing that ever happened to her was also the deadliest. In the end, it was obvious he was right, no matter how eager she was to help and become a part of the inexplicable phenomenon that was Nick Hall. "Okay," she said with a nod. "You're right." She paused. "You may not know who you are, but at least you're a decent man."

"What makes you think so?"

"Well, taking me up on my offer would have been good for you. But you refused to put me in jeopardy."

He shook his head. "Doesn't prove I'm a decent guy. Just that I'm not a raving psychopath. Believe me, no one being hunted like this would be willing to put an innocent bystander in the line of fire, just because she happened to be at the wrong place at the wrong time."

Megan laughed. "Yeah, who knew that the wrong place at the wrong time would be my own office during regular work hours."

Hall liked her already, and her help really could prove invaluable in understanding what was going on. Two heads really were better than one. And even if not, the boost to his psychological well-being would be enormous. She could be the eye of the hurricane raging around him. She was already closer to him than anyone in the world—anyone he could remember, at least. And she shared his secret. Validated his sanity.

Leaving her now to face his predicament utterly alone seemed as daunting as willing his fingers to let go of a rope hanging hundreds of feet above jagged rocks. But he had to do it. The longer he stayed here, the more he endangered her.

And it occurred to him that holing up here might not have been a great idea, anyway. Even if the men after him couldn't identify Radich's car from the road, they could well be able to track its location.

"There is one thing you can do to help," he said.

Megan studied him expectantly.

"Do you have a car?"

She nodded. "It's parked in the back lot. A yellow Ford Taurus."

"Would you mind if I borrowed it? The longer I stay here, the more dangerous. And they know the car I drove here in. But they won't be looking for your Taurus. I just need to drive it somewhere else. Where I can go to ground for a while until the heat is off."

"You sound like a bad crime drama on TV."

"I *feel* like a bad crime drama on TV," he replied.

Hall reached into his pocket and handed her two twenties from the money he had taken from Baldino. "This should cover cab fare to retrieve your car. I'll send you an e-mail telling you where I left it, and where I left the keys." He paused. "Any other exit out to your car other than the main lobby?"

"Yes. There's an emergency exit. I can walk you there. If you stay close, I can make sure no one has a good view of the blood on your shirt. But it's five, so we should wait a few more minutes. The emergency exit is a bit out of the way, so we probably wouldn't run into anyone anyway. But just to be on the safe side . . . "

"Do most people leave right at five?"

"A lot do. At least in this wing. It's not that they're lazy," she hastened to explain. "Believe me, most of them put in sixty-hour weeks. But they can do their work anywhere. They just come here for the receptionist and trappings and to force themselves to get out of their pajamas. So they put in their extra hours at home. But on Fridays everyone wants to get a jump on the weekend, so they leave at five. Or even a few minutes earlier."

Hall nodded. He had had no idea it was Friday. He could have fished this information from anyone, but it hadn't occurred to him to do so.

Megan reached under the desk and grabbed her purse, a large, chestnut-colored soft-leather bag with silver accents. She opened it and pulled out a set of keys, removing her car key from a golden, heart-shaped ring and holding it out to him.

"I do have two conditions," she said, raising her eyebrows. "First, there's a guy in an office four doors down named Kurt Schrom. I like him as a friend, but that's all. He wants me to come with him on ski weekend, and swears he has nothing but platonic interest in me. Can you read in his mind if that's true or not?"

An impish grin came over Hall's face. "It's not," he said.

"Wow," said Megan. "You can find his mind *that* quickly, and dig out this kind of information?"

"No," said Hall, the smile still on his face. "Didn't need to. He's a man. And I've met you. That's all I need to know to answer the question."

Megan's eyes danced in amusement, pleased by the compliment.

"And the second condition?" asked Hall.

"Once you elude all the bad guys and figure this out, you have to promise to let me be a part of it. Whatever *it* is."

"You got it," he said, taking the proffered key and sliding it into his pants pocket. "But I think the odds are extremely long that I'll survive. As near as I can tell, you're the only one in Bakersfield *not* trying to kill me."

"I have every confidence in you. You woke up in a dumpster and there were several attempts on your life. And now, you're about to leave here in a car, willingly loaned to you by someone who was a total stranger and thought you were a serial killer just a few minutes ago. Pretty impressive."

Hall shook his head. "I've been lucky, not good. ESP and internal Internet gives one some major advantages."

"You seem to have a certain quality, a certain resourcefulness, that has gotten you to this point," she thought at him. *"You'll get through this. And when you do, remember your promise."*

He sighed. He knew in his heart he would never see this bright, energetic girl again. He would die having an effective memory of less than a day. But why argue the point further?

"Don't worry, he broadcast to her. *"This is one promise I'll remember."* He paused. *"And thanks for your help. You should have an e-mail with the location of your car within the hour."*

8

John Delamater bent over a black-and-white marble chessboard and studied a complex position from the recent world championships. Both sides had all of their pieces carefully deployed, and both were missing a rook, knight, bishop, and three pawns that had been traded in earlier exchanges. Each piece, from the queens down to the lowliest pawns, had been painstakingly positioned to maximize both their offensive and defensive capabilities.

Delamater was a thin, olive-skinned man with black hair, dark, deep-set eyes that seemed too close together and too small, and a sharp nose. "Mate in seven from this position," he announced to the muscular Russian approaching. "Dusek missed this in Helsinki and ended up losing the game."

Delamater motioned to a chair on the other side of the small oak table. "Sit down, Vasily," he said.

Vasily Chirkhoff did as requested. He was getting on in years, but you wouldn't know it from his level of fitness or musculature. He had served in the Spetsnaz and then worked his way up the KGB. But political and social upheavals in Russia had seemed never-ending, and he had decided that being the alpha wolf in a country of wolves was still more challenging, and less rewarding, than being an alpha wolf among the sheep of America. He had come to the States ten years earlier and never looked back.

Now he lived the life of decadent luxury. The food was better, the weather was better, and there were more entertainment choices; only the hookers were better in Russia, on average, but he had more than enough money to compensate for this shortcoming.

The fact that his last name, Chirkhoff, sounded like the American slang, *jerk off*, had been pointed out to him on several occasions when he arrived, but never by someone who wasn't tasting his own blood soon afterward. After he had been in the States six months, word had spread in the circles in which he traveled, and no one ever made this mistake again. Even so, he had made the decision his first year in America to introduce himself simply by his first name, Vasily, and after a while most people forgot he even had a last name. As his reputation grew, the name Vasily had become instantly identifiable to anyone who mattered, and he was no more in need of a last name than Moses, Plato, Rembrandt, or Elvis before him.

He had a knack for languages and soon spoke English with great fluency, even able to impersonate a native American the way that American actors could pretend to speak with a pronounced Russian accent if the role so required. It wasn't perfect, but native speakers just assumed he had an unplaceable accent from one of the fifty states.

Delamater had hired him two years earlier to lead various teams of men, whose exact identities he was sometimes told, sometimes not, on various assignments. The pay was excellent, as was the quality of the support, so he was well-satisfied.

Even so, he wasn't sure how much longer he would stay in Delamater's employ, although he expected that when the time came for divorce, it would be a messy one. The man was meticulous in ensuring all roads led to Vasily, and not to him. Only the Russian knew Delamater was pulling the strings. To anyone else, Delamater was a ghost—untraceable.

And Delamater was more of a psychopath than he was. And that was saying something. Or maybe he was just insane. Although Delamater never discussed it, Vasily was certain his boss had been a chess prodigy and would have easily been an international grandmaster had he chosen to pursue the game.

A framed poster hung over the chess table. The poster had a photo of a chessboard and pieces made of gold and silver, surrounded by famous chess quotes, such as, "When you see a good move, look for a better one," a quote supposedly once uttered by the chess great, Emanuel Lasker. Vasily had no doubt that Delamater's favorites were the two quotes attributed to Bobby Fischer, the American. The first: "I like the moment when I break a man's ego," and the second: "Chess is war over the board. The object is to crush the opponent's mind."

Vasily's own favorite was from the Russian, Bogolyubov. He loved the playful arrogance behind it, which always made him smile. "When I have White, I win because I am white. When I have Black, I win because I am Bogolyubov."

Vasily stared at the exceedingly dangerous man across the small table. A man whom Vasily had come to respect for his brilliant, strategic mind. While brilliance in chess strategy often failed to translate into the real world, this was not the case with Delamater.

But there was often a fine line between genius and insanity, which men like Bobbie Fischer, the Unabomber, and countless others throughout history had shown. Vasily sensed it was only a matter of time before Delamater crossed this line—if he hadn't already.

Delamater was kneading his temples and his mood seemed even darker than usual, as though he were ready to tear the heads off small animals with his bare hands. Or maybe with his teeth. His reputation for ruthlessness rivaled even that of Vasily's, so the big Russian felt uncharacteristic tension whenever Delamater's aura reached this level of chilling, black-hole darkness.

"You're making a rare personal visit, Vasily," began his wiry boss. "So let me guess. Nick Hall is still alive."

Vasily nodded.

"*You* backgrounded him. So I hold you personally responsible. What did you miss?"

The big Russian shook his head. "I've spent the past hour checking my work. I didn't miss anything. He's a marine biology PhD. Period. No record of any military or other self-defense training. Never owned a gun. Was held up four years ago by a kid with a knife and didn't resist."

Delamater glared at his guest with inhuman intensity. "And yet he's gotten through a dense net of your hired hands."

"So far," acknowledged Vasily.

"And the latest?"

"We had him dead to rights, but he slipped the noose. We no longer have a visual on him."

"Is he still driving Radich's car?"

"Yes. When last we saw him he was cutting across several lanes of traffic like a movie stunt-driver. Cassella got off a shot but didn't stop him, and wasn't in a position to pursue."

"If Hall's in a car that's known to us, explain to me why we need a visual."

Vasily returned his stare without blinking. "We're close to having a GPS read on it, but we don't have it yet. Soon, John. Very soon. Like most people in his line of work, Radich took great pains to make sure his car wasn't easily traceable. But we're close. Any minute."

"Close isn't good enough," spat Delamater through clenched teeth. "Hall could have easily ditched the car already."

"Yes. He could have. But he didn't. Trust me."

"Why didn't he? Because you think you know who he is? Haven't you already learned that you don't? Yes, if he was consistent with the picture you provided of a helpless marine biologist, you'd be right. He'd never consider the perils of driving Radich's car, even if he thought he'd slipped cleanly through the pursuit. He wouldn't know how to steal another. He'd be totally out of his element. But if he was the man you thought he was, he'd be dead already."

"His luck can't hold forever."

"I don't believe in luck."

"We'll get him," replied Vasily with absolute conviction.

"See that you do. Soon. Offer an extra hundred grand on top of what you've already offered to the lucky man who kills him. If Hall manages to catch his breath and start talking, it would be very . . . *inconvenient* for me."

Vasily nodded solemnly. He was well-paid and well-treated. While Delamater lived sparsely like a monk, as far as Vasily could tell spending all his free time playing chess, Vasily lived like a king, with a huge house, indoor pool, and all the women he could want.

But he had no doubt that any inconvenience felt by Delamater would be redirected his way, ten-fold. And that would be very, very bad.

9

Megan Emerson returned to her office with her mind spinning and her feet partially off the ground. Wow. Had that really happened? Had she really had a telepathic exchange with another human being? How freaky was that? And how electrifying.

She was dying to share what had happened with someone, but she knew they would think she was nuts without Hall's ability to demonstrate. He had also warned her that displaying public knowledge of him or his abilities was probably very bad for her health.

But what had happened was just so fricking *incredible*. It almost seemed as though she must have imagined it all.

She had moved from Los Angeles to Bakersfield only a few months earlier, determined to get a business off the ground and lured by the far better rents—both office and apartment. The cost of an office was still a stretch, but having clients come to such a nice facility gave her the air of professionalism that was important. She was branching out, determined to make this work.

She had left a number of friends, as well as a past love interest, behind, and while she had kept her relationships alive with her friends, she had severed all ties with Darren Ortman. She had learned the hard way, her first year at UCLA, that a long-distance relationship—even if the distance could be covered in a few hours—could turn into a nightmare in a hurry, and she wasn't about to make that mistake again. And they had been beginning to drift apart anyway.

But starting with a clean slate was scary. And difficult. And although she loved the creative end of things, her social life was almost non-existent, and her life in general had become almost insufferably boring outside of work.

Enter Nick Hall. Center stage. Unshaven. Hair in disarray. Wearing baggy clothes and a blood-stained shirt.

Who could have known he'd be so intriguing? And alluring.

When it came to hitting her buttons, he had achieved a perfect score. Injured and capable of bringing out her Florence Nightingale instincts. Check. Bright and obviously well-educated. Check. Often looking like a lost little boy because he had no idea who he was. Check. International man of mystery. Check. And fricking capable of reading minds and surfing the fricking web in his fricking head. Check. And mate.

Megan had wanted with every ounce of her soul to run off with him on a great adventure. But he had made a good point, and she wasn't suicidal. Too bad, because unlike marriage, this was an adventure she was certain she wanted to undertake.

Her parents had gone through a messy divorce, so she was jaded about people and relationships. She had often wondered if humans were even psychologically built for marriage. Yes, it was probably genetically ingrained in the species for people to mate up to help raise children, like those tuxedo-wearing Emperor penguins that were always the subject of documentaries.

And maybe mating for life made sense in prehistoric times when many died before their kids were through puberty. She had never forgotten what she had learned in a history class at UCLA: that the average life expectancy in the Roman empire had been in the twenties, below the age at which the vast majority of people even married in today's world. It was true that many Roman's died during childhood, skewing the average lower, but still . . . *Till death do us part* seemed far more achievable when your death came in your twenties or thirties rather than at eighty.

She was still young, but she was getting to the point at which she had to think about what course she wanted her life to take. She had become as morose as she could ever remember. Maybe the move to Bakersfield at this time in her life had affected her more than she thought. She hadn't lost her memory like Hall, but she had severed a large part of her past life just as well.

She had always been outgoing, but without question the move had dampened this personality trait. She knew she didn't need a man for happiness, but she did need *something*. She lived alone. Yes, she had made a few friends in her apartment complex and had gone out dancing and to a few bars, but while she had been hit on a number of times, she hadn't found anyone she really liked. She was about to start online dating. Why not? Everyone was doing it these days, and if you went to bars, you couldn't exactly complain about the quality, and motives, of the men you met there.

In fact, she needed to stop going to bars for a more important reason: she had started drinking more than she should, probably to fill a void within. She had to get this under control. She had always been the kind of person that the expression, "high on life" was made for, stupid as it was. So why did she seem to need alcohol lately for this purpose?

She frowned as she thought about it. Maybe she should have insisted on helping Nick Hall anyway. You only go around once in life. In addition to the mystery of the man and the many silly romantic buttons he had pushed, there was something about his personality, beyond all of these other factors, that she had liked. A shyness. A vulnerability. An intelligence.

On the other hand, who knew what amnesia did to a personality? Hard to be overbearing when you were so confused. Maybe he was a total jackass when he remembered who he was. Maybe he was in a hot-and-heavy relationship. But even if he did turn out to be taken, or a total jerk, it didn't matter. Even if she had no interest in him, it didn't matter. Because telepathy was *awesome*. Beyond awesome. Talk about adding spice to your perspective. She would kill to be a part of whatever he was involved in.

She just wasn't quite ready to die for it.

He had agreed to come back for her when he learned more about who he was, and what he was up against. Even so, she knew the chances she would ever see him again were small. The e-mail message he would be sending soon, telling her where to retrieve her car, would most likely be the last she would ever hear from him.

Megan leaned back in her chair and closed her eyes, replaying her encounter with the homeless-looking man who had burst into her office. Replaying their telepathic communications with each other.

Her eyes shot open as the door to her office bolted inward once again.

Two men entered and closed the door behind them. Both were fit and intense, one bald as a billiard ball and the other blond.

"*What is this about?*" she demanded. "You can't just barge—"

"Shut up!" said the blond, removing a gun with a long, thin barrel attached, which Megan recognized immediately as a silencer.

She felt queasy and suddenly found it hard to breathe. She had no doubt why these men were here, but they had missed Nick Hall by eight or nine minutes. He was even now on the road, driving away from them as quickly as he could in a yellow Ford Taurus.

The bald intruder held a small electronic cube in one hand and a cell phone in the other. He walked the few steps to the chair in front of her desk and set the cube-shaped device down on it. He glanced at the screen and then nodded at his partner, a grim look on his pock-marked face.

He removed a business card from the card holder on her desk. "Her name is Megan Emerson," he said into the phone. "Works at the address we're at now. I'd advise you to find where she lives and send someone to stake it out, just in case." With that, he ended the connection.

The blond turned toward Megan, the gun in his hand never wavering. "So tell us about your visitor," he said.

She shook her head in pretend confusion. "What visitor?"

He removed the cube-shaped device from the chair and lifted it into the air, gesturing to its digital readout. "Have you ever seen one of these?" he asked

She shook her head.

"It's a very expensive piece of equipment. It's basically a blood-hound in a box. And right now this one has been keyed to the scent of a man named Nick Hall. I have no idea how it works, but I'm told it can detect a smell at one part per hundred billion—which even an actual bloodhound can't match. And do you know what it's telling us? It's telling us that the guy we're looking for, Nick Hall, came into this office." He nodded at the chair in front of her desk. "And sat in this chair."

Megan swallowed hard.

"So last time I'm going to ask nicely," said the blond ominously. "Tell me about this visit. And more importantly, tell me where he is now."

Megan's breath caught in her throat. "Your device must be wrong," she croaked, intending to say this with confidence and defiance, but barely rasping it out. "Or maybe he broke in when I wasn't here."

In a blur the blond was behind her, gluing a huge palm over her mouth and pressing her body back against his. He lowered his other hand, still holding the silenced gun, and pulled the trigger without hesitation. Megan felt a blinding pain in her upper thigh the same instant she heard a spit sound issuing from the barrel of the silencer.

She screamed into the man's hand, which was now pressed into her mouth so hard she thought her teeth might cave in.

"I'm going to release you," he whispered into her ear. "Scream and I'll take out your knee. Do we understand each other?"

She nodded.

The man removed his hand as tears of pain and fear began to slide down her cheeks. He had shot her! Without blinking. Just to prove to her that he was utterly ruthless. The man was a *monster*, and a fear and hopelessness greater than any she had ever known seeped into her soul.

"Last chance," he said calmly as blood poured from her leg and soaked her pants. "Where is he?"

Megan fought to ignore the barrage of nerve signals hammering into the pain centers of her brain. Tears continued to roll down her face, almost of their own volition. She had to tell this savage what he wanted. Nick Hall had abilities that should allow him to protect himself, as he had done before. But even if not, she didn't have a choice. "He left about ten minutes ago. In my car. It's a Ford Taurus."

"Give me the license plate number."

She unconsciously shifted weight and the daggers of pain intensified. She grimaced and shifted her weight back the other way. "Okay," she said, calming herself enough to dredge this information from a suddenly uncooperative memory. She opened her mouth to recite the number when a powerful thought exploded into her head. A *telepathic* thought.

"Megan, stop! Find a way to stall! I've read his mind, and he'll kill you the second you give him your plate!"

"License plate!" the man hissed, moving in front of her and pressing the barrel of the gun into her knee.

"I'll be there in just a minute," broadcast Nick Hall. *"Hang on!"*

"I'll give it to you," said Megan to the blond killer. "But I can do better than that. I know exactly where this Hall is going. Exactly."

The man smiled. "Where?"

Megan raised a hand and pretended a wave of dizziness was coming over her. Every second counted. But she also couldn't risk getting *too* cute. These were not patient men. "You have to. . . promise . . . not to kill me," she said as slowly as she thought she could get away with, pretending her injury had sapped most of her strength.

"Of course. Tell me what I want and we'll leave. Simple as that."

"How close are you, Nick?" she broadcast hastily, with as much force as she knew how to use.

"Maybe thirty seconds. I'm sprinting as fast as I can. Keep stalling. You're doing great."

"How do I . . . know. . . I can trust you?" she said weakly.

The blond shook his head in annoyance and glanced at his bald partner. "Look. There's only one thing you can be sure of," he said, returning the gun to her kneecap. "If you don't tell me where he is in *three seconds*, you'll never walk again."

"Okay," she said frantically, and realized that her tears had stopped and she was thinking as clearly as she ever had. Knowing Nick was on his way had given her hope, and the adrenaline in her system was doing its job, allowing her to temporarily function at a high level despite her injury and circumstances. "There's an old. . . abandoned warehouse. . . about twenty miles . . . from here. On a road . . . called Franklin. He'll be . . . hiding. . . there. But he's planning to. . . to booby-trap the place. In case he gets company."

"*Brilliant!*" came an encouraging voice in her head. "*Just a few more seconds.*"

"But I know how . . . I know how to . . . bypass his trap. He's placing explosives . . . at the main door. But there is a loading dock. On the northeast side. You just have to—"

"*Hit the floor! Now!*"

Megan froze.

"*NOW!*" broadcast Hall so powerfully that if the word had been spoken it might have burst her eardrums. She dropped to the ground.

And less than a second later, so did the two men near her.

Both of their backs had been only a foot or two from the outer wall of her office, and Hall sent multiple silenced slugs through the flimsy wall material and into their bodies. They were dead before they could come close to comprehending what had hit them.

Megan realized vaguely that Hall must have read their precise position from their minds. They hadn't even known he was there, yet he had been able to shoot them at point blank range; so close that even a novice shooter couldn't miss.

Hall entered a second after the two men had fallen, probably having been able to detect the cessation of their thoughts immediately. He closed the door and rushed over to Megan on the floor, whose leg was continuing to seep bright red blood.

Hall glanced at the two men he had killed, and an anguished expression came over his face. He then turned to Megan, and his eyes moistened at the sight of her injury. "I am *so* sorry," he whispered. "This is all my fault."

He pulled a pair of shears from a black metal canister on Megan's desk and cut strips of cloth from one of the attacker's shirts. He folded one of the pieces several times to form a thick bandage and tied it down tightly with the other strips of material. He accessed the web to learn the best way to deal with a gunshot wound, but he didn't find anything magical, just to staunch the flow of blood as best he could—pressure was key—get her to emergency personnel immediately, and be on the lookout for signs of shock, which would cause her to pass out if she had lost too much blood.

"I left your car a few feet from the back exit," he explained while he was tending to her injury. "I'll drive you to a hospital as soon as I'm done. I'm afraid we can't risk an ambulance. They called in your name. Whoever they're working for knows you spoke with me. And I read from their minds that they'd been ordered to be sure there are no loose ends. The people after me won't let you live no matter what now. But these two never got to tell anyone that I took your car."

He stared at her with absolute resolve. "I promise you, Megan, you're going to be okay. I won't let anything happen to you. *I swear it.* This is all my fault."

"It *isn't*," she said, her voice now faint. "*You* didn't shoot me."

Hall carefully lifted her from the floor and sat her in her wheeled desk chair, placing her large purse gently on her lap to hide her injury, and pushed her between the bodies of the men he had killed and out of her office. He suspected Megan Emerson hadn't been pushed any distance in a desk chair since she was nine or ten, if ever, but this was by far the best method of transportation available.

"*Thanks for coming back for me,*" broadcast Megan telepathically, too weak for speech but still able to get her thoughts across.

"*I'm just sorry I was so late,*" he replied in the same way. "*I was already a mile away when they began to examine Radich's car in your lot. I picked up their thoughts and knew their bloodhound device would lead them right to you. I got back as fast as I could.*" Even though he was using telepathy, it was easy for Megan to detect the undertones of guilt and self-reproach in his words.

"*What's your blood type?*" Hall thought to ask.

"*O positive.*"

A man appeared in the corridor as Hall continued wheeling Megan as fast as he could toward the exit, but he didn't waste time slowing down. Not surprisingly, the man's mouth was agape, not entirely able to believe what he was seeing. "It's my turn for a ride next," said Hall as he raced by the other occupant of the hallway.

The man turned to follow their progress, but didn't respond. Although Megan couldn't read minds, she was pretty certain he was thinking something like, *What a couple of morons*, or *That is some messed up shit.*

They made it to the car parked outside, and Hall lifted her into the passenger's seat and belted her in. He slid in behind the wheel and started the car. "Hang in there," he pleaded as the car began to move.

10

"We're missing something," said John Delamater. "Was your man at the mini-mart any good? This Cody Radich?" he asked Vasily.

"Very," replied the Russian. Unlike several of the men on the current manhunt, who had no connection to Vasily, Radich had worked with him often.

"Get him on speakerphone," ordered Delamater. "Don't give my name, but vouch for me and tell him to answer my questions."

Four minutes later Radich's voice issued from a speaker that Delamater had placed beside his beloved chessboard on the small wooden table. Vasily insisted that Radich repeat everything that had happened, down to the smallest detail, along with his every thought and impression, no matter how insignificant. Delamater leaned close, with his right hand rubbing his chin, as he listened to the man's account of what had transpired.

When he had finished, Delamater gestured to the phone, and its mute button.

"Hold on," said Vasily as he muted the connection.

"If Radich is telling the truth," said Delamater, "I can't see how Hall made him. He has to be hiding a mistake." He motioned again for Vasily to unmute.

"Any chance your gun was visible?" Delamater asked Radich.

"None."

"Any chance you were pretending to read the wrong magazine? One that didn't make sense for you? *Ladies Home Journal*? *Vogue*?"

"*Popular Mechanics*," hissed Radich, in a tone that made it clear he was offended by these questions, but he was enough of a professional to keep his temper in check when speaking to someone he would have to assume was Vasily's boss. "And before you ask, the magazine was right side up."

"Any chance you looked out of place?"

"No. I was dressed casually. No tattoos that would suggest I was military or mercenary. Nothing."

Delamater had Vasily put his assassin on hold once again. What was he missing? There was something about Radich that gave Delamater a sense he was competent and really hadn't made any blunders. Delamater was a good judge of character and had learned to trust his instincts, which had served him well. He turned to the Russian. "Do you think he's covering up a mistake?"

"I don't," said Vasily without hesitation. "He's one of the best I've ever worked with. Smart, experienced, and detail-oriented. I spoke with him earlier. He's as mystified as we are."

Delamater gathered his thoughts and motioned for Vasily to un-mute. "Okay," said Delamater. "So somehow, miraculously, this guy gets the drop on you. Even though he has no way to know you aren't just a harmless customer? Is that what you're saying?"

"That's what I'm saying," replied Radich woodenly.

"And you just *took it?* You didn't make any move against him? Against a marshmallow like this guy?"

"I was going to," came the frustrated reply. "But the instant before I was about to try to disarm him, he jumped out of range. Like he knew I was going to attack before I did. It was uncanny."

Radich paused. "And as I explained to Vasily, your intel on this guy is *shit*. Based on the intel, I tried to get him off-balance by suggesting the safety on Baldino's gun was still on. According to the profile I was given, this guy shouldn't have even known which end of a gun to *point*. Not only did he know Baldino's Glock didn't have a traditional safety, he knew it had a fucking five-pound trigger pull. This is lower than most guns, which is one of the reasons the Glock is so popular. But *I* didn't even know the exact spec on the trigger pull."

Delamater tilted his head in thought. "How do you know he was right?"

"I looked it up afterward. He was right."

Delamater's eyes brightened for just a moment. An important piece of the puzzle had clicked into place. He thanked Radich and motioned for the Russian to end the connection.

Vasily opened his mouth to speak, but Delamater held up a forestalling hand. He needed to complete his thinking without interruption.

Hall's four implants were working, after all.

It was the only way to explain how Hall could pass as an expert, could possess detailed information on Baldino's gun. The bastard had his own personal Internet connection.

Hall had lied when he had said the system wasn't working.

But why?

Being able to stealthily surf the web, using thoughts alone, would confer a considerable advantage on someone. But it was hard for Delamater to believe this had been responsible for *all* of Hall's success. Access to the Internet couldn't help him dodge bullets.

But regardless, this could change Delamater's calculations dramatically. He would now have to weigh additional options to determine if a change in strategy was in order.

Delamater had human resources at his disposal that Vasily couldn't even begin to guess at. If you kept palms well greased and didn't ask for much in return, it was easy to corrupt even those thought to be incorruptible. People were greedy and power-hungry, especially the ones who had risen to positions of prominence. Unless you truly believed in something to the deepest depth of your being, as did Delamater, all men were whores in the end.

There was an old joke that had always struck Delamater as defining of the human species. A man asks a woman if she would sleep with him for ten million dollars. She agrees. He then asks if she would sleep with him for a dollar. She is aghast. "What kind of woman do you take me for?" she asks. To that, the man responds, "We have established what you are, madam. Now we're just haggling over the price."

Such was true of humanity in general. He was a rare exception, but the vast majority of humanity would do *anything* for the right price, be it money, power, prestige, or sex. The idea of a man selling his soul to the Devil was a mainstay of fiction, and people found it plausible that someone would strike such a bargain, even when they knew exactly who it was they were dealing with.

But before he committed to a course of action, he needed to speak with his brother. Seek the council of the only man alive whom he fully respected, and whose respect he truly valued. He needed to inform him of this triumphant new development.

His brother was working hard on a project of his own, one with far less lofty goals than Delamater's own project, but one whose chance of success was far higher. His brother had always believed he was wasting his time on this project. That despite his obvious genius at getting past the first monumental hurdle, it still wouldn't matter: what he hoped to achieve with implants was still fifty years away and couldn't be rushed, no matter what the strategy. Delamater had no doubt this stunning new development would get his brother to reevaluate his position, possibly even to drop what he was doing and join Delamater's efforts.

"Vasily," said Delamater finally, breaking from his reverie. "I need you to go out to Bakersfield immediately and take personal charge of operations. Amateur hour is over," he finished, knowing full well they had not sent amateurs, but also that Vasily was a cut above the rest. He gave the Russian a curt nod of dismissal.

Vasily rose. "I'll call you when I'm on the ground."

He took a few steps toward the door to let himself out, but turned before he reached his destination. "I may have misread your expression when the call ended. But it looked like you had figured something out. Something important. If so, it could be vital that I know about it."

Delamater nodded. "You're right," he said, shooting Vasily an icy stare. "You did misread my expression."

11

Hall pulled out into traffic with Megan Emerson in the passenger's seat. She had closed her eyes, but because he couldn't read her mind unless she was broadcasting to him, he wasn't sure if she was still conscious. Returning to her office had reduced his chances of survival, but he had never considered any other course.

Did this tell him anything about himself?

He took it as a good sign, but he wasn't sure it made any kind of definitive statement about who he was—or who he had been. Would a coward or a thief *remain* a coward or a thief, even if his memory slate was wiped clean? Or could he somehow become courageous and noble?

Could not knowing you had a history of cowardice allow you to suddenly become brave? Were bravery and altruism learned qualities or innate ones?

He knew he had no time to consider these questions now, or even to appreciate the software in his implants that made no attempt to search the web in response to his ponderings, realizing he wasn't looking for answers in cyberspace.

After he had left Megan's office he had attempted to find himself on Facebook, as he had with her, using La Jolla and San Diego as locations to narrow it down, but he hadn't had any luck. It had seemed like half of San Diego was named Nick Hall. But even after scanning through them all, he had gotten nowhere. Perhaps he didn't live there after all. Or he was one of the few people on earth without a Facebook account.

He called up directions to the nearest hospital, but even as he did so he concluded that taking Megan there would be a mistake. He vaguely remembered that hospitals were required to alert the police whenever they were visited by gunshot victims, and confirmed it on the web moments later.

After a few minutes deep in thought he arrived at a plan, which he didn't like at all, but which was the best he could come up with. He had no idea how much time he had, but he had to err on the side of extreme urgency.

Hall searched cyberspace and located a nearby motel that was dirt cheap and off the beaten path, the Kern River Motor Lodge. He pulled into its gravel lot seven minutes later, having risked racing there at twice the speed limit where traffic would allow and having ignored five red lights.

He left Megan in the passenger's seat and entered the tiny shack that was the lobby, asking for a room that would minimize neighbors and maximize privacy. The attendant, an obese middle-aged man with a braided beard, didn't seem to find the request the slightest bit unusual. Nor that Hall checked in as John Smith, paying in cash. All of which led Hall to believe that the motel did plenty of business with prostitutes serving married men concerned about their anonymity.

Hall had chosen even better than he had hoped.

He pulled around to the end of the stubby, L-shaped line of rooms and carried Megan inside. Her eyes fluttered open for a few seconds while he moved her, and she might have tilted her chin the slightest bit in a nod, but he couldn't be sure.

The room was small and dark, with nothing but a bathroom, bed, end table, and a small TV that looked to be ten years old. It smelled of mildew.

Hall lowered Megan gently onto the bed and picked up the phone on the end-table, a relic of a bygone age when everyone didn't have their own cell phone. It probably hadn't been used in years.

He dialed 9-1-1, and his call was answered on the second ring.

"I'm in room one eighty-seven at the Kern River Motor Lodge," he said hastily. "My wife was trying to cut open a package and stabbed herself in the leg pretty bad with a pair of scissors. She's lost a lot of blood and can't walk."

"Is she conscious?"

"Yes. But send an ambulance as fast as you can. She may need some blood. So make sure the paramedic has O positive with him."

Even as he said this he looked it up online and realized this was unnecessary: O positive was the most common type of blood. He was getting facile at using the Internet, like it was just another part of his mind, and mining cyberspace for information was becoming as fast and effortless as calling up a well-known fact from memory.

"We'll dispatch an ambulance right away," the young woman on the phone assured him.

"*Thank you*," said Hall in genuine relief. "And please ask the ambulance to kill the siren when they get close. Our baby and toddler are both sound asleep, and I don't want to freak them out on top of everything else."

Five minutes later two men knocked on his door. An ambulance was parked in front, but without the siren it hadn't attracted gawkers. Since it was the dinner hour, the motel was largely uninhabited in any case.

Hall ushered the men in, each holding a canvas medical bag, and they sprang open a collapsible stainless steel gurney in front of them. Megan was on her back on the bed. Hall had elevated her leg on a stack of two pillows.

"Please just fix her up here," said Hall. "No need to take her to a hospital."

Hall read the mind of the shorter of the two paramedics, a Hispanic, and fished out his name: Hector Garcia.

"I'm afraid in a case like this," said Garcia, "we *have* to take her in. We can stabilize her here. But we're required to bring her to the hospital as soon as possible."

They walked over to her unconscious body and examined Hall's makeshift bandages, while Hall slipped into both of their minds effortlessly. He divined that Garcia had considerable experience and was more senior than his partner, Tony Kosakowski. Garcia pulled a bright LED light from his bag, and both men examined Megan's wound.

Garcia tensed and was immediately alert. *She had powder burns around the entry*. Dispatch had said this was a scissor wound, but he now had no doubt it was a gunshot wound. Which meant they had been lied to.

Hall cursed inwardly as he picked up these thoughts, but decided it was just as well. He and Megan couldn't have afforded to be taken to the hospital anyway, where they would be sitting ducks, even if Garcia hadn't figured out Megan had been shot.

Hall removed Baldino's gun from the waistband of his pants and pointed it at the two paramedics standing over Megan. "We need to talk," he said, and both men's eyes widened as they saw the gun pointed their way.

"What's this about?" said Kosakowski, his face now pale.

"Look, I don't mean you any harm," said Hall. "I just can't have you reporting a gunshot wound or taking her in. You need to work on her here."

"Gunshot wound?" repeated Kosakowski stupidly.

Hall read Garcia's frustration at being partnered with such a Newbie, who probably would have missed the telltales if he had seen the shooting personally. *Don't mean us any harm, my ass*, thought the short paramedic bitterly.

Hall knew that Kosakowski hadn't bought his claim either, and that both men were alert for even the slightest chance to escape or turn the tables. He couldn't blame them.

"She needs an IV," said Garcia. "It's already set up in the ambulance."

Hall searched the paramedic's mind and discovered it wouldn't be difficult to move the IV pole and paraphernalia into the room. "Hector," he said, "I need you to start working on the girl right away. Tony, I need you to bring the IV equipment in here, as quickly and discreetly as possible."

Both men's mouths fell open, and Hall was blasted by panicked thoughts of tremendous intensity. He should have realized that using their names would elevate their state of alarm ten-fold, since this level of familiarity was an indication of bizarre, almost certainly psychopathic premeditation on his part. Was this a trap for them? Was the girl just a lure? Was he after them personally for some psychotic reason? What kind of crazed stalker asshole *was* this guy?

"Tony, I know you're thinking of calling for help the second you leave this room," said Hall. "Don't try it. Cooperate and both of you will be just fine. But, Tony, if you try anything—*anything*—I'll have no choice but to kill your partner. And then I'll find you at . . ." He paused and tilted his head. "Eighty-two fifty-eight Big Orchard Road, and kill you as well."

If the use of their names had troubled them, Hall's knowledge of Kosakowski's address hit them like a supercharged cattle prod.

"Look, I can read minds," explained Hall. "That's how I know your address. So if you call anyone from the ambulance or try anything, I'll know about it instantly. Let me demonstrate," he continued, turning to Garcia. "Think of a three digit number."

Garcia hesitated.

"Now!" demanded Hall.

Garcia did as Hall asked, despite thinking he was certainly dealing with a madman.

"Six seventy-three," said Hall, and the paramedic's eyes widened in amazement. "Think of another one."

Garcia did so.

"Two eighty-nine," said Hall immediately, and an observer wouldn't have had to be able to read minds to tell from Garcia's expression that Hall was correct once again.

Hall quickly repeated this demonstration with Kosakowski. "Look, I can do this all day, but you need to start helping this poor girl."

Of all the Twilight Zone shit, thought Kosakowski. *What the fuck is this?*

"Not *Twilight Zone*," said Hall. "Reality. Now hurry up. And remember: I can tell the instant you even *think* of trying anything."

Kosakowski nodded and left the room, mumbling to himself. Hall read from his mind that he was totally freaked out and was fighting to not even think a disloyal thought, let alone act on one.

Hector Garcia bent to his task while Hall looked on.

"This girl was lucky," said the paramedic after his examination. "Clean shot through her inner thigh. Didn't nick anything important, like bone, or even worse, her femoral artery. And you did well bandaging the wound. I can stitch this up with a half dozen dissolving stitches, and spray some quick-clot foam on it. Once I bandage her and give her an infusion of Lactated Ringer's and antibiotics, she'll be good as new in no time."

"Lactated Ringer's?" said Hall suspiciously. "Doesn't she need blood?"

"No. I've had a lot of experience with this. From her blood pressure, blood oxygenation levels, and other indications, she's lost a lot of blood, about twenty percent. But this isn't enough to require a transfusion. But she does need volume resuscitation to maintain good pressure." He paused. "Trust me. I'm giving her the best care I can."

Hall nodded. "I don't need to trust you. I *know* you're telling the truth. And thanks," he added sincerely. He tilted his head. "If her blood loss wasn't enough to require transfusion, why did she go into shock, then?"

Garcia shrugged. "The less you weigh the more you feel the impact, in general. And it isn't full-on shock. Her blood pressure dropped enough for her to feel faint, and her psyche just went with it. She'll be alert in no time."

Kosakowski returned with everything needed for an infusion. Hall had monitored him while he was out of sight, and while the man was still wondering what parallel universe he had suddenly fallen into, and fearful for his life, he continued to have no plans for a double-cross.

The men positioned Megan on the steel gurney, and Kosakowski started an IV while Garcia went to work, cleaning and patching her wound. A bag of clear liquid soon hung from a hook on a thin steel pole, with IV tubing leading from the bag, through a pump, and into the back of Megan's hand.

Five minutes later Garcia was finished, and Hall knew the paramedic was satisfied with his work, and certain Megan would make a
full recovery. Which was good enough for Hall.

"How long until you've infused enough . . . what did you call it?"

"Lactated Ringer's," said Garcia. "Another forty minutes should
do it," he said.

Hall had been deep in thought while the paramedics worked, and
had come up with a plan, having decided that staying at the hotel
would be too dangerous. He had also realized another mistake he
had made, so on his way out of the room he removed Megan's cell
phone from her purse and tossed it gently under a bush, so it couldn't
be used to track them.

Hall explained what he wanted to the two men, and within minutes they were in the ambulance, en route to the Bakersfield Amtrak
station.

The station was a twenty thousand square-foot brick and glass
structure that Hall had learned in cyberspace had opened at the turn
of the new century, and served as the main hub for both train and bus
transportation to and from the city.

Hall instructed them to take a circuitous route so they would
arrive just after the infusion was complete. Halfway there, Megan
opened her eyes, and she continued to gain strength by the minute.

While Kosakowski drove, Garcia also cleaned and re-bandaged
Hall's wound, which he deemed to be fairly minor, a diagnosis Hall
had already made on his own.

Finally, the IV line was removed from Megan's hand and she was
given a clean bill of health. Rest and good nutrition, they were told,
would have her back to normal in no time. The bandages around
her thigh were more obvious than Hall would have liked, so he decided to take one of the ambulance's light weight, disposable fleece
blankets with him when he left, as well as one of the green nylon
windbreakers stored in the vehicle, which he put on and zipped up to
conceal the bandages on his upper arm.

They pulled up near the train station and parked, and Hall reluctantly confiscated all the cash the two men had on hand, totaling one hundred and eighty-nine dollars between them.

"I can't tell you how much I appreciate what you've done for us," said Hall to the two men as he and Megan prepared to exit. "And I'm truly sorry I had to threaten you. I consider guys like you heroes. You don't deserve to be treated like this. I just didn't have any choice. And the money I've taken is just a loan. If I survive long enough, I intend to return it. Doubled."

Hall read that both men were beginning to believe he was sincere, and that they might live through this. At this point, getting their money back was the least of their concerns.

"Once we're gone," continued Hall, "I'll still be reading your thoughts for a time. To make sure you don't tell the cops we're here. But by tomorrow your thoughts will be your own. And I promise to never intrude upon your privacy or trouble you in any other way again. At that point, you can go to the authorities and tell them all about us."

He paused. "But I'd advise against it. Not for *my* safety. I already have every adult male in the area—and maybe some females for all I know—trying to kill me. But the only reason this girl is injured, and now is in as much danger as *I* am, is simply because I crossed paths with her. I've read the minds of the people after me, and they plan to kill anyone I come into contact with."

Hall frowned deeply and lowered his eyes for just a moment. He had become Typhoid Mary, carrying distilled death. No matter what, he vowed to stop endangering innocents in this way, regardless of the cost.

"And I can't guarantee you can even trust the police," he continued. "For your own safety, *please* pretend this never happened. *Please*," he pleaded for good measure. He knew the absolute sincerity in his voice was reaching these men, but only time would tell if they would heed his warnings.

They stared at him for several long seconds.

"Who *are* you?" whispered Garcia finally.

Hall sighed. "I only wish I knew," he replied.

And without another word, he and Megan exited the ambulance and began walking slowly toward the station.

12

Megan walked gingerly, and Hall had insisted on carrying her purse. Even so, he asked if she needed rest after only ten or twelve steps.

"*I'll be okay,*" she assured him telepathically. "*Hector loaded me up with enough painkillers to numb a dinosaur. And I'm already embarrassed by how much of a baby I've been.*"

"*Not at all. You've been through a severe trauma.*"

"*That's not the way Hector made it seem when he reviewed my case. I got the feeling he's treated people in some of the rougher neighborhoods who could take a minor bullet wound like this and then play a game of full-court basketball.*"

Hall laughed as they entered the building. "*They also weigh more than a hundred pounds,*" he replied.

"*I'm not sure it's entirely a weight thing. I've always been a little squeamish at the sight of blood. Especially when it's my own. I'm glad I was out when Hector treated me. I'll try to be less of a wimp in the future. I have a feeling I'm going to need to be.*"

Hall nodded somberly, but didn't reply. He had already apologized more times than he could count for dragging her into this, and while becoming injured and a target was horrifying to her, she was a realist. She was in this now whether she liked it or not, and wasting focus or emotional energy lamenting her position would reduce her chances of making it out the other end. She was taking this better than Hall had any right to hope she would, for which he was thankful.

They entered the station, which was a combination of mint green steel beams, glass, and red brick walls, and he carefully sat Megan in one of the padded chairs that were linked together in rows, spreading the bright blue fleece blanket he had taken from the ambulance over her lap. The station was really beginning to bustle, and Hall guessed that Friday after work hours was one of the busiest times for train and bus travel.

"Don't go away," he said, moving into the scattered crowd.

Five minutes later he was back. "I was checking out schedules," he explained as he returned.

"Where are we going?" asked Megan.

"I don't know. We can afford two train tickets to Merced, Fresno, or Hanford. Or two bus tickets to San Bernardino or Perris. They all leave within the next hour."

"No trips to larger cities? I'd think the bigger the city, the easier it would be to lose ourselves."

"There's a train leaving for LA and a bus to San Francisco in this time frame, but we can't afford the tickets. Not if we want to have enough cash left over for a hotel. Remind me to steal from richer people next time," he added with a grin. "Which brings to mind a quote from Margaret Thatcher: 'Socialism is great—but eventually you run out of other people's money.'"

"So you remember a quote from Margaret Thatcher, but you can't remember anything about who you are?"

"I'm afraid that's how this seems to be working," replied Hall.

Megan nodded toward her purse, which Hall had placed beside her on an empty seat. "I have a Visa with a five thousand dollar credit limit. So money isn't a problem."

Hall paused in thought. "Won't they be able to trace it?" he asked. There was no need for him to specify who he meant by *they*.

"Not nearly as easily as the movies would have you think," said Megan.

Hall frowned. He had learned that knocking someone out with the butt of a gun, without actually killing them, wasn't as easy as movies would have you think, either. Wow, he thought sarcastically, if you couldn't trust Hollywood . . .

"For them to access my Visa information in real time," continued Megan, "they'd have to have some major credentials. Or very impressive capabilities."

"You're probably right. But I think we'd better assume they'll be able to, just to be on the safe side."

A few seconds later a sly smile spread over his face. "But maybe this isn't such a bad thing. Maybe we can turn this in our favor."

"How?"

"What if I buy us two tickets to eight or nine different destinations. Even if they're able to pull the Visa records and see all eight or nine, so what?"

"We're going to be busy little travelers, aren't we?" said Megan in amusement. "Good thinking. If that doesn't confuse our followers, nothing will." She paused. "Wait, I have another idea," she added excitedly, shifting positions abruptly as she did so, which turned out to be a mistake. A look of nausea swept over her face, and she grabbed the arm of the chair for support and closed her eyes.

"Are you okay?"

Megan took a deep breath. "Yeah. Got dizzy. Still a little light-headed, I guess."

She looked up at his concerned face, more deliberately this time. "As I was about to say, let's choose a destination. You go and buy tickets to the *other* eight or nine places that we *didn't* choose using my credit card. Then, just before we leave, I buy tickets to our *real* destination in cash. That way, if they can access my purchase records, we're not giving them a bunch of false leads and one real one. We're giving them *all* false leads."

"Very clever. You seem to have a knack for this."

Megan reached inside her purse, opened her wallet, and handed Hall her Visa card.

"So where do you want to go?" asked Hall. He reeled off the destinations he had already mentioned once again. "Any of these sound good?"

"Is there really a Paris, California?"

"I guess so. But it's not spelled like the one you're thinking of. It's fairly near here. I'm surprised you haven't heard of it."

"I only moved here a few months ago from LA," she explained. "I have to say, though, I've always wanted to go to Paris. Although something tells me the one in California might be just a *hair* less romantic than the one in France. Maybe it's the spelling."

Hall grinned. "I guess the Paris in France is for lovers. The Perris in California . . . Well, let's just hope it's good for fugitives."

Megan flashed an incandescent smile. "I'm game," she said. But just as Hall was about to leave to begin purchasing tickets, she stopped him. "I just had a thought, Nick. We can go to LA, after all. We don't have cash for a hotel, and we wouldn't want to use my credit card, but I have friends we can stay with."

"*No!*" snapped Hall, and then instantly regretted taking this tone. "No," he repeated more pleasantly. "We can't bring anyone else into this. I would have never guessed they'd find out I was in your office—and they did. We can't risk your friends' lives."

"You're right," she said softly. "I wasn't thinking. Let's stick with Perris. How much time do you think we have?"

"That bus leaves in thirty-eight minutes, exactly," he said.

She raised her eyebrows. "You didn't know which destination I would choose. Are you telling me that you memorized the departure times for all possible choices?"

"Not at all. I'm just taking advantage of the personal web access in my head. I signed up for a free notebook app while I was reading the schedules. One with plenty of storage in the cloud. I figured it would be helpful to *think* information to this app. So I can see the cities and times for each trip in my, um . . . mind's eye, so to speak. I've added a small digital clock at the bottom of any page I call up, so I can get the precise time whenever I want."

Megan looked impressed. "So when you said thirty-eight minutes, you didn't mean thirty-seven or thirty-nine, did you?"

"No. And the web has endless calculators, so I can be precise with respect to much more difficult calculations than this."

Hall left once again, this time returning with tickets to nine destinations, not including Perris. They were waiting patiently for five minutes prior to departure, when they planned to purchase two tickets with cash, when a train and bus pulled into the station at the same time, both packed with passengers who were now disembarking.

Added to the ever-growing crowd in the terminal waiting to leave, the increase in chatter in Hall's mind was maddening. He suspected if he ever found himself in a dense concentration of people, like inside a football stadium during a big game, his sanity would be a quick casualty.

The chairs on either side of them began to fill in with passengers. Hall put his head in his hands and tried not to scream. Now the noise was coming through his ears as well as his mind.

A kid wanted some candy. A man was fantasizing about sexual acts he would perform with his girlfriend when they reached their destination. A couple was arguing about who worked the hardest. A man was tallying up how much he stood to lose financially if he divorced a wife he now despised. It never ended. A woman who was about to visit her mother for three days was freaking out, trying to remember if she had shut the garage door when she left, and deciding to call a neighbor, just to be sure.

Hall almost bolted upright as he read this thought. He extended his mind, this time entering the minds of anyone who was departing Bakersfield. The buzzing was still intolerable, but at least he now had a purpose. Five minutes later he rose and faced Megan Emerson.

"Change of plans," he said, reaching for her hand to help her up.

13

Vasily Chirkhoff arrived just before midnight at the Bakersfield Municipal Airport in a small chartered jet, and Cody Radich met him and escorted him to his rental car. While the Russian had been in transit, Radich, with the help and resources of John Delamater, had made significant progress in picking up Hall's trail once again.

WeOfficeU had long contracted with the Adams Janitorial Services company to send a two-person crew to their Bakersfield location each night after hours, with responsibility for cleaning the bathrooms and conference rooms, vacuuming out each of the two hundred and ten offices, and emptying the individual trash containers in each.

Only four hours earlier, a woman named Larissa Hochhalter, who was one half of this crew, had been covering the same ground at WeOfficeU she had covered for years. During this period of time she had thought she had seen it all. She had interrupted office residents having sex, had come across managers passed out drunk, and offices that had been literally torn to pieces by irate wives or lovers. But when she had entered Megan Emerson's office to vacuum, minding her own business, she encountered something that even *she* couldn't take in stride.

After she had stopped screaming, she had called 9-1-1 to report two very dead bodies resting comfortably on the floor, with patterns of blood leakage and spatter that were like demented modern art.

Delamater had learned of this only minutes after the Bakersfield police had been notified, and Vasily continued to be impressed with the wide variety of sources he had cultivated. Although, in this case, Delamater had probably recruited a single player with access to the national police computer system, and had set up the system to alert him to anything of possible interest in the vicinity of Bakersfield.

In this instance, though, they didn't need outside intel. Vasily and Delamater already knew their hired guns were dead at this location.

The men had called Vasily from WeOfficeU to give them Megan Emerson's identity, but had never called back. And repeated attempts to contact them had failed. Vasily tracked their cell phones, and learned the phones hadn't moved a millimeter in hours. Either they had both left their phones behind in the office, which was so unlikely as to defy imagination, or they were recently deceased.

The fact that Nick Hall had prevailed against *two* experienced killers this time was becoming alarming. At first Vasily had tried to convince himself the man just had a six-leaf clover in his pocket. But after this, he agreed fully with Delamater that they were missing something big.

They had been caught off guard by this development and didn't have a crew ready to retrieve the bodies and scrub the premises, which would have been a challenge in a locked office building in any case. And who knew how many bullet holes, and how much blood, would have to be concealed and cleaned.

Had they removed the bodies they might have been able to delay an investigation, but not forestall it entirely. And this move, as well as others they had contemplated, like torching the entire building, added more risk than benefit. No matter. They always retained the capability of remotely frying the phones of anyone in their employ, which they had done to the two phones long before they were discovered. The mercs wouldn't be carrying any identification, and they couldn't be traced in any way to Vasily Chirkhoff or John Delamater.

Now they just had to be sure to stay at least one step ahead of whoever would be investigating the murders. Given that they had started *many* steps ahead, this shouldn't be a problem.

Radich and Vasily had traced Megan Emerson's phone to the Kern River Motor Lodge, and from there, with a little investigative work by Radich, they learned of the ambulance that had made a visit there, and of the woman and man who had left in it. A pair who matched the descriptions of Nick Hall and Megan Emerson. The girl was wounded, although the severity of her injury had not been clear.

Apparently, Hall had played the Boy Scout and had stuck around to help her.

What an idiot, thought Vasily in frustration. *What a soft, sniveling idiot.*

How could they be having trouble getting this guy?

Vasily had sent a handpicked team of men to hunt him, each of whom could bring down a Grizzly with their bare hands. And yet none of them had managed to club the helpless baby seal that Nick Hall represented. It was *insanity*.

If Hall had any survival instincts at all, he had ditched the girl the moment she was patched up. But for some reason, only because nothing with this hunt had gone as planned from the very beginning, Vasily fully expected Hall to stick around to ensure her safety.

Radich had found Megan's phone at the motel, under a bush, and had destroyed it so those investigating the murders would never be led to the Kern River Motor Lodge, or the ambulance that represented their single best lead. Staying a step ahead of the legitimate investigation was even easier when you could sabotage those behind you.

It was nearing one in the morning when Vasily and Radich pulled quietly into the Blue Ridge Luxury Apartments complex and killed the engine.

Vasily prepared himself mentally to put on an American accent and called a number he had already entered into his phone. At one in the morning, it could be hard to get someone to answer the door, and they wanted to minimize the attention they drew to themselves.

The land line he called was picked up after three rings, and a word was mumbled into it that Vasily could only assume was *hello*.

"Hector Garcia?" said Vasily.

"Yeah," came a mumbled reply, only slightly more intelligible than Garcia's first syllable had been.

"Sorry to trouble you in the middle of the night like this," said Vasily, "But my partner and I are with the FBI, and it's urgent that we speak with you."

"What's this about?" said Garcia, less groggy this time as adrenaline began to hit his bloodstream.

"We're right outside your door, Mr. Garcia. If you could let us in, we'll be happy to answer your questions."

"Who *are* you?" said Garcia, a question that showed an unexpected level of suspicion, even for this hour. Vasily had already told him they were with the FBI, but he apparently wasn't taking this assertion at face value. Good for him.

"My name is Jim Anderson," replied Vasily, using the name that appeared on his flawlessly forged FBI credentials. "My partner is named Troy Shaw," he added.

"I'm not opening the door until I see your IDs and badges," said Garcia.

"If you have a peephole, I'll hold them up to it."

"No. Take a photo of them and text it to my TV. I'll give you the address."

"This is ridiculous," said Vasily, losing his patience. "What's wrong with the peephole?"

"If you aren't really FBI, you could shoot me through the door."

Vasily turned toward Radich and rolled his eyes. "If we weren't really FBI and wanted to kill you, you'd be dead *already*. You think a killer's going to call you and make sure you're awake?"

There was a long pause. "That's probably true also. Okay. Hold up your ID to my peephole. I'll be down in a minute or two."

Five minutes later they were inside Garcia's apartment. Before they began any exchange, Vasily asked if they could conference in their colleague, and soon Delamater's face appeared on Garcia's TV. Garcia grew more impatient and agitated by the second.

"Okay, let me tell you why we're here," began Vasily once Delamater had joined them. "Six or seven hours ago, you and your partner, Tony Kosakowski, were called to the Kern River Motor Lodge. We want to know everything about the woman you patched up there, and the man who was with her."

"Why?"

"There was a double murder less than an hour before you arrived at the motel. And these two were both involved." Vasily sighed. "I know it's unusual to visit you in the dead of night like this. But every minute we don't apprehend these two, the trail grows colder."

Garcia shrugged. "There's nothing to tell. The girl had had an accident with a pair of scissors—stabbed herself in the leg. It was actually pretty minor. They really shouldn't have called us. We stayed for a few minutes to make sure she was going to be okay, and then we left. Altogether, we couldn't have exchanged more than a sentence or two, all of it medically related."

Vasily considered. A scissor wound didn't sound likely. He would have guessed a gunshot wound. But it was possible that after she or Hall had shot his men, one of them had managed to stab her with scissors before bleeding out.

"Where did you take them?" asked Radich.

"We didn't. The girl was fine. So we just left." He paused. "If you check the hospital log, it will show that we never brought them in."

"*Why are you lying to us?*" said Vasily ominously.

"I don't know what you're talking about."

"We have a witness who saw them enter the back of the ambulance."

Garcia looked flustered, but recovered quickly. "They did," he said. "We had them in the back for a few minutes while we were working on the girl. But then they returned to their room."

Vasily glanced at the television to see if Delamater wanted to jump in, but it was clear he was willing to let Vasily continue at this point. "Mr. Garcia, we don't have to rely on eyewitnesses. I can play the satellite footage of what went on outside of the motel if you would like. Showing them leaving in your ambulance."

This last was a bluff, but Vasily was sure it wouldn't be called. He had no idea why Garcia was being so uncooperative. He was sure the man now believed they were with the FBI. They could have easily beaten the information out of him, but given their cover they had assumed he'd give it to them willingly. And the current body count was already sure to be attracting enough unwanted attention.

Vasily leaned in toward the paramedic menacingly. "Frankly, Mr. Garcia, I'm having trouble understanding why you're lying to us about this. These people are dangerous criminals. On the loose. Do you know what obstruction of justice is?"

The big Russian allowed this to sink in for a few seconds. "If the next words out of your mouth aren't the truth, you're going to become intimately familiar with this term. And jail time."

Garcia took a deep breath. "Okay, okay. I'll tell you the truth. The truth is the girl had a gunshot wound, not a scissors wound. When we got there, the guy with her forced us to work on her. At gunpoint."

"Now we're getting somewhere," commented Delamater dryly from the TV. "Why wouldn't you want to tell us about this?"

"The guy told us everyone was after him. Trying to kill him. And he warned us that if we went to the authorities we'd probably end up dead ourselves. He said the people after him would kill anyone whose paths he had crossed."

"And you *believed* him?" said Vasily.

"I didn't know what was going on. But there was something persuasive about him. He threatened us repeatedly, but there was something about him," he said, holding out his hands helplessly, as if unable to find the right words. "Like, I don't know . . . like he was a decent guy who was at the end of his rope. Like the type who wouldn't willingly hurt anyone."

"You do realize," said Delamater, "that this guy is a paranoid schizophrenic. Thinking the entire world is trying to kill you. Nothing about that suggested *paranoia* to you?"

"There was more to him than that," said Garcia. He hesitated. "He had some . . . unusual . . . characteristics. Hard to believe characteristics. Which made what he said more believable."

"Like what?" said Vasily.

Delamater jumped in immediately to cut off any possible answer. "Don't bother with this now, Mr. Garcia," he instructed. "We can circle back to it later. Right now, we need to know where you took them."

"I dropped them both off at the main Amtrak station on Truxtun Avenue. I have no idea where they went after that."

Delamater asked several additional questions. What Hall and the girl were wearing, anything else they might have said about their destination, and the like. When these had been answered, he said, "Mr. Garcia, I have some questions of a more sensitive nature I need to ask. I'm going to ask my colleagues to return to their car for a few minutes. When I'm done, they can return so we can conclude the interview."

Vasily's blood began a slow boil. The bastard had cut off the paramedic before he could explain Hall's *unusual* characteristics, because he wanted this information for his ears only.

Prick.

If it had been anyone other than Delamater, Vasily would have told him to shove his secrecy up his scrawny ass. Nick Hall had made Vasily's people look like incompetent assholes. And now, when he might finally get some clarity on how this could be, Delamater was playing games.

Vasily glared at his boss with enough intensity to melt lead, but the serene look never left Delamater's face. "Thank you, gentlemen," said the image of Delamater to the two mercenaries. "I'll let you know when we're finished."

14

Delamater was now absolutely convinced Hall had Internet capabilities, but this was his chance to learn the true extent of these capabilities. Apparently, Nick Hall hadn't been the least bit shy about demonstrating them to the two paramedics.

"Mr. Garcia," he began, "let's circle back to the unusual characteristics you were speaking of."

"Yeah. About that. I, um . . . I'm not exactly sure what I meant by that. Just that he seemed like a good guy. A smart guy."

A predatory smile played across Delamater's lips. "You're lying yet again, Mr. Garcia. I thought you had gotten that out of your system. This is the last time I'm going to let this slide. If I detect even a hint that you're not being one *thousand* percent forthcoming, I promise I'll make an obstruction charge stick."

Garcia looked like a trapped rat. "Look, you'll think I'm crazy."

Delamater shook his head reassuringly. "Not at all. Because I already know what you're going to tell me. And I know it's not crazy."

"You know about his ESP?" said Garcia in shock.

Delamater couldn't keep his eyes from widening, but he managed, barely, to maintain the placid expression on his face that he had worn throughout the interview.

What? he thought in dismay. *Hall had developed ESP?*

Delamater's thoughts raced around his head so quickly he became dizzy, having to reach out and steady himself on a table out of sight of the camera that was transmitting his image. He had a well-earned reputation for his ability to maintain a poker face, for his machine-like unflappability, but these traits had just been tested like never before.

"Right," Delamater finally managed to get out. "His ESP. We know all about it."

"What's the deal with that?" said Garcia in awe. "I mean, is he some kind of mutant? Or are there more like him?"

"I'm afraid that's classified," said Delamater smoothly, having already recovered his equilibrium. "But I need you to tell me everything about this. How he revealed this to you. Every last thing you can remember. It might be important."

Garcia spent the next few minutes recounting what had happened with respect to Hall's psi ability.

Mind reading was completely impossible, Delamater knew, but he also had no doubt that this was what was going on, anyway. It explained so much of what had happened. How Hall had known that Radich was at the mini-mart to kill him. How he had managed to stay at large. He had two impressive capabilities: thought-controlled web access *and* the ability to read minds.

Delamater would have to ponder the implications of this new development long and hard. Should he continue on course, or should he now switch gears entirely? Could he now come up with a more optimal strategy? *When you see a good move*, he thought, *look for a better one.*

He decided he would tell his business partner that Hall's implants were working to surf the net, but he would keep the ESP angle strictly to himself. At least until he figured out how best to use this new reality.

"Are there any other impressions from this encounter that you want to report?" asked Delamater. "If there's even a chance an impression or hunch might be useful, I urge you to share it with me."

Garcia scratched his head. "Well, there may be one thing. Just before they left, I asked him who he was."

"And what did he say?"

"He said, 'I only wish I knew.'" Garcia paused. "Maybe he meant this on a deep, philosophical level. You know, like do any of us really know who we are? But I got the impression he really *didn't* know. Like he had lost his memory."

Delamater nodded. This wasn't entirely surprising, but still very good to have confirmed. "That *is* interesting," he said. His hands flew over a cell phone touch screen for several seconds. "I'm texting Anderson and Shaw that it's time to rejoin us," he explained.

He looked down at the message he had written: *Knock. When Garcia answers, kill him. Then visit his slumbering partner, Tony, and make sure he never wakes up.*

Delamater hit *send* and the text message raced into cyberspace.

"We'll be out of your hair in just a few minutes," he told the paramedic. "Thanks a lot for your help. "

"You're welcome," replied Garcia. "Hopefully you can understand my paranoia. And why I didn't level with you at first."

"Absolutely," said Delamater. "You can never be too careful," he added with a friendly smile. "There are a lot of dangerous people out there."

15

Megan Emerson slowly drifted awake, her half-conscious mind vaguely becoming aware that her inner thigh seemed to be throbbing painfully. She glanced at a digital alarm clock through lidded eyes. It was nine o'clock! Why hadn't her alarm gone off?

Now fully conscious, she realized with a start that she had never seen the alarm clock she was looking at before, and memories of last night's events came flooding back to her.

She had been asleep for thirteen hours.

She sat up in the bed and was relieved when no dizzy spell came over her. She felt strong. Other than the throbbing pain in her thigh—the IV pain killers Hector Garcia had given her long since out of her system—she felt like herself again.

Nick Hall's change of plan had been just what the doctor ordered. A bus ride to Paris, followed by a hunt for lodging, was not what her body needed. She smiled as she remembered what had happened the night before. If you had to be running for your life, it was good to be doing so in the company of a mind reader.

When Hall had picked up the worried thoughts of a woman leaving her home unattended for several days, wondering if she had remembered to shut the garage door, it occurred to him that any number of passengers would be going on extended trips and wouldn't be returning to their homes that night. And many wouldn't be returning for *several* nights.

Not surprisingly, in the city's main train and bus terminal, he had found dozens that fit this bill, and raided their memories for intel. Were their homes totally abandoned in their absence? Or were they leaving spouses or kids behind to man the fort? In the days of hired dog-walkers, there could be dogs left behind as well; dogs who would be unlikely to welcome uninvited houseguests. Hall checked for this as well.

When he discovered a traveler leaving an empty home, he probed more deeply. Had they hidden a key on the premises? Was their home alarmed, and if so, what was the combination that would deactivate it?

Hall had found what he was after in fairly short order. A shack would have done nicely, but just by chance the first home that was abandoned, and for which the owners, Carl and Terry Glandon, had hidden a key, happened to be in an upscale neighborhood only a fifteen-minute cab ride away.

The setup was nearly perfect. Each house was on a considerable parcel of land, and only two neighbors had a clean view of the Glandons' front door and garage. Even so, Hall had had the cab drop them off a few blocks away, and they didn't approach the house until his psi reconnaissance told him the coast was clear. There was a small chance one of the neighbors would turn out to be unreadable, like Megan, and could be watching them through a window, but they decided they had no other choice but to take this risk.

They retrieved the key, hidden in a small steel box inside a hollow, decorative rock near the front door, entered, and disarmed the alarm, well within the sixty-second window they had before it went off.

The house was spectacular: a split-wing design, with a four-car garage, blue granite countertops, a beautiful pool and spa, soaring ceilings, and a covered patio with a gleaming stainless steel barbecue grill.

Hall had raided the Glandons' well-stocked kitchen, making sure Megan was well-fed with nutritious and easily digestible food, and then, even though it wasn't even eight, they had both retired to separate rooms for some much-needed sleep. While a long conversation was very much in order, Hall insisted they wait until morning when they could think more clearly; and when Megan had had a full night to regain some of her strength.

Megan was impressed with how Hall had handled himself. And his strategy had been excellent. When their pursuers tracked them to the station, and then learned that they had booked trips to nine different destinations, they would never guess in a million years that she and Hall would instead stay in Bakersfield. Even if they did, the Glandons' lovely home would be the very last place in the entire city they would think to look for them.

Megan was wearing shorts and a T-shirt she had borrowed from the woman of the house, which engulfed her, and a white terry cloth robe that could have fit two of her inside. She rubbed sleep from her eyes, deciding this was the most comfortable bed on which she had ever slept.

She noticed a small piece of notebook paper folded on the nightstand, which she opened with great trepidation. Had Nick Hall decided to abandon her after all? Was this a Dear Jane letter? She held her breath, looked down, and began reading:

Megan. Good morning.

I'm writing this at two in the morning, after waking up from six hours of sleeping like a corpse (probably a bad choice of words). I can't remember the last time I was in bed by eight. Then again, since I can't remember my own name, maybe this isn't surprising. Anyway, I should be back by nine or ten this morning.

I don't know what we're up against, but we can't risk using your Visa again, and our cash supply won't last long. And we both need clothing and some spare bottles of Aleve—I left a bottle I took from the Glandons' medicine cabinet in the end table drawer. Help yourself, but be sure to eat a good breakfast first.

Anyway, I gave it some thought, and I'm planning to drive Carl Glandon's Mercedes to The Golden West Casino on South Union Avenue. Their web page says they host all-night, no-limit Texas Hold'em games. I've never played before, but I like my chances. I'm not an ethicist, but I have to believe that being able to read the cards and strategies of everyone at the table isn't playing fair, but again, I feel I have no other choice. I've learned that adherence to a strict ethical code is a lot harder when you're fighting for your life. And now, unfortunately, I'm not the only one involved. Sorry again . . . .

I hope you're feeling better. Remember, don't turn on or off any lights that can be seen by the neighbors or go near any uncurtained windows. See you soon.
Nick

Megan folded the note back over again with a smile on her face. She opened the drawer and found the small bottle of Aleve Hall had left for her, and then padded into the kitchen to make breakfast. She was still recovering, so she didn't want to eat too much. She microwaved a frozen bagel, slapped on some cream cheese, and had two glasses of orange juice.

She was just finishing up when Hall entered the kitchen and removed the green windbreaker he had taken from the ambulance and had probably worn all night, revealing a crisp, unwrinkled shirt that actually fit. His pants were new as well. He had showered and shaved before leaving and finally looked like a human being.

"You clean up well," said Megan by way of greeting.

"Yeah, well, you have to keep up with fashion. The dumpster look I was going for when you met me was so . . . I don't know . . . *yesterday*," he finished with a grin.

He held out a large Nordstrom's shopping bag filled with women's clothing. "I got you a few things on the way home," he said. "I would've been back earlier, but I had to wait until they opened. How are you feeling?"

"Much, much better."

He slid the bag over to her and she looked inside. He had bought three different outfits in two different sizes, both of them petite. "Not bad," she said. "Not exactly what I'd buy myself, but good enough. And I'm sure at least one of these will fit." Megan raised her eyebrows. "Shop for women's clothing often?" she asked.

"God, I hope not," he said with a wry smile.

"How did you do at the poker table?"

"As well as you would expect. I cleaned out two tables full of players. When I knew I had the best cards, I bet big. When everybody had crap, and so did I, I knew I could get away with bluffing and they'd eventually fold. And when I knew I was beat, I got out early."

"Did anyone get suspicious?"

"*What?*" he said with an exaggerated look of innocence. "Of a guy dressed like a homeless person, who looks and acts like a poker patsy, and steadily cleans everyone out?" He paused. "Actually, the good news is that you only have to show your hand when someone calls you at the end. So the players rarely got to see my uncanny instinct for knowing when to bluff. For all they knew, I was just getting lucky all night and really did have great cards."

"How much did you, um . . . win," she said finally, having first thought the word, *steal,* and hoping she hadn't done so forcefully enough for him to read. She knew he already felt guilty—no sense rubbing it in.

He pulled a sheaf of hundreds from his front pocket, an inch or two thick. "Twenty-two thousand," he said. "And change."

Megan whistled. "Wow. I would have thought that much cash would take up more space."

Hall tilted his head. "Well," he said after a few seconds, "a hundred dollar bill is .0043 inches thick. So two hundred and twenty of them are just under an inch. Of course, these aren't fresh from the mint, so there's a bit of air between each of them."

"Showing off a little, Dr. Cyberspace?" she said with an amused twinkle in her eye.

"What? Are you saying that the thickness of a hundred dollar bill isn't common knowledge? Hard to believe."

Megan laughed. This would have been fun if it weren't for all the scary assassins trying to end their lives. But even though she had been shot, she now felt safe. Safer than she had any business feeling; a clear denial of reality.

But Nick Hall and his abilities, and his obvious resourcefulness, made her think she would be okay. She knew this was a dangerous optimism to have, but she couldn't seem to shake it. The excitement of the adventure seemed real. The fact that she might be dead by the next day, *surreal.* Besides, she told herself, either trying to think on the bright side or else sinking even deeper into the quicksand of denial, the Creator had already imposed a death sentence on every human ever born. It was just that these sentences in most cases were a little less . . . imminent.

"As fun as it was to play poker when I knew everyone else's hands," said Hall, serious once again, "and it *was* incredibly fun, I can't deny it, I do know how wrong it was. But it was also necessary. We have too much going on to have to worry about funds. And I'm looking forward to mailing our two paramedic friends their money, with a hundred percent interest, as soon as I have the chance."

A faint smile came over her face. "Have you had breakfast?"

"I have." Hall gestured toward the family room. "How about we grab a drink and get comfortable. We have to start trying to figure out what's going on. Not to mention what we're going to do about it."

Megan removed a plastic bottle of water from the Glandons' refrigerator and Hall grabbed a can of Diet Mountain Dew, a twelve pack of which he was delighted to have discovered the night before. The moment he saw this drink he learned something more about himself: he wasn't a coffee or tea guy. Instead, he realized, whoever he had been in the past was just as addicted to Mountain Dew as many others had become to Starbucks.

They settled into the Glandons' large, vaulted family room, on comfortable beige couches, thankful that the two-story window behind them faced the Glandons' backyard and pool, which was fenced in, so there was no danger of being seen. They set their drinks on a red cedar table between the couches, being sure to use coasters so they would be good houseguests—although they decided that *guests* might not be the exactly appropriate word for it.

"I'd love to regale you with stories about myself," began Hall, "but I'm afraid I'll have to remain a closed book to both of us for the time being." He shifted on the couch. "But tell me about you," he said, sipping from the green and red can of Mountain Dew.

It was awkward for a baring of souls to be such a one-way affair, but Megan knew it couldn't be helped. So she gave him an abbreviated summary of her life. She was born in Iowa. Two older sisters. Her father was a dentist, her mother a receptionist. She told him about their bitter divorce when she was fifteen, and how each had used her against the other as a human pawn. About attending UCLA to be as far away as she could get from her parents, neither of whom she had fully forgiven. About her dream of building a major graphic design firm, and her doubts that she could really do it.

She stopped short of telling him her misgivings about marriage. About being unsure if she ever wanted to go this route, and if she did, if she ever wanted to have children. After all, she wanted to give him a sense of who she was, but it wasn't as though he was her shrink or bartender.

Hall seemed to hang on her every word. She understood why he was so interested in learning about her. They were fighting for their lives together. And he had no past of his own. But she also didn't want to be the sole focus of attention.

"I'm afraid that's it. For now, at least. And you can't be told the essence of a person, anyway. That's something you have to experience. Their sense of humor, their values, their demeanor, that sort of thing. My favorite flavor of ice cream doesn't seem all that important at the moment."

Hall tilted his head. *Chocolate peanut butter*, he thought.

Megan's eyes narrowed. "*Hey!* I read that," she said. "So have you become able to read *my* mind, too?" she asked worriedly.

Hall winced, obviously embarrassed that she had caught his unspoken words. "No. Still can't," he said. "But you caught me. I must have thought that pretty loudly. I hope you aren't offended, but I took a thorough look at your Facebook page while I was playing poker. Among other surfing expeditions. You know, when I had dropped out of a hand and was bored."

"I see," she said noncommittally.

"You don't post there very often, and I have a feeling I wasn't a power user either, but I have to say that Facebook does a good job of sharing background information. I've read most of your two hundred and fourteen 'likes.' Chocolate peanut butter is one of them. I also know your favorite books, bands, movies, sports teams, activities, and interests. Really sorry about that."

She stared at him for a moment and then said, "Don't be. I guess I posted them for a reason. And now I don't have to waste time telling you what I like," she added with a smile. Her smile vanished quickly and she looked deeply into his eyes. "So you still can't read me?"

"Right."

"Any further thoughts on why not?"

Megan didn't want to admit it, but when he was in her office and had wondered if his inability to read her thoughts was due to her having an unusually weak mind, this had struck a nerve, an insecurity she had thought had been completely excised. But apparently not. She had struggled in grade school and her first two years of high school, especially in subjects like math and science. She was convinced her mind *did* work differently than others. For a long time in school she was sure she was an idiot, and her self-esteem had plummeted.

But it gradually dawned on her that she wasn't an idiot. Not totally. In math and science, yes. But in the realm of creative thinking, she came to realize she was a sighted person in the kingdom of the blind. Because as much as she seemed unable to process algebra and geometry, she was a savant when it came to pure creativity.

And not just in graphic design. In everything. Coming up with ideas for the company picnic. Throwing parties. Wording invitations. Writing poetry. She came to be thought of as a one-woman idea machine. The kind who could take four or five mundane office items and turn them into fifteen different stunning decorations.

And she could figure out the most complex fictional mysteries. She was almost always able to see the coming plot twists, even when those who excelled at academics missed them entirely. So maybe she did have a different style of intellect. She thought her self-esteem had become off the charts high, but Hall's offhanded remark had shown her that the scars of her early struggles in school still remained, as did deep-seated doubts.

"Scoping you out on Facebook wasn't all I did last night," said Hall. "I did some research on ESP as well. But nothing I learned suggested a reason why a mind reader might be unable to read certain people. On the other hand, it wasn't as if I found a manual on exactly how ESP works in the first place. Because no one knows. After all, no one's had it before. Not really. If they had, parapsychologists wouldn't need to perform statistical tests in an attempt to demonstrate it. They could demonstrate it instantly, beyond question, the way I did with you and the paramedics."

"Do you think there are others out there you can't read?"

"I'd be amazed if there aren't. You're unique, but I can't believe you're *that* unique. The question is, how many people are like you? One in a hundred? One in a thousand?"

"You haven't encountered anyone else you can't read so far, though, right?"

"Right. As far as I know. Although I haven't made much of an effort to find any. But we'll probably never figure out why you're different. Why are some people allergic to peanuts while most people aren't? There are endless examples of significant traits appearing in the population at very low levels."

"And I'm sure you could cite them all for me, couldn't you, Dr. Cyberspace?" said Megan wryly.

She took a long drink from her bottle of water, savoring the cold, refreshing liquid as it traveled down her throat. Fearing for her very life had changed her perspective, freed her from petty, everyday worries, and seemed to make her better able to appreciate simple pleasures.

"So how is it that you knew to come back for me? You hear hundreds of voices in your head all the time, right? From miles around you? So how did you know when those men had found your car in our lot?"

"Great question. Their thoughts when they saw the car, and were licking their chops to come after me, emerged like a neon sign from the sea of noise. And this isn't the first time this has happened. I've had thoughts stand out this way before. And they've always been thoughts that were vitally important for me to know. If it wasn't for this, I'd be long dead."

"Wow, Nick. It almost seems like you have a higher power looking out for you."

Hall shook his head. "As much as I can use all the help I can get, I don't think that's the explanation. I'm pretty sure I know what's going on."

She raised her eyebrows questioningly.

"It's called the *cocktail party effect*. Have you heard of it?"

Megan searched her memory. She had heard the phrase, but she didn't know anything about it. She admitted as much.

"Has this ever happened to you, Megan? You're in a big crowd, where dozens of conversations are going on at the same time, totally focused on your own conversation. The endless other conversations around you are like white noise, and you aren't listening to them at all. But then you hear your name from somewhere in the room. Clear as a bell. It just kind of stands out from the background."

Megan nodded thoughtfully. "Now that you mention it . . . yeah. I totally know what you mean."

"Almost everyone has experienced something like this. So how did your name suddenly stand out from a jumble of noise you weren't paying any attention to? Well, this curious effect has been thoroughly studied."

"The cocktail party effect?"

"Right."

"Good name for it," said Megan with a smile. "So how does it work?"

"The gist of it is that people soak up far more information than we realize. All the time. At the subconscious level, we're monitoring everything. But our subconscious can't bring all of it to our conscious attention or we'd drown. Too much information. So in the party example, your brain is taking in all of the conversations around you, but sparing you from having to deal with them. So you can focus on your own conversation. But when your subconscious hears your name, or the words, 'run, the house is on fire,' or something else of great interest to you, it decides that this is important information and brings it to your conscious attention. It seems like magic. It's not that you're suddenly paying attention. Part of you was *always* paying attention. You just didn't know it."

"That is so cool," said Megan. "How'd you even know where to begin looking that up?"

"I didn't look it up. That's something I actually knew—*without* the Internet. Because I think it's very cool, too, so wherever I learned it, probably in a class at some point in my sordid past, it must have stuck with me. I think I've forgotten a bunch of fascinating examples of this effect, but I do remember one more. Take a new mother, completely exhausted. She can sleep soundly through the loudest thunderstorm, no problem. But if her baby makes the softest whimper, she bolts awake like she was electrocuted. How does *that* work? The answer, again, is that the mom's subconscious heard both events. For the thunderstorm it said, 'Just a stupid thunderstorm. No need to disturb the weary boss.' For the baby, it heard the low whimper and shot it up to her conscious mind immediately for further attention."

"Fascinating," said Megan. "So your guess is that the same effect is working with your psychic background noise."

"Exactly."

"Makes sense to me. And it seems I owe my life to this effect."

"You and me both," said Hall.

Megan hadn't thought it possible to explain how Hall had been alerted, out of the blue, to information that was critical to him. But this only went to show, when you didn't know what you didn't know, you could fool yourself pretty easily.

16

Hall asked to pause the conversation briefly while he cast his mind out as widely as he could, straining to detect anyone who might suspect where he and Megan were now hiding. He had done this periodically since they arrived, just as an added precaution. Once again, he detected nothing that might worry them.

"So let's get back to you," said Megan when he had finished. "You have brain implants that let you surf the web. You have ESP. And you've lost your memory. Those three things have to be related. You couldn't just coincidentally have that much weird stuff going on inside your head."

"Yeah, it's a real party in here," he commented, rolling his eyes. "I'm almost certain the Internet and ESP are somehow related. The memory loss, not as much. I did seem to have some head trauma when I came to in the dumpster. And I read the thoughts of the first guy who tried to kill me. Apparently, I had led them on a big chase. But I don't remember that. So maybe I had the ESP and Internet going for me, and only lost my memory recently."

"If the Internet ability and ESP are related, the next question is: are they related on purpose?"

Hall shrugged. "I have no idea."

"You seem awfully articulate and educated to me. You think maybe you invented the implants? Used yourself as a guinea pig? You think you might be a mad scientist?"

He smiled. "I prefer the term, *angry*."

Megan laughed.

"It's a valid question," said Hall. "But the answer is no. I don't have memory of myself, but I know what I know. And I know what I *don't* know. Remember how I knew the Margaret Thatcher quote?

Well, I'm sure I know nothing about the brain, or how implants might work. And I'm sure I know nothing about ESP."

"Why don't you tell me everything that happened to you before you met me."

Hall did so as thoroughly as he possibly could, describing how he had killed Baldino at the Shell gas station, the incident with Radich at the mini-mart, and how he had narrowly avoided another assassin heading toward him on the road, all compliments of the cocktail party effect.

"So why do you think they're after you?" asked Megan when he had finished.

Hall told her his theory that maybe he had read something he shouldn't have in someone's mind, but she was skeptical. "It seems to me they don't even *know* about your ESP," she said. "I think they're after you for your web surfing ability alone."

"Why do you say that?"

"It's obvious," she replied. "The killers after you all thought they could surprise you. If they would have known about your psychic abilities, they would never have made that assumption."

"You're right! That *is* obvious. How did I miss that?" he said, shaking his head. "So do you think the guy at the top of the pyramid, the guy in charge, knew about it but didn't tell them?"

"No," replied Megan without hesitation. "He'd be setting up his men to take a fall for no reason. Either tell them what they're up against, or have them act as spotters. Have them find you and then call in the people who *do* know what they're up against. The people who actually have a chance to stop you."

"I think you're in the wrong line of work," said Hall admiringly.

"So they must be after you because of your web surfing ability," continued Megan, pleased by the compliment, but choosing to ignore it and forge ahead. "*Not* because of anything having to do with your psychic ability."

"But then why try to kill me?"

"Maybe this is military technology that's supposed to be top secret. Like whatever is going on at Area 51. Do you feel like a rogue soldier?" He certainly had the body of an elite soldier, she had to admit, although she was careful not to project this thought.

"No. I'm even more sure I was never a soldier than I am that I didn't invent the technology in my head."

"Well, then it seems to me that you can't be the prototype with this technology. Otherwise, they would be trying to catch you rather than kill you. To study you. If they knew about the ESP, they'd want to take you alive as well."

"Exactly what I've been thinking."

"If you *were* the prototype, the question wouldn't be who would want to grab you for study. The question would be, who *wouldn't?* Every industrialist and every corporation on earth, not to mention the government and military of every country on earth, would want you desperately. The industrialists because the technology behind your web surfing abilities would be worth trillions of dollars. And governments and militaries because of the huge advantages this technology would give them. And if the Internet capability alone is enormously valuable, combining this with ESP is *unstoppable*. You could be a one-man army. A one-man force of nature."

"I don't know about that."

"I don't think you've fully grasped the possibilities," said Megan. "Which is a good thing. I think if you really were a power mad asshole, you'd have done so right away. But think about what you can do. Forget about ESP for a second. While you're sitting here sipping your Mountain Dew and talking, you could be booking a flight, calling a cab, communicating with multiple people, transferring funds, trading stocks. You get the idea. And anyone with your implants gets an unlimited knowledge boost. You have instant access to trillions of pages of information. You can obtain instant biographical information on anyone you meet, the way you did with me. And the more powerful the person, the more information is online. Plus, you can turn the cloud into your virtual memory, storing anything you want to remember there. Like the train and bus schedules from last night."

Hall nodded. "And if this technology can convert video and audio into vision and hearing without the use of my eyes or ears, I don't see why it wouldn't be able to go the *other way*. To convert my vision into *video*. If so, I could record anything I'm seeing and hearing and save it in the cloud." His expression reflected awe and fear at the possibilities inherent in the technology.

She stared at him thoughtfully. "It looks like I haven't fully grasped the possibilities either."

"They are pretty staggering," he said. "And sobering."

"And I think we're only scratching the surface. Let's think about special forces soldiers with your implants. They can access any information they need in real time, without anyone knowing they're doing it. Maps, floor plans for raids, what have you. They can access language translation programs to convert signs and conversations to English for them. You think that might be helpful? They can communicate to each other without anyone knowing it. Their ability to use stealth and deception would increase dramatically. A soldier with these implants could go into a war zone pretending to be with the Red Cross, and while helping to move rubble and not outwardly in communication with anyone, could be deploying entire teams of soldiers. Anyone with implants could direct drones, call in air strikes, and paint targets—not with bulky lasers—but with their *eyes*, while they're having tea and crumpets and engaging in polite conversation."

"And *with* ESP in the picture?"

"Then all bets are off," replied Megan. "You could get every intimate secret of every billionaire and politician—and believe me, most of them have *lots* of secrets. You could probably find enough to get many of them thrown in jail, even if it's as relatively minor an offense as cheating on taxes or insider trading. But even if not, I'd bet, at minimum, they have secrets that could embarrass the hell out of them. So you could blackmail the most powerful men in the world. Or you could fish through the mind of the NSA's top programmer for backdoor access codes to their computers, and have access to unparalleled records, phone conversations, and intelligence from around the world."

Megan paused for a drink of water and then continued. "Cheating at poker to win a few thousand dollars is like an adorable schoolyard prank compared to what you could do. You could read the minds of CEOs to get insider information for stock trading. Read combinations to wall safes, the same way you read the combination to deactivate the alarm to this house."

Hall was staring off into space now, pondering the possibilities. "And that's not all," he said softly. "I could be the ultimate identity thief. I could go to a charity event filled with rich people and read their account numbers, passwords, their mothers' maiden names—the works. I could be dining on expensive lobster while raiding their accounts, transferring their money to accounts I set up in the Caymans, and wiring money to a team of mercenaries to take over a Pacific Island for my own personal use."

"Why stop with individuals, even if they are super rich. You could get into corporate accounts. *Government* accounts."

Hall whistled. "You're right about this. I never thought through the angles. And I'm sure there's a lot we're still missing. Right now, I've been a hunted animal. Running blindly and barely staying ahead of the dogs. But if I could get off the mat, get my bearings . . ."

"Now you're getting the picture."

"Yeah. I could be pretty formidable. With a little time to set myself up in some hidden evil lair and gather my minions around me, I could be . . . Well, I could be— "

"A veritable one-man army," Megan finished for him. "You could give *Superman* a run for his money."

Hall grinned. "He'd still kick my ass in a fight, though."

"Maybe. But you could rob him blind, learn his secret identity as Clark, and call in an air strike on him." She raised her eyebrows. "Kryptonite-laced missiles?"

Hall laughed, and then excused himself to make use of one of the Glandons' bathrooms. His expression was somber when he returned. "Now I know why someone might choose to kill me rather than capture me. I'm potentially very dangerous. But you have to wonder if I'm *already* the bad guy here. What if I *did* set up an evil lair somewhere and the men after me—at least the people pulling their strings—are trying to stop me for noble reasons. Like if the

Joker wakes up one day without a memory and wonders why this evil Batman dude is trying so hard to kill an innocent guy like him."

"I don't believe that for a second," said Megan, shaking her head vigorously.

Hall looked unconvinced. "Why not?"

"You'd make the worst supervillain *ever*," she said. "You don't know anything about weapons. You risked your life to save someone you didn't know. And while fighting for survival, you're determined to repay a few hundred dollars to some paramedics as soon as you can."

Hall sighed. "I hope you're right," he said. "You have no idea how much I hope you're right."

Megan had meant what she had told him earlier. She really did believe that when all was said and done, only experience with a person could give you a sense of their spirit—their values, their dreams, their demeanor, and their sense of humor. And she had already gotten a strong sense of Hall's spirit. So much so that she was willing to bet her life that he wasn't the bad guy in these proceedings.

She swallowed hard as she realized that she couldn't bet her life on this.

Because she already had.

17

Colonel Justin Girdler entered his office, as he did on most Saturday mornings. And Sunday mornings as well. He was in the middle of more important projects than he could manage in two lifetimes, but he guessed this went with the territory.

The colonel had been head of PsyOps for six years before being asked a year earlier to do the same from the Black Ops side of things, which he supposed suggested a certain level of trust in his judgment.

He had to admit it was a great change of pace. The projects were more interesting, on the whole, and his power was virtually unlimited. Being completely off the radar did have its advantages. First and foremost among these was not having to suffer the ridicule he knew many poorly informed members of the military heaped on him and his unit behind his back.

PsyOps used to have a glamor to it. An intimidating, nefarious connotation. You really couldn't find a cooler sounding name, even though many of its responsibilities were pretty mundane. It stood for Psychological Operations, under the purview of special forces. It dealt in deception and mob psychology, among other things, to sow dissension in the ranks of the enemy, lower morale, and exploit psychological weaknesses, although he had heard the term "mind fuck" used in conjunction with his group on more than one occasion.

The great Chinese strategist and tactician Sun Tzu had probably been the father of PsyOps, and Girdler had made everyone in his command memorize what he believed to be a central tenant of PsyOps, written by Sun Tzu thousands of years earlier:

All warfare is based on deception. Hence, when able to attack, we must seem unable; when using our forces, we must seem inactive; when we are near, we must make the enemy believe we are far away; and when far away, we must make him believe we are near.

And even though fictional, the Greek's use of a wooden horse to breach an enemy's defenses was a striking example of the power of a simple PsyOps mission; one that had ended the ten-year siege of Troy.

In popular culture, psi, with an "i," stood for psychic phenomenon. It stood for the paranormal. For *para*psychology. Psy with a "y," on the other hand, was just plain old *psychology*. PsyOps: Psychological Operations.

Yet many had come to believe the military spelled its *Psy* with an "i," especially after the turn of the century when the organization had been painted as a bunch of loons, helped along by books and movies such as *The Men Who Stare At Goats*. This movie may have been the single biggest public relations blow PsyOps had ever been dealt, and had the military of a hostile country wanted to conduct their own PsyOps mission to hurt the standing of America's PsyOps branch, they could not have done a more impressive job than releasing this film.

So in 2010, PsyOps had been renamed, for the *stated* reasons of making the name more user friendly, more descriptive, and less intimidating at home and abroad. The group officially became Military Information Support Operations, or MISO—and jokes about Japanese soup abounded—although, after all this time, the new name still hadn't been fully adopted, since PsyOps personnel tended to hate it.

Colonel Girdler had disliked the name change as well. But having been high up in the organization at the time, though not quite yet its head, he had to publicly pretend otherwise, something he had detested. He and his group found ways to exploit the political nature of those they opposed on the world stage, but he personally hated politics. Which was one of the reasons moving over to Black Ops had been so appealing. The less accountability, the fewer political games that needed to be played.

He was sipping his second cup of coffee at his desk, having spent the first several hours of the morning with his nose buried in printed briefings, when Maggie, his PDA, interrupted him. "Colonel Girdler, you've been forwarded an eyes-only e-mail message, marked urgent. Please acknowledge."

"Acknowledged," said Girdler. "Forwarded by whom?"

"No human has seen this message yet, Colonel," replied Maggie's flawless female voice pleasantly, "so there is no *whom*. But there is a *what*. It was forwarded by the NSA's Expert System in Fort Meade."

"Very interesting," mumbled the colonel to himself. "Did Nessie forward it to anyone else?"

"NSA's Expert System forwarded it to you as the primary recipient," replied his PDA, her programming not allowing her to use the computer's nickname unless Girdler instructed her to do so. "Major General Nelson Sobol was cc'd. No one else received it."

This was unusual, thought Girdler. Nessie had obviously intercepted the original message and decided to limit the group who received it to only two people, him and Sobol. Nelson Sobol was his boss, although Girdler rarely reported to him and functioned almost entirely autonomously. But Sobol was technically in charge of all American Black Ops units around the globe, and while his job didn't officially exist, only a handful of people on earth wielded as much power as he did.

"So when you said no human has seen the message, you just meant that Sobol hasn't read it yet?"

"Correct, General Sobol has yet to acknowledge receipt. And given that he is at his annual three-day retreat with high-ranking members of Congress and the military, this status may not soon change."

The colonel smiled, reflecting once again how lucky he was. Sobol could have his power, but Girdler would rather have acid poured in his eyes than attend a retreat like the one his boss was at now.

"Would you like me to read the message to you?" asked Maggie.

"No. But put its history on screen."

He glanced at the data now on his monitor. The e-mail message in question had been sent two mornings earlier to a Fresno, California police hotline, and to thirty-eight high level civilian and military leaders in such agencies as the NSA, FBI, CIA, and HSA; to publicly disclosed e-mail addresses in each case. Colonel Justin Girdler had not been among the intended recipients.

As Girdler had known would be the case, the NSA computer had blocked the message from going to anyone when it had first come in, deeming it to have been spam and not worth anyone's time or attention.

But the message had obviously undergone a major change in status since this time. The colonel was tempted to ask Maggie what had prompted the change, but he decided to read it first before digging any further.

"Maggie, display the message please."

The e-mail message appeared on his screen below the background information Maggie had already placed there.

From: Nick Hall

Subject: Urgent, life in jeopardy

I awoke this morning in a locked warehouse without any memory of who I am, hearing voices in my head. I may be insane, in which case I'm only imagining sending this message. If you receive this then I am not insane. A man was here when I awoke, and he left ten minutes later, but I was able to read his mind. Not just read, but fish anything out of it I wanted to. I know how all of this sounds. But bear with me.

Girdler looked up from the screen and barely suppressed a groan. *Are you shitting me*, he thought angrily. He had read somewhere that more than half a percent of the population was schizophrenic, which amounted to well over two million people in America alone. And the colonel was pretty sure he had heard from every last one of them.

But this message had been delivered by the NSA's top computer, which integrated data from thousands of government, military, and civilian sources. It was also the most advanced computer ever built, and its software had been allowed to evolve itself to maximize efficiency. It weighed countless pieces of data and countless probabilities to reach its decisions.

Even so, it almost seemed like the computer was playing a practical joke on him. If it were April first he would have been sure of it. Sure, send the message from the ESP nutcase to the head of Black PsyOps. Very amusing.

It was true that PsyOps had once experimented with parapsychology, but enough educated people believed there was something to it that it would have been malpractice for the military not to at least have attempted to investigate this area. But they had abandoned these projects years ago, even though the ridicule they had sparked still remained.

But this wasn't a practical joke. Because the NSA's Expert System didn't make mistakes. Not mistakes this big. There had to be more to this than met the eye. But what?

There was only one way to find out. As silly as he felt, he needed to finish reading, and then ask Maggie why the most impressive computer system ever built was suddenly taking this crazy message seriously enough to warrant his urgent attention.

18

Megan Emerson waited impatiently for the hostess to seat a young family.

"A table for two, please," she said when the woman returned. "I have a friend coming to meet me."

The hostess, a tall brunette, led her to a table, while Megan concentrated on counting diners. The four-star restaurant was small, dark, and cozy, and several blocks from any other concentration of people, which was ideal for their needs. Megan thanked the hostess, sat facing the door, and took a proffered menu that said, *The Maple Terrace,* and under this, *Award-Winning Fine Dining.*

"How's it going in there?" came Hall's telepathic thought.

"I need a few more minutes," she replied. A waitress brought her a glass of water with a lemon slice already in it, which was a pet peeve of hers. Even when she specifically requested no lemon, half the time she got it anyway.

When the waitress left, Megan rose from the table and walked the short distance to the kitchen, barging in before anyone could stop her. A young woman with her hair tied back into a bun, wearing a white chef jacket, looked up from where she was plating a piece of salmon covered in glazed walnuts and spinach. To the chef's left, a single busboy was placing a drink order on a tray.

"Can I help you?" said the chef, looking perturbed. "Customers really aren't supposed to come back here," she admonished.

"Sorry about that," said Megan. "I was looking for the restroom."

A quizzical expression came over the chef's face, as though she couldn't believe anyone could be so stupid as to confuse the kitchen with the restroom, especially in a restaurant that was so small and had only a single dining area.

Megan apologized and quickly headed back to her table, stopping at the restroom along the way to be sure no one was inside.

As she was reseating herself she broadcast to Hall. *"Okay, I've got the count."*

"Good. So I'm reading eighteen people, including you."

"That's right," she replied with a smile. *"There's a waitress and hostess in the main restaurant, and a busboy and cook in the kitchen. Along with me and thirteen other customers, that makes eighteen. How far away are you?"*

"The odometer says I'm exactly a half mile."

"Have you noticed any loss of ah . . . intensity?"

"None. And while I can detect the usual babble from all around, I can focus in and detect individuals in the restaurant in isolation of the others." There was a pause. *"I'm going to go out to two miles."*

After their conversation in the family room of their borrowed home, at Megan's encouragement, they had tried numerous experiments under the category of, "What other tricks might Nick Hall be able to do?" He had complained the entire time that he felt like a total idiot, but he had been a good subject and had given it his all.

In the end, they were unable to discover a single new ability. He couldn't move anything through telekinesis. He had strained until Megan thought the veins in his neck would burst, but he couldn't even get a piece of facial tissue to move a hair.

He couldn't start a fire with his mind, which wasn't surprising after his failure at telekinesis. He tried teleportation for fifteen minutes. Nothing. Levitation. Nothing. Transmutation. The same. Megan had brought in a black ant on a stick from the yard, but try as he might, he wasn't able to kill it with his mind, or even slow it down.

Then, getting inspiration from the X-Men, Megan had forged a tin-foil helmet several layers thick for Hall to wear, but it hadn't stopped the voices swirling in his head in the slightest. She wanted to try lead as well, and he agreed that the next time they came across a bank vault or other lead-lined room, he would do the experiment. No matter how ridiculous he might feel by the attempt, no one was more eager to find a way to turn off the voices than he was.

"I'm two miles out," broadcast Hall. *"I'm still reading eighteen people. And they still seem to be the same intensity."* There was a pause. *"Are you still reading me telepathically as clearly as before?"*

She told him that she was. They continued their range-finding mission with great success. They learned that their ability to communicate telepathically ended rather abruptly at just over five miles.

With respect to others, Hall's ability to pick up the thoughts of the people in the restaurant was lost at between six and ten miles, with most dropping off his radar at six or seven, and only one managing to hang in there until mile ten. Before the experiment had begun, they had bought untraceable, disposable cell phones, which allowed them to communicate after Hall was out of telepathic range.

Hall finally joined her at the restaurant, a little more than an hour after she had arrived. When the waitress approached to take their order, Hall tried one further experiment. He thought the word *stop* at her, at the top of his mental lungs.

"Did you hear that?" said Megan to the waitress. "I could have sworn I heard someone say *stop*. But I'm not sure from where."

The waitress looked genuinely perplexed. "I didn't hear a thing," she said.

"Oh my god, there's a tarantula on your arm," Hall thought hard at the waitress for good measure.

The woman calmly thanked them for their order and left.

"Well, Megan, it's looking like you're one of a rare breed who can read my directed thoughts. I tried to reach several other people telepathically while I was on the road, also, with no luck."

He sighed. "I'm beginning to think that maybe you're *more* wired for ESP than average, rather than less. Maybe part of it is that your mind is just naturally able to block me. Instinctively. Like a Venus fly trap that closes when it feels a touch."

Megan shrugged. "Maybe. But if so, I have no conscious awareness of it."

There was a long silence, during which Hall seemed lost in thought. "Who knows," he mused finally, almost to himself. "Maybe you've got some Neanderthal DNA in you somewhere."

"What's *that* supposed to mean? Are you saying I look like a Neanderthal? Or that I'm as dumb as a Neanderthal?"

Whoops, thought Hall. "Sorry," he said, wincing. "I wasn't saying either of those things. I mean, you're super petite. Nobody looks more like a Homo sapiens than you do. And you're obviously very bright," he added for good measure.

"Nobody looks more like a Homo sapiens than me?" she repeated. "Wow. That's one I've never heard before. You really know how to flatter a girl," she added wryly, her eyes sparkling in amusement.

Hall couldn't help but smile. Whoever he was, he knew one thing for sure: he wasn't very smooth with women. "Let me explain. I told you I researched ESP last night at the poker table, when I wasn't in a hand."

"Go on," said Megan. He didn't need to read minds to know she was wondering what this had to do with Neanderthals.

"I came across a fascinating blog that postulated that Neanderthals had psi powers. Before Neanderthals went extinct, they shared the globe with Homo sapiens. For well over a hundred thousand years. Although they were geographically separated for most of this time, with Homo sapiens inhabiting Africa, and Neanderthals Europe and Asia. There are a number of theories about what happened to them. But many years back, a science fiction writer named Ben Bova wrote a novel called *Orion*. Apparently, in the novel, Bova wrote about a meeting between the narrator, a human, who had traveled back in time, and a group of Neanderthals. I read a fascinating passage from the book that really got me thinking."

"Did you, um . . . save this passage?" asked Megan. "You know, in the cloud?"

"Didn't really need to. I can call it up online pretty fast."

Megan grinned. "If only you came with a printer," she said. "If the passage isn't too long, why don't you read it to me."

Hall thought about this for a few seconds and shrugged. "Okay. Sure. Give me a second to call it up and find the right place."

There was a brief pause. "Okay, here we go." Hall cleared his throat and began reading.

The Neanderthals had no fear of strangers. Warfare and conflict were virtually unknown to them. At first I thought that might be because their telepathic abilities made it impossible to attack someone without his sensing it beforehand and being prepared to retaliate. I was wrong, although I had been on the right track.

They were peaceful because their telepathic abilities allowed them to understand each other much more thoroughly than speech permits true understanding. It was not that they constantly read each others' minds, I gradually learned. But the Neanderthals were trained from birth to communicate their feelings, their emotions, as well as rational thoughts and ideas. When a Neanderthal was angry or upset or afraid, everyone around him knew of it instantly, and they all did their best to get to the cause of the problem and solve it. Similarly, when a Neanderthal was happy, everyone knew it and shared in the joy.

How alone we Sapiens are! Locked inside our skulls with our individual personalities, we make feeble attempts at communication through speech, where the Neanderthals shared their thoughts as naturally as warmth flows from a fire. There were no psychotherapists among them—or, rather, they were all psychologists.

They were a gentle people, in spite of their powerful muscular bodies. Their innocent brown eyes reminded me of the doe and fawns I had seen my first day in this time. They did not, probably could not, dissemble.

Megan didn't seem all that impressed. "That's nice, but it *is* science fiction. No way that it's true."

"You're almost certainly right. But according to the blog I read, there is just the tiniest chance that it is. We don't know much about Neanderthals, and scientists have conflicting interpretations of what we do know. Many think Neanderthals were actually *smarter* than us, not dumber, based on a bigger cranial capacity and better stone tools. Many others think this is ridiculous. If they were smarter than us, why did they go extinct?"

"A good point."

"Some think they couldn't speak. They didn't have the physical apparatus we have for it. Those who believe they were smarter than us think their brainpower didn't matter in the end. Without our ability to communicate through complex language, their smarts couldn't help them in the long run."

Megan raised her eyebrows. "But if they couldn't speak, maybe they evolved ESP, instead. Is that what you're saying?"

"They thrived for tens of thousands of years. Possibly without language. So who knows, maybe they had psychic powers. I would have thought this was the most ridiculous theory I had ever heard—if I had read about it two days ago. *"Funny,"* he thought at her with a smile, *"but I'm suddenly less skeptical about the possibility of telepathy than I once was."*

Megan nodded. *"Yeah. Another good point,"* she replied telepathically. "So maybe Neanderthals did have ESP at that," she finished aloud.

"And some scientists think they were able to interbreed with us. Again," he hastened to add, "not that there's any chance *you're* part Neanderthal. I was just trying to figure out why you're different, and I was kind of thinking out loud."

"And I thought nothing could top some of the bizarre conversations I've *already* had with you. But I think this might do it."

The waitress returned and set two dishes in front of them, both of them colorful works of art as well as meals. They thanked her and then resumed.

"But you said this science fiction passage really got you thinking," said Megan. "Just that I might have some Neanderthal DNA, or something more?"

"Something more. About the nature of Homo sapiens. Our history is riddled with brutality, wars, violence, and the like. We all know that. But I've been forced to overhear thousands of people's thoughts since I awoke in that dumpster yesterday. And they aren't pretty. I haven't mentioned this to you, but people think the nastiest things pretty routinely. Even friends. Even couples who have been married a long time. I might even say, *especially* these couples. People are selfish, nasty, and brutish. They fantasize about sex acts that defy imagination. This one likes latex, and that one likes to masturbate on women's clothing, and the other one likes having a tongue stuck in his ear. Not to mention some who have engaged in, or fantasize about engaging in, sexual acts that I plan on never repeating, even to myself."

Megan inhaled deeply and nodded. She had long known the truth of what Hall was saying, and it went far beyond just sexual fantasies.

"And sexual thoughts are only the beginning of why it would be a disaster if we could read each other's minds," continued Hall, right on cue. "And I'm not talking about just being able to read each other's *surface* thoughts, which would be bad enough, but being able to read each other's *innermost* thoughts. The problem goes far beyond just reading all the white lies we tell each other dozens of times a day to spare each other's feelings."

"Like telling your friend you like her new outfit when you actually despise it?"

"Right. You could argue that these lies are at least told for the right reasons. But what I'm talking about is far worse. People wishing other people were dead. Wives learning what their husbands are really thinking about when they're pretending to be listening to them, and vice versa. Or what their partners are thinking about during sex. Spouses learning of the sordid details of past infidelities, both real and fantasized. Subordinates who *despise* their bosses. You think there are any employees only *pretending* to laugh at the bosses' jokes? Coworkers who badmouth colleagues behind their backs. Kids learning what their parents really think about their fifth grade art projects, and their general criticisms and disappointments. And parents reading the hatred toward them that nearly all kids feel at one time or another. And revealed prejudices, even among the best and most open-minded of us. Not necessarily just against blacks, or whites, or Asians, or homosexuals, or Arabs. But against the obese. Rednecks. Snobs. Sluts. Believe me, I've been reading minds. *I know.*"

"It's an awfully bleak picture," said Megan. "But I can't argue with anything you've said. When you knew the flavor of my favorite ice cream and for just a second I thought you could read me, I was panicked. I like you Nick—maybe a lot—but humans aren't wired to let someone inside our innermost sanctums. I feel like I'm not bigoted and have led a good life—but everyone has secrets. Like you said, sexual fantasies, embarrassing moments, thoughts they've had and things they've done that they aren't proud of."

Hall nodded slowly. "So if I'm stuck with this ability, and word gets out, I'll be a pariah. No one I can read will be willing to come *near* me."

Megan lowered her eyes. As much as she had come to care for him in a short period of time, if he could read her every, innermost thought . . . . She shuddered just thinking about how impossible that would be. "I guess our species just isn't wired for full disclosure," she said.

"So this ability may make me formidable, but it's like the curse of Midas. Seems like a good thing at first blush . . ."

They both fell silent, alone with their thoughts for several minutes while they tried to enjoy an expensive lunch that was growing cold. Finally, Hall said, "Now that I've depressed us both, I should probably mention that it isn't like the species is beyond redemption. It goes without saying that I've read a lot of positive thoughts and emotions as well. Selflessness. People going out of their way to please, or help, or surprise each other. Devotion to kids or parents. Generosity and compassion. I've read all of this too. Some of it is faked for outsiders, but a lot of it is real."

"So do positive thoughts outweigh venomous thoughts?"

Hall laughed. "I haven't really done that experiment. And most thoughts are neutral. You know, like, 'I wonder if it will rain tomorrow?' But regardless of the good will that would come from reading each other's positive thoughts, nothing could mitigate the total disaster that mind reading would cause."

"Yeah. My guess is that if everyone could read minds the way you do, society would tear itself to pieces in hours. Probably with our bare hands and teeth."

19

Megan and Hall fell silent. Megan looked around at the fellow inhabitants of the restaurant. Dining pleasantly with others, secure in the knowledge that their inner thoughts and feelings, and outer expressions of these thoughts and feelings, could be diametrically opposed without anyone being the wiser. Separated by an impenetrable wall.

But if this impenetrable wall ever came crashing down, civilization would not be far behind.

"I have absolutely no doubt that you're right," said Hall grimly. "We've lost a lot of privacy already. There are cameras everywhere, and everyone is a narcissist. Our generation grew up thinking that everyone wants us to Tweet them our every thought. We can't wait to post pictures of a date on Facebook, before the date is even over. Or go on reality television and expose every facet of our lives. Or sext each other naked pictures which end up in cyberspace for all eternity. The privacy that our parents knew is long gone.

"But at least we still have *some* control," continued Hall. "We can still hide our *thoughts*. We can choose *what* to post on Facebook. So while we've gone a long way toward eliminating our own privacy, the mind is the last bastion of privacy we have. If this is ever breached, society self-destructs," he finished, mirroring Megan's reasoning exactly.

A thoughtful expression came over Megan's face as something clicked about the science fiction piece Hall had found so thought-provoking. "You had read hundreds of minds already when you came across that passage about Neanderthals, hadn't you? So you'd already come to this conclusion."

"Yes. That's really why I found the passage so interesting. Why it struck home. Only if a species evolved ESP gradually, so it became a part of their psychological makeup, like the Neanderthals in the story, could ESP be a positive force. Introduced suddenly in a species evolved to shield its thoughts, like ours, it's catastrophic."

Megan nodded.

"The real Neanderthals probably didn't have ESP," continued Hall. "The theory is probably wrong. But if they *did*, they would almost surely have developed a gentle, open-minded nature. Like that described in the novel. Pretty easy for a tribe to weed out those who are psychopathic, or who aren't team players, when it's impossible for anyone to hide anything. They almost would have had to evolve into kind, compassionate, ultra-pacifists. So when Homo sapiens crossed into Europe forty-five thousand years ago, Neanderthals wouldn't have had a *chance*. Can you imagine having absolutely no concept of selfishness, deception, ruthlessness—and then you come across *us*. Talk about a mismatch. Neanderthal extinction would have been a certainty."

Megan forced a smile. "When I picture them the way they're described in that story, I suddenly find myself wishing I *did* have Neanderthal DNA. Nice save, Nick. Anyone who can call a girl a Neanderthal, and then convince her it was a genuine compliment, is awfully good."

Hall laughed. "You know, I don't know who I am, but I'm beginning to think you're my type. I'm not hitting on you or anything. But if we weren't running for our lives . . ."

"You'd ask me out to a lunch like we're having now?"

"Assuming I could afford this place," he replied in amusement. "I don't think the old me could take a tiny poker stake and turn it into over twenty grand. But on the subject of you and me . . . Well, it's probably a good thing you can't read my mind."

The corners of Megan's mouth turned up into an impish smile. "I wouldn't find any naked pictures of me in there, would I?" she said, gesturing toward his head.

"Nah," he said shyly, looking more than a little embarrassed. "Not at all." He paused and raised his eyebrows. "But now that you mention it . . ."

Megan hit his arm playfully. "Stop that," she said. And then tele-pathically, she added, *"It's a good thing you can't read my mind either."*

Hall gazed at her meaningfully, but chose to let this go. *"As disastrous as full-on mind reading would be, you have to admit, wide-spread telepathy would be awesome."*

"Absolutely," replied Megan.

Telepathy was something that would be heralded by society, she realized, if ESP could be limited just to this. Rather than invading the inner sanctum, this was just another form of communication. Society would have to make certain adjustments, but nothing that couldn't be done. True, you couldn't stop someone from shouting into your brain, which could be disruptive, but there was nothing to prevent people from shouting into your ears right now. Only the conventions of polite society prevented this behavior. And rules of etiquette would develop quickly for telepathy as well.

Still, she didn't doubt that unforeseen issues would arise. Cheating was one that occurred to her even as she had this thought. If everyone could communicate telepathically, she was pretty sure the average SAT score would rise dramatically. But she also had no doubt that the ingenuity and genius of humanity, its can-do spirit—the flip side of the negatives they had been speaking of—would find a way to make telepathy a blessing.

A busboy removed their empty plates from the table and they ordered dessert. Hall frowned for just an instant as his eyes followed the waitress's receding figure. Megan caught his frown and guessed the reason behind it. "Mind reading again, Nick?"

"If only I could prevent it," he said.

"So what was she thinking?"

Hall sighed. "You really want to know?"

Megan nodded.

"Okay, here goes. She thinks you're cute, but that the outfit you're wearing is unflattering and you're too skinny. And she doesn't like your hair style. She thinks I'm probably a jackass for standing you up for over an hour, and annoyed that this resulted in the table being tied up for as long as it has been. Now that we've ordered dessert, she's wondering if we're ever going to leave. And she thinks any man who would keep a girl waiting for over an hour is probably a bad tipper."

Megan digested all of this and shook her head. "I am so glad I'm not you," she said. "I don't know how you're handling this as well as you are."

"Mostly because of you, Megan," he replied earnestly. "You're a big part of my coping mechanism. And I'm probably not handling things as well as you think."

Megan found herself drawn to his expressive brown eyes, and she lost herself there for several long seconds. If she was going to fall for a guy, did it really need to be in the context of the most complicated and bizarre set of circumstances in history?

"So any other epiphanies last night?" said Megan, breaking out of her trance.

"Nothing too earth-shattering. The ESP thing is driving me batty and making me wish I weren't human a lot of the time. But being able to surf the web with my thoughts is more amazing than I could ever explain. I must be a super nerd. Because being able to learn about anything that crosses my mind, effortlessly, is like the ultimate nirvana to me."

"I don't think you're a super nerd because of that," said Megan, fighting to keep a straight face. "I think you're a super nerd because you use words like *nirvana*."

Hall laughed, and for just a moment a smitten expression flashed across his face, but he quickly concealed it.

"I had a memory last night of a presentation given by an author of kids science fiction books maybe twenty years ago. I don't remember anything but the content, but I remember this quite well. The guy spoke about writing—and technology. About how the rate of change was accelerating at an insane pace. He talked about how big a deal it had been when he was a little boy when his family went from a black-and-white to a color television. He said he remembered when they got their first microwave oven, and they all gathered around with their mouths open to watch it boil a glass of water, as if by magic. He remembered going on a family outing to marvel at the wonders of the first ATM machine in their neighborhood.

"He talked about how lucky kids were—again, I think this was about twenty years ago when I was little—to live in the computer age. He said that in his day, they had a device called a typewriter. He described how it worked, how mechanical keys would strike a ribbon of ink and slam into a piece of paper. And he said that the thing was, if you made a single mistake, you'd often have to start the entire page over again. A mistake of a single letter! You could try to correct it by backing up and using correcting tape, but that often failed. Or you could brush this white paint over your mistake and try to line it up again, and type on the dried paint. But usually, for him at least, one wrong letter typed and he'd have to start the page from scratch."

"We really do take technology for granted, don't we?"

"That's why this guy's talk was so fascinating. He reminded kids how lucky they were. That with a computer, one could make endless changes, effortlessly. Move sections of text around to see where they fit best. Improve a sentence a hundred times. He said that anyone who had been able to write a novel using a typewriter was truly a *god*. He was a successful author, but he insisted that if he would have had to use a typewriter, he couldn't have done it."

Megan thought about how limiting graphic design would be without computer technology, and had trouble even imagining it.

The waitress returned with their desserts, outwardly as pleasant and professional as anyone could want. Megan didn't even want to consider what she might be thinking this time.

Megan pushed a spoon into the tiramisu she had ordered and brought it to her mouth as Hall continued.

"This author said his father had worked in the office equipment field when he had been a kid. One day, his father took him into his office and told him about a revolutionary new invention. You took a piece of paper with text or images on it and you put it on this machine. And *thousands* of miles away, an identical copy of the paper came out the other end. It was called a *fax machine*. He said when his dad told him about it, it seemed like something from *Star Trek*. Like the transporter machine. He thought his dad was making it up."

"And the fax machine became practically obsolete overnight."

Hall swallowed his first bite of the chocolate ganache and nutella crepes he had ordered, and paused for just a moment to savor it. "Exactly," he continued. "He made this exact point. The Internet came along, so instead of faxing documents, you could just attach them to e-mails. He considered the Internet humanity's greatest achievement. A single repository of all human knowledge, including images, audio, and video, that could be instantly searched for the occurrence of any subject matter or phrase. And one that allowed users to jump off the page to reference a related topic millions of pages away and then jump back again in an instant.

"Of course, even at that time, kids had grown up with the Internet, so they weren't as impressed as he was. But he drove the point home. He said that in his day, if you wanted to know Grover Cleveland's date of birth, it would take you hours. You'd have to go to the local library, go through a card catalog, find a book about him, and search by hand for his birth date. Now it takes you seconds to find out. And if you wanted to know a dozen recipes for asparagus, you were out of luck. Period. There was no way possible to get that information. Now, of course, you search for 'asparagus recipes' and you get hundreds instantly."

"It really is amazing," said Megan. "I wonder what he would have had to say about *you*."

"He'd be astounded, that's for sure. Even our generation would be astounded by this. Although a lot of the research I did last night suggested many people think a marriage between man and computer is inevitable."

"Maybe some implants and artificial limbs, but it isn't like we'll stop being human any time soon."

"I'm not so sure about that. Last night, I found some writing by a guy named Ray Kurzweil that spoke to this."

"You really are a super nerd, aren't you?"

"Sure seems that way."

"You kept *busy* last night. When did you find the time to fleece two tables of unsuspecting gamblers?"

"I've always been good at multitasking," he said in amusement. "At least I *think* I have."

"So go on."

"This guy writes about what he calls a singularity event. A point at which humanity sort of combines with computers—I guess I'm the start of this—and then quickly evolves into something transcendent. He says it won't be long. Not thousands of years. Not even hundreds. Sooner than anyone thinks. He believes we're just a hair away from a tipping point."

"Based on what?" asked Megan.

"We all know the rate of computer advances is exponential. That power and memory and speed doubles or so every twelve to eighteen months, and has done so for decades. Well, a lot of things are like this. Internet nodes. The speed of sequencing DNA. And so on. But Kurzweil explains how exponential growth sneaks up on you. If you double a penny every day for forty days, at the end you'll have over ten billion dollars. But in the first week you hardly notice. When one penny doubles to two pennies, who cares? But when five billion dollars doubles to *ten* billion, *that's* what you call a noticeable increase. So in the beginning the line for growth on the graph seems to barely be going any higher. But there comes an inflection point at which the graph almost looks like it's going vertical. When each step taken becomes *enormous*."

Hall paused. "According to Kurzweil, we're just about there. And when that happens, we'll make more progress in a year or two than we did during the entire twentieth century. We'll reach this man/machine transcendence faster than anyone realizes."

"Do you think he's right?"

"A lot of scientists thought he was far too optimistic when he first wrote about this. But I checked predictions he made in 2000 for where we'd be today. His were the most aggressive of anyone's, and he's not that far off, especially when it comes to computer technology. The speed and power of the 6G WiFi system now in place is even *more* impressive than his predictions, which were considered ridiculous at the time."

Megan nodded soberly. There were a lot of things *she* had once considered ridiculous. In the past twenty-four hours she'd had to re-think much of what she thought she knew. There was no doubt that getting to know the phenomenon that was Nick Hall was changing her perspective dramatically.

She lowered her spoon and stared happily at the man across from her. Yes, getting to know him was definitely changing her perspective. In more ways than one.

20

Alex Altschuler walked through the computer lab, thick with oversized monitors and electronics debris of every type, past a dozen workstations, past a door leading to the adjacent facility at which rodent, and occasionally primate, experimentation was conducted, and to a set of glass doors, on which the words *Theia Labs* were stenciled in blue. He opened the doors and quickly paid for his pizza before returning to his office.

As usual, he was the last one in the lab—although, to be fair, it *was* Saturday at six p.m., and a number of his team had put in a full day's work anyway. Also, as usual, he was eating alone.

He was a scrawny geek; a fact of which he was well aware. A *brilliant*, scrawny geek. He had skipped ahead in high school and had finished his doctorate at MIT in Electrical Engineering and Computer Science in only four years. He well knew that his appearance fit the geek stereotype exactly, right down to the glasses on his face, an appliance that was accelerating toward extinction.

But God had played a practical joke on him. He had a condition where his eyelids were very tight to his eyeballs, and he didn't tear a lot. So no matter how many times he struggled with contacts that others raved were the essence of comfort, he ended up being miserable. And the idea of his eyes being sliced and then hit with a laser was something he couldn't get comfortable with, even knowing intellectually that the procedure worked perfectly almost all of the time, just as he could never bungee jump off a bridge, even if he intellectually believed he would survive the ordeal. After vision correction eye surgery had become fully automated a few years before, and the price had plummeted, he was one of the few remaining holdouts.

There were two diametrically opposed male stereotypes that had been around forever. The dumb jock stereotype. And the brilliant, socially awkward, unattractive, uncoordinated geek—with bad eyesight—stereotype.

And while there were endless counterexamples, in Altschuler's experience, these stereotypes were stereotypes for a reason. It seemed to him they had an evolutionary basis—at least somewhat. Every male was competing for mates. The most successful passed down their genes to numerous offspring, ensuring their traits would survive. Strong, handsome, tall, athletic men didn't need any other redeeming qualities to find a mate. Mates found *them*. If they were brilliant this was just a bonus.

But if you didn't possess these positive physical traits, being very bright could compensate—at least to some degree. You could use this intellect to accumulate wealth and power, which were also appealing to a mate, ensuring the spread of these characteristics to future generations.

Altschuler lifted a piece of his meat lovers pizza, which was spewing irresistible aroma molecules into the air around him like lava from Mount Vesuvius, and tore off a large bite. He finished shoving the entire piece into his mouth without once taking his eyes from the large monitor in front of him, covered with the complex computer code he had been writing.

The progress he had been making this year was nothing short of *stunning*. He felt sure that Theia Labs was on the verge of any number of revolutionary, world-changing breakthroughs, which his boss and Theia's CEO, Kelvin Gray, continued to insist they sit on for inexplicable reasons.

Gray, who stomped all over the geek stereotype by being a triple threat: handsome, charismatic, *and* brilliant, had recruited Altschuler only three years out of MIT, luring him away from Intel by making him a financial offer he couldn't refuse. One that easily outdistanced even the most aggressive offer he had received from other global electronics, computer, and Internet behemoths. In just a year, Altschuler had built a nest egg that he might not have managed in three years at his previous job. Another few years and he'd have the house on the beach, the Lamborghini, and everything else he needed to signal to women that he was loaded.

The irony, of course, was that the only girl he really wanted, Heather Zambrana, wasn't the type to be impressed by wealth. Which was one of the many reasons he liked her so much. She was a few years older than he was, reported to him, and although better looking for a woman than he was for a man, was a certifiable geek, just like him. But unless she left the company there was no way for him to even ask her out, which was maddening, but also a great relief to his inner insecure geek, who was sure she would reject him anyway.

His work at Theia Labs was fascinating, but infuriating at the same time. At the tender age of twenty-seven, when he had joined, he had been put in charge of two dozen scientists, almost all of them his elders, and been given the title of Executive Vice President of research, second in line only to Kelvin Gray. At twenty-seven this was extraordinary.

And yet the title was strangely a paper tiger. He wasn't treated like an executive or partner. Gray was demanding, but rarely visited. His boss worked out of a small suite of offices in nearby Madera, connected to two very well-equipped computer and electronics labs. A large one for the use of those who also worked there, and a smaller, but still impressive lab for Gray's personal and private use. Gray also worked out of his home much of the time.

Altschuler's responsibility was to lead a team of computer geniuses, along with a group of ex-pharma people doing animal experiments on the brain, with the goal of determining the precise neuronal real estate with which visual and auditory impulses interacted; the precise data stream required to perfectly mimic the visual and auditory signals naturally delivered by the eyes and ears.

On a second front, they had been trying to decode pure thought into language. A primitive version of this capability had been available for years, but it was orders of magnitude less capable than the system for which they were shooting. Kids all over the world were controlling video games with their minds, using headsets spouting numerous electrodes that touched their heads as they played. But the input for this system was derived empirically, and was different for each person. Users had to train it, concentrating on making a cursor on the screen perform different movements until the game's computer could map the electrical patterns their brains generated when they tried to do this.

The leap in technology required to go from controlling simple movements with thought, to getting a computer to correctly read an exact stream of words thought to it, chosen from an unlimited vocabulary, was similar to the leap in technology between an abacus and a supercomputer.

But progress during the past half-year had been almost unprecedented in the annals of technology. Impossibly rapid.

Yes, Altschuler knew his own unparalleled genius had a lot to do with it, suffering no false modesty when it came to his computer skills. But it was Kelvin Gray's suggestions that were making the virtual simulations and animal experiments sing. The man was *uncanny*. He would suggest novel positioning and interactions of electrical signals within the neuronal matrix, positionings that were far from obvious, and they would work, for reasons that were often still not clear.

The same was true for tweaks to the data stream, and modifications to the sets of algorithms they were using, which Altschuler believed to be among the most complex and revolutionary ever attempted. Altschuler had had to convert Gray's insights into code and hardware, which in itself was daunting, and in his opinion, had been somewhat miraculous. But without his boss's insights, he had to admit, they'd still be taking baby steps instead of sprinting like an Olympic champion.

They were ready for human trials. Animal experimentation and virtual simulations, as comprehensive as they were, could only take them so far. For all Altschuler knew they were there already, able to mimic the data stream sent by both the eyes and ears with absolute perfection.

If their current results really could translate, Altschuler believed they might have the absolute cure for blindness *and* deafness. And on their other front, they were ready to come out with breathtaking applications for thought-to-data conversion.

But Gray kept putting him off. He hadn't been allowed to publish any of their findings. They had certainly made breakthroughs that would instantly translate into blockbuster products, yet these weren't even discussed.

Ultimately, Altschuler knew, Gray wanted to combine the technologies and algorithms they were establishing to enable humans to surf the web with their thoughts alone, using brain implants. This would introduce additional challenges. Fortunately, scientists had been inserting implants into animal brains for decades. As early as 1998, iridium microelectrodes coated in Parylene C, implanted in the dural matter of monkeys, were found to be well-tolerated and operational after three years. And improvements had been made since this time.

The chips would require minimal power, but this was still another obstacle to be overcome. The chips would get their juice from fuel cells able to convert glucose into electricity. And while such technology had been available for years, it would take careful experimentation, when the time came, to be sure not too much heat was given off from this reaction, and that the implants weren't stealing too much of the glucose the brain devoured at ten times the rate of the rest of the body.

Gray had a number of top people working on problems such as this at Theia's Madera site, but he never discussed particulars, nor disclosed the progress made by these groups.

As for Altschuler and his team, they had prepared endless patents, but Gray wouldn't even let them work with a patent attorney. Gray was sitting on a winning lottery ticket, but refused to cash in.

It was *maddening*, thought Altschuler, for maybe the tenth time that day, as he continued to attack the pizza in front of him. He was starting on his final slice when a call came in on his cell.

"Alex, it's Cameron Fyfe," said an intense voice. "Are you alone?"

Altschuler was immediately on guard. Fyfe was Kelvin Gray's silent partner. He was a venture capitalist responsible for financing the entire show, and he had controlling interest in Theia. And Altschuler had only met him once before. Despite Altschuler's lofty, symbolic title, he was treated by both Fyfe and Gray as just a hired hand.

As though, outside of his expertise, he might as well have been the janitor there.

This Fyfe kept a very low profile. He must have been worth tens of millions, minimum, but there was very little about him online— Altschuler had checked. Occasionally he was written up for donating to this charity or that, but he managed to keep his business interests strictly out of the public eye.

It was odd for Fyfe to be calling. Even odder for him to begin the call with "are you alone?" Not exactly a standard greeting.

Altschuler confirmed he was alone, removing his glasses and cleaning them on his shirt, a nervous habit he had picked up years earlier. "What can I do for you, Cameron?" he asked. He resisted the urge to call the man Mr. Fyfe since this would be too subservient for the second-in-command of the company.

"I'll get right to the point, Alex. A year ago, I told Kelvin that if he didn't begin to make more than marginal progress, I was going to pull the plug on Theia Labs. Beginning six or seven months ago, from all accounts, your progress has been unprecedented. You've made Mount Everest look like a bunny hill. Any idea why this might be?"

"As much as I'd like to take full credit, I can't. Kelvin has come up with insight after insight that have been pretty miraculous. His intuition should be bronzed."

There was a long pause. "Last night I was at the Theia offices in Madera," said Fyfe. "I had a meeting scheduled with Kelvin after hours. I let myself in, but his office door was closed. I found out later that the meeting was scheduled for next week, but I had entered it incorrectly in my calendar. Anyway, I overheard snippets of conversation that were quite alarming."

Scheduling mix-up, my ass, thought Altschuler. Fyfe had suspected something was fishy and had purposely eavesdropped. If the eavesdropper had really been Fyfe, which Altschuler was not at all certain of. More likely he had given his keycard to someone else, who had done the eavesdropping for him. Or he had even employed other means entirely, less accidental and less legal, to catch the few snippets of conversation he had.

"Go on," said Alex Altschuler.

"He was speaking with someone named John," continued Fyfe. "I only got pieces of the puzzle. But I did some research later, and I've put together what I think Kelvin has been up to. I suspected something was going on." He took a deep breath. "But not to this extent. *Never to this extent.*"

Altschuler braced himself. If a man like Fyfe, who had probably seen it all, was shell-shocked by something, it had to be very bad.

"Given what I overheard, the mystery of the Scripps *Explorer* has been solved."

"What?" mumbled Altschuler to himself in shock. This was the very last sentence he had ever expected to hear.

The Scripps Institute of Oceanography exploratory vessel, aptly named the *Explorer*, had made international headlines about a half year or so earlier when it had disappeared off the coast of Mexico, with twenty-seven scientists and crew on board. The ship had been doing research over the Middle America Trench, a little known tear in the floor of the Eastern Pacific that ran for seventeen hundred miles from central Mexico to Costa Rica, at depths as great as four miles. The vessel had disappeared without a trace and none of the passengers or crew were ever recovered.

Bits of wreckage had eventually been found washed up to shore, which were identified as belonging to the ship, but the bulk of the vessel was never found. Given the depth of the trench, finding the wreckage was a daunting task. It had been a huge story for weeks, as weeping relatives were interviewed, scientists speculated that it must have encountered a hundred-foot rogue wave, and cable specials were launched speculating about the ship's final hours.

"The Scripps *Explorer?*" repeated Altschuler, blinking in confusion.

"Yes. I think Kelvin arranged to kidnap the *Explorer's* crew and passengers, and then scuttled the ship. Using this guy John as the hired muscle. I think he's been using the passengers as human guinea pigs to perfect Theia technology."

Fyfe paused. "And then killing them," he finished chillingly.

21

Altschuler reeled backwards as though from a physical blow. The world seemed to spin around him.

Did Fyfe know what he was saying? If this were true, it was a massacre on a historic scale.

Perpetrated by Kelvin Gray? How could it be?

Gray may have been annoying in some of his business decisions, and didn't treat Altschuler the way his title and contributions would dictate, but he was a great scientist and a great man. Thoughtful. Generous. Compassionate. Altschuler had seen him scoop up a spider and gently place it outside rather than kill it.

To have been part of this atrocity, to have experimented on and murdered scores of people in cold blood, he would have to be on par with the most heinous psychopaths in history. But even as Altschuler thought this, he realized that many of these famous psychopaths had managed to fool others equally well. They had appeared equally kind. They were equally persuasive and charming.

Somehow, he knew it was true. In some purposely ignored recess of his consciousness, he *had* known for some time. Not the specifics. Not the heinous nature of the crime. No one could have guessed Gray would go *this* far. It was unthinkable.

But the part about experimenting on human subjects?

How else to explain the superhuman insights Gray kept bringing to the table, seemingly from out of nowhere. Altschuler realized that *Gray* hadn't fooled him. Altschuler had *allowed* himself to be fooled. He had been complicit, not asking any questions, even of himself. He had turned a blind eye, refusing to allow even a hint of suspicion to mar the bliss of his denial.

But even had he allowed himself to come to the obvious conclusion, he would never have guessed *this*. Perhaps some human experimentation with ridiculously well-paid subjects, sworn to secrecy.

But he *should* have guessed. Even this. Because the only way to get results this spectacular, this quickly, was to have total disregard for the gray matter of an actual human being. To cut a swath of destruction through a brain, eliminating what didn't work and finding and refining what did. To risk killing scores of subjects. Treading lightly, slowly, *carefully*—even with human subjects—wouldn't do it.

"Are you still there?" said Fyfe.

"I am," said Altschuler woodenly.

"You have to admit, it explains a lot. I've been thrilled by your progress. But in my experience, if you roll snake eyes eight or nine times in a row, it's time to question if the dice are loaded."

Altschuler nodded, disgusted with himself. Even Fyfe had finally refused to turn a blind eye to what was going on, despite all he had to gain by their progress. And venture capitalists weren't exactly known for their ethics. So what did that say about *Alex Altschuler?*

"If what you suspect is true," said Altschuler, "it would *definitely* explain a lot. Kelvin's insights *were* too good to be true." He paused. "So why are you calling me and not the authorities? And how can you be sure I wasn't a part of this from the beginning?" he added, his mouth suddenly as dry as the Sahara.

"Let me answer your second question first. Your name came up in Kelvin's conversation. He and the man he was speaking with, John, had seen no indication you suspected anything. I didn't hear the other end of the line, but my guess is this John was surprised at this. Kelvin actually quoted Upton Sinclair to help explain it."

"Upton Sinclair?"

"Yes. The quote is something like, 'It's difficult to get a man to understand something when his salary depends on his *not* understanding it.'"

Altschuler grimaced. Sinclair had hit the nail on the head in his case. Altschuler's livelihood, and one breakthrough after another, had depended on him not suspecting anything, so his consciousness had obliged. Altschuler took a moment to reflect on how surreal it was for one psychopath to be quoting Upton Sinclair to the other. But there was no rule that said just because you had no conscience, you couldn't still be well-read and cerebral.

"As to your second question," continued Fyfe. "Why am I not going to the authorities? I only have suppositions at this point. I didn't record the conversation, and even if I had, I did a lot of reconstructive surgery, Googling, and applying inductive reasoning to draw the conclusions I have. We need to gather more foolproof evidence. We need to make sure this monster doesn't slip the net."

Altschuler knew that Fyfe hadn't used the pronoun *we* by accident. "What is it that you want me to do?"

"We need to get a confession from Kelvin. As it is, we could never get a search and seizure warrant for his home and office. And we need to know *everything*. *Theia Labs* needs to know. We can't wait months to understand every last detail of what happened while Kelvin's high-priced lawyers are playing games tying up the system. We need to have everything out in the open from the start. To make sure Kelvin is sent to the chair, and to make sure we know the exact score from day one."

"I don't disagree. But given what he's done, I don't think he's the confessing type."

"No. That's where you come in. You, working with a specialist I've worked with on occasion. A man who is a combination private investigator and bodyguard, with an office in San Francisco. A man with impeccable credentials and exceptional reliability. He works alone, but if necessary, he can also field and manage a team of fellow professionals very quickly. His name is Ed Cowan. He's the very best. Ex-Army ranger. Very smart. Very fearless."

That makes one of us, thought Altschuler, swallowing hard.

"I need you to go to Kelvin's house—tonight—wearing a bug. It will be very tiny, don't worry. And Ed Cowan will be listening in nearby, which means that you can't be in better hands. Anyway, I want you to tell Kelvin you've figured it all out. That you overheard one of his conversations, like I did. And you want in."

"I want in?" repeated Altschuler in dismay.

"If you confront him, you'll get nowhere. Worse, you'll tip him off and he'll destroy all evidence. But by telling him you want in, you're using the carrot and the stick strategy. If he *could* get you involved, he'd have total control over you. He'd *own* you. And the project would benefit from your genius applied at the source. That's the carrot. If he plays dumb, he has to know you won't buy it, and you might turn him in. That's the stick. The combination can't help but work. He'll *welcome* you in. Believe me, he's *dying* to tell someone like you what's really going on. This will work. Trust me. I'm sure of it."

Fyfe said it with such absolute conviction Altschuler almost took it as a fact. Almost. Fyfe hadn't gotten to where he was by letting any uncertainty enter his rhetoric when he was trying to be persuasive. But Altschuler hadn't gotten to where *he* was by letting anyone else's passion stop him from using his own considerable analytical ability.

"You can't be sure of how he'll react," said Altschuler. "And we both know it. So what if you're wrong? What if Kelvin decides to kill me? After all, he's already responsible for multiple murders. What's one more?"

"He won't. Trust me. He may be a ruthless psychopath, but he's also brilliant. He'll do what's in his best interest. And if he does threaten you, then show him the bug. Tell him that Ed Cowan is outside and that if anything happens to you, the same will happen to him in short order."

"I don't know . . ." said Altschuler.

"*You can do this, Alex.* You *have to* do this. I'm not pointing fingers, but you *should* have caught on before anyone. And you didn't. And people have died. You're going to do this for several reasons. First and foremost, because you know it's the best way to be sure Kelvin pays for what he did, and the world knows him for the monster he is. But also for yourself. This is the chance of a lifetime for you. If you do this, I'll install you as CEO of Theia Labs."

Fyfe paused. "Now I know what you're thinking. Yes, when this comes out it will be the shitstorm of the century. It will dominate the international news for seemingly forever. But everyone will know you weren't involved. And the smoke *will* clear. And when it does, Theia will still have the intellectual property gained from Kelvin's atrocities."

"But the IP couldn't be more poisoned," said Altschuler. "The whole thing immediately brings to mind the sick medical experiments conducted by the Nazis in World War II."

"I know that! I don't want to be associated with what Gray did any more than you do! But what would you recommend? That we pretend these advances weren't made?" asked Fyfe in exasperation. "If Adolf Hitler cured cancer, would we refuse to use the cure?"

Altschuler sighed deeply. "I don't know," he whispered stubbornly.

"*Of course* we'd still use the cure," insisted Fyfe. "And you know it. And it would be the *right* thing to do. Well, it's the same with this. And the public will come around to appreciate that. Not immediately, but they will. And if we tie the system into the input coming in through the eyes, rather than cyberspace, we could well have the cure for blindness on our hands. And deafness. You think that won't ultimately be embraced, despite being tainted?

"And this is only the beginning," added Fyfe. "Theia Labs will survive, and will soon thrive. Trust me, when the smoke clears, we'll be in a position to break Facebook's record as fastest to reach a hundred billion dollar market capitalization. And you'll be CEO, with tens of billions of dollars of stock."

Altschuler realized that Fyfe was using his favorite strategy, the carrot and the stick, to persuade *him*. But he had to admit, it *was* effective. Combing the stick of guilt with the carrot of becoming CEO of the next Facebook or Apple, along with the certainty of untold wealth, was as persuasive as it got.

"I know I'm asking a lot, Alex," continued Fyfe. "And I know it's scary. But I need your help. Are you in?"

Altschuler swallowed hard and nodded, only remembering Fyfe couldn't see him several seconds later. "I'm in," he whispered finally.

"You're doing the right thing," said Fyfe. "Ed Cowan is at Theia Labs' outer door right now. Let him in. And let's nail this murderous bastard tonight."

22

Colonel Justin Girdler had made finding Nick Hall his top priority. After reading the e-mail message Hall had supposedly sent three times, and learning why its status had been changed, he had set wheels in motion and then had locked himself in his office, turned off Maggie, and spent hour after hour just pondering the implications of what Hall's message, if true, really meant. This he followed with several more hours of discussion with his second-in-command, Major Mike Campbell, and he believed they were very much on the same page.

The colonel still had no guarantee the message was real, but given the implications, he'd be a fool not to prepare as though it was.

Before he finally went to sleep after a very long day—or tried to get to sleep in any event—he decided to read Hall's message one last time.

He called it up on his TV.

From: Nick Hall
Subject: Urgent, life in jeopardy
I awoke this morning in a locked warehouse without any memory of who I am, hearing voices in my head. I may be insane, in which case I'm only imagining sending this message. If you receive this then I am not insane. A man was here when I awoke, and he left ten minutes later, but I was able to read his mind. Not just read, but fish anything out of it I wanted to. I know how all of this sounds. But bear with me.

The man was a hired killer named Billie Peterson, who works for a man named John Delamater, whom he's never met. I may not remember who I am, but I was able to fish out a lot from Peterson's mind beyond just his name and the name of his boss.

I'm at a large warehouse outside of Fresno, California. Peterson doesn't remember the exact address so I can't get it from his mind, but it's on Albany Avenue. I stayed in Peterson's head after he drove off, but lost him when he was about six miles out, so this must be the range of my ESP ability. There seem to be only about fifteen to twenty other people I can pick up within this six-mile radius, so the warehouse is fairly isolated.

Anyway, Peterson's boss, John Delamater, is working with someone else—the man who runs the warehouse. Peterson doesn't know this guy's name. He only knows that he's a "big-shot scientist" who purposely vacates the premises during Peterson's infrequent visits. Peterson was told nothing about what was going on at the warehouse, and managed to learn only that it involved experimenting on humans to perfect some sort of brain technology—technology that would allow people to surf the web with their thoughts.

He did know my name, however, which is more than I can say. It's Nick Hall. Apparently, I am the last of twenty-seven men and women who were experimented on, and Peterson got the word to kill me later tonight. He replaced another of Delamater's men on this duty a month ago, and has killed three others of these mysterious twenty-seven. Peterson wasn't given any information on who these people are, how they got here, or even their names. He only knew mine because he overheard someone say it, and that I was the last of the "lot."

Given I've been the last man standing for three weeks now, he assumed I'd been the most promising subject in getting the Internet to work, but had finally been a failure. They've been using a drug to force memory loss on their subjects to keep them off-balance and not let them realize what's going on. Without my ability to read thoughts, this would have worked well, and even with my ability, it's disorienting and scary not to know anything about yourself or what has been happening.

Anyway, Peterson and his predecessor incinerate the bodies. After he left, I tried to activate the Internet with my thoughts, and I got it to work. Perfectly. After only ten or fifteen minutes of experimentation, it's insane how effortlessly I can use it. Either I lied to this scientist when I said it wasn't working, or the scientist lied to Peterson. I've been locating e-mail addresses and sending out this distress call. I know this sounds like the ravings of a lunatic, but it's not. At least I don't think it is.

Peterson will be coming back tonight. He's planning to lie to me to get me to accompany him to their incinerator, telling me he's learned who I am and can clear up the mystery of how I happen to be here. But given that I now know what he really intends, and can read his mind every step along the way, I am confident I can escape.

Anyone who gets this message, please reply. I'll check this e-mail address often, and I have no doubt I'll need help once I escape. I know you won't believe this, but I'm begging you to take just a little time to look into it. Find the warehouse, and this will prove the truth of what I'm telling you.

Girdler read the message one more time for good measure and then turned off his television and stretched out in bed. He had divorced three years earlier, and while he had been in a few relationships since this time, he was currently sleeping alone, which suited him just fine. He could analyze the psychological aspects of the most devious totalitarian regimes, but women would forever be as inscrutable to him as Sanskrit.

When he had first read the message that morning, he had been impressed with the sender's vivid imagination. The idea of ESP working this powerfully, and this flawlessly, was impossible. On the other hand, the military already had teams that could issue simple commands with their thoughts—as long as they were hooked up to special helmets. Industry had made great progress in the past decade driving games and devices with thought in the same way. So perhaps this was less impossible than it might have once been. Still . . .

When Girdler had finished the message the first time, he had finally decided it was time to find out why the NSA Expert System had reawakened this message from the dead. He learned that when it had first been sent on Thursday, Nessie had automatically searched for correlations across hundreds and thousands of dimensions, which had taken on the order of a second. The computer had discovered that there had been a Nick Hall on board the Scripps *Explorer*, a ship that had launched with twenty-seven men and women on board, the exact number he had mentioned in his message.

This information had been dutifully noted, but the identity of the twenty-seven people lost at sea was in the public domain. So given an unauthorized, unknown sender, and the preposterous contents of the message, Nessie had decided some crackpot had used Nick Hall's name and the number twenty-seven for twisted reasons of his or her own.

But that had changed when the system learned that Nick Hall's fingerprints had been discovered at the scene of a double murder in Bakersfield, California. The same Nick Hall who had voyaged on the *Explorer*, and who was *supposed* to be resting in peace miles under the ocean.

Nessie routinely sucked in the contents of all military and law enforcement computers around the country, and if Nessie could have registered surprise, she would have done so when she got around to digesting the news out of Bakersfield.

Nessie had recognized that this was a game-changer instantly, and that it was time for a human to be brought into the loop. It had been a good decision.

For his part, Girdler had immediately instructed Maggie, his PDA, to send a message to law enforcement systems stating that the fingerprint results reported earlier had been in error. Had any investigator gotten to the point of realizing these were the fingerprints of what should have been a very wet corpse, which was unlikely, they would have no trouble believing that an error had been made. How could this *not* be an error?

Shortly after this the colonel had used his considerable authority to call all other agencies off the Bakersfield murder investigation, putting this responsibility under his auspices, and giving himself the fictitious title for this purpose of Special Investigator, Transdepartmental Affairs. Most would know this was a bullshit title, but since word that he and his team were in charge of the investigation would come from on high, this wouldn't be a problem.

They had found an abandoned warehouse where Hall's message had indicated it would be, and part of Girdler's team was still collecting forensic evidence, but as yet the findings were inconclusive. It did appear that much had been taking place within the space until very recently, when the insides had been torched and the warehouse abandoned. The company who had rented the space turned out to be a shell company that led nowhere. Blood and other fluids were found at or near the scene, and were being analyzed.

General Sobol had finally read Hall's message, and after a brief text exchange during which Girdler had assured him he was following up vigorously, they had scheduled a call for late afternoon the next day to discuss the situation further.

Girdler was well aware, of course, that there were explanations for the e-mail message and Hall's fingerprints that were still more probable than the contents of the message being true. The Bakersfield killer could have had access somehow to Nick Hall's fingerprints. He could have sent the e-mail and planted the fingerprints at the crime scene as a twisted practical joke, or to throw off the hunt, which it was doing.

Perhaps the real Nick Hall had never voyaged with the *Explorer* on its fateful trip in the first place. He was *supposed* to have been on board, but there were no witnesses left who could say for sure, one way or another. Or maybe he had been the only one to miraculously make it to shore after the ship went down, and the resulting trauma had caused memory loss and psychosis.

But Colonel Justin Girdler was now convinced the entire contents of the message were genuine, as preposterous as they were. And he was determined to find out for sure as quickly as he possibly could.

23

Kelvin Gray ended his phone conversation with John Delamater with mixed feelings. He should have been ecstatic beyond all measure. He was so close he could *taste* it. But he still had a few hurdles to go before he could celebrate the way he deserved. And knowing that these hurdles were keeping him from his just deserts was not only stripping him of the triumph and ecstasy he should be feeling, but actively *pissing . . . him . . . off.*

He unclenched his locked jaw and took several cleansing breaths.

Settle down, he told himself. He now had a clear handle on his two remaining problems, and it wasn't time to be overeager, to let emotion and justified impatience cloud his judgment. He emerged from his home into the front yard, gazing up at the starry night sky for several minutes, letting the calm of the heavens seep into his being.

Nature had bestowed tremendous gifts upon him. He didn't believe in God, but at times he thought, in many ways, compared to the inconceivable stupidity that was the average human, he was one: a god among men. Some people had been gifted with mathematical, scientific, and technical genius, like Alex Altschuler. Some with verbal and linguistic genius. Some with physical superiority. And some with the ability to read and manipulate human beings like so many pre-programmed puppets. But he alone possessed all of these gifts in combination. And more.

Even at a young age he had recognized his gifts and been thankful for them. He had known he had to give back. Give back to the pathetic species he had risen above. Help to transform society and lift it to a plane closer to his own.

Men like Newton and Einstein had done this in their time on the pure science front. On the technology front, Bell had invented the telephone, and Martin Cooper the cell phone; both monumentally important advances. Tim Berners-Lee had devised the hypertext transfer protocol that would become the World Wide Web. Steve Jobs had been instrumental in ushering in revolutions in personal computing, computer animation, music, tablet computers, the use of the Cloud, and Siri, the prototype for modern PDAs.

Gray had known from a young age he was destined to join these visionaries on the pantheon of the gods—to *exceed* them—someday. And that day was fast approaching.

He would cure blindness and deafness. And that would just be his warm-up act. He would integrate the Internet into the human mind, expanding human memory, capacity, and capability to undreamed-of heights.

This monumental feat had required him to decode and translate human thought, to turn it into a lexicon that was limitless. Precise. Perfect. The applications were so wide-ranging, even *he* couldn't fathom them all as yet. He would transform the human race, propel it to summits it wouldn't otherwise have reached for decades or even centuries.

Gray fully expected to eventually be recognized as outshining all others who had come before. History would one day conclude, properly, that his profound contributions marked the tipping point in humanity's transformation and ultimate transcendence.

The untold billions of dollars that would come with this fame and adoration would be icing on the cake; but only that. He was far too altruistic to be concerned about money.

Gray considered contacting Nick Hall, but decided he would make this the second of the two tasks before him. First things first.

He returned inside, finished preparations he knew he needed to make right away, and then removed a bottle of expensive Merlot from his custom-built wine cellar, which he maintained at a temperature of fifty-seven degrees and a humidity of sixty-five percent.

He uncorked the Merlot and brought it, and a large wine goblet, into his living room, which had a vaulted ceiling and was filled with ultra-modern furniture, sculptures, and paintings. He sat in one of two chairs in the room, each with elegant brushed nickel frames and white leather seats, and closed his eyes, letting the first small mouthful of wine roll lazily over his taste buds. The Merlot had a black cherry bouquet with a touch of black licorice, along with oak, plum, black currant, and even a touch of spice mixed in.

It was excellent. But it wasn't his best. He had been saving *that* bottle for the ultimate celebration.

A bottle that he would be uncorking very soon.

He continued savoring the contents of his oversized goblet, willing himself into a profound state of relaxation. When he had finished three quarters of the glass, his doorbell rang, a short melody that was amplified throughout his five thousand-square-foot residence. He could have installed a wireless intercom system, but that would have been pretentious.

Kelvin Gray opened the door to reveal the unimposing presence of Alex Altschuler. The kid was an off-the-charts genius, whose contributions to the project had been incalculable, although history would only record that it had been Gray who had had the impeccable judgment to recognize his full potential when others had not, elevating him at a young age to a prominent leadership position. Like Steve Jobs, he had gathered a strong team around him, and like Jobs, he would justly get the credit for being the visionary behind the breakthroughs his genius had made possible.

On the scientific and technical side, Alex Altschuler was nearly as talented as Gray himself, although the kid was ridiculously inept on all the other dimensions on which Gray excelled. Still, someone capable of being his equal on even a single dimension deserved considerable respect.

"Alex. Hi. What brings you here at this time of night?"

"Can I come in?"

Gray swung open the door and gestured toward the inside of his home. "By all means."

Altschuler entered, immediately removing his glasses and using the bottom of his shirt to clean them.

"Are you okay?" asked Gray. "You look a little . . . ill."

Altschuler forced a smile. "I'm ah . . . fine."

Gray nodded. "Must just be the lighting in here," he said, almost to himself. "Let's get comfortable and you can tell me why you're here," he added, leading Altschuler to the living room he had just left. Gray gestured to the other brushed nickel leather chair facing his, and Altschuler sat, nodding his thanks.

"Wine?" offered Gray, gesturing to the expensive bottle on the table. "It's a 1991 French Merlot. Quite good."

Altschuler nodded, looking as though he wanted to rip the entire bottle from Gray's hand and down it in one gulp. Gray removed a second goblet from a recessed alcove and poured Altschuler a glass, setting it on the mirrored table between them.

Altschuler picked it up gratefully, but he had developed a palsy and was forced to take a big sip so the waves of wine he was generating wouldn't crest over the lip of the glass. He shakily set it back down as Gray looked on with an amused half smile.

"This is your first visit ever," noted Gray. "To what do I owe the honor?"

Altschuler removed his glasses once again and begin to fidget with them. His breathing was shallow and his face gaunt. "I want in," he said simply, but while he had clearly intended on saying these words forcefully, he practically choked on them, and they were croaked from his mouth more than spoken.

Gray smiled at him serenely. "Excuse me?"

"I want in," repeated the scrawny scientist. "I know what you've been up to. I should have figured it out long ago, but I've finally gotten there. And I want in."

Gray considered him for several long seconds, forcing him to twist under his hypnotic, rattlesnake stare. The only unknown in this blinking contest was how many times Altschuler would blink before Gray leisurely did so for the first time. "I don't have any idea what you're talking about."

Altschuler swallowed hard. "You've been experimenting on humans. I know you have."

Gray didn't respond.

"It was the only way you could have had the insights you did," continued Altschuler. "The only way you'd know to recommend trying to put four very specific nodes of the brain in play at once. There was no way to come to this insight from theory alone. It had to have come about empirically."

"If you say so," said Gray calmly.

"I, um . . . I *do* say so."

Altschuler removed the wine from the coaster, his hand shaking worse than before, and drained the remaining contents of the large goblet in a matter of seconds. "And I've confirmed it," continued Altschuler. "I overheard a few conversations you've had over the past month," he said, setting the glass back down. "Conversations that allowed me to piece together where you got your subjects."

Gray looked on, appearing only mildly interested.

"You worked with an outside person or group to down the Scripps *Explorer*. And somehow, they removed everyone on board. And brought them to you for use as human subjects."

Gray swirled the wine in his glass, watching it absently, his hands as steady as a surgeon's. "Ingenious, wouldn't you say?" he responded finally, and Altschuler practically fell out of his chair at this relaxed admission. "The world is absolutely convinced they're all dead. In Davy Jones's locker, hundreds and hundreds of miles from me. Hell, I've even heard some lunatics are insisting the North American Trench is the new Bermuda Triangle. That the Triangle has shifted, presaging a shift in the Earth's magnetic field."

Altschuler blinked stupidly, waiting for Gray to continue.

"What's so ingenious about this strategy, is that when everyone thinks you're dead, no one comes looking for you. So I'm free to experiment however I like. And then, when I ah. . . *incinerate* the evidence, no one cares. You can't be wanted for murder for killing what's already presumed dead."

Gray took another sip of wine. "Are you sure you want to be a part of this, Alex?" he asked in amusement. "You should see your face. You look horrified. Hardly the expression of someone who wants to roll up his sleeves and pitch in."

"Not true. There are a number of experiments I'm eager to try. With me intimately involved, our progress will accelerate significantly. We'll both be richer than God."

"Pretty bold wanting to join me. I would have expected you to go to the authorities."

Altschuler shook his head adamantly, as if even the thought of turning Gray in was abhorrent to him. "Let me join you, Kelvin."

Gray frowned and opened the drawer of the table beside him. He removed the gun he had placed there in preparation for this meeting and pointed it at his underling. "Thanks for the interest, Alex. Really. But I'm afraid I'm going to have to say no."

Altschuler's eyes bulged. "No? No! Do you have any idea what you're passing up? My bandwidth added to yours—with human subjects—the sky's the limit."

Gray noted with clinical detachment that now that the preliminary accusations were out of the way, Altschuler had developed more of a spine, even with a gun pointed at him. Interesting.

"Ah, but it turns out I've already made the breakthroughs I need," said Gray.

During his phone conversation with John Delamater only an hour earlier, his partner had explained his reasons for believing that Nick Hall's implants were working perfectly, after all. And these reasons were absolutely convincing. Which was why Gray had been so ecstatic. Or *almost* ecstatic, in any case.

"The very last of the twenty-seven subjects from the *Explorer* was the key," explained Gray. "A man named Nick Hall. We've now positioned the four implants in precisely the necessary locations, and the algorithms have been tuned to utter perfection. We damaged a number of inconsequential areas of Hall's brain in the process, but he doesn't seem to miss any of them."

Gray took another sip of wine, pausing to savor it before he continued, his grip on the gun never faltering. "I just found out before you got here that the program was an unqualified success. You see, I hadn't known. It turns out that Hall lied to me. We were very close, he said. A minor adjustment and he was sure we'd be there. And then

I made the adjustment, and perfected a system that will revolutionize the world. But instead of reporting this historic achievement, Hall reported the opposite. He said he had lost the signal entirely. That it had been a significant step backwards."

Gray raised his eyebrows. "Between you and me, Alex, I think this Hall got it into his head that if I finally perfected what I was after, he'd be killed. He was right, of course. But when he convinced me progress had halted, I decided it was time to kill him just the same. We'd already painted a bit much on his neuronal canvas, and it was best to take the ground we'd gained and start on a new batch of abductees. Maybe from the new Bermuda Triangle again. Fuel the crackpot theories." He laughed, the gun vibrating in his hand as he did so. "Maybe that's how the Bermuda Triangle thing got started in the first place. Wouldn't that be ironic?"

"You still need me for the implementation, Kelvin. To make sure this works with *everyone*, and not just your subject twenty-seven. And to *improve* it. This Hall is just a prototype. You and I both know there are still a lot of hurdles to jump before the system will be fully polished and scaled up for mass use. You *need* me. And if I'm in this with you, you can count on my silence. I have too much to gain, and too much to lose, to be stupid about this."

Gray laughed. He finished his wine, set it on the table, and laughed again. The gun was still in his right hand, but he was resting it in his lap, unconcerned that Altschuler would try anything. Even though the kid was toughening up, it was a miracle he hadn't wet his pants.

"That would be true," replied Gray finally. "If anything about your offer was genuine. But the funny thing is, I got a call from an associate of mine. Just before you arrived. The same guy who arranged for the unfortunate sinking of the good ship *Explorer*. He's been keeping tabs on you, Alex. For a long time now. And do you know what he told me?"

Altschuler shrank back, as if trying to hide behind his glasses.

"No guesses, Alex? Surely someone as brilliant as you can figure this out. He said that you'd be coming over and professing your interest in joining forces with me. But that it would be total bullshit. He said you were trying to set me up."

Gray opened the same drawer from which he had taken the gun and this time removed a pair of handcuffs. He tossed them the short distance to Altschuler. "Cuff your right hand to the chair," he ordered. "Never used these to handcuff a *man* before," he added as Altschuler followed his instructions." He shrugged. "I guess there's a first time for everything."

Even without the tip-off from Delamater, Gray would have known Altschuler's offer to join him was fake. There was no way his subordinate would have had the balls to get involved. And it wasn't just Altschuler. Almost no one else would have. That was yet another dimension of Gray's superiority. He alone had the steel to make the hard decisions. To make the brutally difficult tradeoffs; the very tradeoffs that begged to be made to move the species forward.

Not that being the rare man capable of doing what was necessary didn't come at a high cost. No one mourned the loss of twenty-seven good people—innocent people—more than Kelvin Gray did. It was a tragedy. But they were giving their lives for a much higher cause. Everyone died. But how many in the history of the world ever died to catapult the entire race forward to undreamed-of heights? There was no more honorable way to exit this existence. And twenty-seven heroes, or even twenty-seven *thousand*, was a small, small price to pay for what was being gained.

Gray had never shed literal tears for them, because this wasn't his way, but the sacrifices they had made tore him up on the inside. Nothing had ever brought him more pain. But part of his greatness was the willingness to endure this kind of pain for the greater good. Something people like Altschuler were incapable of understanding.

"I just have one more loose end after I take care of you," explained Gray. "And then there's nothing between me and immortalization."

"Loose end?"

"Yes. This Nick Hall I was telling you about. He was a visiting scientist from the Woods Hole Oceanographic Institution in Massachusetts who was lucky enough to join the La Jolla contingent on the *Explorer*. Seems he managed to escape from us recently. We've been trying to kill him, but he's managed to slip the noose a few times. It would be nice to have him alive for follow-up testing, but it isn't an absolute requirement. We have all the data recorded for the positioning, intensity, and signaling parameters of his implants. But now that I know his implants are working, my life is greatly simplified. Because I left a backdoor in his implants I can use to instant-message him. So I can reach out to him, wherever he is. Lure him in and then capture him again. Or kill him. Either way, no more loose ends. Easy to do, since my friend John has also learned that Hall has no memory of being experimented on."

Gray paused for a moment and then smiled. "With all the amne-sia-inducing drugs we gave him during the past seven months, it's not surprising. The slightest tap on the head would probably cause him to re-lose his memory, even without an additional dose. Hell, after the number of doses he's had along the way, putting on a *baseball cap* might be enough to do it."

"So once you've captured or killed Hall, then what?"

"Well, then I go through the FDA to get the implants approved for blindness and deafness, and separately, for thought-controlled web access. But now that I know the precise placement, we can be ever so cautious and plodding. Proceed with the utmost concern for pa-tient safety. All the while knowing that we'll nail it on the first try. A miracle."

Gray locked his eyes on Altschuler. "Had I not taken this short-cut, Alex, we'd have never gotten there. I'd have never been able to make so many wild attempts; wild attempts that resulted in scores of deaths. The FDA would have pulled the plug long before this. So it isn't just that we would have been delayed crossing the finish line by eight or ten years if I hadn't considered the subjects expendable. It's that we would have *never* finished the race." He frowned. "It will still take a few years to get proper authorizations and approvals, even though the implants will work perfectly right out of the gate. But we'll have gone through all the right channels. The technology will be as clean as a whistle."

Gray shook his head sadly. "I only wish the public could know that the members of the *Explorer* gave their lives in the service of mankind. Alas, I'm afraid this won't be possible. Society, pathetic as it is, would not react well to this knowledge."

Altschuler was glancing nervously around the room.

"What's the matter, Alex? Run out of questions to ask to stall me? Are you expecting someone?"

"What are you talking about?"

"I'm afraid your mercenary buddy won't be coming to save the day. What's his name? Ed Cowan perhaps? Well, my friend John only had one of his men nearby tonight, so we have to wait a little. I've actually been stalling *you*, not the other way around. John told me his man would take out Cowan, which he's now had ample time to do, and then come here to take you, um . . . off my hands. Which I really hate to dirty more than I have to."

Altschuler blanched and shrank into the chair in horror. Gray suspected he would have rolled up into a fetal position had the chair allowed it.

Gray shook his head sadly once again, a kindly grandfather having to share troubling news with a beloved child. "You're a very talented man, Alex. And I wish this could have turned out otherwise. But you're weak. Like the vast majority of your fellows. So it's up to men like me to move the species forward. I'm just sorry you had to get caught up in the gears."

He gestured to the bottle beside him. "More wine?" he asked pleasantly. It was a shame to waste wine of this quality on someone who wouldn't live out the night, but he considered it a noble, last supper sort of gesture.

Altschuler's eyes were vacant, and he was long past the point of being able to respond. Gray was pouring himself another glass of Merlot when the door chime sounded.

"That would be John's assistant, arriving to take you off my hands."

Gray walked over to the wreck of a man across from him and undid his cuffs, forcing him ahead at gunpoint.

The bell chimed one more time and then was silent as they made their way to the entry foyer. As they reached it, Gray ordered Altschuler to unlatch the door and open it. He thought for a moment that Altschuler might pass out, but his soon-to-be-deceased subordinate managed to carry out his instructions.

The door opened slowly to reveal a tall man with blood-soaked bandages on his left arm and right leg.

"*Ed?*" whispered Altschuler in disbelief.

At that instant a terrible realization hit Kelvin Gray. *Delamater's man had failed.* Instead of eliminating Ed Cowan, Ed Cowan must have eliminated *him*.

Gray desperately yanked the gun from Altschuler's back and began to raise it, *but he was too late.* A gun had appeared in Cowan's hand as if by magic, swinging up to point at Gray's head, which towered above his shorter human shield.

Cowan depressed the trigger, giving Gray only a thousandth of a second to process the deafening explosion before his head was almost torn from his shoulders by the high caliber slug, and leaving him no time at all to reflect on what a tragedy the world would now suffer from the loss of a veritable god like himself.

24

Ed Cowan had showered and dressed his wounds while Alex Altschuler had gotten right to work cracking Gray's home computer for evidence—after having another large glass of wine to steady his nerves and wait for his hearing to return. Cowan had fired his gun practically *in* Altschuler's ear. Not that he had complained. The man had also saved his life.

Altschuler still couldn't quite process just how blatantly psychopathic his boss had truly been, and how badly he had been fooled by the man's charm and charisma. Gray had been totally devoid of a soul. Altschuler's meeting with Gray, which had included being threatened at gunpoint and his boss's face exploding like a watermelon, was like a nightmare from which he couldn't quite awaken.

Cowan borrowed fresh clothing from the deceased Gray, since the men were of roughly equal size, and he and Altschuler worked through the night. Cowan had sent a man to Altschuler's home and office, and as expected, he had found and removed several listening devices.

Before sunrise, still in Gray's house, they had amassed mountains of unimpeachable evidence of Gray's involvement in the kidnapping and imprisonment of twenty-seven people who had been on board the *Explorer*. And the murder of twenty-six of these.

They discovered the location of the warehouse at which the abductees had been kept month after month, while Gray was using their brains as his personal playground. They learned of the specialized amnesia drug Gray had used, one that had only recently been discovered by street chemists, accidentally, while they were trying to improve the date rape drug. This nasty cousin, however, was able to erase recent memories, along with a lifetime of core, sense-of-self memories, while leaving all other memories intact. It was so potent and horrific, it made the date rape drug from which it had spawned look like a harmless chewable kids vitamin. And they had learned the full name of the man Gray had been working with, John Delamater. Cowan had run this name through his computer and sources and had come up empty, and he was convinced this was an alias.

Gray was a meticulous note-taker and his notes, video, and rantings made it clear he thought of himself as so god-like, so smart and invulnerable, that he wasn't the slightest bit nervous about keeping a treasure trove of incriminating material on a relatively insecure home computer. As though he was sure he would never be caught, but if he was, he *wanted* the evidence of his involvement to come out, since he considered his actions praiseworthy. Hitler and the Third Reich had similarly kept meticulous records of their atrocities, which had astonished the allies after these records were seized.

While the evidence implicating Gray was overwhelming, Delamater continued to be an enigma. His ability to organize teams of mercenaries and assassins was well-documented, as was the military precision with which he had carried out the raid on the *Explorer*. But where he could be found, and who he really was, wasn't clear at all. They ran across notes explaining that Delamater had access to Gray's computer, and had warned him not to write anything more about him than he had.

Gray may have wanted to advertise his involvement for posterity, but John Delamater had threatened to kill him if he ever wrote anything that someone could use to identify him. While Gray almost *courted* attention, Delamater guarded his privacy with all the ferocity of Cerberus guarding the gates of hell.

There was more to the Madera facility than met the eye. There was a hidden basement room under Gray's private labs. The implant machine Gray had used on his prisoners, which combined a top-of-the-line MRI to visualize the brain with a robotic placement device capable of inhuman precision, had been removed from the warehouse just a few days earlier and stored in this room, along with hundreds of finished and fully programmed implants, awaiting the next batch of victims.

The bug Altschuler had been wearing had transmitted his encounter with Gray flawlessly, and Ed Cowan had had no trouble recording the conversation. Cowan had described for Altschuler his run-in with one of Delamater's men, and how he had been able to disarm his attacker after being shot in the arm.

Both men had apparently possessed high-level martial arts skills, and while Cowan downplayed it, Altschuler could only imagine the battle royale that had ensued, resulting in Cowan suffering a knife wound in his leg to complement the hole in his arm. In the end, Cowan had won the day, but had been forced to kill his assailant, whom he would have loved to interrogate. As it was, the man had no identification or cell phone on him, and while a potential lead, did not look to be a path to the mysterious Delamater.

Altschuler and Cowan had reported immediately to Cameron Fyfe the night before, but at five in the morning they decided it was time to give the man another update. Cowan and the diminutive scientist sat together on Gray's maroon leather sofa facing a three-dimensional image of Fyfe on a television screen that occupied almost an entire wall.

Fyfe listened with very few interruptions for fifteen minutes as they detailed all they had found. When they were finished, Alex Altschuler said, "I think we're overdue calling the authorities. We've got recordings of Kelvin admitting to the crimes. And enough evidence on his computer to cover a tropical island." He paused. "And I'm pretty sure you're supposed to report when you gun someone down in self-defense, you know . . . fairly promptly."

Ed Cowan shook his head. "I recommend waiting another forty-eight hours," he said. "It's not exactly standard procedure, and we'll have some explaining to do about the delay. But if we report what we know now, there's no way it doesn't leak. And I'd bet good money this John Delamater has his fingers in at least one of the organizations that'll be called in."

"So you're saying if we report this, we lose the chance to get this guy?" said Fyfe.

"Very likely."

Fyfe pursed his lips in thought. "Alex, what do you think about this?"

"I'm not sure," said Altschuler. "This would be bad enough if we were just sitting on two deaths, even if they were in self-defense. But like you said earlier, Cameron, we're sitting on the story of the century."

Altschuler frowned. To be precise, Fyfe had called it *the shitstorm of the century*, but Altschuler hadn't felt the need for this level of accuracy. "And how likely is it that we catch this guy, anyway?" he asked. "Even if we don't risk tipping him off by alerting the authorities?"

"Good question," said Cowan. "I've put traces on Gray's phones and computers. Delamater may be so good that he has safeguards in place that will alert him to this. But if not, if he reaches out to Gray, we can nail him. Even if he doesn't, my team will have a lot to go on now. Operational details on the *Explorer* raid. A dead man with dental records who worked for Delamater. And we can do further work with his name. There's no guarantee we'll find him, but if we go to the authorities, I think our chances will be reduced significantly."

Fyfe nodded, and it was clear he had made up his mind. He had a reputation for being decisive, and this was well-earned. "I say we do whatever we can to get this son of a bitch," he hissed with a chilling intensity. "This bastard deserves to die miserably. We *cannot* let him get away with this."

Fyfe's 3-D image on the TV stared intently at Cowan. "Ed, spend whatever money and resources you need. Let's work around the clock. If we don't have him in forty-eight hours, we won't delay any further. We'll go to the authorities and lay everything we have out for them. Alex, does this work for you?"

Alex frowned, but did not dissent. He wasn't cynical by nature, but after recent events it was hard not to be. He didn't doubt that Fyfe was outraged and sincerely wanted Delamater to fry, but he couldn't help but wonder how much Fyfe was motivated by the pursuit of justice, and how much by an interest in putting the best face on this for Theia Labs. The nicer he could tie a bow on this case, the better it would be for Theia's rehabilitation in the public eye.

"Okay," said Fyfe. "Alex, I need you to send a global e-mail to everyone who reports to Kelvin—or *reported*, past tense, I guess, is now the more accurate way to say this. Anyway, let them know he'll be out of pocket for several days and won't be responding to calls or e-mails."

Fyfe sighed heavily. "Let's hope we find Delamater and anyone else involved before forty-eight hours passes—which I guess would put us at Tuesday morning. Regardless, whenever we do alert the authorities, I'll call a press conference for just afterward. As Alex said, this will be a huge story. *Huge.* I'll prepare two sets of remarks. One if we catch Delamater, and one if we don't. In both cases, I'll be stating our remorse, outrage, and intent to move forward and put this behind us through philanthropy and improving human lives." He stared meaningfully at Altschuler. "And I'll be announcing Alex as our new CEO."

The thin scientist blew out a long, tired breath. He had dreamed of being a CEO of a transformative tech company someday. But never like *this*. Who could have? It was as if Altschuler had been second-in-command to Adolf Hitler, who had just died while captaining the *Titanic* into an iceberg. And now he was being named the new captain.

Congratulations, Alex, on your promotion.

"It goes without saying," continued Fyfe, "that we keep anything and everything having to do with Kelvin Gray and with these implants strictly between the three of us until the press conference. Ed can give his hired team assignments, but not even a whiff of the true background. And the same goes for you, Alex. Not even the hint of this. To *anyone*. Agreed?"

Altschuler and Cowan assured him they understood the importance and agreed entirely.

"Anything else for now?" said Fyfe.

"Yes," said Altschuler. "As you no doubt heard Kelvin say on the recording of our meeting, one of the *Explorer* crew is still alive. Nick Hall. We need to bring him in as soon as possible. In fact, he should be part of the press conference."

"You're absolutely right," said Fyfe. "Good point. Any idea how to do that?"

Altschuler nodded tiredly. Recent events had nearly depleted his reserves. If he didn't get at least a few hours sleep very soon, he would be useless.

"As a matter of fact," he said, managing the briefest flicker of a smile. "I do."

25

Megan Emerson and Nick Hall had been kissing passionately for five minutes on the Glandons' couch, and the small part of Megan's brain still capable of rational thought wondered how Nick was managing to keep his hands from roaming, even a *little*. Either she was losing her touch or he had an iron will.

Then her mind turned to the real question. *How had this happened in the first place?* Had *she* made the first move? She couldn't seem to remember. One second they had been talking and the next . . . not.

Please tell me I didn't make the first move, she thought to herself.

"*I'm not sure which of us did*," replied Nick Hall telepathically. "*It just sort of . . . happened.*"

"*Damn!*" thought Megan, separating momentarily from the embrace. She had forgotten that she couldn't think strong thoughts in the form of words without Hall picking them up. "*You weren't supposed to hear that.*"

"*Sorry*," replied Hall. "*But if it makes you feel any better, whichever one of us initiated this is a genius.*"

Megan smiled. She leaned in and kissed him for another full minute before separating once again. "I'm going to the fridge for a bottle of water," she said aloud. "Want anything?"

"Can you get me a Diet Mountain Dew?"

"You do know it's still morning, right?"

He shrugged. "Think of it as coffee. Cold, yellow-green coffee."

Megan walked gingerly to the kitchen, trying to ignore the giddy feelings that were now gushing from her like water from a broken fire hydrant. She needed to concentrate. What had *happened*? Was this a wise thing to be doing?

The long conversation they had started over their late lunch on Saturday had continued seamlessly when they returned to their temporary home, and had magically morphed into a late *dinner* conversation. Nick Hall didn't have to know about himself to be entertaining, and thoughtful, and witty. With some people it was like pulling teeth to keep a conversation going for five minutes. With Hall, it was effortless.

They had returned from lunch and then, snap of the fingers, they had looked up and it was time for dinner—with little sense of the hours moving by. Both were equally surprised it had become so late. She had read this was a clear sign you were engaged and enjoying yourself. Five minutes in a dentist's chair could seem like an eternity, but five hours doing something you really enjoyed seemed to pass in the blink of an eye.

The Glandons would be gone for a week, and they had decided their best strategy was to stay put for at least another day. So after dinner they had watched a movie, and then Hall had insisted she get to sleep early to help her get back to full strength.

Once again, they had retired to separate bedrooms for the night, where she had slept as soundly as she ever had in her life. After a laughter-filled breakfast they had gone to the family room and had begun considering their next move in earnest when . . . *this* had happened.

So now what? Didn't they have too much going on to get entangled? To get . . . physical? And were her feelings for Nick Hall real or artificial?

She had already acknowledged he had hit all the right romantic buttons when he first appeared in her office. And even though he had put her life in jeopardy in the first place, he had also saved it. Now her life was literally in his hands.

So was falling for him just a survival mechanism programmed into her genes by natural selection? Was she subconsciously trying to have sex with him to have more of an emotional hold on someone upon whom her life now depended?

Not that sex was even possible in her current condition, she realized. Nothing like a gunshot to the upper thigh to kill off working through even the first page of the Kama Sutra. Was that why Hall had been such a gentleman?

"*Nick,*" she broadcast as she pulled a water bottle and can of soda from the refrigerator, "*I've noticed you've been practically sitting on your hands. Is that because you're afraid to hurt me?*"

There was a pause. "*Yes. I can't tell you how much I'd love to lie to you,*" replied Hall from the family room, "*and pretend it's because I'm such a gentleman. But I've noticed you wincing in pain when you re-aggravate your injury. So I'm trying to prevent any outbreaks of horrible screaming while I'm kissing you.*"

While he had been broadcasting she had made her way back to the family room and handed him his drink, resuming her place close to him on the couch.

How incredibly thoughtful, she thought, making sure she did so in such a way that Hall wouldn't "overhear" it. Even she had forgotten about her injury while they had been kissing.

She decided her feelings had to be real. She couldn't imagine fooling herself to this degree. And even if she was, she decided she didn't care. It didn't matter if her amorous feelings for Nick Hall *were* just part of a pre-programmed survival instinct, a possibility that would have never even occurred to her before she had met him.

The only thing that mattered was that she wanted him. *Bad.*

How long did it take an upper thigh to heal, anyway?

"Listen . . . Megan," began Hall. "I've been thinking." He sighed and took a large swig of the yellowish liquid inside the can. "You are . . . well, you're *amazing.* I can't even describe the way I'm feeling about you. But I think we might be making a mistake."

She gazed at him calmly, but didn't respond.

"I'm a shell of a man. With no past. And a pretty scary future. Neither of us know what you're getting into here if you form any kind of attachment to me. What I'm getting into. Hell, I could even be married for all I know. Just because I don't have a ring doesn't mean much. I didn't have a wallet or a memory either when I awoke in that dumpster."

"I know all this," said Megan.

"I know you do. I just don't want to hurt you. Or me. You're an incredible woman, and I really think my feelings toward you are . . . well . . . real. But I can't be sure my emotions aren't just playing me for a fool. Because you're the most important person in my life. The *only* person in my life. So maybe subconsciously, I'm trying to have a deeper relationship with you just to have more of an emotional hold on you. I don't think this is the case, but I don't know." He frowned in frustration. "Am I making any sense?"

Megan grinned. He had basically re-created her thinking exactly. If that wasn't a sign from on high, nothing was. "Perfect sense," she said, leaning in and kissing him once again. "And I'm willing to take my chances. You can't deny that we're very good together. I'm convinced this would be true even if it weren't for everything else going on."

Hall nodded, palpably relieved. "I couldn't agree more."

Megan gestured toward the stairs, which led to the Glandons' master bedroom. "Sex right now—in my current condition—would be a very bad idea," she said. "But if we're very, very careful, I'm willing to bet we can still find a way to get closer. To relieve some of the stress we've been under." She raised her eyebrows. "Ever been intimate with a Neanderthal before?"

Hall laughed. "My memory may be gone," he said, a look of infatuation on his face, "but I think I can say with great confidence that you'd be the first."

26

Hall gazed happily at Megan as she lay naked on her back next to him, the Glandons' satin sheets covering her body and her eyes closed. She wasn't sleeping, but no face had ever looked more relaxed, peaceful, or satisfied.

The *satisfied* part of that equation had been a challenge for both of them given her condition, but in the end they had managed to relieve tension in a way that was surprisingly tender and romantic, without worsening her injury.

Hall glanced at the clock on the end table. It was already past noon. It seemed impossible. He knew they should have spent the past several hours planning their next move, but sometimes the body and heart had a mind of their own.

Hall studied the contours of her face. She was cute enough, but she had suddenly become irresistibly appealing to him out of all proportion to her physical attractiveness. He was convinced his emerging feelings for her were all about her energy and personality, rather than simply her looks. He had a funny feeling that this was a rarity for him. Nick Hall decided then and there that the universe must have a way of evening things out. He was possibly the unluckiest man in the world—and the luckiest—both at the same time.

Megan's eyes fluttered open and she smiled when she saw him watching her. She had a serene expression on her face and Hall kissed her gently on the cheek. She almost purred she seemed so content.

"For some reason I'm a little hungry," she said softly.

"For food?" said Hall with a salacious grin.

"Among other things," she replied, returning his smile. "How about if I make us some sandwiches?"

Hall shook his head. "Don't move. I've got this," he said, leaving the bed before she could protest.

He entered the Glandons' walk-in closet and threw Carl's blue robe around himself. "What kind of sandwich would you like?"

"Surprise me."

"You got it," he said.

Hall glided into the kitchen and decided what he really wanted to do was kill the Glandons so he and Megan could live here forever, although this hardly seemed fair to the poor Glandon family, who had so far been very generous.

He opened the refrigerator to take inventory of just what he had to work with when a glowing box, filled with words, popped up in the corner of his internal field of vision and hovered there. It was a standard IM text box, with a box underneath for a reply, and a small *send* icon underneath.

And it had appeared there all on its own.

Hall closed the refrigerator, fell into a kitchen chair absently, and turned his full attention to the words in the box.

To the man able to surf the Internet with his mind. Hello. I'm sending you an Instant Message through a backdoor in your system. Please confirm you're alive and well by thinking a short message into the reply box and hitting send.

Hall's heart leaped to his throat. This was an earth-shattering development, which could be very, very good, or very, very bad. He considered sending a reply but decided against it.

He didn't know anything about the sender, but he did know this: they wouldn't give up just because he failed to respond to their first volley. He just hoped they couldn't use this backdoor into his personal Internet to track his location. But even as he thought this he realized that if this had been possible, he'd already be dead.

A minute later another message came in. *I understand why you might be reluctant to reply. But trust me, I have no way to track you by your reply.*

Apparently his reaction had been on the predictable side. Hall thought about it for just a moment before deciding to continue to play possum and see what happened next. He tried to do additional research on the web, but he couldn't focus. Finally, almost five minutes later, a new IM came in. A longer one. He was both desperate to read it, and terrified of reading it, at the same time.

Hall took a mental breath, centered the text box in his mind's eye, and began to read.

Okay. I don't blame you. It's my understanding that you've lost your memory and lots of people have been trying to kill you. But I want to help. I know that we have to establish some trust, so I'll go first. I'll keep this brief, but if we have a conversation, I can give you far more details.

Your name is Nick Hall. You were a marine biologist at the Woods Hole Institute of Oceanography in Massachusetts.

Hall stopped reading and searched his mind. Sure enough, he knew the Woods Hole facility like the back of his hand. He still couldn't remember his past, but he had little doubt the person behind the message was telling the truth. Not only about Woods Hole, but about his name, which the sender of the message didn't realize he already knew.

Hall continued reading.

You were a visiting scientist on board the Scripps Explorer along with twenty-six other people, scientists and crew, most of them from the Scripps Institute of Oceanography in La Jolla. Seven months ago, a team of mercenaries led by a man named John Delamater kidnapped all twenty-seven of you and brought you to a warehouse outside of Fresno, California, where you were held as prisoners. The rest of the world believed that the ship had gone down and all were lost—and not a soul was looking for any of you in California.

Nick, by now I'm sure you'll have guessed what you were doing there. A man named Kelvin Gray, who Delamater was working with, was using all of you as guinea pigs to perfect brain implants that would allow you to do what you're doing this second—accessing the web with your thoughts. I'll give you a few seconds to call up Gray's image.

Hall found Kelvin Gray almost immediately. He stared at the man's photo on the website of a company named Theia. The man looked to be in his late forties, but Hall suspected he was even older than this and was just naturally youthful in appearance. Somehow, along with Gray's general handsomeness, the photo managed to convey competence, self-assurance, and intelligence. The face was eerily familiar. Like someone you were sure you knew, but couldn't quite place.

A new box filled with text appeared in Hall's vision.

As you've no doubt discovered, Gray is listed as CEO of a company called Theia Labs in Fresno. My name is Alex Altschuler, and I worked for Gray. But I knew nothing about this kidnapping or experimentation. You can find my bio on the Theia Labs management page.

Hall was soon staring at a photo of Alex Altschuler, an unimpressive specimen of a man wearing glasses, which had become something of a rarity. But his background, as outlined in his brief bio, was spectacular, and his academic achievements attested to an extraordinary intellect.

The message box returned.

I was Gray's second-in-command and helped lay much of the groundwork for the technology that you're making use of now. But there was much I didn't know. I only learned about the Scripps Explorer and his experimentation last night—and I can prove this to you beyond a shadow of a doubt.

Early this morning, I also just discovered that Gray contracted out much of the work that led to the miracle technology behind your implants, to teams of scientists and engineers who only knew very specific pieces of the puzzle. Gray used his seven months of experimentation on twenty-seven people to guide his teams, and he alone integrated all of the pieces. I had no knowledge of any of this, and neither did Theia's biggest investor, Cameron Fyfe.

It was Fyfe who uncovered what Gray was doing in the first place, and we arranged a sting operation to get the evidence we needed to send this guy to the chair. Unfortunately, things didn't go as planned, and Kelvin Gray ended up dead.

The text ended. Perhaps because Altschuler was pausing as he dictated to his PDA, or perhaps because he wanted to give Hall time to ponder what he had already disclosed.

Several seconds later a new box appeared.

I'm afraid it gets worse. Much worse. Gray was interested in speed and results in his experimentation, and considered his prisoners expendable. Twenty-six of the twenty-seven died during the experimentation.

You were the twenty-seventh.

Hall's mouth fell open. Twenty-six people killed! It was unthinkable.

"Nick, are you still out there?" came Megan Emerson's telepathic thought. *"You sure aren't the world's fastest sandwich maker. You sure you've got this?"*

"Sorry," he shot back quickly. *"Got distracted. Be with you in a few minutes."*

He turned his attention once more to his internal text box and continued reading.

Now that I've told you all of this, I'm aware you could go to the authorities with it. I'm asking you not to. Why? First, because I can't be sure who you can trust. If John Delamater was able to pull off one of the most impressive kidnapping operations in history, I wouldn't put it past him to penetrate law enforcement agencies. Second, we're trying to keep this quiet for a little longer in the hope of nailing Delamater before it's too late. We plan to reveal everything to the world very soon, and we ask that you not jeopardize our plans to get Delamater by revealing what I've told you prematurely. I hope you can appreciate the level of trust I'm showing by telling you all that I have.

So let me go on and tell you our plans going forward. First, we want you to come in so we can protect you, using people we know we can trust. We want to restore your memory—more on that later. And while I know nothing we can do can make up for the atrocities committed by the head of our company—for twenty-six innocent people dead, sacrificed in Gray's attempt to perfect the implants—we will not stop trying. We will tell the world what happened and try to make amends as best we can to the families of the victims, and to you.

We will let the world decide our fate, but obviously, the results Gray achieved are astonishing—you know this better than we do. Despite the atrocities committed to get to this point, we believe society will eventually see beyond this and let us test this technology, first for use by the blind and deaf, and then as a commercial Internet product.

Hall shook his head. He agreed with this man with respect to a cure for blindness and deafness, but he was convinced the regulatory authorities would never let the internal Internet see the light of day.

Needless to say, the message continued, *in addition to millions in cash, we will grant you and the victims' families shares of Theia Labs as part of our efforts to make amends: shares that should soon be worth tens of millions of dollars. This is not a bribe for silence or forgiveness, just a sincere attempt to compensate in some minor way for what was done to those on board the Explorer.*

Regarding your memory, Gray used a street drug called Erase 190 on you and your colleagues to create amnesia. Repeatedly. He did this for a number of reasons, including keeping you off-balance and keeping you from remembering each other and trying to work as a team. I wasn't even aware this drug existed until last night, but apparently it is a very potent, very scary cousin of the date rape drug, and if overused, can cause memory loss at the slightest physical trauma. Even after it has been discontinued.

The good news is that an antidote is possible, although it does require some of the initial brew. I don't know why this is true, but I've been assured that it is. If you whip up the antidote using a different batch, even of the same drug, it won't work.

Fortunately, Gray had some of the batch he used on all of you stored in his house, as well as a few vials of antidote. When you come in we can give this to you immediately. This should work to restore your memory very quickly. But I won't lie to you. At this point there are no guarantees. At the risk of being indelicate and crass, your brain has been fucked with pretty good.

I know this is a lot to take in, and I know you've had a rough few days. I blame myself for not catching on earlier. But I didn't. And I can't go back in time and change what happened. All I can do is try to make it as right as possible from here. I've now laid all of my cards on the table. Please respond.

Hall felt totally numb. He had no doubt there were deep truths in Altschuler's message. But was it *all* true, or just enough of it to get him to walk blindly into a trap?

Then it occurred to him. Altschuler hadn't mentioned his psi abilities. So maybe no one but he and Megan knew of them, just as she had conjectured. If Altschuler was lying to him, trying to set a trap, he would never be able to keep this from Hall.

How can I be sure this isn't a trap, Alex? he thought into the text box, and then mentally hit *send*.

Thank you so much for responding! Altschuler texted, and Hall could almost feel the man's excitement. *You won't regret this. As to your question, I'm not sure what I can do to convince you I'm sincere. Especially after what you must have been through. But I'm willing to try my hardest. If there is anything you can think of that will allow you to trust me, just tell me what it is.*

Do you have the antidote to the Erase 190 with you?

Yes.

The web says Theia is in Fresno. Are you there now?

I'm in Madera, but it's basically the same location. You spent seven months in a warehouse fairly near here. Do you remember this at all?

Hall searched his memory but drew a blank. He responded that he didn't.

He queried a maps program using his internal system and learned Altschuler was one hundred and twenty miles from his current location. He then called up the address of the grocery store nearest the Glandons' house.

Okay, he texted. *You have ninety minutes to get to the Vons Grocery on the corner of Roosevelt and Pike in Bakersfield.*

Hall didn't have to wait long for Altschuler's response. *Ninety minutes! Impossible. I'd have to leave this second and drive ninety the entire way.*

Then you'd better get started, hadn't you? You want me to trust you, you'll have to earn it. You get no time to plan. And you'll be going on a wild goose chase, starting in Bakersfield. How wild this goose chase gets is all about how much I grow to trust you. And this depends partly on how well you follow instructions.

Hall thought for a few seconds and then continued. *Bring the antidote, no weapons, and come alone. Wear a baseball cap and don't take it off. When you arrive, I want you to hang out next to the eggs.*

Hall knew this would be a well-defined location at the back of the store, since groceries always put staples like milk and eggs at the back, forcing customers who needed these things to traverse the entire store so they would be tempted by impulse purchases as they went. Hall thought about ordering Altschuler to balance several eggs on his head and spin like a top, but he resisted. He wasn't sure how this silly thought had popped into his head, but it brought a much-needed grin to his face.

Send me your cell number, continued Hall. *I'll call you with more instructions once you've had a few minutes to appreciate Vons' fine selection of eggs. The more comfortable I am that I can trust you, the more likely I'll come to you. Or have you fly to where I am.*

Altschuler's reply arrived in very short order. *Are you sure there is nothing I can do to prove myself to you short of recklessly breaking every traffic law?*

I'm sure, texted Hall. *And one other thing.*

What?

You'd better have started five minutes ago. Because you're already running late.

27

Hall rushed back to the bedroom. Megan was lying on her back, just as he had left her.

Upon seeing him enter, an amused smile came over her face, and she rolled her eyes. "Let me get this right, Nick. You take almost fifteen minutes to make a few sandwiches. And then, when you return . . . you don't even have the sandwiches?"

Hall couldn't help but laugh. "Something came up," he said. He lifted the sheets and gazed appreciatively at her naked form. "I can't believe I'm saying this," he muttered, shaking his head. "But I need you to put your clothes back on."

Hall told her the reason for his delay—and lack of sandwiches. As they both dressed, he read the text of his IM exchange with Alex Altschuler.

Megan was stunned.

Hall had been on the Scripps *Explorer*? The most famous ill-fated voyage since the *Flying Dutchman* or the space shuttle *Challenger*. He had been experimented on for seven months? Incredible!

And she was fascinated that he was a marine biologist from Woods Hole. Judging from his brains and geekiness, she would have guessed if he were a scientist, he'd be a mathematician or physicist, not a scientist so far on the cool and romantic side of the ledger.

"And none of these revelations brought back your memory?" she asked him.

Hall shook his head no. He told her that now that he had more to go on than just a name he shared with hundreds of others, he had spent a few minutes Googling himself, and had learned some additional information. He had obtained his undergraduate degree in biology from Indiana University in Bloomington, and his PhD in Oceanography from the Florida Institute of Technology. He had been an only child and his parents were deceased as of two years earlier. And he was unmarried.

He had decided to wait to dig further. There was always the chance he would have his full memory restored, and he'd prefer to wait for this to happen rather than rely on a cyber footprint of limited depth and questionable reliability.

"If this guy," began Megan, and then, drawing a blank, said, "what was his name again?"

"Alex Altschuler."

She repeated his name a few times, since she didn't have an Internet boosted memory to draw from. "If this Altschuler does turn out to be on the level, do you plan to tell him about your psi ability?"

"I don't think I should. They still haven't found the people trying to kill us. And this could be the ace in the hole we need to save our lives. I think we need all the advantages we can get." He frowned. "What do you think? Am I using faulty logic here, just so I can delay my pariah-hood?"

Megan shook her head. "No. I agree entirely. When you have your memory back and they catch the guys hunting for you—us—then you can consider it. But it's our best weapon right now."

"Yeah. But breaching people's privacy without their knowledge couldn't be more unethical. I just don't want to get used to doing this. I'm counting on you to keep me honest. And to make sure I don't turn into a monster."

She nodded with a grim expression, acknowledging the seriousness of the request. "Why do I suddenly feel like the bride of Frankenstein?" she said, attempting to lighten the mood.

"I don't know," replied Hall with just the hint of a smile. "Did Frankenstein marry a Neanderthal?"

28

Seventy minutes later, Megan pulled into a spot in the Vons parking lot and killed the engine of Carl Glandon's Mercedes. She wore oversized sunglasses, baggy clothing, and her hair was tucked neatly inside a Stanford baseball cap, all of which the Glandons had generously provided.

Hall had driven by a police station on their way home from lunch the day before and had scanned the minds inside. To his surprise, none of them were looking for Megan Emerson in connection with the dead men in her office. He'd have thought a double murder in Bakersfield would have been at the top of the cops' radar. But maybe whoever was behind this had retrieved the bodies before the authorities had found them, to stifle an investigation.

Still, as relieved as they were by this development, it would be careless not to at least make some effort at disguise.

"*Okay,*" she broadcast to Hall, who had remained in their borrowed home. "*I'm in the lot.*"

"*Great. Hold on a second. I'll find out how our boy is doing.*"

Hall called up the IM screen he had used before. *You have ten minutes, Alex,* he sent.

I'll be there in five, came the reply inside Hall's internal text box, no doubt sent by Altschuler's PDA while he raced to his destination like a caffeine-addled maniac. To make time this good, he must have been going nearly a hundred on the highway the entire way.

What kind of hat are you wearing?

The only one I could find on short notice. It's a pink women's tennis visor. It's as close to a baseball hat as I could get.

Hall laughed out loud. Altschuler had certainly been willing to go the extra mile to obey his instructions.

Hall transmitted this information to Megan. Five minutes later, right on schedule, she reported seeing a scrawny man in a ridiculous pink visor enter the store. She waited another five minutes, scouring the lot, but Altschuler appeared to have come alone. Hall was counting on the cocktail party effect to alert him if there were already other men in the grocery store waiting.

Megan entered the store and walked to the egg area.

"I see him now," she broadcast to Hall. *"I'm pretending to be choosing some cheese slices. He's about twenty feet to my left."*

Hall detected only seven minds in Megan's vicinity. He entered each of them until he found Altschuler. Megan had served her duty as spotter flawlessly.

"Find him?" she asked.

"Yeah. Give me a few minutes to explore, and I'll get back to you."

Nick Hall entered Alex Altschuler's mind once again and began to dig. His first impression was that the guy was largely harmless, and this was borne out after several additional minutes of perusing his memories. Hall read the memory of his recent call with Fyfe and his encounter with Gray. Altschuler was smart and ambitious, but he had actually wet himself during this encounter, although not enough to be detectible. This was a memory Hall felt bad about reading, and vowed to forget that he had.

Unbelievably, everything Altschuler had texted to Hall was one hundred percent accurate. The events had unfolded precisely the way he had said. Not even any white lies to make himself look better. And the stuff he had written about how sorry he was and how he wanted to do right by the victims' families and society had been absolutely genuine. Hall had thought these were platitudes issued by a heartless executive performing damage control, but these Boy Scout utterances had been entirely sincere.

The man was excited, and nervous, about his upcoming elevation to CEO, and saw it as a huge opportunity. He also was excited about the progress Gray had made and how it would revolutionize the world.

But at the same time, he felt profoundly guilty for feeling this way, given the atrocities Gray had committed to achieve this progress. And guilty for not realizing what Gray had been up to earlier. His empathy and remorse were very deep, and very real, and Hall could not have been more astonished.

He relayed what he had learned to Megan, who was as surprised as he was by his findings.

"Let's bring him to the house," suggested Hall telepathically. *"He's harmless."*

Megan took a deep breath. *"You ever misread anyone before?"* she asked.

Hall couldn't blame her for wanting to be sure. Everyone else who had been looking for them wanted them dead, but he reassured her that he was absolutely certain about this particular individual.

Megan approached the man in the glasses and pink visor, who was nervously hovering next to dozens of rows of egg cartons sitting on a low, refrigerated shelf, not exactly sure what to do with himself. He had such a worried expression on his face, and his eyes were shifting around the area so quickly, it looked to Megan as though he were expecting an entire team of commandos to descend from the ceiling.

"Alex Altschuler?" she said.

From his shocked look, he had been expecting many possibilities, but Megan Emerson wasn't one of them. "Who are you?" he replied.

"Nick Hall sent me. He's decided to trust you, after all."

Altschuler eyed her suspiciously. "Really? Just like that?"

"Apparently so," she replied with a shrug. "Follow me."

"Where are we going?"

"I'm taking you to Nick," she said, beginning to lead him out of the store. "He's just a few miles from here."

"No kidding?" said Altschuler in genuine surprise. "I would have bet my life he wasn't in Bakersfield."

Megan smiled. "Good thing you didn't bet, then," she said dryly.

"Oh, and by the way," she added. "Feel free to take off that ridiculous visor."

29

Megan turned the corner and pointed out their destination ahead, a truly impressive home.

"You two have been staying *there?*" said Altschuler incredulously.

"For two days now. The owners are on vacation."

"How did you know they weren't coming back yesterday or today?"

"We, um . . . overheard them."

"And, what . . . did they forget to lock the door?" said Altschuler.

Megan shrugged. "Let's just say we were fortunate and leave it at that."

She pushed a button near the dash and the leftmost door on the Glandons' four-car garage slid smoothly open. She pulled in and quickly closed the door behind them.

Megan opened the car door and exited. Altschuler followed suit, throwing the door open and narrowly missing Nick Hall, who had entered the garage to be a one-man welcoming party.

As Altschuler stood, Hall held out his hand. Altschuler shook the offered hand with a look of disbelief, obviously not expecting access to Nick Hall to have been this easy, especially after the text messages they had exchanged. Both men introduced themselves, even though this wasn't necessary. Both knew full well whose hands they were shaking.

"Welcome to our hideout," said Hall.

"Thanks," said Altschuler. "But aren't you worried that a neighbor just saw us pull in? In a car I presume belongs to the people who own this place? Someone could be calling the cops right now."

Hall reappraised the man in front of him. He had known the man was a genius technically, but hadn't expected him to be this savvy. Hall had been monitoring the neighborhood psionically and had broadcast to Megan when the coast was clear. But this wasn't something he could tell Altschuler. "I set up cameras pointed at the houses on either side of us," he lied. "With the feeds coming into my personal World Wide Web. No one saw you come in."

"Impressive," said Altschuler. And then, changing gears, added, "Thanks for bringing me here. I can't tell you how much I appreciate your trust."

They entered the main residence and Hall offered his guest a drink, which he refused.

"Did you bring the antidote?" asked Hall.

Altschuler pulled a small glass vial from his pocket, its lid screwed on tightly. "Drink this. Within thirty minutes to a few hours, your memory should return." He grimaced. "If it's ever going to return, that is. I can't guarantee it."

"For some reason, I thought it would need to be injected."

"It's a nasty, super-potent cousin of the date rape drug," explained Altschuler. "The one that deviant assholes slip into girls' drinks."

"Got it," said Hall. "Having to inject it would make it a little less . . . stealthy, wouldn't it?"

Hall put out his hand and Altschuler gave him the vial, which he chugged down immediately.

Altschuler shook his head in amazement. "How did you decide to trust me so completely—so suddenly? I can't believe you just took that without analyzing it first. I mean," he hastened to add, "it is what I said it is. But still . . ."

"Megan is a great judge of character. And she decided you were trustworthy. That's good enough for me."

"*Yeah?*" thought Megan wryly. "*I wouldn't have trusted him as far as I could throw him.*"

Hall suppressed a smile while they adjourned to the family room.

For the next forty-five minutes, Altschuler filled them in on the entire situation as thoroughly as he could, including Fyfe and Cowan's roles. Hall had already read all of it from his mind, but this was helpful to Megan, and it was another great test of the bespectacled scientist's veracity.

Once again, he told it straight. The only area in which he wasn't totally honest involved his own feelings of guilt. They were stronger even than he let on, and he was beating himself up over not having caught on to what Gray was doing in time to save lives.

Hall found himself liking and admiring this man, and wondering if he could have been as upstanding as Altschuler if their situations were reversed.

When Altschuler was finished revealing everything he knew, he couldn't contain himself any longer. He had to know more about Hall's implants. He asked questions for the next thirty minutes, and had Hall run through various diagnostic programs to assess the implants' performance more precisely.

Altschuler was ecstatic over what he learned. The system worked better than he could have ever dared hope. Kelvin Gray may have been a man with no soul, he told them, but there was no denying he was a genius.

Finally, when he had run out of questions, at least temporarily, Altschuler said, "I came here with the goal of getting you to come back to Fresno with me. How about it? I won't tell anyone you're there."

"Other than your friends Cameron Fyfe and Ed Cowan, correct?"

"Right. Those two, and the three of us, will form a crisis management team. We'll spearhead the search for John Delamater. And go public with the atrocities committed by Kelvin Gray."

"Where would we stay?" said Megan.

Altschuler smiled, pleased with himself for having thought far enough ahead to have a good answer. "At the Fresno Homestead Inn. Ed Cowan has already gotten you a suite there, under an alias. It's an extended stay hotel, and the suites are really nice."

"Extended stay hotel?" said Megan.

"Yes. You know, like the Residents Inn. Although I think the Homestead is even better. They cater to businesspeople on long assignments, people relocating, and so on. In fact, Theia houses our relocating employees there until they find permanent residence. They're separate units, about seven hundred square feet. A few rooms, a small kitchen, free breakfast." Seeing that Megan's expression remained unchanged, Altschuler added, "You'll love it. Pool, business center, weight room . . . ." Altschuler trailed off and rolled his eyes. "Why do I suddenly feel like I work for the hotel?"

Megan and Hall both laughed.

"We're going with him to Fresno, aren't we?" broadcast Megan.

"It really is our best option. And I trust this guy implicitly."

"And you really like him, also, don't you?"

"A lot," he replied. Hall locked his eyes on the thin scientist. "What the hell," he said. "Let's go to Fresno. We accept your proposal."

Altschuler was delighted. "Fantastic!" he said.

"Naturally, we'll want to take your car," said Hall. "Give me a second and I'll call a cab to get us back to the Vons parking lot. The local cab company lets you schedule a pickup online," he explained.

"Let's have it pick us up away from the house," suggested Megan.

"Right. I'll send it to Primrose, which my map program says is one street over." He looked away for several seconds. "Okay. Done," he announced. "A cab will pick us up in fifteen minutes. While we wait, let's straighten up and put everything back the way we found it."

To Megan, he added telepathically, *"When we leave, you two can go first, so I can reset the alarm and return the key to its hiding place."*

"You really think these people won't know someone was in their home?" said Altschuler.

"They may notice some things out of place. Scratch their heads over some missing food. But trust me, they'll eventually convince themselves they're misremembering these details, since no other explanation could possibly make any sense."

"Maybe they'll think they had a poltergeist," said Megan dryly.

The corners of Nick Hall's mouth were beginning to turn up into a smile when they abruptly reversed course.

Hall gasped and sank to the ground.

He held his head in both hands, and his eyes appeared to bulge from their sockets.

The antidote had taken effect all at once. And like a wall of snow barreling down a mountain during an avalanche, his memories, his knowledge of himself and his past, came crashing down into his mind.

It was almost too much for him to handle, and he continued to reel from this terrible blow for several seconds.

"Nick?" said Megan worriedly.

Hall finally took a deep breath and picked himself up off the ground, rising to his full height. He had managed to absorb the blow and his mind had now righted itself.

His memories had returned! He didn't even have the need to search them. He *knew* who he was.

"I'm back," he whispered, and tears began to roll down his face.

He had been living a nightmare. Even *he* hadn't realized how emotionally traumatic it had been to live without a past, without an identity, with his sense of self stripped totally away.

Megan gave him a warm hug. "I'm so thrilled for you, Nick," she said, her eyes moistening as well.

"Thank God," whispered Altschuler, and Hall could read in his mind how glad he was to be able to undo the damage suffered by at least one member of the *Explorer* expedition. "So it all came back? You remember everything?"

"Everything," replied Hall happily.

But then a puzzled expression came over his face and he looked away. A few seconds later he looked back and said, "Well, *almost* everything."

Nick Hall blew out a long breath. "There does seem to be this one little gap. . . "

PART TWO

"The dead keep their secrets. And in a while we shall be as wise as they."

—Alexander Smith

"Who are you? Why do you hide in the darkness and listen to my private thoughts?"

—Juliet, from *Romeo and Juliet*, (modern translation)

30

Colonel Justin Girdler rushed up to the small military helicopter that had just landed inside Fort Bragg, a TH-67 Creek, ignoring the wind that blasted his salt-and-pepper hair as though he were in a wind tunnel. He shook the hand of the man who jumped out of the helo, his second-in-command, Major Mike Campbell—a man he had handpicked for this position, ruffling more than a few feathers by jumping him over others who had served longer.

Campbell was in his mid-thirties and almost seemed like a son to Girdler—the son he should have had. His own son, who had been born when Girdler was in his late thirties, was graduating high school with spiked green hair, tattoos and piercings covering his entire body, and no future.

Justin Girdler was disappointed in his only child. But more than this, he had deep feelings of guilt, believing that the path his son was on was largely *his* fault. Divorced. Rarely at home during the boy's formative years. And worse still, a psychologist by training. He was the head of PsyOps after all. There was a saying he had heard on occasion: show me a shrink's kid, and I'll show you a fucked up mess. In his experience this was largely true. Even worse if the poor bastard in question was the kid of a *child* psychologist. At least his own son hadn't had this cross to bear.

"I appreciate you coming in person for this one," said Girdler.

"Not at all, Colonel. Of all the unusual shit we've been involved with, this has to take the cake. Worth a two-hour helo ride."

In their line of work, it wasn't unusual to be working on a Sunday morning, but Girdler appreciated Campbell's attitude nonetheless. He could have had Campbell teleconference in, but he liked the personal touch. And he hadn't seen the major in weeks now as their responsibilities seemed to have drawn them in opposite directions.

Girdler also wanted his second back at Fort Bragg so the major could man the main office while Girdler flew to Edwards Air Force Base, which happened to be just ninety miles outside of Bakersfield, where he also maintained an office. Girdler had no doubt Nick Hall had left Bakersfield behind since the time his fingerprints were found, but going to the last known location of one's quarry was sound operating procedure.

Even if the man they were seeking had fled into the heart of the country, with the colonel in California and Campbell in North Carolina, one of them should be fairly close—at least measured in distances that could be covered quickly by military aircraft. In the days of electronics connecting people in numerous ways and flawless 3-D teleconferencing, which was now as simple to implement as a phone call used to be, geographical proximity was not as important as it once was.

But Campbell wasn't sure if he fully embraced this development. He had read a short story when he was a kid about a future in which a teleportation device had been invented that had become as ubiquitous as the telephone. It was a miracle of technology, but the twist to the story was that it caused an increase in suicides.

Why? Because you could never get away from people you were desperate to get away from. Your ex-wife. Your mother-in-law, who could pop over for a quick lunch every day, no matter how many thousands of miles away you moved. When you could travel anywhere instantaneously, every person on earth was as good as your neighbor. Perfect 3-D teleconferencing was moving the world in this direction.

Colonel Girdler drove the major a half mile away to a private conference room with the highest level of security on the base, which was saying a lot. Bragg was home to the US Army Special Operations Command, of which PsyOps was a part. Now that Girdler headed the Black Ops version, he could base wherever he wanted, and in fact had offices at several military installations around the country, which he shared with Campbell—including the one at Edwards.

Major General Nelson Sobol's 3-D image appeared on a thin screen that hung on the conference room wall, right on schedule. The general was inching toward the finish line of his endless off-site retreat, and Girdler could sense right away that he was in a foul mood. Perfectly understandable. But still unfortunate.

"Gentlemen," said Sobol in greeting, nodding to Girdler and Campbell in turn. That was it for the pleasantries, as the general immediately asked for a status report on the Hall situation.

Girdler gestured at his second-in-command to begin.

"I'll keep this short and to the point," said Campbell, also sensing Sobol's less than optimal mood. "If there is anything on which you would like elaboration, General, just let me know."

Sobol gave a curt nod to acknowledge that this was understood.

"We began by investigating the warehouse described in the message. It was quite large, as Hall had indicated: twenty-five thousand square feet. It had also been cleaned out, and then torched, the day after Hall's putative message was sent. A very professional, high-heat, high-intensity fire."

While Campbell spoke, Girdler sent several photographs of the warehouse, inside and out, and the surrounding area to the corner of both their monitor and the general's.

"How do we know it was cleaned out?" said the General.

"We found two witnesses—not easy to do, as Hall was right about the place being isolated—who saw several men loading up a moving van with items from the warehouse. Mostly chairs, beds, and interlocking steel panels."

"I'm sure your witnesses didn't get a count," said Sobol, "but if you had to guess, would you guess there were twenty-seven beds?"

Girdler nodded. "There are alternative hypotheses to cover this, but this information is consistent with the warehouse being separated into twenty-seven . . . sleeping quarters would be a polite way to phrase it," he said. "But a prison cell is a prison cell. So while this isn't absolute confirmation, it is . . ."

"Consistent. Yeah, I get it. Go on."

"We haven't found the location of the incinerator spoken of in the message," continued Campbell. "Yet. But we did find trace amounts of blood in the warehouse's parking lot and a thin trail of gasoline beginning about fifty feet away from the blood residue," he added, while Girdler highlighted the location of the blood and line of gasoline on one of the photos on the monitor.

"The blood workup came back two hours ago," said Girdler. "The blood belonged to a man named Billie Peterson, the same name Hall mentioned in his message. Peterson is a mercenary with special forces training. Got drummed out because there were questions about whether he was overzealous in his use of force."

Sobol nodded, almost imperceptibly, at the mention of Peterson, a man who had figured so prominently in Hall's message, but his expression never changed.

"Assuming we can believe everything in Hall's message," continued Girdler, "and the warehouse and Peterson have certainly been borne out, there is an obvious scenario that would account for what we found."

Sobol nodded slowly as he considered what scenario would best fit the data.

"Right," he said after a few seconds of thought. "Peterson takes Hall to his car in the lot to drive him to where the incinerator is. He thinks he's luring him there, like a helpless sheep to the slaughter, with promises of information, not knowing that Hall is aware this is a ruse. But Hall turns the tables, using his mind reading ability to get the jump on him. Who knows, maybe he slams the car door into Peterson, bends over and gets a large rock, whatever. But I'm guessing you would have told me if you found Hall's blood. So somehow Hall bests this guy, who is ten times more capable than he is."

"Right," said Campbell. "Which is consis—supports the idea that Hall is smart and that this ESP might be real. Real enough to compensate for unequal skills."

"Then Hall steals Peterson's car and races off," continued the general. "Peterson is injured, but gets a shot off, puncturing the gas tank, and leaving a trail of gas behind the car. Since gas tanks only explode in the movies, Hall drives on until he runs out of gas. Which still could have taken a while, depending on the location of the puncture."

"That's the reconstruction of events we tend to find most probable," said Girdler.

"Find the car yet?"

"No," replied the colonel. "Not surprisingly. Anybody who could pull off something like the Scripps *Explorer* would clean up after themselves whenever they could. The way they sanitized the warehouse is a good example."

"Remind me of the name of this mastermind Hall fingered?" asked Sobol.

"John Delamater," said Campbell.

"Right. Anything on him?"

"Nothing," replied the major. "It's almost certainly an alias. It didn't light up any of the computers."

"Our best guess is that the car ran out of gas in Bakersfield," said Girdler. "Assuming, of course, that our analysis is on track. Which may well not be the case."

"Bakersfield. That's the location of the double murder where Hall's prints were found, right?"

"Exactly," confirmed the colonel. "And we've now identified the two victims as mercenaries—both with connections to Peterson."

Sobol nodded slowly, his expression still grim. "It does appear to keep adding up, doesn't it? If you had to bet, you'd bet big at this point that Hall's message had a lot of truth to it."

Girdler quickly ran down how they had looked into other murders around this time and had connected these in as well. A murder in a Shell gas station, and the murder of two paramedics.

"We pulled strings to have our people take over these investigations as well," said Girdler. "We retraced the route the two paramedics took the last few days they were alive. And we spoke to witnesses. We're almost certain the paramedics interacted with Hall. One of the men, Hector Garcia, had a girlfriend who told us he had insisted he met a man who could read minds. Perfectly. And fish out any information he wanted without any apparent effort. But the man had warned Garcia to keep this quiet, saying he would be in danger if he didn't. Garcia also told his girlfriend he had dropped this man off, along with a woman, at the Bakersfield Amtrak station."

The colonel nodded at Campbell to pick up the narrative. "We accessed all of the cameras in the train station," said the major. "And sure enough, we did get a match to Hall. Using an image taken just before he boarded the *Explorer*. He was with a girl—turns out the same one who belonged to the office where the double murder took place. Megan Emerson. They stayed for a while and then left in a cab."

"Have you found the cabbie?"

"Yes," said the major. "His log shows that he dropped them both in the middle of Serene Oaks, a wealthy suburb of Bakersfield. Our guess is the girl had a car parked on the street there. Other than this, we can't find any connection. We checked with the neighbors, but no one saw anything suspicious, nor did any remember seeing Hall and Emerson. One couple was out of town, but their doors were locked and their alarm set."

The general eyed Campbell dubiously. "Please tell me you checked it out anyway, Major."

"We did. We contacted the alarm company and broke in just before this call, but the place was empty."

"So they were dropped off in a neighborhood," said Sobol, "and either had a car there, met someone, or had another cab pick them up to confuse their trail."

"That's our guess," said Major Campbell. "Although we haven't found any evidence any other cabs had a pickup in Serene Oaks around that time. There are very few street cameras in this neighborhood, and none of them picked up Hall. We've been tracking cars that came into range of any cameras in the area, the night they were dropped off and even the next day. But there are a shitload of them, and we haven't found anything noteworthy. We've also been accessing the cameras of any store or gas station in a ten-mile radius, starting a full day before the cab dropped them off and going forward. "

"So basically the trail is cold," commented the general, giving them no credit for their progress so far.

"For the moment," said Girdler. "But we'll pick it up again."

"Hall sent out an e-mail. Have you tried to reply to it?"

"Yes," said the colonel. "We sent a message. With a tag to tell us when it's opened. So far he hasn't read it. Why he hasn't read it remains a mystery. Maybe he's been too busy to check his messages. Maybe he canceled the account for some reason. But it could be that he doesn't even remember he sent the message, or set up the e-mail account, so he wouldn't know how to access the account or even think to try."

"Yes, he did say he'd been given amnesia drugs," said Sobol. "But it's doubtful he was given another dose between the time he sent the e-mail and the time he escaped. What would be the point? As far as Peterson knew, Hall hadn't learned or experienced anything that day he needed to forget."

The colonel nodded. "This is true," he said. "But we're guessing they used a fairly new drug called Erase 190. If this is the case, further memory instability going forward, even without dosing, wouldn't be uncommon."

Girdler paused. "So that's basically all we have right now, General," he finished.

Sobol nodded slowly. "Okay," he said. "So what are your thoughts on this, Colonel? And your recommendations going forward?"

Girdler took a deep breath. He glanced at Campbell, who shot him a look of encouragement. "I believe Hall's e-mail message is accurate," he said. "I believe some private citizen or company kidnapped those aboard the *Explorer* and brought them to a warehouse just outside of Fresno. I believe the kidnapper experimented on them all, resulting in the deaths of everyone but Hall. I believe whoever was behind this perfected what they were after, that somehow Hall developed ESP, and that he escaped. That's what I think happened."

The colonel paused and stared at Sobol for his reaction.

"I tend to agree," said the general. "It looks like Hall's message so far is checking out to be absolutely credible."

"On the assumption this is the case," continued Girdler, "my first and highest priority recommendation, therefore, is that we locate Nick Hall as soon as we can." A pained look came over the colonel's face. "And terminate him with extreme prejudice."

31

Several seconds of total silence settled over the proceedings.

"Let me understand," said Sobol dryly. "A team kidnaps the entire crew of an oceangoing vessel. Imprisons them for many months. Conducts illegal experiments on them. Then kills all but one of them. And your highest priority recommendation is to terminate the one surviving *victim* of all of this?"

"Yes, sir."

"Major Campbell, do you agree with this recommendation?"

"Yes, sir, I do," replied the major.

"Okay, now you have my attention. I'm sure you recognize that while Black Ops powers are broad, they aren't unlimited. Killing an innocent civilian isn't exactly in the charter—even if you stretch it far enough to cover the Pacific ocean. So on what grounds do you make this recommendation?"

"We've given this a lot of thought, as you might imagine," replied Girdler. "These implants have led to mind reading. And not just surface thoughts. Hall could apparently dig out of Peterson's mind anything Peterson knew. The same with Hector Garcia. Do you have any idea of the implications of this?"

"I've been busy, Colonel, but I did manage to prepare for this call. So, yes, I have thought about what this would mean."

"Then you must see that this guy is far too dangerous to let live. ESP—true, potent, absolutely perfect ESP—is a power that can never see the light of day. We'll be the instruments of his death, but whoever did this to him put this death sentence on his head. We're just the executioners, doing what needs to be done. I'm sick about it. But if we allow ourselves to be compassionate, we stand to lose everything."

"Surely you're overstating the case, Colonel? He's one man."

"Would you want to be in the same room with him?"

A slight smile came over Sobol's face. "I can't say that I would. I may have committed an . . . indiscretion . . . or two," he said wryly, "that I wouldn't want him to read. But so what? I wouldn't want to be in the same room with a trained attack dog, but that doesn't mean it isn't useful. I say we capture and study this guy. Can you imagine someone with these abilities working for *our* side? And what if we can use him to figure out how to give others this ability?"

"That's exactly what we're afraid of," said Mike Campbell. "It's too much power for any man. Even a man who is a perfect angel, with a perfect moral compass. It's absolute power and it's corrupting. Remember your Sunday school, General? Satan, himself, began his career as an angel. If *he* could be corrupted, even while an angel in heaven, what hope does a mere man have?"

"But it's far worse than just what Hall could do if he turned," added Girdler. "If we let him live, we open Pandora's box. We all but ensure the start of an international ESP arms race."

Sobol stared at him as though he hadn't heard correctly.

"Every country will search for the key to unlock ESP," clarified Girdler. "Both to use as a weapon and to achieve parity if some other country gets there first. With disastrous results no matter how you slice it. ESP arms race."

"Has Hall's condition become international news in the past five minutes?" said Sobol sarcastically. "Because the last I heard, the only people who have any suspicion of it are the three of us, and the girlfriend of a fallen paramedic."

"You don't think other countries would get wind of this?" said Girdler, refusing to back down. "With all due respect, General, you know they would. One way or another. And if Hall is left at large, very quickly. He's apparently not shy about showing off his ability. If we try to harness him for our own ends, this will eventually leak out as well. *If* we can even contain him, which I suspect we can't. How bad would we panic if we thought Iran or Russia or China had a program that was yielding perfect psi ability? Would we pull out all the stops to start a crash program, General?"

"Of course. We'd have no other choice."

"And neither will they when they learn about our program. Anyone who can't harness this ability, in a world with those who *can*, would be at a devastating disadvantage. And suppose a straightforward way to confer this ability could be found? And don't underestimate the ingenuity of humanity. We put bloodhounds to shame once we're following the scent of a breakthrough. If this were to occur, and ESP became widespread, it's game over. An extinction level event. If you think this through, we're not a species who can read each other's inner thoughts without self-destructing. We're teetering on the brink right now, even without this destabilizing influence."

Sobol now looked more thoughtful. "Even if we eliminate Hall, isn't there a chance this has already leaked more broadly?" he asked. "Unlikely, but not impossible. If an arms race is about to begin, can we afford to throw away a winning hand?"

"There is no arms race without Hall," replied Girdler. "Think about it. If we kill him and bury this story, everyone thinks he went down with the Scripps *Explorer*. Any rumors that he was ever even alive after this tragedy will be seen as crackpot conspiracy theories."

He paused. "This isn't to say that we let those responsible for this atrocity escape justice. We can wait and see who comes out with breakthrough advances and then quietly investigate, taking care of them before anything is public. Before they go public, the first thing they'll do—they'll *have* to do—is file patents. They'll delay doing this until the last second, but we can have Nessie tie into the patent computers and sound the alert the moment something is filed.

"The people behind this *will* be brought to justice," insisted the colonel. "And we can consider making use of what they learned. Although there are plenty of issues with this as well. But keeping Hall alive is a recipe for disaster. The existence of his abilities *will* get out, even if we can contain him. Which is a huge *if*. And it *will* boomerang on us—and the world."

"I'm not as certain about that as you are, Colonel. If I had ESP right now, what would I read in your mind? That your superior officer is a lobotomized jackass for not immediately agreeing with you on this?"

Girdler smiled. Perhaps Sobol *could* read minds. "Not at all, General. I'd be thinking that I appreciate your insight, and the fact you're open-minded enough to listen to me and consider the merits of my argument."

"Uh-huh," said Sobol skeptically. "While I don't share your views entirely, Colonel, you do make some compelling points. I need some time to think this through. I'll call you back in forty-five minutes."

With that, the screen went dark.

Forty-five minutes later they were staring at Sobol's dark visage once again. "I've looked at this from several angles," he began. "I think you made some excellent points, gentlemen. But I'm afraid I can't support your recommendation. First, we don't have the power to kill an innocent American citizen who has displayed no intent to endanger this country. Second, now that you've made me painfully aware of the unstable nitroglycerin we're holding, I'm counting on you to take the proper precautions to make sure your doomsday scenario doesn't come to pass. The three of us are the only people authorized to know about this. Period. And I want a list of recommendations for how to contain this secret. And how to contain someone with these abilities."

"I urge you to reconsider, General," said Girdler. "Trying to harness Hall and ESP is more likely to boomerang and bite us all in the ass than playing around with *germ warfare*, for Christ's sake."

"You have your orders, gentlemen," said Sobol firmly.

Both men nodded. "Roger that," said Girdler. And while he managed to say this in a neutral tone, his eyes blazed with a steady defiance.

32

Girdler and Campbell sat in silence for several minutes after Sobol's virtual presence no longer inhabited the small conference room. The major finally broke the silence. "How surprised are you?" he asked.

"I don't know. I thought the arguments were convincing. I know you well enough, Mike, to know that you're not just humoring me, and you thought so too. Not that you'd ever just humor me on something this important."

Girdler shrugged. "But I suppose this threat is too insidious for the general. If Hall had his finger on a button that could detonate a hundred nukes around the world, this would get Sobol's attention. But he can't really see the potential for disaster as easily with just one poor son of a bitch who can read minds."

"At least *we'll* be in charge of containment. The people most aware of the danger. At least that's *something*."

"It's not good enough, Mike," said the colonel, shaking his head. "I don't care what our orders are. When the world is in flames, I won't feel better about myself because I was only following orders. That's what the Nazis said at Nuremberg."

Campbell frowned. "Look, Justin, you know I'm on your side on this one. But some could argue *we're* the Nazis here. We're the ones recommending the assassination of an innocent man. It's not comforting to know that our goal is now the same as those who committed mass murder on Hall's colleagues."

Girdler's eyes fell. "No, it's gut-wrenching to have to advocate for this." He returned his gaze to Campbell and shook his head morosely. "But we have no other option. Hall has to die. It isn't his fault. If they had given him a drug that turned him into a crazed killer, it wouldn't be his fault either. But that wouldn't change the cold equations."

The colonel paused. "Hall may be a great guy. He probably is. And he may mean very well. Right now. But what if this changes? What if he becomes unstable? He's the sword of Damocles and Pandora's box rolled up into one."

Campbell sighed heavily. "You're right. We have no other choice. It would have been hard enough to do this if Sobol were on board. Now it's even worse. We do something that goes against everything we believe in on one level, and our reward is a court martial—with no possible defense."

"Not necessarily. It depends on how it goes down. If we kill him cleanly, we can pretend we were never able to find him. Or if not, we can claim it was an accident. He forced our hand."

Campbell considered. "Okay, but even if we can do this and still save our own necks, Sobol is now a believer in ESP. So won't he insist on us starting a program to look into this—Hall or no Hall?"

"It's a good point. But I'll be the one running any program he wants initiated. I'll just make sure we never get anywhere."

"But can we count on Sobol not mentioning this program to anyone? Isn't there a danger in having a program running, even one we sabotage? What if what we're doing becomes known? Won't this start an arms race anyway?"

"No. Sobol wouldn't breathe of word of it to anyone. He couldn't. Without being able to produce Hall to demonstrate ESP, people would think he was out of his mind. They'd think he was back to having us try to stare goats to death. He wouldn't say word one until we produced some unambiguous evidence. And even if I'm wrong about that—which I'm not—a living Hall is still the key. Without him, whatever gets out will be seen as a load of conspiracy theory crap that no one will take seriously. We can even leak that rumors about Hall were part of a PsyOps mission to get other countries to waste resources on ridiculous ESP projects, and to sow panic that the US has cracked mind reading."

The major stared at Girdler for several seconds, weighing his points. "Okay," he conceded finally. "That makes sense." He paused. "But we do have one more problem."

"Finding Hall in the first place?"

"No. Not that finding him won't be challenging enough. But that wasn't the problem I meant. When we do find him, have you considered how we go about killing him?"

"I have," replied the colonel. "And you're right. This could be . . . problematic. How do you sneak up on a guy, with intent to kill, who can read your thoughts from six miles out?"

"Exactly," said Campbell.

"It's a very good question," said Colonel Justin Girdler. "I only wish I had a good answer for you."

33

When the cab dropped them at the Vons parking lot, Nick Hall and Megan Emerson entered the store while Alex Altschuler waited for them in the parking lot in his black BMW. They quickly picked out sunglasses that covered much of their faces, and baseball hats, using a tiny fraction of the loot Hall had amassed cheating at poker, having decided not to steal these items from the poor Glandons.

They emerged five minutes later, and Hall insisted Megan take the front seat with Altschuler during the relatively quick drive back to Fresno. It had taken Altschuler ninety minutes to arrive, but it would take over two hours to return at a pace that was at least within shouting distance of the posted limits.

Megan and Alex Altschuler chatted and got to know each other while Hall remained silent behind them. He had announced at the outset he needed time to think. To get reacquainted with himself. And that he didn't plan to be sociable during the early part of the drive.

As they pulled out into the street, Nick Hall allowed himself to face the full horror of the massacre that had taken place. Bad enough to contemplate the murder of twenty-six people when this was just a number. But with his memory restored, he now could run down an inventory of who was on the ship. He knew them all. While it was true that several were little more than strangers, many others he had known for years, and were colleagues and in some cases friends. People he had worked with and laughed with. People who shared his passion for oceanography. Tara Cohen, Ashok Patel, and Gavin Hirsch. Don McBride and Andy Chen. Latisha Lewis and Min-sue Ahn. The list went on and on. It was a tragic, senseless loss of a truly wonderful group of human beings. How could they all be gone?

He allowed himself to wallow in the misery of their loss for ten minutes and then forced himself to put this massacre out of his mind.

For now. He would continue to mourn their loss in the days and weeks ahead.

So now he knew who he was again. And much of who he was, he liked. He had been hard-working, determined, and successful. He was a loyal friend and someone who set high moral and ethical standards for himself.

But there was much about himself he now didn't like, even detested. He had been arrogant. Smug. He was an only child. Bright. Funny. Athletic. But his success had gone to his head. He had become selfish. In short, he had begun to think he was hot shit.

It was funny what waking up in a dumpster without a memory could do for your perspective. And reading minds could take anyone down a peg. He had thought when he walked into a room, everyone inside had been holding their breath, waiting to be dazzled by Nick Hall's entrance. By his lean, athletic body and ruggedly handsome face.

What an arrogant, self-delusional fool he had been. He had now read the minds of dozens of women he had passed. While a few had reacted positively to his appearance, an equal number had been decidedly unimpressed.

How had he gotten so full of himself? And how had his friends put up with him?

And seven months ago he had been engaged to a woman named Alicia Green. Beautiful, but on the cold side. Okay to talk to, but not . . . Megan Emerson.

But seven months ago he would have never given Megan a second look. She had a cute face and appealing figure, but she wasn't nearly hot enough for the great Nick Hall. She would never have made the first cut for the superficial asshole he had been.

When his parents had both died in a car accident two years previously, he had mourned for six months and then asked Alicia to marry him, more to get a feeling that he was moving forward with his life than out of a passion that couldn't be denied. Alicia was a perfectly fine woman, with a spectacular appearance. He had thought he was her equal in the looks department, but given his new perspective, he knew he was not.

But so what? That shouldn't have been so important anyway.

He had been about to settle. He hadn't been passionately in love with Alicia Green. And while they mouthed the words, she hadn't been in love with him either. Not really. Maybe it was telling that he had looked her up on Facebook while the cab was taking them to Vons, and she was already in another relationship.

And why was it that his mind and heart wanted to focus on Megan Emerson, even when his fiancée was now also part of his memory? Was it just proximity?

He didn't think so. What Megan had brought him was contrast. She wasn't as beautiful as Alicia, by any means, but she was more energetic. Warmer. More fun to be around. Without Megan he would never have known he was missing anything. He would have thought he had hit gold with Alicia Green.

And he couldn't blame Alicia for moving on. She thought he had died seven months ago. And in a way, he *had* died. He was not the same man she had been in love with—if that's truly what it had been.

Too much was going on for him to contact her now, but after his return from the dead became public, he would have no choice. He would call her. He would explain he had seen she had moved on, and that this was probably for the best.

He wouldn't blame her. He wouldn't pretend even for a second she had betrayed him by entering into a new relationship so quickly. He would wish her well and explain that he had been traumatized and changed.

Once he had become, temporarily at least, the most famous man on the planet, he suspected she might make a strong effort to hang on, but it wouldn't work. If she knew the truth, she wouldn't let him and his mutated psionic mind get within ten miles of her, anyway.

He wasn't certain how this would play out with Alicia. But he *was* certain that he wasn't the same man he had been seven months before. Even if Megan Emerson walked out of his life forever, she had already shown him there could be so much more to a relationship than he had known. And while looks deteriorated with time, a great personality and great chemistry only strengthened.

The funny thing was that the last seven months were still completely absent from his memory, even though everything prior had returned. He had done some research into amnesia and learned this wasn't impossible.

He remembered the Scripps *Explorer* exactly, and all the colleagues with whom he had embarked. He remembered beginning to feel woozy. And hearing what sounded like multiple helicopters off in the distance.

Was he getting seasick? Hallucinating? He had never been prone to seasickness, so he was very confused.

Then several people around him fell to the deck. His mind was too far gone to realize he had been drugged, which was obvious in retrospect. Whether by gas in the air or by something in the food or drink was unclear. His last memory of the ship was falling to the deck, closing his eyes, and noting in the back of his mind that the helicopter sounds were coming closer.

Next he remembered a small room with a small bed, locked from the outside. And a television that could only play movies and wasn't connected to the Internet. And then a man had come by with a clipboard, asking about his health but refusing to answer any questions. A man he now knew to be Kelvin Gray.

And then he awoke in the dumpster.

But it wasn't as though the events on the *Explorer* seemed to have happened only days before. The memories felt old. Felt like there had been a seven-month gap since he had experienced them.

He had no idea how he had escaped, but after having experienced using his psi ability to good effect, it wasn't a surprise that he had. His escape must have gone horribly wrong, though, for him to have needed to hide in a dumpster.

He thought about Megan once again. He had to tell her. About what a jackass he had been. And about Alicia. He needed to get this off his chest. And he owed it to her.

He had thought he might have been drawn to Megan because she was the only person he really knew. She had anchored him. Kept him sane. She was his only friend in an entire world of strangers. But now that his full memory was back, he felt just as dependent on her. Maybe more.

So he would tell Megan of his past, and pledge to her that he was a changed man forever. He didn't need to tell her what a jackass the old Nick Hall often was, he knew, but it was something he refused to hide from her.

The black BMW continued to glide quietly along California 99, eating up the miles with effortless power and grace. The conversation up front had died down temporarily, and the absolute quiet within the luxury car, even at highway speeds, spoke of some impressive automotive engineering.

"Are you okay back there, Nick?" thought Megan at him after several minutes of silence. *"I know you wanted some time to think. And I know you'll tell me what's bothering you when you're ready. But can you give me a hint? I mean, you're an innocent oceanographer, right? It's not like you remembered you really are a supervillain with minions somewhere, right?"*

Hall smiled. *"I'm sorry, Megan. Didn't mean to worry you."*

He thought about what else he might tell her right now. He knew they had a conference call scheduled for the moment they arrived at the Homestead Inn, to include the three of them, Cameron Fyfe, and Ed Cowan. So he wasn't sure when he would have time to really tell Megan what was on his mind, and about Alicia. As great as telepathy was, when he had this discussion, he wanted to be alone with her. And to be able to read her body language. And to be able to hold her.

"Everything is okay," he continued. *"Just needed to sort out a few things. I'll tell you all about it when we get some time alone. But for now, just know that, if anything, I've come to appreciate you even more than I did when I had no identity. Which is saying a lot."*

"Great," thought Megan, but in such a way that Hall sensed part of her was still waiting for the other shoe to drop. *"I look forward to being alone together."*

"*Me too*," thought Hall.

But with his past and Alicia Green as the primary agenda, he knew he didn't really mean it.

34

They arrived at the Homestead Inn, and it was as nice as Altschuler had advertised. A fairly large number of people resided there, but while Hall would have still given his right arm to get rid of the constant background chatter in his brain, he was becoming ever more adept at ignoring it.

They walked straight through the lobby, having no need to check in, keeping their heads down to avoid the cameras there, and onto the grounds. Ed Cowan had assured them there were no cameras covering the grounds or the rooms themselves, so once they were through the lobby they didn't have to look down at their shoes anymore.

They located the keycards Cowan had hidden for them—so they wouldn't have to use their own names to rent a suite, and were soon inside. A bowl of fresh red apples sat on a table to welcome them, along with a plate of home-baked chocolate chip cookies, which sent a schizophrenic message about the Homestead's position on the health of its guests.

Within minutes they were in the small living room section between bedrooms, and Cameron Fyfe and Ed Cowan were displayed in split screen on the TV hanging on the wall, in full three-dimensional splendor.

Cowan and Fyfe began by peppering Hall with questions about his ordeal. He told them he remembered a first meeting with Gray and then nothing else. With respect to his escape, and how Megan Emerson had ended up joining him on the run, he answered as truthfully as he could. But given he didn't want to disclose his psionic ability, he had to fabricate more of the story than he would have liked. He left the events at the mini-mart out of the narrative entirely.

When he had finished describing a somewhat fictionalized version of events in Megan's office, Fyfe and Cowan both looked skeptical.

"Just to be absolutely sure I'm not missing anything," said Fyfe, "let me try to recap. The first guy, the guy at the Shell, got distracted by some kids setting off a firecracker. And when he turned, you were able to slam a door handle into his skull."

"Right."

"And then two men were threatening Megan in her office, but they left the door open a hair."

Hall nodded.

"And you were able to slip behind them quietly while they were concentrating on Megan."

"Exactly," said Hall.

The venture capitalist's face remained impassive, but Cowan's eyes narrowed. "Uh-huh," he said. "So two trained killers, who were stupid enough not to close the door all the way, didn't hear you sneaking up on them? And you were able to take *both* of them out?"

"That's right. I'm not saying I wasn't lucky. But you know the old saying: I'd rather be lucky than good." Hall shrugged. "And maybe this Delamater ran out of talented bad guys."

"The same Delamater who managed the flawless assault on the *Explorer*?" said Fyfe. "The kidnapping of the century?"

Hall ignored him, deciding to forge ahead with the rest of the chronology instead. When he had finished, Fyfe said, "A fascinating story, Dr. Hall. . . . Nick," he amended, since Hall had insisted they use his first name. "You are, indeed, a very lucky man."

Fyfe leaned forward and stared intently at Hall, his eyes probing. "But are you *certain* there isn't anything else you'd like to tell us?" he asked, almost as if daring Hall to answer.

Hall shook his head. "That's it. I wish I could remember my seven-month imprisonment, but I can't. I don't think that's ever coming back."

"That's okay," said Fyfe. "We have more evidence than we need already. And you at least remember that Kelvin Gray was behind it."

"True," said Alex Altschuler, who had been largely silent up until this point. "But it would have been nice to have eyewitness testimony, from a Scripps *Explorer* survivor, that *we* weren't involved, Cameron.

Regardless of the evidence we present, you know the public will have lingering doubts."

Fyfe smiled, which was a rarity. "More than just lingering," he said. "And with good reason. If this had been perpetrated by the CEO of another company, I'd have trouble believing the majority investor and Executive Vice President of research had been totally clueless. Even if they were responsible for bringing the CEO down in the end."

Hall knew with absolute certainty that Altschuler hadn't been involved, but he knew this using a means he couldn't disclose. So if they wanted eyewitness testimony, he wouldn't feel the slightest bit guilty in stretching the truth to assist. "But I *can* deliver testimony that will help show you weren't involved," said Hall excitedly. "Gray spent five minutes boasting to me about how great he was."

This was an absolute lie, but it did fit in with what he had learned about the man. "He bragged that he was the only scientist involved. How he was so smart he was using hundreds of other scientists to translate his findings into reality, and was still able to keep them all in the dark. He mentioned Theia Labs and specifically said that not a single person in the company had any idea of what he was doing. He boasted that no one at Theia would believe a bad word about him, anyway. Even if you showered them with evidence."

"Very interesting," said Fyfe, but his expression suggested he didn't entirely trust this statement either.

Hall realized it *was* a bit of stretch to believe he could only remember one short interaction with Gray, but during this lone meeting Gray just happened to have said the exact words needed to absolve Theia personnel.

"I guess your luck is rubbing off on all of us," continued Fyfe. "This will go a long way toward getting everyone comfortable with new management and the people Gray left behind at Theia."

Hall went on to describe his web surfing capabilities, and then the group discussed their plans to catch Delamater and hold a press conference at nine or ten in the morning on Tuesday. Fyfe would fly out to Fresno immediately afterward to meet Hall in person, which he was eager to do, and present him to the FBI.

This normally wouldn't have been so intimidating, but the authorities were sure to be *livid* they hadn't come forth sooner. Especially when they learned that Kelvin Gray had been killed and left to rot in his own private wine cellar days earlier. Not to mention that Hall could have cleared up several unexplained murders in Bakersfield.

"I'll call the press conference for New York," said Fyfe. "Arguably the news epicenter of the world."

"What do you plan to tell the press to get them there?" asked Altschuler.

Fyfe frowned. "I've given this a lot of thought. I *could* tell them I know, with absolute certainty, what happened on the mysterious voyage of the Scripps *Explorer*. Then I could tease the true story beforehand. I'm sure this would get the press there in droves."

"But you aren't sure if that's what you want?" guessed Hall.

"Very good. Under the circumstances, a very modest, low-key press conference might be the better choice. So I won't get swarmed and tied down. So I can make a quick exit and wait for the world to digest things. So I think I'll just tease this to a select few journalists, who will end up thinking they've won the lottery. Believe me, within hours of the press conference finishing, this will be the number one news story in every country in the world."

"And you plan to reveal everything you have on Gray?" asked Megan. "No matter how bad it makes your company look?"

"That's right," said Fyfe. "We'll tell the world about the *Explorer* and apologize for Gray's heinous acts. After this, the press conference and Theia Labs will be in a tailspin. That's when we'll announce Nick is alive and show a video statement from him, which should begin to pull our propeller back up."

He turned to Hall. "Nick, as soon as possible, I need you to tape a brief statement and a demonstration of your implants. Both with respect to web surfing and your view of the technology's use for blindness and deafness."

"Tape a statement?" said Megan. "Wouldn't this be more effective if Nick was at the press conference in person?"

"Yes," replied Fyfe. "But we can't risk him traveling across the country and making a personal appearance while this Delamater is still out there. And I can't have him fielding questions. I've already mentioned how pissed off the FBI will be by all of this. If the public got to question him before they did, this would rub salt in the wound. They'd take pissed off to a new level."

"What's the point of demonstrating the web surfing aspect of the implants?" asked Hall. "Why create buzz for a technology that can't possibly ever see the light of day?"

"Why not?" snapped Fyfe. "Because of how it was obtained?"

"That's one of the reasons, yes."

"Let me worry about what becomes of this technology," said Fyfe, with a can-anyone-really-be-this-naive expression. "Just give the best demonstration you can. Visual, auditory, and thought-controlled Internet connection."

"So when this all settles out, you really think you can market the Internet aspect of this technology?" said Hall skeptically.

Fyfe answered in the same way he had answered Altschuler earlier. No technology had ever been more tainted, but it was too important and useful not to be adopted. "You can't stop progress," finished Fyfe. "Not the kind of progress this represents."

"I hate to rain on the parade," said Hall. "But I don't think it will ever get approved. For reasons beyond how it was obtained. The visual and auditory aspect, yes, for blindness and deafness. But not for a personal, thought-driven Internet. At least not in the US. Not when the government thinks through all the implications."

From the looks on the faces of Cameron Fyfe and Alex Altschuler, it was clear they had no idea what he was talking about.

"I don't get it, Nick," said Altschuler. "You've been *raving* about the technology. You've said it works flawlessly, and is profoundly useful. You said you're already having trouble imagining life without it."

"I am. And that's the *point*. That's the very thing that makes it too dangerous for widespread use. It's absolutely, one thousand percent addictive. Think of how many people are addicted to their cell phones.

Who can't carry on a conversation at dinner without checking it every ten seconds. Think of those *already* addicted to the Internet. The *old style* Internet. And online virtual worlds, like *Second Life*, and role playing games like *World of Warcraft*, *Sim City*, *Guild Wars*, and the like, which are growing in popularity every year."

He had become so facile at using his internal Internet connection that the exact figures for the growth of this demographic hovered in view of his mind's eye, but he ignored them.

Hall took a deep breath and pressed forward. "A scary and ever-growing number of players are becoming so addicted they live more of their lives in the virtual world than the real. And the technology in my head makes this a *hundred* times worse. It's totally immersive. People will become so addicted they won't leave their beds for days at a time. The technology works *too* well. You'd have better luck asking the government to approve widespread use of LSD."

Altschuler looked highly troubled by the picture Hall had painted. Fyfe, on the other hand, looked almost amused.

"And just to make one final point," continued Hall. "Any idea how many traffic accidents immersive web surfing will cause? How many annual fatalities?" He paused. "Ten thousand? Five hundred thousand? Five *million*?"

Fyfe shook his head condescendingly. "Nick, you make some good points. But let me tell you, an army couldn't keep this out of the hands—minds—of the public. The government will talk about addiction. And about safety. They'll wring their hands. But it will go forward. Do you know how many car accidents have been caused by cell phones? Do you have any idea?"

Hall effortlessly queried cyberspace and the answer hovered in his view. In 2010, years before hands-free cell phones in cars were mandated in all fifty states, it was estimated that more than twenty percent of the nation's annual accidents were cell phone related, which amounted to roughly one and a half million. And after cell phone use in cars was restricted, this number of accidents was actually thought to have stayed the same, or even to have increased.

"No," said Hall, not seeing the need to quote these statistics. "How many?"

"I don't know for sure," said Fyfe. "But a lot. A hell of a lot. But Americans are fully prepared to overlook dangers, and even clear evidence and proof of fatalities, to have their tech toys. The government will just make a law like they did with cell phones. You know, you must have your hands free and no texting. Who cares if you know for sure that many millions will ignore the law, and thousands will die each year because of it. Same thing with this. The danger of addiction and traffic fatalities will be gladly overlooked and accepted. Cell phones still cause numerous deaths, but nobody has the nerve and audacity to suggest we stop using them."

No one spoke for several long seconds.

Megan Emerson finally broke the silence. "Sorry, Nick," she said softly. "But I think Cameron's right."

"I *know* I'm right," said Fyfe.

"There are other issues," said Hall. "Privacy issues. Porn issues."

Altschuler couldn't help but laugh as his agile mind considered the porn angle. "It would certainly shake things up in the world of sex, all right. In the old days, if you were bored with your partner, you had to *imagine* you were with someone else. These implants would allow you to actually 'see' someone else—no imagination required. Even if your actual eyes were open and focused on your partner, you could choose to view a porn film in your mind's eye instead."

"Yeah, brave new world," said Fyfe in disgust.

"Sex isn't even the real issue here," said Hall. "The real issue is that I don't see any problem with reversing direction, so that you can convert anything you see or hear into video and audio. So everyone becomes a perfect spy. Every human interaction is potentially recorded. Two people never can be certain of absolute privacy. The consequences of this are *incomprehensible*."

Altschuler nodded thoughtfully. "The cloud could become a repository of every word ever spoken in the presence of someone else." He shuddered. "It does have a Big Brother vibe to it," he said grimly. "And just to bring it back to sex for a moment," he added. "Sleep with a girl, and nothing can stop you from 'filming' the act with your eyes, and posting videos of the entire encounter online before you've even finished."

"*Now he tells me,*" Megan shot telepathically to Hall. "*I'm not about to see a YouTube video labeled, 'How to be intimate with an injured Neanderthal girl,' am I, Nick?'*"

Hall laughed.

"Do you find the idea of invading a woman's privacy amusing, Nick?" asked Fyfe.

"No. I was laughing at another thought I had," replied Hall.

Fyfe stared at him a few seconds longer and then continued. "My point stands no matter what argument you make. This is progress. This is an invention that is as big a leap forward as the fire, the wheel, and electricity. And it will *not* be denied. Society will adjust—or turn their backs on any unpleasant side effects. Maybe they'll make it an imprisonable offense to post images of others taken without their knowledge or consent. Who knows? Expert systems are getting smarter all the time. Maybe the Internet itself will police this kind of behavior."

"Oh yeah, *that* makes me comfortable," said Hall sarcastically. "Let's turn cyberspace into Skynet."

"Skynet?" said Fyfe, raising his eyebrows.

"You've never seen the Terminator movies?"

Cameron Fyfe shook his head no, and Hall decided not to elaborate.

"Look . . . Nick," continued Fyfe. "Adjustments will certainly have to be made. And who knows. You may be right," he added in a way that suggested he didn't believe this for an instant. "But once we've had our press conference and the investigation is wrapped up, it'll be out of our hands. Society will either accept this technology, tainted and potentially dangerous though it may be, or it won't. Simple as that."

Hall nodded. Fyfe's arguments were better than his own. If he was forced to bet who would end up being right, it was the jaded, street savvy investor for sure.

"Either way," continued Fyfe. "There is one thing I'm certain of. As the first man to ever use this particular technology, voluntarily or not, you're about to become a key figure in history."

35

"So Hall has ESP," said Colonel Justin Girdler to his second-in-command. "But can it be beaten? Any chance someone who knew Hall was out there could find a way to mask their thoughts? Mask their intent?" He paused for a moment in thought. "You know, like thinking about your tax return while having sex," he added, with just a hint of a smile.

Girdler hadn't needed to resort to this strategy for decades, but almost all young men in their prime had used it at one time or another. If a nineteen-year-old male having sex allowed his mind to become fully consumed by the experience, he would find it to be very short-lived. Embarrassingly so. The only way to beat a hair-trigger response was to think of *anything* but the allure of your partner and what you were doing: baseball, math problems, grocery lists, and in extreme cases, images that were sexually repulsive. At certain times, if you wanted to last more than a few minutes, it was the only way.

"It's been too long since that was necessary," said Campbell in amusement. "But I get what you're saying. Could the man we send to kill Hall do his job by rote? While forcing himself to concentrate on his favorite cars, favorite movies, whatever?"

"Exactly."

"I don't see this as viable," replied Campbell after a few seconds of silence. "First, we'd have to tell whomever we send about Hall's ability. You can't just ask someone to kill Hall by habit, while trying their damnedest not to focus on what they're doing, without telling them *why*. And even if you did, it wouldn't work. Remember the guy at the warehouse that Hall read, Billie Peterson? Hall could read far more than just what Peterson was thinking at the time. He has *perfect* ESP. He'd be able to cut through any deceptive surface thoughts to our man's underlying intent with ease."

"Both excellent points," conceded Girdler. He was annoyed with himself. He knew the implications of Hall's deep ESP far too well to have raised such an obviously flawed idea. He had little patience for stupidity, especially when this stupidity was his own.

The colonel pursed his lips in thought, searching for another angle of attack. "So Hall estimates his ability has a range of about six miles," he continued. "But thousands and thousands of people could be within that kind of range. And he can't read them *all*. Right? So if we were five miles away, it isn't likely he'd have any idea we were important to read."

"Which would suggest we could take him out with a sniper at long range. He'd never know to read the mind of the sniper. No way to see it coming."

"Maybe. God only knows neither of us has any clue how this works. But we do know a very impressive and capable group of people are trying to kill him—who may well know about his ability by now—and he's still alive. And some of *them* aren't. So I wouldn't bank on him missing the mind of the sniper." He paused. "But it isn't a bad idea to try out if we can't come up with anything better."

"What about taking him out with a missile or a drone strike?" said the major. "We just make sure we're more than six miles away when we pull the trigger."

"I see two problems. First, six miles was just his guesstimate. We should assume twelve in our thinking to be on the safe side. That's assuming his range hasn't increased as he's learning to use this new ability."

Campbell shrugged. "Well, even if it has, this just increases the number of minds that are thrown at him. Which makes finding ours even more of a needle-in-a-haystack problem for him."

"That's a good point as well."

"So what's the second problem?"

"Presuming we find him in mainland USA," replied Girdler, "this isn't something I'm prepared to authorize. Yet. Unless we find him hiding out in an massive cornfield somewhere in Indiana. Regardless, it'll be awfully hard to convince Sobol that we were trying to capture him alive as ordered, when we blow him off the face of the earth with a drone or a missile."

Campbell frowned. "There is that," he conceded. After further thought, he added, "Okay, so the two of us can't get near this guy without him reading our intent. And anyone sent to kill him can't get near him either. Either he can magically sense when he's in danger, or the closer they get the more likely he reads them coming. Either way, you make a great point about the failures of the other group trying to kill him."

Girdler's jaw tightened at being reminded, yet again, of the group of psychopathic assholes with whom they were now allied, at least with respect to their mutual interest in seeing Nick Hall dead. If the murder of twenty-six human beings wasn't enough to ensure Girdler wouldn't rest until he had these men's heads on a spike, the fact that they were forcing him to target an innocent man heightened his rage even more.

"So our only option is to play our own people," said Campbell.

"You mean *play* as in *mislead?*"

"Yes."

"I agree. Given we're disobeying direct orders, we'd need to do that anyway. But I get where you're going with this. Since Hall will read the minds of whomever we send, we should make sure they think we're after him to pin a good citizenship medal on his shirt."

Campbell was about to reply when his computer PDA came to life. "*Major Campbell,*" said the soft, feminine voice. "*You asked me to alert you if significant new information was discovered on the Hall case. Please check your incoming messages.*"

Campbell checked his computer and his face brightened.

"Did we find him?" asked Girdler.

"Not yet," said the major. "But we have picked up his trail again," he added enthusiastically. "We forgot to tell Adams to stop checking footage near the area where the cab dropped them. Good thing. A camera in a nearby Vons spotted Nick Hall and Megan Emerson buying a few hats and sunglasses."

Campbell threw the footage on the big screen in the room. The store cameras were pointing down at an aisle which included a vertical sunglass rack, which could be rotated around to access sunglasses on all four of its sides.

Megan Emerson slowly turned the rack, stopping when she found the most oversized pair of women's sunglasses they had. She put them on, looked into the tiny mirror at the top of the display, and shook her head, obviously knowing how bad they looked on her. Hall laughed, leaned forward, and kissed her warmly on the lips; a kiss that was returned—with *interest*. Their body language suggested this wasn't the first time.

"You've really got to hand it to this guy," said Girdler dryly. "He's running for his life and he still manages to score with a girl he picks up along the way."

"Well, sure," said Campbell. "But he has an unfair advantage. When you can read a girl's mind, you always know the right thing to say."

Girdler laughed. "I don't know," he said. "I'm convinced I wouldn't be able to understand any woman. Even if I *did* know her every thought." The colonel's brief smile vanished. "When was this taken?"

The major checked the time stamp on his computer. "Shit! Five minutes ago," he said excitedly.

"Incredible! I can't believe they're still in Bakersfield."

"Me either."

Campbell checked some notes on his monitor. "Unfortunately, the cameras lost them when they left the store. Adams is checking other cameras in the area, but we'll still need some luck to find them."

Girdler picked up a phone and began barking orders, deploying a number of human resources in the area to descend on this particular Vons. He instructed them to look for people who might have seen Hall and Emerson, inside the store and out—especially anyone who might have seen the couple enter a car in the lot. He also made sure all video footage from all cameras anywhere nearby would be channeled through Nessie.

When he was through, he rose from his chair and turned to his second-in-command. "I'm going to scramble a jet and accelerate my travel plans. It's your baby until I land. You're a better field manager than I am anyway. Make sure it counts. We may not get another chance this good for a long time."

Campbell nodded grimly.

"Call me with updates when I'm in the air. And I'd like to keep brainstorming on ways to kill Hall when we find him."

Girdler looked at his watch and did a quick calculation. "I should be wheels down at Edwards in two hours," he said. "Have a helo waiting to take me to Bakersfield the second it lands—or within fifteen miles of Hall and Emerson if they've been located, wherever they are."

"Roger that," said Campbell.

36

With the conference call finished, Hall asked Altschuler if he could have some time alone with Megan. The bespectacled computer scientist was happy to oblige, offering to bring in Chinese for dinner, and even though Hall and Megan had both had a sandwich before they had set out for Fresno, they hadn't eaten much all day and welcomed the prospect of having the suite to themselves.

Altschuler studied the two of them before he left. They weren't touching, but Hall could read in the scientist's mind that their body language was still somehow giving them away. Altschuler had already come to suspect they had become more than just two people thrown together by fate, fighting for their lives. They had become friends. *More* than friends . . .

Hall read that Altschuler was wondering if he had asked for time alone with Megan just to get laid. Under normal circumstances, the computer scientist was thinking, he couldn't blame Hall for this. Altschuler was as horny as the next guy, and Megan Emerson was cute. But there was a lot going on here, so it would have been nice if Nick Hall could manage to keep it in his pants a while longer.

The possibility of barging in on them in the middle of this activity wasn't something Altschuler was relishing either. "Um, the Chinese place is close by," he said, "and they're fast. So I'll be back real soon," he added, hoping this would ensure they kept their clothes on. "I'm guessing twenty minutes."

"Thanks, Alex," said Hall. He wished there was a graceful way to reassure the man that they were only going to be talking while he was gone. At least for the most part.

The moment Alex left, Hall drew Megan into his arms. He could now remember his past, baseline behavior, and the level of affection he typically required, and knew that his current need was many times greater than normal. He wasn't sure if their ordeal had caused this, or if this was the Megan Emerson effect—or a little of both. But there was no doubt that his lips sought Megan's out as eagerly as if he were still in high school.

He motioned for her to sit on a kitchen chair while he jumped up and sat across from her on a stretch of the tan granite island in the middle of the suite's kitchen.

Hall began by telling her the good news. He hadn't mentioned it earlier, but he had been making more of a concerted effort to identify others he couldn't read. This required sighting hundreds of people and carefully trying to read each one, matching a visual identification with a mental one. Once inside Vons, and twice during the drive to Fresno, he had seen someone with his eyes who he couldn't *see* with this mind. Two men and a woman. It was an encouraging development to verify that Megan wasn't the only one. He had known in his heart this would have to be the case, but it was a relief to at least know there were others out there with whom he could have a normal relationship. Well, normal-ish.

Megan was thrilled by the news, and even resisted making another Neanderthal joke.

With this out of the way, Hall knew it was time to broach more difficult topics. There was no easy way for him to tell her what she needed to know, so he just did. He told her that his ordeal had changed his perspective, had allowed him to assess his previous personality and behavior almost as an outsider. To see himself as others might see him. And he wasn't thrilled with what he saw. He described his past arrogance, superficiality, and selfishness, and vowed to do everything in his power to stay changed forever.

Megan wasn't the least bit concerned. "All I know is the Nick Hall I've seen since you barged into my office. You're being too hard on yourself. Anyone who had an out-of-body experience, who could view their past from above like you've been able to do, would find things about themselves that needed improving. And everyone changes and grows from their experiences. But I know that your essence didn't change."

Hall considered. "Well, I'd like to think I was a decent enough person, despite my flaws—at least at my core."

"I'm *sure* you were, Nick. We all have lots of different facets. I don't want to get all philosophical on you, but we're different people in different situations and around different companions. We're all shaped by genes and events. Not entirely. And not to use this to excuse bad behavior. But it's true. So much is a matter of perspective." She paused. "Did you ever see the play, *Wicked*?"

Hall nodded. "Yes. My parents took me to see it on Broadway when I was a teenager."

"Me too!" said Megan excitedly. "What a great show. The musical numbers were *incredible*."

Hall smiled. "I'm not much of a Broadway musical kind of guy, but even I have to agree with that."

"The reason I bring it up is that seeing it really changed the way I look at things. Things often aren't black and white. Or are black when viewed from one angle, and totally white from another. The genius of the play is that it takes a classic story we all grew up with, *The Wizard of Oz*, and instead of telling it from Dorothy's perspective, retells it from Elphaba's perspective—the Wicked Witch of the West. And everything changes. Not that it's always the case, but this demonstrates one case in which there are hidden motivations, things that we weren't aware of that change *everything*. Elphaba wasn't wicked at all. She was painted this way by the *real* villains. She never really planned to hurt Dorothy—she just needed to make it look that way. People and situations can be multi-faceted, and a lot can depend on which facet you happen to be looking at."

Hall nodded, considering her words carefully. Megan Emerson continued to surprise him. She thought in ways he had never encountered before. She was fun and playful, but she had a depth to her that wasn't immediately apparent. Which he guessed spoke to her exact point.

"You're absolutely right," he said simply.

"You talked about the cocktail party effect," continued Megan. "Maybe we should call this the *wicked effect*. And it applies to *us* right now more than anyone. Look at the crazy situations we're finding ourselves in. With life-and-death decisions to make, involving revolutionary technologies and abilities. And then consider the paramedic, Hector Garcia. Tell the story of your encounter with him from *his* point of view, and Nick Hall is a dangerous, gun-wielding mutant—possibly from outer space—and a thief. From my point of view, you're a gentleman and a hero. You risked your life to save mine. And you would never have carried out your threats against them no matter what the circumstances."

She stood up, rose to her full height, and leaned against the edge of the granite counter on which he was sitting. Their faces were now approximately at the same level.

"So I'm sure you've done some annoying things in your life. I'm sure you aren't proud of some of them. But give yourself a break. There's more to most of us than meets the eye. And it's who you are now that counts the most." She sighed. "Besides, this gives us something else we have in common."

Hall raised his eyebrows questioningly.

"I haven't been very happy with myself recently, either. The move from LA was hard. I've become moody and not very fun. And I've been drinking too much."

"You haven't had a drink since I've known you," said Hall. "And the Glandons had a well-stocked bar."

"Believe me, I *know*. Don't think I wasn't tempted. Very tempted. But I knew I had to get back to my roots, find myself. And this experience is the perfect opportunity to do so. So I'm all for taking each other the way we *find* each other. We can learn from our past mistakes. But we're not allowed to ruin *the now* by beating ourselves up over *the then*."

"Very deep," said Hall. "I mean that," he hastened to add, realizing this might have come across as patronizing or sarcastic otherwise. "And in a good way,"

Megan leaned in as if to initiate a kiss, but Hall pulled back. He had vowed to tear off the band-aid that was Alicia Green quickly, even knowing it would pull dozens of hairs up by the roots when he did.

"There's one other thing you need to know," he said wearily. His expression suggested he had just swallowed poison. "Before I joined the *Explorer* expedition, I was engaged to be married."

This time it was Megan who backed away. She lowered her eyes and didn't reply.

Hall felt as if the world were suddenly moving in slow motion, with minutes passing between each new beat of his heart. But he had to stay silent now, as difficult as this was for him to do, and let her process this new information.

Finally, after five or six seconds that seemed like an eternity, Megan lifted her head and met his gaze once again. "Look," she said softly, trying to keep the hurt from her voice and failing. "You get involved with a man with no past and you take your chances. You did warn me. And we've only known each other a few days. So . . . congratulations. I'm happy for you."

"That's just it," he said. "*I'm* not happy for me."

He went on to passionately explain how he was feeling, how he had changed. And that even before the *Explorer* expedition, he had been coming to the realization that he and Alicia weren't in love. Not really. He had continued to fool himself, but he doubted he would have done so long enough to actually walk down the aisle. He had proposed more as a reaction to his parents' deaths than anything else. He and Alicia had both been superficial, getting married for the wrong reasons.

No matter what happened from here on out, Hall assured her he was going to break it off with Alicia. He had no idea what the future would hold, but being with Megan had already shown him he had set the bar too low. That a girl could be more fun to be around than he had known. That discussions could be more lively and engaging. Besides, he wasn't sure if he even believed in the concept of marriage anymore.

"Funny, a few days ago I was thinking the exact same thing," said Megan. "But I didn't believe in ESP then, either—so things can change. I'm not saying they have, by the way—I'm just saying they *can*."

She paused. "Are you sure about your feelings for Alicia? Sure that when the circumstances change and you get your life back, everything since the dumpster won't all seem like a bad dream?"

Hall shook his head. "No, my past before I met *you* was more the bad dream. My current feelings aren't going to change."

He was sure of this, but also concerned. He felt more vulnerable now than at any time in his life. Megan was one of the few people impervious to his psi ability with whom he *could* have a relationship. He continued to feel dependent on her, and this was worrisome. The more irreplaceable and important a person was in one's life, he supposed, the more vulnerable and afraid one became of losing them.

And Megan was as irreplaceable as it got.

But as he thought about it, he was forced to admit to himself that her importance had nothing to do with her being one of the few who wouldn't see him as a leper. Even if every woman on earth were throwing themselves at him, he couldn't imagine wanting to be with anyone else. It was time to admit that his feelings for Megan would be the same, regardless of the presence or absence of the ESP curse that Kelvin Gray's experiments had brought into his life.

There was something about this last thought that troubled him. Something about Gray's experiments. What was it?

He slapped the palm of his hand hard on his forehead as he realized what it was.

"What?" said Megan, tilting her head in confusion.

"I've been such an idiot," he said. "We need to change our strategy. And we need to do it immediately."

37

Megan scratched her head and reseated herself at the kitchen chair facing him. "What strategy?"

"We can't keep my psi ability secret anymore."

"Why not? I thought your reasoning made a lot of sense."

"It did. But it doesn't anymore. First, and believe it or not, least important at the moment, I need to get rid of this curse. I'm not going to do that alone. Alex may not have been responsible for these implants, but he's one of the top electronics and computer experts in the world, and he knows these systems. He could remove them. Or find some other way to kill off my psi ability."

Megan considered. "That makes sense. And the most important reason to keep this secret was for our safety. But once the press conference is over, and the story is out there, no one will have any reason to kill us anymore."

"I'm afraid we have to tell him immediately," said Hall.

Megan blinked in confusion. "I know you're eager to lose the ESP, Nick. But we're still probably targets. And your ability could save our lives. Why so urgent all of a sudden?"

"Because I've been short-sighted and naive. When I agreed to come to Fresno with Alex, I somehow convinced myself the web surfing technology would never get approved."

"I know," said Megan. "And I thought the arguments you raised with Fyfe were good ones."

"But you've already said you thought his were better."

Megan winced. "On paper, yours are better. But he does know mob psychology and that people would sell their own mothers for the latest gadget. He's cynical, but I'm sure he's also right."

"I'm sure he is, too. That's the problem. The plan is to go public with all of this Tuesday morning. Have me shoot a demo of the technology. But here's the thing. What if the exact placement of my implants is entirely responsible for my ESP? What if this ability is a simple side effect? I'd be bringing about the very disaster I wanted to prevent. Bringing the implant technology to the attention of the public would be like opening Pandora's Box. The internal Internet we can and will adjust to. But if this brings ESP along for the ride . . ."

Megan frowned deeply. "Yeah. That is a big problem."

"So I'll confide in Alex, and *only* in Alex. Immediately. Make him understand the magnitude of the issue. You know I've rooted around in his mind and I've come to trust him completely. He's not perfect, but he's a good man in general. Well-meaning. And he can keep a secret. Especially one this important."

"I'm sure you're right. And you've proven to be a great judge of character. At least when it comes to women," she added with a broad smile. Then her smile vanished and she couldn't help but mumble under her breath, "At least your *recent* judgment."

Hall hoisted himself off the granite counter and reached out for Megan's hand to pull her up from the chair and into his arms, when there was a tentative knock at the door.

Hall smiled. He had read that Altschuler was coming for a while now, and that even though the scientist had a keycard of his own, he wasn't about to throw the door open without warning.

Hall helped Megan up from the chair, but decided he shouldn't be holding her when Altschuler came through the door.

"Come in, Alex," said Hall loudly.

Turning to Megan, he added telepathically, "*Well, here goes nothing. This should be . . . interesting.*"

38

Vasily Chirkhoff stared into the pale blue eyes of the girl seated across from him at the elegant La Gastronomie Restaurant and Wine Cellar. She was stunning, with a body to match. Also exceedingly pricey. But you got what you paid for, and she was the ultimate provider of what was called in the business, the *girlfriend experience.*

The restaurant was French and five-star, with white satin tablecloths, elaborate chandeliers, and huge, baroque oil paintings in equally baroque frames. If not for the tables, it could have been a room in the Louvre. But Vasily's philosophy was that when one was spending this much on a companion, one shouldn't cut corners on dining. And the Russian had money to spare.

The waiter came over to take their order. Vasily ordered the 1998 Gaja Barbaresco, which cost three hundred dollars a glass, one for him and one for the girl, who called herself Jasmine. He loved the name as much as he loved everything else about this exquisite creature, who was unsurpassed with her mouth, but who wasn't shy about begging him to take advantage of her two other ports of entry as well.

"It's an Italian vintage," explained Vasily to the girl. "Piedmont, to be precise. From the winery of Angelo Gaja." He smiled. "You will love this," he added. "Guaranteed."

"I love *everything* you give me, Vasily," she said with a sly smile.

They had each finished half a glass when their salad course arrived, and Jasmine told Vasily that it was the best wine she'd ever had. The one problem with call girls, he knew, was that they tended to tell you what you wanted to hear. So even if she thought it tasted like piss—which she probably had actually tasted, come to think of it, while entertaining men who were into that sort of thing—she would tell him just what she had. But in this case, he tended to believe it was true. The Gaja Barbaresco was just *that* good.

Vasily's phone vibrated in the middle of a mouthful of his lamb salad, which contained wilted spinach, warm pommery mustard vinaigrette dressing, feta cheese, and pine nuts. He frowned. He was old school about answering his phone during dinner. He wanted to soak in the taste and texture of the meal, its presentation, and the God-created, immaculate sculpture sitting across from him. Still, he glanced down to see who was calling.

His frown deepened. It was John Delamater, his principle benefactor, and the only person he would allow to interrupt the ambiance he had created for himself. Vasily hadn't heard from Delamater since the man had changed plans and called Vasily off the hunt for Nick Hall.

"I'm so sorry, my dear," Vasily said to his companion, "but I need to take this."

Jasmine smiled serenely. "Of course," she said.

He turned away from her and answered. "Yes?"

"Vasily. Sorry to disturb you. But I wanted to thank you for your two years of service. You have been quite competent and dependable, and I have appreciated that."

Vasily's heart constricted. Delamater was ruthless and wasn't the type to call with a random thank you. It sounded as though he was being fired. But Delamater wasn't the type to *fire* people, either. His personnel changes were far more. . . permanent.

Vasily lowered the phone and took a quick survey of the room, but didn't see anything suspicious. On the other hand, his quick survey had taken a few seconds longer than it should have.

He looked across at Jasmine, whose eyes were becoming droopy, and he knew: Delamater had managed to slip something into the wine. He was always on guard when visiting with Delamater, knowing this day would come, but the chess grandmaster had easily bested him, not caring in the least that Vasily's call girl companion would inevitably become collateral damage.

Vasily cursed himself. He had become predictable. His tastes in women, restaurants, and wine too easy to exploit. And now he would pay for this with his life.

"I planned a fail-safe if you tried to kill me, John. Photos and video of you that will be released to authorities upon my death. Believe it. So there had better be an antidote," he threatened as lethargy began seeping into his bones. "Or your precious identity is blown."

"Yes, Vasily, I've known about your fail-safe for some time now. But rest easy. It's been thoroughly disarmed. Nothing will be released."

His calm tone made Vasily certain he was telling the truth. Which meant Vasily had miscalculated twice. He had always believed Delamater would end his employment face-to-face. That he was so psychopathic he would want to kill Vasily with his own hand, savoring the moment when the Russian was facing a gun, knowing he had only seconds to live. That was when Vasily planned to reveal his insurance policy. His ability to expose an identity Delamater held so dear. But Delamater had easily outmaneuvered him.

A feeling of total contentment settled over Vasily as he continued to drift into a stupor. It was a measure of the regard Delamater held him in, he knew, to have chosen a drug that would lead him to his death gently rather than in agony, as many other choices could have done.

"Why?" asked Vasily.

"It was necessary," replied Delamater. "I only wish this weren't the case."

Jasmine had already fallen forward onto her half-eaten Hearts of Romaine salad and several waiters were rushing over to check on her condition. Vasily ignored them. "I'll be waiting for you in hell, you *bastard*," he said. "And I'll take my revenge across all eternity." He had tried to put some venom into this with the last of his energy, but the words came out soft and dreamy.

"Very poetic," said Delamater. "But I'm afraid I'm destined for the other place."

Vasily tried to respond, but his tongue was now too thick, and he collapsed onto the table as had Jasmine before him, unable to hear the gasps and confusion erupting in his favorite restaurant.

39

Alex Altschuler entered the suite with a sack full of cardboard boxes filled with steaming cuisine.

They spread the boxes on the small kitchen table, stuck spoons in each, and passed around the heavy beige plates they found in a cabinet. Soon they each had a pile of rice covered with multiple chicken and beef dishes. Hall allowed Altschuler to finish half of his plate before he decided not to delay getting to the point any longer.

While Altschuler continued to eat, Hall told him he wanted to reveal something important, and swore him to absolute secrecy. He would be able to tell no one, including Fyfe or Cowan. *No one.* If Altschuler thought that might be a problem, he needed to tell them now.

The bespectacled scientist was perplexed and a bit wary, but he said he would keep it a secret. Hall read from his mind he was absolutely sincere in this, as he had expected.

While Altschuler and Megan finished their meals, Hall explained how he had come to realize he could read minds, and provided additional background information. Altschuler was skeptical and taken aback, as anyone would be, but not after Hall provided an unimpeachable demonstration of the effect.

"Holy shit!" said Altschuler after the demonstration. "Holy mother of God. I wouldn't have been this shocked if aliens had flown out of your ass." But as he thought about it a moment longer, he decided it wasn't as impossible as it had first seemed. After all, hadn't Gray managed, with Altschuler's unknowing help, to get Hall's *implants* to pick up his thoughts? Wasn't this a form of mind reading? And as part of their functioning, the implants needed to amplify electrical impulses coming from parts of Hall's brain. Could this amplification have been responsible?

"Let me explain why I told you about this," said Hall. "Mind reading turns out to be a curse."

"Really? It seems like it would be awesome," said Altschuler with the enthusiasm of a geek being told the next installment of his favorite comic book had arrived.

"That's only because you haven't spent even a second thinking about it," said Hall. "When you do, you're going to be very uncomfortable being anywhere near me. Although," he hastened to point out, "I promise not to root around your mind for anything embarrassing. Or anything that would expose any vulnerabilities."

Altschuler swallowed hard. Holy Hell! Hall was *right*. His head was packed with thoughts and memories of which he wasn't particularly proud. He thought about some of the pornography that appealed to him and shuddered. And there was far more. Ugly thoughts. Ugly deeds. Thoughts and actions he had regretted. Insecurities in areas he would never want exposed.

A sick expression came over his face. "Can you turn it off?" he asked

"No. But I can turn it down. And I can choose what thoughts I focus on, and whose mind I mine for information. I'm trying to stay out of your thoughts," Hall tried to reassure him once again, "but there isn't a human alive who won't grasp the horror of having their every secret and private thought violated."

Hall raised his eyebrows. "But maybe you think it's only horrific to have *your* mind read. Maybe you think being on the other side of the equation, being the one *doing* the reading, would be great fun. If so, think again. First, the chatter never ends. Second, people tend to be judgmental and unkind. Even people who like you. Even women I pass who think I'm reasonably attractive are often critical about some aspect of my appearance."

Altschuler grimaced. Hall was far closer to the standard of male handsomeness than he was. He wondered how many people he passed in malls thought the word *geek*, or *loser*, or *ugly* as he walked by. He was already self-conscious. What would a week with ESP do to him? He'd probably never leave his house again. Would he then decide to lash out at society?

The computer scientist's mouth fell open as he had a sudden realization. Then his jaw tightened and he glared at Hall. "You've promised not to invade my mind. *Now.* But you already have, haven't you?"

Hall remained silent, but his guilty expression said it all.

"So *that's* what the visit to the grocery store was about. While I was hovering over a bunch of egg cartons you were roto-rooting my brain. That's when you decided you could trust me. Because you *knew* you could trust me."

"That's right," said Hall softly. "And why I know I can trust you now. You're a good man. With far more integrity than most."

Altschuler was glad to learn of Hall's high opinion of his integrity, but he still felt violated. And Hall was right, he did want to get away from him as quickly as he could. It was a visceral reaction that was very strong, and standing his ground took some real will power. He wondered how Megan Emerson had managed it for so long. Not only managed to stay in the same room with Hall, but, he had no doubt, to get far closer even than this.

Hall went on to describe the six-to-ten-mile range of his ability, how certain thoughts could pierce through the noise, due to their intrinsic nature or to the cocktail party effect, and how he could choose to focus on the thoughts of single individuals and separate them out.

Hall and Megan then made many of the points they had discussed with each other over lunch. Points about society and the catastrophic nature of ESP if unleashed.

But Altschuler needed no convincing. His mind was so agile, he was often way ahead of them.

"So why confide in me about this?" he said when they had finished.

Hall sighed. "I need your help."

"To turn off your ESP?" guessed Altschuler.

"Yes," said Hall. "But also for something even more urgent. What if my ESP is a side effect of the implant technology?"

"This has occurred to me also," said Altschuler. "And it *is* possible."

"If this turns out to be the case, there's no way Theia can go forward with this technology. Which would mean canceling Tuesday's press conference and burying the technology."

Altschuler frowned. Of course! Hall was absolutely *right*. "Are you willing to confide in Cameron Fyfe?" he asked.

"No. Not yet."

"Then this will be a problem. Without him knowing why, there's no way we can convince Cameron to call off the press conference. Let alone to bury the technology."

"I realize that," said Hall. "But now that *you* know, we have three minds working on the problem. Four if you count yours twice," he added with a wry smile. "So let's think this through for a few minutes."

"Okay," said Altschuler. He paused for several seconds. "First and least important—for now—is killing your psi ability. There are a number of things that could be tried, but there are no guarantees that it can be shut down without doing irreparable damage."

"Wouldn't removing the implants do it?" asked Hall. "Almost for sure?"

"Maybe. Maybe not. There are two likely possibilities. Perhaps the precise, to-the-micron placement of the four implants triggers this, and will do so in everyone. But even if this is the case, removing them would be dangerous for you. The techniques are as non-invasive as we can make them, but your implants aren't just on the surface of your brain. These are buried deep. Placing them, and removing them, can't be done without causing some neuronal damage. The brain is quite plastic and can recover—and also compensate—but I've seen your file, Nick. Kelvin Gray repositioned the implants dozens of times trying to find the right configuration. He did the same with twenty-six others until their brains were so chewed up they turned into vegetables or died."

"So you're saying Nick's brain can't take any more abuse," said Megan.

"I wouldn't risk it. Along with the physical abuse, he was given a steady diet of Erase 190 to further muck with his brain chemistry.

Even the minor damage incurred by removal of his implants at this point could be the straw that broke the camel's back."

"But you said there are other things you could try," said Megan hopefully.

Altschuler nodded. He opened his mouth to speak, but Hall cut him off.

"You said there were two likely possibilities as to how I developed ESP. The first is the exact placement of the implants. What's the second?"

"That the merry path the implants took through your brain was cumulatively responsible. It could be one-in-a-million coincidence. If invoking ESP requires the exact recipe; the exact pathway Gray took as he repeatedly plowed through your brain; the exact level of electrical output; the exact level of neuronal damage done as a result; the exact length of time they were at any given position, and so on, it might never be replicated in anyone."

"Or it might require the exact pathway, but with length of time and these other factors not being critical, correct?" said Megan. "More open to minor variations. So, difficult to achieve, but not impossible."

"Correct," replied Altschuler. "We're in uncharted territory. Anything is possible."

"Did Gray keep accurate records?" said Megan.

"Yes. Say what you want about him, but he was a brilliant scientist."

"We need to delete them from his computer," said Hall. "Can you do that?"

Altschuler thought about this. "Yes," he said. "But we should keep a copy for our own use. It would help us unravel what happened to you, and make sure it never happens again. And it may lead us to a way to reverse your ability."

Hall thought about this for a moment and then nodded his agreement.

"What about our imminent problem?" said Megan. "The press conference?"

"If the web surfing and ESP effects of the implants are separable," said Altschuler, "we're in good shape. If not, we're screwed."

"So we have to hope that Nick's ESP is a result of months of experimentation rather than their current configuration," said Megan.

"Right," said Altschuler. "No one else being fitted for these implants will ever have them take the same path they took through Nick's brain. Now that we know the correct placement, they'd be placed there and we'd be done with it."

"So how do we find out which possibility is correct?" said Megan. "Computer simulation? Animal models?"

Altschuler frowned deeply. "No good. Not for this. We'd need to set the implants in another human subject. If he or she develops ESP, we're screwed, like I said. If he or she can surf the web, but *can't* read minds, we still can't be sure we're in the clear—not with an 'n' equal to one—but at least it will make us a *lot* more comfortable."

After a few seconds of silence, the computer scientist issued a heavy sigh. "I'll volunteer," he said.

40

Both Megan and Hall stared at Altschuler in shock.

"I'll volunteer," he repeated. "It's our only option if we want to still go forward with disclosure. Or avoid having an ugly battle with Cameron Fyfe over this."

"But even if you're only experimenting on *yourself*," said Megan, "isn't this still illegal?"

"Let's just say that, like Nick's ESP, we'd keep this our secret. The world will know about Kelvin Gray's experimentation on unwilling victims, but not about this. So if it does give me the ability to surf the web with my thoughts, as we expect, I won't let on."

Altschuler removed his glasses and began cleaning them on his shirt. For once, not because he was nervous, but because they needed cleaning.

"Now that I think about it," he continued, "this experiment is critical. And not just for the reasons we've been discussing. For all we know, Nick is unique, and the current configuration will only work on *him*. For ESP *or* the Internet. So fitting me for implants does two things. It provides a confirmation that the placement of Nick's implants, and his subsequent web surfing abilities, can be duplicated in others. And it helps us determine if ESP and web surfing are separable effects."

"If they *aren't* separable," Hall pointed out, "you'll be cursed as well. Cursed with learning what people really think about you and each other. Cursed to end up a pariah. And cursed with hearing nonstop voices in your head, and slight echoes whenever anyone speaks."

"I'm willing to take that chance," said Altschuler, slipping his glasses back on. "And it will only be temporary in my case, anyway. Since I'll have virtually no damage to my brain, it will be safe for me to reverse the implants. But I can assure you, Nick, no matter what, we'll find a way to cure you of your psionic ability."

Hall glanced at Megan, but her expression was difficult for him to read. He turned back to Altschuler. "If you did this, could we know where we stand before Tuesday morning?"

"Yes. We'd need to get started immediately and work through the night, though."

Altschuler told them about the equipment Gray had hidden in Theia's Madera facility. While the robotic device Gray had used could be programmed to place implants at precise coordinates in the brain, a human surgeon was required to make the initial incision and guide the procedure.

"How did Gray do it?" asked Megan.

"About a year ago, he spent several months getting trained to do animal surgeries in our labs. Said he wanted to be more hands-on." Altschuler frowned deeply. "I guess now we know the real reason he wanted to acquire these skills."

"So where does that leave *us*?" asked Hall.

"I have an expert in mind," said Altschuler. "A woman named Heather Zambrana. She's done animal surgeries in the pharmaceutical business for years. One of five people on our team who position implants in animal brains. I trust her more than anyone in the company. And she's single, so she won't have to hide our little cabal from a husband."

Hall could read that Altschuler had long had a romantic interest in Heather Zambrana as well, which he hadn't acted on because she reported to him. Altschuler found her shy, bright, and attractive, although he was convinced the hardcore geek in her led her to hide her physical appeal rather than spend any effort on hair, makeup, or clothing that would reveal or enhance it. Hall didn't care if he had a crush on her, as long as this didn't color his assessment of her trustworthiness. After a little more fishing in Altshculer's mind, Hall became convinced that it hadn't.

"So your recommendation is to let this Heather into our exclusive club?" said Hall.

"Yes."

"And there's no other way?" asked Megan.

Altschuler shook his head. "I'm afraid not," he replied. "But there isn't much to worry about. Not when we have a mind reader in our group. As much as I hate to suggest it, we can use Nick here to verify my opinion of her trustworthiness. We can drive by her condo and he can read her. If it turns out she's unethical, can't keep a secret, or," Altschuler added with a grin, "has always longed for the day when she could announce the existence of working ESP to the world, then we can choose someone else."

Hall laughed. "Sounds like a good plan."

"If she does pass the test, Nick, I'll need you for two other things," said Altschuler.

"Go on."

"First, you'll need to demonstrate your ESP to her. Without that, she'll never believe it."

"Very true," said Hall. "I barely believe it. And I'm the one who *has* it."

"Also, I'll want to scan your brain using the ultra-high-resolution MRI at our main facility. I need to confirm Kelvin's data as to the final positioning of your implants. Hate to find out after my procedure that he entered a wrong digit, and end up with impaired brain function."

Hall nodded soberly. This was a good point.

Hall read the computer scientist was ready to leave. Before they did, he needed to remind Altschuler of a tactical issue he had forgotten. He had already read from Altschuler's mind that he had come up with several security precautions all on his own. Cowan had been confident that Delamater had lost them after their trick with the credit card at the Bakersfield train station. But Altschuler hadn't wanted to take any chances, especially since people who entered Hall's sphere, like Megan Emerson, had also become targets.

It had been Altschuler's idea to have Cowan secure the suite, even before he had been sure he could lure Hall back to Fresno. And he had asked Cowan to rent a car, which couldn't be traced back to him, and leave it in the Homestead parking lot. With the keys inside. And there had been one other item as well.

"Alex, before we charge out of here," began Hall. "Given that we've agreed that only the three of us, and soon Heather, can know about this little operation, don't you think we should be sure to avoid our . . . neighbors."

Altschuler's face was blank for a moment, until he remembered the security next door. "*Very* good point," he said appreciatively. Then, with an accusing look, he added, "I thought you weren't going to read my mind from here on out."

"Well, I can't help reading some thoughts. I mostly meant I'd try to keep it clinical. Avoid probing for anything that might be sensitive. But the truth is I read about your ideas for security when we first got here," explained Hall.

"Does anyone want to fill me in?" said Megan.

"Sorry," said Hall. "Alex asked Ed Cowan to post a two-man security detail in the bungalow next door if we agreed to come to Fresno with him. He didn't mention it because he didn't want to freak us out."

"And they're in place now?" asked Megan.

"Yes. I read them when we arrived. They're very dangerous men. Cowan told them to watch us and make sure we aren't hurt, but that he doesn't really expect any trouble, so not to be too commando about it."

"Do you think we can get out of here without them knowing it?" asked Altschuler.

"Fairly sure," replied Hall. "I can read them to choose the timing. We'll go on my signal, through the patio. If we're on the quick and quiet side, we should be okay."

Hall paused in thought. "So after we recruit this Heather and you scan my brain, then what? We go straight to your Madera lab for the procedure?"

"Right. But no need for you come with us at that point. Assuming I can surf the web, but I can't read minds, we'll still want to have the press conference. So I'll drop you back here so you can start preparing a tight presentation we can film before Tuesday. You'll want to get across what happened to you. And figure out the most compelling way to demonstrate your miraculous web surfing capabilities. This will take some creativity."

"And what if the implants *do* give you psionic abilities?" said Hall.

"Then we destroy all the data—except where it applies to vision and hearing. And we'll never disclose the success of the program. If anyone ever suggests it was successful, we'll deny it adamantly."

"This is like being in some kind of insane, alternate reality," pointed out Megan. "I mean, *listen to you*. You're talking about the fricking cure for fricking deafness and blindness like it's a *consolation* prize." She smiled from ear to ear. "I mean, how awesome is just that? There aren't even any words for it. It'll go down in history as perhaps the greatest achievement of all time. If there wasn't any taint to the technology, they'd create a special Nobel Prize just for you, Alex. They'd rename a fricking state after Theia Labs."

Altschuler grinned. "No truer words have ever been spoken. I was thinking through these problems like they were mathematical equations. Thank you for reminding me of the human aspect to all this. We'll truly be bringing a miracle to the world, no matter what."

"So worst case," noted Megan, "Cameron Fyfe is disappointed because he can't have his entire cake and eat it too."

"You're absolutely right," said Altschuler. "If Nick comes to trust him enough to tell him why we've pulled back on the Internet aspect—assuming this even becomes necessary—that's great. But if not, who cares? He'll just have to settle for becoming one of the wealthiest and most beloved men on earth. With the data destroyed and Hall not coming forward, there won't be anything he can do about it."

41

Megan Emerson waited in the suite, idly flipping through TV channels without finding anything she could focus on, waiting to hear from Nick Hall. Finally, almost ninety minutes after they had left, he called her on his disposable cell phone, since Heather Zambrana's condo and Theia Labs were both out of range of their telepathy.

Apparently, Hall's mind reading had shown Heather to be just as trustworthy as Altschuler said she would be, and they had brought her up to speed. She was now fully on board. He told Megan the three of them were now on their way to Theia Labs so he could have his brain scanned. He was driving the rental, and Heather and Alex were taking Heather's car. This way, Hall could return to the hotel later while Altschuler and Heather continued on to the Madera facility for the procedure.

Feeling better after hearing from him, Megan took a long, hot shower, which was truly a slice of heaven, and re-bandaged her thigh. It was coming along beautifully. In a day or two, she decided, she'd be willing to risk actual sex with a man with whom she was rapidly becoming infatuated.

She settled in to watch a long romantic comedy on pay-per-view, and before she knew it, the movie was at its end, and the inevitable misunderstandings between the two romantic leads were finally being cleared up, allowing true love to blossom.

Megan caught motion at the edge of her field of vision.

It was the door. Swinging open!

Before it had completed its arc, a man with light blond hair slid inside the room and drew a gun, raising it to a firing position in front of him. Megan instinctively threw herself from the couch as a silenced projectile whistled by her ear.

The man was trying to kill her.

A specialized electronic device had been shoved into the door's keycard mechanism, no doubt to emulate a key, and the gunman disengaged the device and slipped it into his pocket. The assailant was lean and his motions were calm and practiced; professional. The level of competence and sophistication of the attack reeked of John Delamater. If she had been on the other side of the couch, the opening door wouldn't have been in her line of vision, and she'd be dead already.

Not that it mattered. She had only bought a few additional seconds of life. She was now on the floor—a sitting duck—and her visitor would not miss again.

The man reached for the door and gently pulled it closed behind him with one hand while raising the gun once again with the other. But just as he was pulling the trigger, a silenced shot from outside ripped through the door and into his arm, causing his aim to be off.

The man didn't miss a beat, despite having been shot. Ignoring both his arm and Megan Emerson, he dived against one wall and out of the line of fire as two more silenced bullets punched though the door.

"Need reinforcements," he hissed into an unseen microphone. "I'm inside Hall's suite. One or more hostiles are outside the front door. Hurry!"

All the drapes to the room were already closed, but just as Megan's assailant said his final word a bullet crashed through the outside wall of the bungalow, missing him by less than a foot. He rolled past the splintered door and into a standing position behind it, drawing a second gun and lying in wait for anyone who tried to enter.

Megan jolted awake. What was she *doing*? Why was she acting like a spectator in this drama? Now was her chance.

She stayed low to the floor and crawled for almost ten feet, sliding open the door to the suite's small patio and rushing through. She rose to a crouching position and hastily surveyed the area. While the walking paths between suites were relatively well lighted, it was a cloudy, moonless night, and much of the sprawling complex was too shrouded in darkness for her to be certain another gunman wasn't lying in wait.

It didn't matter. She had no choice. She laid her torso on the flat upper beam of the short, decorative wrought iron fence that surrounded the patio and swung her legs to the other side.

Just as she stood she heard an explosion of sound from within the suite as the door was kicked open by her protectors, who must have been the two bodyguards Ed Cowan had stationed next door. Her racing heart quickened even further as she rushed across the lighted pathways and into the darkness, as quickly and quietly as a cat.

Inside the suite, the man who had attacked Megan was perfectly positioned behind the door and took out the first of Cowan's men to burst through with a shot to the torso. The second man through slammed his fist into the intruder's bloody arm and sent his gun flying. But the wounded assailant ignored the severe pain and evened the score by launching a series of rapid-fire open-handed strikes at the bodyguard's arm, causing him to drop his weapon and forcing him to immediately square up his stance and switch to a hand-to-hand posture.

Cowan's man was good, but the intruder was better, managing to hold his own even though injured, blocking attempted blow after attempted blow with a flurry of well-honed martial arts moves.

This is where Megan's would-be protector made a fatal mistake. He pulled a lethal switchblade knife from his pocket, sprang it open, and lunged at his adversary, who grabbed his knife hand as it was coming down and used the bodyguard's own momentum to break his wrist and drive the knife into the man's own chest. This was done so expertly that the motion of the bodyguard's arm was smooth and continuous, from the beginning of his lunge to the moment his lungs began filling with blood.

It was late on a Sunday night, and only a few nearby residents who were up and about bothered to look through their windows to determine the cause of the loud crack they had heard when the door was kicked in. But since the door in question wasn't in direct view of any other unit, they soon shrugged and went about their business.

On the grounds, Megan Emerson kept to the darkness, certain her jackhammering heart could be heard in the next city, giving away her position as surely as if she were inside a macabre Edgar Alan Poe tale.

Megan watched the lobby, which fronted the grounds and which represented the only way to enter the large community of temporary residents that didn't involve climbing fences or walls. Two men, who had the unmistakable physical aura of trained killers, rushed through the lobby doors. They tried their best to look casual, but failed miserably.

Megan flattened herself against the dark ground. After the two men passed her on the way to their comrade, she rose to a crouch and rushed to the lobby doors. But just as she was about to push through, she spotted two additional men across the lobby, chatting casually near the exit to the street. In her state of heightened awareness, and heightened paranoia, she was certain these two were also part of the assault force trying to kill her.

How many of them were there?

She retreated back into the darkness and called Nick Hall, trying to shield the light of the phone with her body and hands. "*Nick,*" she whispered frantically the moment he answered, "all hell's broken loose. Delamater's men are swarming the place."

Hall had just finished the MRI scan and was in the rental car, heading back to the hotel. "Are you hurt?" he asked anxiously, and then quickly added, "what about Cowan's men next door?"

"I'm okay," she whispered. "Our neighbors tried to stop them but failed. I'm hiding on the grounds."

"Okay," he said, his voice raw with barely contained emotion. "Do whatever you can to stay hidden. Stall if they catch you. I'll be in range in about five minutes and can read what you're up against and help you. Good luck, Megan."

The tone of his voice said so much more than just good luck, and she could tell he was dying to tell her what she meant to him, but he wanted her attention *off* her cell phone and *on* staying alive.

Megan looked across the grounds to the weight room and considered using it as a hiding place. No good. It was still well lighted inside, even after eleven at night, and had several windows. The men after her would be able to see in. She wouldn't be able to see out. Very bad idea.

While Megan weighed her limited options, the man who had originally attacked her managed to re-close the door and was tending to his injury. The two men who had rushed to his aid were now fanning out over the grounds, both pretending to be on a casual stroll, with their weapons hidden.

Megan saw them as they crossed lighted areas and knew they would likely close in on her before Hall got into range. There were limited hiding places available, and since they were being methodical, it was only a matter of time. And not much time at that.

She needed to move. If she stayed where she was she'd be discovered in seconds.

Megan worked her way soundlessly to the pool area. The pool and spa had been closed since nine-thirty and the water inside of both was still as ice.

Sitting next to where patio chairs had been stacked for the night, on four small wheels, was a large, rectangular laundry cart, with a shiny steel frame and royal blue fabric walls. It had been emptied and was awaiting dozens of wet towels that would be deposited inside by hotel guests the next day.

Megan realized it was her only hope. The pool area was well lighted, for safety reasons, so they would never expect her to hide here. She approached the fabric container and carefully folded herself inside.

Where was Nick? How much longer until he was in range?

But even as she considered this, she knew it didn't matter. These men were very good. It might take them a few extra minutes to check the wet towel container, but they would—long before Hall could arrive. His ESP was remarkable, but there was no way it would save her this time. Not from *these* men.

Too bad. It would have been fun to joke with Nick about it. *Why did I hide in a laundry cart?* she imagined asking him. *Because not everyone's lucky enough to find an open dumpster when they need one*, she would answer with a smile.

Yeah. Someday they'd have a good laugh over this. Unfortunately, that laugh would have to wait for the afterlife.

42

Nick Hall was out of his mind with worry. He had felt panic before, but never like this. Not even in the Shell gas station bathroom.

He had lost numerous friends and colleagues on the Scripps *Explorer*. But the prospect of losing Megan Emerson was *unthinkable*. It was psychologically debilitating.

He felt so *helpless*.

Hang on, Megan, he pleaded to the gods, glancing up at the dark, moonless sky. *Please hang on*.

He pressed down even further on the gas pedal and the rental car jumped to above eighty. As he approached red lights, he flicked on his brights and laid on the horn, sounding a single long, blaring warning, and then burst through the intersections like a rocket.

Part of him wanted to up his speed even more, but he wasn't on a freeway, and he could only be so reckless before it caught up to him. The streets were largely deserted at this late hour, but if a single approaching driver didn't hear his warning, or was at the exact wrong place at the wrong time, they'd be carting him away in a body bag.

While he drove he shot his mind out to its limits, searching for the familiar mental presence of Megan Emerson. But he was still out of range.

He streaked past the smattering of cars on the road ahead like they were standing still, and since the road had three lanes, he was always able to find a way to slide around these glowing speed bumps without slowing. He ignored thoughts such as "*shithead*" and "*where's the fire, asshole*," coming from the drivers he passed. Not a single driver gave him the benefit of the doubt. Not even one considered that a life-and-death emergency might be the reason he tore past them at twice the posted speed limit.

As he neared an upcoming intersection, he slammed on the brakes without knowing why, realizing only as a car shot by in front of him, just clearing the intersection before his squealing, decelerating car barreled through, that his mind had picked up the panicked thoughts of the crossing driver before Hall had seen him. The cocktail party effect had reared its magnificent head once again.

He regained his speed and was soon nearing ninety, on a street with a posted limit of forty-five.

Hall cursed in frustration as he picked up the minds of two cops in a squad car heading back to the station. They weren't prowling for speeders, but it didn't matter. They didn't need a radar gun to tell he was breaking every traffic law in the book. And even if he could have slowed fast enough to escape their attention, Megan couldn't afford *any* delay.

He pressed the gas pedal even further toward the floor as a siren began sounding behind him, its red and blue strobing lights visible for miles in the dark night, like an angry UFO flying after him. The blare of the siren diminished as he picked up even more speed and left his pursuers farther and farther behind.

The cops had been chasing him for almost a minute when a light switch went on in his head. *Hallelujah!* Finally, he felt Megan's impenetrable mental presence. She was still alive!

"*Megan*," he broadcast as forcefully as he could. "*I'm in range. What's the situation?*"

"*Nick, thank God!*" came the quick reply. "*I'm hiding in a towel cart near the pool. There are two men combing the grounds for me, and at least two more in the lobby.*"

"*Got it*," sent Hall. After a short pause, he added, "*I'm reading the two on the grounds. They've checked the weight room, outside bathrooms, tennis courts, and maids' closets. One of them is coming to check the pool area now.*"

"*I'm lucky it took them this long. Nick, you can't get me out of this. You can't. But I'm glad I'll at least get to say goodbye. I just want you to know—*"

"Megan, Megan, Megan," he interrupted excitedly. *"They're not with Delamater! They're US special forces."*

Hall had read that they had come after both of them—him primarily—and were told if either he or Megan so much as developed a hangnail, their heads would roll.

"I have no idea how they fit in, but they have strict instructions not to hurt you."

"Nick, they shot at me! Twice."

The face of one of the men hunting Megan appeared above her, visible in the eerie glow from the small lights illuminating the pool area. He raised his gun and pointed it at her at point blank range.

"They only shot tranquilizer darts," sent Hall, slowing the car dramatically, knowing he couldn't reach her in time and that he'd be of no use to her dead.

"Megan, I'm going to get you out of this," he insisted. *"Somehow. I promise. Take the pill he offers. It's legit."*

"You have two choices," whispered the man looming above Megan, and she felt as helpless as if she *were* a wet towel. "This is a dart gun. I can shoot you in the leg and put you out. But that will be more painful than necessary. Or I have a pill in my pocket that will do the same thing. Your choice."

"Who are you?" said Megan.

The man ignored her. "You have three seconds to choose. If not, the default is shooting you." He paused. "Three, two . . ."

"Give me the pill," said Megan.

The man reached in his pocket and handed her a clear green capsule. She placed it in her mouth and swallowed. *"See you on the other side, Nick."*

A tear escaped from the bottom of Nick Hall's right eye and slid slowly down his cheek. *"Stay strong, Megan,"* he broadcast as he pulled off the side of the road to take his own medicine from the cops behind him. *"And you'll be seeing me again on this side. You can count on it."*

43

Colonel Justin Girdler was the sole occupant of the lone safe house in the area, in Merced, about fifty miles northwest of Fresno. If this wasn't enough distance from Hall to avoid being read, then the task was truly hopeless.

Major Mike Campbell, still in North Carolina, appeared on one of his monitors, and both men had a separate screen nearby, each displaying identical video, imagery, and tactical information.

Just before Girdler had touched down in California, Campbell had finally tracked Hall and Emerson to the Homestead Inn. But given Hall's ESP, they had decided to do nothing but monitor the hotel while they chose the best course of action.

When Hall and Emerson had separated, and the girl was out of Hall's range, Girdler had decided to seize on this unexpected opportunity. His plan was bold—and risky. He was forced to make numerous assumptions. And if even one of these was wrong, the plan might fail.

But his first assumption, that Megan Emerson was important to Nick Hall, was coming true. The footage of the two of them embracing in Vons was an obvious indication they had a physical relationship. But this didn't necessarily indicate just how much she might mean to him. What Girdler and Campbell were now seeing on their monitors, however, did.

Girdler watched Hall's car scream along the road, and he got a sense of speed even from the satellite imagery. *He's really hauling ass*, he thought, and even in the middle of directing a mission, part of his mind couldn't help but reflect on what a good pun that would make. *Hall* was *Hall-ing* ass.

"Have you found Megan Emerson on the satellite imagery yet?" he barked at Campbell in annoyance, still not quite able to believe the mission had gotten *this* out of hand, and that the girl had escaped the bungalow and into the night.

"Not yet. But we're certain she's still on the grounds. Somewhere."

"How the hell are the satellites missing her?"

"It's dark and the contrast isn't great," replied the major. "Satellite imagery isn't magic, and even the IR isn't infallible. In this case, our men on the ground will find her before the satellite does." He smiled as an update came in the moment he had made this prediction, just to make a liar out of him. The Satellite had found her first, after all.

"Check that," said Campbell, and then opened a channel to their team at the Homestead Inn. "The girl is hiding in some kind of container by the pool."

"Roger that," said Lieutenant Dan Hubbard, who was nearest to the pool. "She'll be unconscious in less than a minute."

Girdler nodded. Unfortunately, the two unknown hostiles who had thrown a wrench in the works on what should have been a routine operation were both dead. He'd have to send a clean-up team to handle that and try to learn who they were, and where they fit in. But first things first.

He turned his attention once more to the most ballsy piece of driving he had ever witnessed. Hall was literally playing Russian Roulette with every red light he encountered. At this rate, Hall was likely to end his *own* life before Girdler did.

"Mike, are you sure Nick Hall and Megan Emerson didn't have a prior relationship? He's driving like he's on *fire*. Like *her* life means more to him than his own."

"We can't be sure they didn't know each other before, but we can't find any evidence. As far as we can tell, they met for the first time on Friday."

Before Girdler could ask additional questions, Lieutenant Hubbard reported back that they had found the girl by the pool, as expected. They were now transporting her to the small U-haul truck parked in the lot, propping her up *Weekend at Bernie's* style and pretending she had had too much to drink.

Meanwhile, on the left half of the monitor, Hall had stopped, and two cops were cautiously approaching him, guns partially drawn.

"Can't blame the cops for being nervous," said Campbell from thousands of miles away. "Any maniac driving like that and then refusing to pull over—I'd act the same way."

"Have you located their commanding officer yet?"

"Coming in . . . now," said Campbell. "I'll pull strings and send them packing."

"Good. Do it fast," said Girdler.

"Roger that," said Campbell, who then muted the audio and picked up a phone.

Girdler watched with great interest as the tiny images of the two cops frisked Hall, none too gently. They began a discussion, and from the gestures and body language he could pick up, he guessed they had asked Hall for ID and none was forthcoming. That should hardly have surprised them at this point, thought the colonel.

They appeared to be exchanging heated words with Hall a few minutes later when one of the cops pulled a cell phone from his pocket. Girdler couldn't read his expression precisely, but he had a perfect idea what he must be feeling. Confusion and anger. If this didn't piss him off, nothing would.

After a brief conversation, he returned the phone to his pocket, and had an even shorter conversation with his partner. Seconds later they retreated back to their car, shaking their heads the entire way, and drove off into the night, leaving Nick Hall with his mouth wide open.

"Nice work, Mike," said Girdler. "That set some speed records."

"Thanks," said the major, unmuted once again. "More good news. As hoped, Megan Emerson had a cell phone. A disposable, as we guessed. And she's only ever called a single number. Putting it on screen now."

Perfect, thought the colonel. So far, everything was going as planned. Well, *as planned* if he didn't count having one of his men shot, being interfered with by two mysterious bodyguards who were now dead, and Megan Emerson running around the hotel grounds like an invisible rabbit.

"Calling the number now," said Girdler. "I'm conferencing you in, Mike. But mute your end of the call."

"Roger that."

On the monitor, the small, poorly illuminated image of Nick Hall, still standing beside his car, answered his phone without hesitation. *"Who is this?"* he demanded. "If anything happens to Megan, I swear to God I'll—"

"Nothing will happen to the girl, Nick," interrupted the colonel, knowing that the way Hall had answered the call, while not definitive, greatly increased the chances he really could read minds. He appeared to be certain the caller wasn't Megan Emerson, the only person who had his number. Unless he had some other way to know, it was likely he had learned this from the mind of one of Girdler's men at the hotel. "My name is Justin. Justin Girdler. And my men have Megan Emerson, safe and sound."

"Who are you?" hissed Hall, with a fury hotter than molten lava. "And what do you want?"

If Girdler's assumptions were correct, Hall already had a very good idea who he was. He had almost certainly already read the minds of Girdler's team at the hotel, who were told that both Emerson and Hall were the targets of the operation, and neither was to be harmed. Hall had also learned that they were elite members of the US military. Girdler had been counting on him gleaning this information from his men.

"I'm a special forces colonel," replied Girdler. He had made sure the team he had deployed wasn't aware their orders had originated from PsyOps. If Hall had known this was the case, he might immediately guess they were on to his ESP, which wasn't something Girdler wanted to reveal. "We just need to talk to you, Nick. That's all. We don't want to hurt you."

Hall conducted a rapid search through cyberspace, looking for Girdler's name in conjunction with *military*, or *special forces*, or *colonel*, but came up with nothing. "So you kidnapped an innocent woman just so you could *chat?*" spat Hall in contempt.

"I have to admit that we screwed the pooch on this one. We thought you were in the room with her," he lied. "Someone's head's gonna roll over this mistake. I apologize about Megan Emerson. Again, we were primarily after you."

"Why?"

"*Really*, Nick? You can't guess? We both know you were on the ill-fated *Explorer* expedition. Since *you're* the only survivor, it occurred to us that maybe you *caused* it. That wouldn't normally have been the first conclusion we jumped to. But we learned you were alive when we found your prints. *At the site of a double murder*. Sound familiar?"

There was a long pause. "So the US military is now investigating domestic crimes?" Hall asked suspiciously.

"Look, I don't have time to go over the complex web of US agency jurisdictions. But even if I could, it wouldn't apply in this case. The *Explorer* was in international waters and was an international story. So I'm in charge. So I'd really appreciate it if you'd stop running and spend some quality time answering questions. Very civilized questions. If you stay where you are, we'll come to you in a U-Haul truck. Megan Emerson is in the back, unconscious, but not harmed in the slightest. If you take a short road trip with the men inside, rather than attempting to run again, or attempting an ambush, we'll release her." He paused. "And you have my word you won't be harmed."

Girdler was glad Hall couldn't see his face right now, or the game would have been up. No words had ever tasted so bitter coming from the colonel's lips. Deception was one thing. Giving your word to an innocent, helpless man, with full knowledge your *word* didn't mean shit, was beneath contempt. Girdler felt like puking.

"Yeah. And how do I know I can trust you?"

The colonel took a deep breath and tried to remember why he was taking the actions he was. That the emergence of psionics, or the prevention of such emergence, would be a turning point in human history. "You realize we're watching you on satellite this second. That's how we knew you'd been stopped. Obviously, we were the ones who called off the cops."

"Obviously," repeated Hall.

"In addition, you're on a god-damned cell phone. So you're a painted target. If I wanted you dead, I could send a missile straight up your bony ass this second."

His reasons for *not* taking this action went far beyond the inability to explain such action to Sobol. Using military assets to fire a missile at a civilian on US soil was only possible, or forgivable, if that civilian were holding a nuclear detonator at the time. But he suspected Hall wouldn't consider this, so his point would be persuasive.

If Girdler's guess was right, Hall thought he still had an ace up his sleeve. He had no reason to expect the colonel knew anything about his psionic ability. So Hall would expect to be able to verify Girdler's trustworthiness for himself five or ten miles out. If he learned the colonel was lying, he would still have plenty of time to escape from men who didn't know the kind of advantage he could use against them.

"Well?" said Girdler. "What do you say? Do we have a deal?"

44

Nick Hall reached out and searched with his mind. Sure enough, the men from the Homestead Inn had carried Megan to their U-Haul and were now less than a mile away from him, closing fast. They had received new orders. To pick him up and bring him to a safe house in Merced, forty-five minutes away. They had been told in no uncertain terms that if he cooperated he was to be treated as gingerly as if he were a crystal vase. The boss only wanted to do a catch-and-release on this fish.

Hall could detect the faint outlines of Megan's mind, but conscious or unconscious, it remained unreadable to him. It didn't matter. It was enough to know she was alive, and the men in the truck provided confirmation that she was in mint condition.

"Your men have been approaching while we've been talking, haven't they?" said Hall into his phone.

"Good guess," replied the colonel. "They're almost there. Should I tell them you'll be cooperating? So they can revive Megan Emerson and drop her back at the hotel?"

Hall sighed deeply. "I'll cooperate," he said.

"Good choice, Nick. I'll let them know. They'll be there shortly."

In less than a minute, a fourteen-foot U-haul truck, painted a familiar orange and white, arrived on the scene, and pulled off the road near Nick's rental car. The back of the truck rolled up to reveal two men, each carrying both tranquilizer guns and real guns. Megan had been carefully strapped in against one wall, her head against a pillow.

Hall couldn't believe his reaction to seeing her. It was like a crushing weight had been lifted from his chest. He felt intense relief and elation, and the raw power of these emotions took him by surprise. He stepped into the truck and went straight for Megan, kneeling down next to her and making sure she was in perfect health.

One of the men rolled the back of the truck back down and the vehicle began moving. A light was on inside, providing plenty of illumination. Another of the men nodded at Hall. "We appreciate your cooperation," he said.

A receiver in the man's ear came to life as a call came in. Hall couldn't hear what was being transmitted through the tiny device, but he could read the words as they registered in the soldier's mind. "Lieutenant," said the voice. "This is Colonel Girdler. New orders. I want you to shoot our new guest with a tranquilizer dart. *Immediately!* No hesitation!"

Hall read that the lieutenant was just as astonished by this order as he was, but the soldier reacted with admirable speed, drawing his tranquilizer gun like he was a gunfighter in the old west. Hall didn't have enough time to even think about diving away as the soldier depressed the trigger.

As Hall felt the sting of the dart, he knew that Girdler hadn't played it straight with him.

So what else had he lied about?

Hall's grip on consciousness slipped away quickly. But the fear that enveloped him just ahead of the darkness was not a fear for himself, but a fear of what might happen to Megan Emerson, a woman who was rapidly becoming his entire world.

45

As consciousness gradually returned, Hall found his right hand had been handcuffed to a heavy steel chair in a large bedroom. And his Internet connection was down!

He had become so dependent on instant access to cyberspace that its absence was jarring. He had integrated this new ability so quickly and so thoroughly into his senses that its loss was as distressing as the loss of an arm, or maybe even an eye, would have been.

Had his implants been removed?

Across from him, a man with salt-and-pepper hair, in his fifties, was watching him intently. He entered the man's mind and answers to this question, and many others, gushed in as quickly as he could assimilate the information.

The man was Colonel Justin Girdler, the head of PsyOps, and they were in the safe house in Merced he had spoken of on the phone. Girdler had been forced to use the safe house because he was going against the direct orders of his boss, a general named Sobol, so nearby Edwards Air Force Base was out.

Girdler was using an electronic device to actively suppress the WiFi in the area. The 6G system was never down. Its coverage was absolute across the fifty states: penetrating and overlapping. But Girdler didn't want Hall to be able to send e-mails and texts, or otherwise make use of the most impressive system to communicate information the world had ever known.

Hall opened his mouth to protest he had nothing to do with the destruction of the *Explorer*, and that the killings at WeOfficeU were in self-defense, but before the first word came out he read that it wouldn't matter.

Girdler knew very well this was the case.

He also knew about Hall's ESP. That was why Hall was here.

Hall continued probing. Girdler's thoughts revealed that no one else was in the house, other than an unconscious Megan Emerson two rooms over and a single man to guard her, whose presence Hall had already discovered for himself. This man had strict instructions not to leave the room under any circumstances. Girdler had made sure he wouldn't be interrupted. Sure there would be no witnesses to what was to take place here.

The colonel not only knew about his ESP, he even had a rough sense of its range. "But how?" muttered Hall out loud.

He paused for several seconds and then his eyes widened in shock as he fished out the answer to his own question. "I sent you an e-mail?" he whispered, as if he was still having trouble believing it. "I alerted you *myself?*" he finished in horror.

"If you read your entire message from my mind," said Girdler, "you'll know not to be too hard on yourself. It was a desperation move. We thought you might have lost your memory again after it was sent, so didn't realize that you had. Your reaction now confirms it."

"And you're also thinking that I've just confirmed my ESP, as well, which was critical to you."

"You're right, of course. Your ability is *amazing*. Just incredible. Intellectually, I had convinced myself you had this ability. But to be faced by the reality is just . . . extraordinary."

Hall remained silent. He glanced at a digital clock on an end table. It was two a.m. He had not been out long. Even now, Altschuler was having his head drilled and technology implanted in the soft tissue of his brain.

"Although you can read my mind," said Girdler, "I'd prefer an actual conversation. This way, instead of going to the effort of randomly picking out what you will, I can direct and organize the presentation of my thoughts. You've no doubt read I plan to kill you here this morning. And why."

"What do you plan to do with Megan Emerson?" demanded Hall.

He already read the gist of the answer, but Girdler was correct. He could get a clearer, more nuanced answer if someone organized their own mind around a subject. He could pick apart memories and specific information, but opinions, future plans, and answers to subjective questions were harder to get a handle on through mind reading alone.

The answer to the question, "Did you like the horror movie you just saw?" could be read instantly. The answer to the question, "Do you *think* you'll like the new horror movie coming out next week?" was far more challenging to read. This answer was an amalgam of preferences for genre, the actors involved, the director, the screenwriter, opinions of friends, reviews one might have read, and so on. And only the person being asked the question knew their own minds well enough to instantly weigh and combine the variables to provide an answer. A trespassing mind reader could not.

"Your friend will be awake fairly soon," answered Girdler. "My associate will give her a second dose and then return her to where he found her, good as new."

Hall read in Girdler's mind that different people responded differently to the knock-out drug, and she was very petite, so giving her a second dose before she regained consciousness from the first would put her at unnecessary risk. The fact that Girdler was unwilling to take this risk was encouraging.

"I'm fairly sure she knows about your ability," continued Girdler. "But without you to demonstrate, no one would ever believe her. Like you, she's innocent. You have my word she won't be harmed."

Hall laughed. "Your *word?*" he said in contempt. "We both know that's not worth a fucking thing."

Girdler reeled, and Hall knew he was drilling into a sore spot.

"Why did you let me wake up?" asked Hall. "I can read how distressing this is to you." Hall wasn't sure it was comforting to know the man who would kill him regretted it to the very core of his being and was sure he would pay a terrible price, psychically, the rest of his life. "So why let me see it coming?" he continued. "Much harder this way for both of us."

"I had to be absolutely certain you could read minds," replied the colonel. "I had to be absolutely certain I wasn't making a mistake."

He frowned deeply. "And I owe it to you to not to kill you from afar, like a coward, without you knowing the reasons why."

"You *owe* it to me?" spat Hall. "Are you serious? Did you ever consider I might prefer *not* to see it coming? That this would be the more humane option?"

"I had to be sure about your ESP," mumbled Girdler miserably. "Killing an innocent man is bad enough. Killing an innocent man on the basis of a mistaken assumption is . . . unthinkable."

"Okay. So having to kill me makes you feel like shit. I get it. So here's an idea. *Don't!* I agree with your position about mind reading being too dangerous to risk unleashing. I really do. I wish you could read my mind just for a second to see this for yourself. I'm working hard to cure myself of this curse and see to it that the recipe is deleted from history forever. Even if I can't rid myself of this unwanted ability, I promise to never admit to having it. To never demonstrate it again. How can I convince you?"

If anything, the colonel's expression became even more morose. He lowered his eyes. "You can't," he said softly. "I believe you. Everything I've learned about you tells me you're a decent man, with high ethical standards."

"*So let me go!*" insisted Hall. "Do the right thing."

Girdler looked as though he had been hit in the stomach. "I *am* doing the right thing," he said, disgusted with himself. Disgusted with an impossible situation with only ice-cold solutions. "I trust your good intentions, Nick. *Now.* But what about tomorrow? Given what was done to your brain, it's a miracle you're still alive. Your mind and memory have been screwed with mercilessly. Since you wrote the e-mail, you've already had a memory-loss relapse. Your mind has undergone multiple, severe traumas, and is potentially unstable. Who knows what will happen going forward? What if you become psychotic? A paranoid schizophrenic who can read minds?"

Hall blanched, now looking as though *he* had been sucker punched in the gut. This was a chilling scenario he had never considered.

"Or what if the power changes you?" continued Girdler. "Power has corrupted good people before. So you're a potentially mentally unstable nuclear bomb who assures me you won't self-detonate. I trust your sincerity when you tell me you won't do anything to let this genie out of the bottle." He shook his head despondently. "But the stakes are too high to leave it at that. It's the Nick Hall that you'll be a year from now I can't be certain of." He nodded toward his prisoner. "And neither can you."

Girdler was *right,* Hall realized. He *was* too potentially dangerous to let live. His mental stability going forward was by no means a given, not with what had been done to him. So was his death for the good of society? He couldn't argue that it wasn't.

But his survival instinct was too strong. He couldn't lay down his life because of what he *might* become, *might* represent. Maybe it was the ethically right thing to do, but it was something of which he was incapable. So he would fight to his last breath to survive, even though he understood intellectually why he should do nothing to resist.

He was once again living the lesson Megan Emerson had taken from a Broadway play. Her *wicked* effect. Seen from one angle, Colonel Justin Girdler was a hero, not shirking his duty—no matter how detestable—of eliminating a credible threat to the safety of civilization. Seen from another angle, Hall was an innocent man, being executed without a trial by a merciless autocrat. And it occurred to Hall that Girdler was the hero from many more angles than he was.

Unlike Altschuler, the colonel had skeletons in his metaphorical closest that were not pretty. On the whole, he was a good man, forced all too often into making impossible decisions no one should have to make, but he was far from a prince in his personal life. Altschuler's decency was fairly white, while Girdler had a lot of gray in his background.

But there was no question that being forced to kill Hall would leave psychological scars that would never fully heal, nor Girdler's commitment to take out his fury at being forced into this situation on John Delamater. Now *there* was a killing he would enjoy. Relish even.

Megan had been steadily struggling to regain consciousness in the other room, and Hall sensed a change in her, finally, that suggested she might be open to his thoughts.

"Megan!" he blasted with as much power as he could. *"Megan, don't open your eyes. If you can read me, answer now. But don't open your eyes, whatever you do."*

There was no response.

"Okay, Colonel," said Hall out loud. "This has been fun. Really. But unlock my cuffs and let me go. Or I'll be forced to kill you where you sit."

Girdler raised his eyebrows.

"Mind reading isn't the only impossible thing I can do," said Hall. "I can also cause your heart to stop. I can use my mind like a steel hand to seize your heart and stop it cold, before you can even *begin* to raise your gun."

Girdler actually smiled. "Very impressive, Nick. You've got balls and can think on your feet in the most stressful of situations. You can't teach that. Believe me, I know. You've heard about the staring at goats thing, haven't you?"

"I've more than heard about it," said Hall firmly. "I can do it. I won't enjoy killing you any more than you'd enjoy killing me. But if you don't release me in ten seconds, you'll force my hand."

Girdler shook his head. "I think you're bluffing. If you really did have this power you wouldn't have had to shoot two men in the back at WeOfficeU. You'd have just stopped their hearts and left the authorities scratching their heads."

"I only realized I could do this yesterday."

"I have no choice but to call your bluff, anyway," said Girdler. "If you really do have this power, you're even more dangerous than I thought."

Hall considered beginning a countdown, but his ESP told him these dramatics wouldn't help. Girdler was willing to take his chances. Hall sighed. His bluff had been called, and he had no choice but to throw in his cards. "To be honest, I'm not sure I'd do it even if I really could," he admitted. "But the truth is, I can't even slow down an ant."

Girdler nodded, relieved, despite the resolve he had shown. Hall read that the colonel had genuinely come to like the man he was about to execute, which made it even worse. And Hall realized he had come to respect his executioner. A bizarre twist, even for the wicked effect.

"So I can't convince you not to do this?" said Hall.

"I wish there were some way you could."

"Well, I hope you can appreciate that on the subject of my death," said Hall, "we're going to have to agree to disagree."

Girdler couldn't help but smile, a bittersweet expression; far more bitter than sweet.

Hall repeated his urgent telepathic message to Megan and then said, "Before you do this, let me tell you everything I know about the bastards chasing me. Everything that happened. If Delamater is going to cost me my life, I want to help you put a bullet in his head."

Girdler became upbeat for the first time, and his mind responded to the idea with the enthusiasm of a dog whose master had just returned home.

Hall slowly began his tale of waking up in a dumpster. Every thirty seconds he re-sent his telepathic call to Megan. Ironically, while he was describing to Girdler how Megan had ended up joining him on the run, he got a response from her, so faint he could barely pick it up.

"*Nick? Where. . . Where am I?*"

"*Megan!*" he broadcast excitedly, and then repeated, "*don't open your eyes!*"

"*Nick, what's going on?*"

"Colonel," said Hall out loud, "I think there's something important I may be leaving out. My memory's not what it once was, as you know. Give me a few minutes to think," he finished, and then closed his eyes.

"*Megan, you were drugged in a laundry cart at the Homestead Inn. Remember?*"

There was a brief pause. "*Yes. I do remember now.*"

"*Good. Whatever you do, keep your eyes closed. You're now in a safe house in Merced, and there's a guard watching you. I'm in a bedroom two doors down from you. A PsyOps colonel knows about my ESP and thinks I'm too dangerous to let live. He's planning to kill me very soon.*"

"*Oh my God, Nick!*"

"*It's okay. I have a plan. And you're the key.*"

"*Tell me what to do.*"

"*The man watching you isn't sure exactly when you'll come to, but he has no worry you can overpower him. You're sitting on the floor in a bedroom, propped against a wall.*"

"*How do you know?*"

"*I can see the room through the eyes of the man in there with you. A few feet to your right is an end table with a lamp on it, about three feet tall, which isn't currently on. Its base is like an elongated, colored teardrop. It might be glass, but I think it's heavy Lucite. Regardless, if you grab it just under the lampshade and bulb, where it tapers, you can use the bottom like a club. The wall outlet where it's plugged in is about two inches from your right hand. Feel around until you find it, and then slowly loosen the plug so it will easily pull out when you swing the lamp. But do it so slowly that you'd lose a race with a glacier. You can't let him detect any movement.*"

"*Will do,*" came the reply.

Inside the room with Hall, the colonel was becoming impatient. "Anything new coming to mind?" he asked.

"Yes," replied Hall. "But give me another minute or two to dig out the rest and then I'll continue."

"*Okay,*" sent Megan thirty seconds later. "*It's done.*"

"*Great work! The guy in there still thinks you're unconscious. Open your eyes just a hair and find the lamp, just slightly above your head to the right. And also locate your guard. He's dead center in front of you.*"

"*I can see both through my eyelashes,*" sent Megan a few seconds later.

"*Great. I need you to count down 'three, two, one, now' in your mind. When you hit 'now,' I'm going to scream at the top of my lungs. Plenty loud enough to carry to your room. This will distract the guy. So the moment you think, 'now,' jump up, grab the lamp near the top, and hit him with all of your strength.*"

Hall didn't want the guard dead, just unconscious. So should he have Megan pull her punch? After all, he had killed Baldino with a single blow. But he was stronger and had been able to torque the hardened butt of the gun into Baldino's head at tremendous velocity. Having no way to judge Megan's strength, or know if she would deliver a glancing blow or a direct one, he couldn't afford to take any chances. Hopefully, the guard would survive.

"*You can't be squeamish about this, Megan,*" he added, having made his decision. "*My life depends on this. So no mercy. Put all the anger and hatred you've ever felt into the blow. The gun he's holding only shoots tranquilizers, and he has strict orders not to hurt you. So even if this fails, you'll be fine. There's no risk. Just reward.*"

"*Okay, Nick. I won't let you down. On 'now.' Ready?*"

"*Ready.*"

"*Three . . . two . . . one . . . now!*"

46

Nick Hall screamed for all he was worth. A chilling, primal scream that caused Girdler to jerk back in surprise. Hall screamed at the highest decibel level he had ever managed, until his vocal cords begged for mercy, and then continued screaming.

At the same time, he was inside the head of the man who was guarding Megan. The man had been startled by a scream that shot through the walls like they were tissue paper, and turned toward it. But just as he completed his turn, his subconscious caught a sound or a movement behind him, and he sensed he was in danger and needed to turn back.

But he was too late. He turned just in time to see the heavy base of a lamp coming toward his head.

And then the guard's conscious thinking ceased, and the mental picture Hall was borrowing from him went dead. Even so, Hall could tell the guard was still alive. Perfect!

"I did it!" screamed Megan telepathically.

"Outstanding!" replied Hall, finally cutting off his scream and sparing his burning throat. *"He has a real gun in an ankle holster. Get it, along with his dart gun, and wait for my instructions. Move very quietly."*

Girdler shook his head at Hall's antics. "Are you done screaming now?" said the colonel. "Do you think someone outside the house might hear you and come to your rescue?"

"Not really," said Hall. "But I figured the universe owes me one last primal scream."

Girdler nodded while Hall read his mind. Hall was under tremendous stress, the colonel was thinking. Understandably. The scream had been pretty bizarre, but he was on death row after all, and every man handled this kind of pressure in his own way.

"I guess I didn't remember anything new, after all," continued Hall conversationally. "Where was I?"

"Before you freaked out," said Girdler, "you were telling me that Megan had been shot. And you were wheeling her outside to her car on her desk chair."

"Right. I knew I couldn't take her to a hospital. So I drove her to a seedy motel."

"And called an ambulance," said Girdler knowingly, as the pieces continued to fall into place. "I'd love to know what happened with that. We interviewed the friends and families of the paramedics who responded."

Hall's face wrinkled up in confusion. "Why didn't you interview the paramedics themselves?"

"They were both murdered."

"No!" bellowed Hall, his eyes widening in horror.

Hall read that Girdler instantly regretted telling him this. Why make Hall feel any worse than he needed to feel? Most men being executed were allowed to enjoy a last, favorite meal. Instead, he was burdening Hall with remorse and guilt.

But Hall had no time to dwell on these senseless deaths that he had caused, even if only indirectly. While he had continued speaking with Girdler, Megan had quietly entered the room behind them. Because he couldn't see through Megan's eyes, he was only able to position her approximately, about six feet in from the left wall. But since she could also hear the colonel's voice through the wall, she was confident she was precisely behind him. She stood there, barely breathing, and waited for Hall's signal.

"Colonel," said Hall, "I've come to like and respect you. And I understand why you feel you have to kill me. But if you'd like to remain alive, I really do need you to toss over the keys to my cuffs and not to move. And this time I'm not bluffing."

"You already admitted you couldn't stop an ant."

"Colonel, I've found there are a small percentage of people I can't read. Megan Emerson is one of them. But while I can't read her mind, for some strange reason, we *are* able to communicate with each other telepathically."

The colonel considered. This was interesting, if true. But he didn't understand why Hall was telling him this now, and making idle threats, rather than continuing his narrative.

"She's free now. Not only free, but pointing a gun at your back from point blank range. How thick do you think these flimsy plaster walls are in here? Specifically the one your chair is leaning against? Do you think the walls could stop a .45 caliber slug fired from six inches?"

"Good try," said Girdler calmly. "But your first bluff was better."

"Was it?" said Hall, sending instructions to Megan.

A boom sounded behind the colonel as a fist pounded the wall where his head was located. Girdler was startled nearly out of his mind, and the shock wave through the wall forced his head forward.

"The next thing through that wall won't just be a fist tap," said Hall. "I know you're a heroic guy, Colonel Girdler. But you can't prevent me from escaping, whether you cooperate or not. So why throw your life away?"

The colonel reached into his pocket and withdrew the keys to Hall's cuffs, knowing any deception he could try would be read. He tossed them to Hall, who snatched them from the air with his free left hand.

Hall read from Girdler's mind that a large part of him was actually relieved at this turn of events. Even though Hall had been granted a stay of execution, Girdler had been granted a stay as well; a stay from taking the role of executioner he was loath to play.

Once Hall had freed himself, he had Girdler kick his gun over to him, and then his dart gun. After he had gathered up both guns, he backed away from the colonel and instructed Megan to join them.

As Megan entered the room, Hall raised the tranquilizer gun and pointed it at the colonel.

"You know you should really use the one with bullets," said Girdler wearily. "I'm sure you can read that if you let me live, I'll still have to try to kill you. The stakes are too high to do anything else."

"I know," said Hall. "But I'm not a murderer. And I like you, Colonel Girdler. I even agree with you." He pulled the trigger and a dart imbedded itself into Girdler's stomach.

"But you'll have to forgive me for not wishing you luck," he added, and then turned to embrace the remarkable woman standing beside him.

47

To say that the past few days had been the most incredible of Alex Altschuler's eventful life was an understatement. He had worn a wire to entrap his boss, had been on the verge of being killed, had lost his hearing temporarily from a gunshot that had blown away much of Kelvin Gray's face, and had been shown unequivocal evidence of perfect ESP.

And now, standing in a secret basement room at Theia's Madera facility, he was able to surf the web with his thoughts alone!

Heather Zambrana had been so excited by the success of the surgery she had hugged him, and he sensed that she considered this a positive experience, something he would have to explore further another time.

He would have to explore this further, of course, *because he could not read her mind.*

Cybersurfing and ESP were not linked! You could have one without the other.

The experiment had been a stunning success in every regard.

He didn't even feel that bad physically. Blood loss had been minimal, and there were no pain receptors in the brain, which was why surgeons could perform brain surgery on patients who were fully awake, ensuring the procedure wasn't adversely affecting vision, speech, or motor control functions. And while the skull *did* contain pain receptors, the pain hadn't seemed that bad, even before Heather had given him a potent pain reliever.

Heather cleared her throat loudly, but Altschuler was so engrossed in putting his Internet connection through its paces he was completely oblivious. He had been experimenting at a furious pace for forty-five minutes. Hall was bright, but Altschuler was in a league of his own, and was an expert with computers and the Internet. So he became more adept at manipulating the system than Hall after less than an hour, and page after page flashed into his mind's eye like they were being fired from a machine gun.

Heather cleared her throat a second time, with equal lack of effect. "Um . . . Alex. If you're feeling okay, I'd like to leave. You can continue experimenting in the car. And I think, um . . . well, you know, we could be more comfortable at my place."

Altschuler froze. What did *that* mean? God, what he wouldn't give to be able to read her mind for just a few seconds.

They had always had a great working relationship, and maybe she had sensed how he felt about her, despite how hard he tried to conceal it. But now he had blown her mind with revelations about Gray, about the *Explorer*, about a fully functioning personal, thought-controlled Internet, and about a man named Nick Hall. He had taken her from the realm of the ordinary and routine to the stratosphere of extraordinary and incredible. The fact that he had chosen her to be the fourth member of an exclusive club safeguarding the most astonishing secret in history couldn't help but enhance his appeal to her. Now they not only shared an incredible secret, but also an incredible *purpose.* How could this not bring them closer together?

But just *how* close would it bring them? And how quickly?

Altschuler was pretty sure Heather wasn't in a relationship. And her condo *would* be far more comfortable than the basement lab. But was she innocently pointing out the accurate fact that it would be more comfortable? Or was this her way of making the sexual innuendo that it would be more *comfortable?*

"Alex?" said Heather after he had stared at her, blinking, for several seconds without a response. "Are you feeling okay?"

"I'm feeling great," he replied finally. "Thanks to you. And you're right. Let's get out of here. We have a lot to do."

They made their way to the ground floor and exited the building. Heather's car was the first and only one in the lot. "And you're positive you can't read my mind?" she asked for the second time as they walked the few feet to her car in the cool night air.

"Positive," he said again. He couldn't blame her for being nervous at the prospect of him having access to her innermost, private thoughts. "Believe me, I know how relieved you must feel."

Just the hint of a smile came over her down-to-earth face, which glowed against the faint light at the front of the facility that was kept on throughout the night. "I'm *mostly* relieved," she admitted. She tapped her head with her index finger. "But there might be a few things in there I wouldn't mind you reading."

It didn't take a genius, which Altschuler was, to know this was a statement worth following up on.

He opened his mouth to explore what this meant when he heard his name from ten feet away in the darkness. "Dr. Altschuler?" said a deep, gravelly voice.

There were two men approaching.

In an empty parking lot at three in the morning, below a dark, moonless sky, being approached by an elderly woman with a cane would be alarming. But being approached by two men who exuded menace froze both scientists in place and sent their hearts racing.

"What do you want?" asked Altschuler, noting that neither man was carrying a weapon. At least for the time being.

The man who had spoken reached into his pocket and pulled out his wallet. He opened it to reveal a government ID. He was a member of a three-letter organization with which Altschuler was not familiar. What was even more troubling was that even when he used his internal Internet to search for it, he still came up empty. Which meant the agency didn't exist and these men were frauds, or it did exist and was so secret it wasn't mentioned a single time on the trillions of pages of cyberinformation available. Either way, this was a bad sign.

Were they working for John Delamater?

"Sorry to bother you this late," said the man, pocketing his wallet. "But we need to ask you and Miss Zambrana a few questions. If you could come with us, our car is parked around the corner."

"And if we don't?" asked Altschuler, certain his face was now as pale as the light surrounding them.

"I'm afraid that really isn't an option," said the man, while his partner remained silent.

"Freeze!" said a male voice from the opposite side of the parking lot. While the two scientists and the two men near them were illuminated by the light of the building, this voice seemed to be coming from the heart of a black hole.

"Raise your hands! Now!"

The two men who were supposedly from the government glanced at each other, and the one who had been speaking shook his head the slightest bit, a gesture that even Altschuler knew meant that he had calculated the odds and decided firing into darkness wasn't a great option. The men raised their hands above their heads with their jaws clenched.

"Alex and Heather," instructed the man giving orders, "quickly backpedal away from them, toward my voice."

While the two scientists, who had both also thrown their hands above their heads, lowered them and did as they were told, a second man emerged from the void and began walking toward the two prisoners, reminding them his colleague still had a gun trained on them. He tossed them each a pair of plastic handcuffs and instructed them to slip them around their wrists and pull them tight with their teeth. Soon both men's wrists were bound.

The man who had yelled for them to freeze emerged from the darkness and approached the two scientists. "I'm Eric Trout," he whispered softly, so the men they had just captured couldn't hear. "Ed Cowan sent me. Stay here, and I'll be back in just a few minutes."

Both men marched off with their prisoners. But while four men left, only Trout returned.

"Where are the others?" asked Altschuler.

"I helped my colleague secure them in an SUV. He's taking them somewhere else for . . . um . . . questioning." He turned toward Heather. "Give me your car keys. I'm driving."

As they pulled out of the lot, with Trout driving and the two scientists in the back seat, Altschuler said, "Thanks for saving our necks.

But how did you find us? And how did you know we might be in trouble?"

"Nick Hall's suite at the Homestead Inn was raided three or four hours ago. Two men Ed Cowan had posted for security were killed."

Altschuler shrank back as if he had seen a ghost. "And Nick and Megan?" he asked, terrified of the answer he might get.

"We don't know. Hopefully, my colleague can learn more from the two men we captured. Once Cowan discovered what happened, he pulled out all the stops to find you. He didn't know who was behind it, or if they would make a play for you as well. My guess is that they were waiting for you to come out of the building. Who knows for how long."

"Where are we going?" asked Heather.

"To a safe house outside of Sacramento. But not directly. We'll need to switch cars a few times at certain parking garages in a certain way to shake any possible satellite surveillance. Although I doubt anyone wasted satellite time on this operation once they knew your location. They expected gathering you up to be a walk in the park. They didn't draw any weapons and remained in the light. I'd bet no one else will learn what happened here for hours. But we like to be on the safe side."

Trout instructed his PDA to contact Ed Cowan and Cameron Fyfe. "They've been awake since the attack on the Homestead Inn," he explained as the call went through. "I need to report in."

Trout was three minutes into his report when Altschuler's phone vibrated.

"Alex, it's me," came the breathless voice of Nick Hall when he answered. "Be careful! Someone was able to track us to Theia Labs, which means they could have tracked you to Madera. Get out of there now! And watch your back!"

"Are you and Megan okay?" said Altschuler anxiously, noting the irony of the timing of Hall's warning as he did.

Hall assured him that they were fine and that Megan was in on the call as well.

"Is that Nick and Megan?" asked Trout from the front seat, having overheard Altschuler while delivering his report. "What's their condition?" he asked before Altschuler could respond.

"They're both unharmed."

"Great. I'm going to conference us all together," said Trout, and then instructed his PDA to perform the magic necessary to tie Megan Emerson, Nick Hall, Ed Cowan, and Cameron Fyfe all together on the speaker phone of Heather's Toyota.

Altschuler brought Megan and Hall up to speed on recent events. He explained that Hall's warning had come too late, but that Trout had intervened. And that the three of them were now in Heather's car.

Next it was Hall's turn, who explained that he and Megan had been kidnapped by the military, and brought to a safe house.

"If they were military," said Cowan, "why didn't they take you to Edwards?"

"I have no idea. Nor do I have any idea who they were. Or what they wanted."

"They didn't tell you what they wanted?" repeated Fyfe in disbelief. "They went to all this trouble and they just let you go? Didn't ask any questions?"

"No, they *didn't* just let us go. I was coming to how we escaped. There was one guy in the room with me, who was about to begin an interrogation, when Megan came to the rescue. The man guarding Megan in another room underestimated her. She managed to clock him in the head with a lamp and spring me. Both men will be out for a long while."

"You do seem to lead a charmed life," said Fyfe, and his tone suggested he found it difficult to believe anyone could be as lucky as Hall continued to be. "Great job, Megan. I had no idea you were so . . . formidable."

"Me either," said Megan.

"But why would the military be after you?" pressed Fyfe. "It doesn't make any sense."

"I have no idea," said Hall. "But whatever the guy in charge wanted, he didn't seem like the type to give up easily."

"Where are you right now?" asked Cowan.

Hall explained they had taken a car from their abductors and gave him their location.

Cowan left the call for several minutes. When he returned, he instructed Hall to ditch his phone, drive to a nearby shopping center, and wait to be picked up in front of the Macy's at the southeast corner of the mall.

"The men I send will switch cars and do other stunts to be sure we lose any eyes in the sky," said Cowan. "After that, you'll be joining Alex and Heather at a safe house in Sacramento—a little over a hundred miles from where you are now."

"Great," said Megan sarcastically. "I've gone my whole life without ever being inside a safe house—whatever the hell a safe house really is, anyway. And now I get to be in two of them in the same day. What are the odds?"

"Look, Cameron," said Hall, changing the subject. "We need to learn what this is all about before I have a coming-out party. Now I have to worry about Delamater *and* the military. So being presented to the FBI on Tuesday is out. You'll need to make up some story at the press conference. Say I disappeared again. Or make up something else. But you have to buy more time until we sort this out."

There was a long silence. "Agreed," said Fyfe finally. "I'll take care of it. And Ed, get some more ex-military for hire to look into this as well. In the meanwhile, I'll work my contacts to try to learn what's going on."

The conversation continued for a few minutes before Fyfe and Cowan signed off. Once they left, Hall had Trout take him off speaker and return the call to Alex's phone.

"Can I be overheard?" Hall said softly once this was done.

"Hold on," said Altschuler, pulling a wireless earbud from his pocket and sliding it into his right ear. "You're good to go," he said.

Hall briefed Altschuler as quickly and efficiently as he could as to what had really happened: that Girdler had learned of his ESP and had decided he was too dangerous to let live, fearing an ESP arms race.

Altschuler was stunned. The implications of this were profound, but now wasn't the time to ponder them.

"The good news is that none of us should have any trouble making it to the safe house," said Hall. "There are only two men in on this. Colonel Girdler, and his second-in-command, Major Mike Campbell. But I read from Girdler that the major wasn't monitoring things when we escaped. Girdler told him he had everything well in hand and ordered him to get some sleep."

"Why?"

"Girdler thought he was being heroic. Killing me is going against orders, and he wanted to keep the major clean if it was ever discovered. Plausible deniability." Hall paused. "But with the men Girdler sent to retrieve you and Heather out of the picture, and Girdler unconscious for a few more hours, there's no one tracking us."

"Good to know," said Altschuler, choosing his words carefully since Trout could hear his end of the conversation. "And alerting this guy's boss may be just the ticket."

He knew Hall was bright enough to understand what he was saying. If this colonel was disobeying orders, Hall needed to have a little conversation with the person above him in the chain of command.

"This occurred to me also. The problem is that his boss, a general named Sobol, doesn't want me on the loose, either. He wants me as a guinea pig. And a weapon. But it's definitely something I'll have to consider. In the meanwhile, how did the surgery go?"

"Perfectly," replied Altschuler, although with Trout in earshot he kept his voice bland and revealed no trace of the enthusiasm he would have been gushing otherwise. "Like a dream."

"Meaning you *can* surf, but you *can't* read minds?"

"Exactly."

"Fantastic! Finally, a bit of *good* news." Hall sighed. "On that note," he added, "I'd better be signing off. I need to lose the phone and get to, ah . . . Macy's. But there are some other topics I want to raise with you, Alex, so stay safe."

"You too," said Altschuler. "I'll see you in Sacramento."

48

Heather Zambrana awoke and glanced at a clock on the end table. It was almost noon. She still could have used more sleep, but the sleep she had managed had done wonders for her after the crazy events of the night before, which had bled all the way into sunrise that morning.

The safe house was a large, fairly nondescript tract home in a moderately affluent neighborhood, with four bedrooms, and spare, utilitarian furnishings. Two of the men who had brought them there, Eric Trout and a man named Tyrone Tienda—both ex-military—had stayed to keep watch near the front and back doors, while the four civilians had all fallen asleep in their clothes.

Megan Emerson and Nick Hall were already sound asleep when she and Alex had arrived, since they had been closer to Sacramento, and had chosen to share a room. This wasn't surprising from what Alex had told her about them, although she was certain they had been too exhausted to do anything but sleep. She and Alex had chosen separate rooms. But she had hopes that this might change—as early as that night.

The purpose of the house was to hide and protect those on the run or in danger, so the timing and nature of its occupants couldn't be predicted. For this reason, it was well-equipped with simple men and women's clothing in several sizes, unopened toothbrushes, and other toiletries.

As she showered and changed clothes, she thought of Alex Altschuler.

He was absolutely *brilliant*. And there was a kindness to him. Also, it was adorable the way he looked at her; like an awkward high schooler with a crush. He wasn't much to look at, true, but looks had never mattered all that much to her; her own or others. So he was ten pounds underweight and she was ten pounds over. They balanced each other out. She was also several years older than him, but if that didn't bother him, it didn't bother her.

He loved science and science fiction and was a fun and interesting conversationalist. She could imagine them attending Comic-con together, each dressed as their favorite superhero. How fun would that be?

She had intended to respect the boss-employee code, as he had been so careful in doing, but these recent developments had changed everything. It was time to go for broke. And if a relationship did develop, he could always change the reporting structure so she no longer reported to him, and disclose a relationship as required in the corporate charter. Or she could leave and work elsewhere. Either way, now wasn't the time to hide behind a silly corporate edict, designed to protect management from sexual harassment lawsuits.

When she and her fellow civilians were all up and about, each now scrubbed clean and wearing the safe house's boring, but fresh clothes, their bodyguards gave them a tour of the house. Their last stop was the panic room, which could be entered just beyond the kitchen.

Trout led them inside, and Heather found it to be quite impressive. About the size of a small guest bedroom, it was fortified with steel, Kevlar, and bullet-resistant fiberglass, and its ventilation system was externally vented. The room was carpeted, which was rare, since these rooms were only inhabited during emergencies, and comfort and appearance weren't high on the list of priorities. A steel workbench stood against a side wall, the purpose of which Heather couldn't even hazard a guess, and above the bench was a gun rack with an impressive array of firepower.

On another wall, a bank of monitors provided twelve different views outside of the house. These same views would be accessible from Trout's and Tienda's cell phones and tablets at all times, and a PDA named Tanya would alert them to anything unusual the cameras might detect. Even so, Trout explained, he and his colleague were paid to be paranoid, so would most often station themselves near the front and back doors, just to be sure.

"I've adjusted the cameras to the settings I prefer," said Trout. "They cover every square inch of the perimeter of the house, out to six yards. I've also chosen a few panoramic views. While there are gaps when you go farther out from the house, I've covered the angles *I* would take if I were going to lead an assault on us."

Heather swallowed hard from yet another reminder that she wasn't in Kansas anymore. "That's very comforting," she said dryly.

An hour after the tour was completed, Heather was sitting around a kitchen table with Alex, Megan, and Nick, eating a ham and Swiss omelet that Megan had made for each of them. They had asked their bodyguards if they could have some privacy in the kitchen, and they had been happy to oblige. Even so, the four civilians kept their voices low.

Altschuler reported on a conversation he had just ended with Cameron Fyfe and Ed Cowan. Fyfe was going forward with the press conference as planned, with one notable exception. He wouldn't be introducing Alex as CEO. Fyfe himself would become interim CEO until he could figure out why the military was after Hall, and why they had sent men for Altschuler. Naming a CEO the US government seemed to want to abduct or kill probably wasn't something that would get strong shareholder support.

Heather gazed at Altschuler, directly across from her, with deep lines of concern in her face. "I'm so sorry, Alex. How disappointed are you?"

"I'm disappointed," he replied. And then, with the hint of a tired smile, he added, "But also a little relieved. Being CEO for the first time is scary. Even more scary when all hell is about to break loose. This way, I'll be a little less in the path of the raging inferno until this dies out. And I can't blame Cameron. I think his decision makes a lot of sense."

"Speaking of being in the path of something deadly," said Megan. "Did Cowan tell you if he learned anything from the men they captured last night?"

Altschuler shook his head. "No. They're special forces operatives, who got legitimate orders from their superiors. But they don't know who ultimately is at the top of the pyramid. Or why they were asked to bring us in."

Heather frowned. "They didn't, you know . . . torture them or anything, did they?" she said.

"No. I asked Cowan the same question. They used truth drugs and set them free. I got the feeling Cowan did this for practical reasons rather than ethical ones. He said torturing government spooks, and especially killing them, was a sure way to kick the hornets' nest, and would have been a very bad move."

"Any leads on Delamater?" asked Megan.

"None. Fyfe had hoped to be able to have him wrapped up with a bow for the press conference. But it's not looking good. Cowan has run up quite a bill, tapping dozens of security-for-hire types, like our two friends in this house, but they haven't gotten anywhere."

He stared at Heather, and his eyes took on a puppy dog quality as he did. "Fyfe did ask about the newest member of our group."

Heather raised her eyebrows. "What did you tell him about me?" she asked. Given that Fyfe wasn't in on Nick's ESP, nor Altschuler's recent implants, she knew this would be a difficult question to answer.

"That I had freaked out because I thought of a possible technical problem with the implants. I told Fyfe I couldn't really explain my concern, because it was out of his depth. But it was a problem that might cause the system to glitch up after a few months. I needed some equipment in Madera to check into it. But even more importantly, I needed *your* expertise," he said, nodding at Heather. "I told him it turned out to be a false alarm, but I was forced to trust you with the *Explorer* situation. Given the world would know very soon, anyway, I took it upon myself to make this executive decision."

"Very creative," said Heather with a big smile, and she could tell Alex was delighted by the compliment.

When breakfast ended, Hall and Altschuler retreated to opposite couches in the living room and closed their eyes for over an hour, each explaining they were doing research. It was a foreshadowing of things to come, Heather realized. Of a future in which, if you came across someone with their eyes closed and looking like a zombie, you couldn't be sure if they were *sleeping*, or if they were balancing their checkbook, writing a novel, or watching a movie inside of their head.

With Alex and Nick out of commission, Heather thought this was a good opportunity to get to know Megan, and they returned to the kitchen table and sipped coffee and talked about a variety of topics.

"So you and Nick are pretty close, aren't you?" said Heather at one point.

Megan smiled. "Given how short a time we've known each other, *very* close. We'd be even closer if it weren't for a pesky injury," she added. She leaned towards Heather conspiratorially. "You and Alex sort of have a thing for each other also, don't you?"

"Did Nick tell you that?"

"No. Nick's not like that. He knows having a mind reader around is a menace, and he'd never share anything private he reads unless he really needs to. But I could just tell."

Heather confirmed that she was interested, and believed that Alex was also.

"So is it something in the water?" asked Megan. "I *think* I like Nick a lot, but given you and Alex are falling for each other, maybe if you force any man and woman together in a pressure cooker like this, their hormones play tricks with their minds."

"There is evidence with certain species," said Heather, "that if there's enough food and space, and their populations have declined dramatically or are under stress, individuals tend to want to mate more often. Sort of nature's way of speeding up the regrowth of a population that has come under pressure. But I don't think that's it. At least not for me and Alex. We kind of had a thing for each other before this. Although we pretended we didn't. That's why Alex chose me to join this group. There were others who were qualified."

"Either way," said Megan with a grin, "I have a feeling we'll have two couples tonight trying to, um. . . rebuild the population, so to speak. It'll be like we're in some kind of surreal summer camp. Where boys and girls pair off to practice their night moves, avoiding the watchful eyes of the camp counselors."

"The counselors being Eric Trout and Tyrone Tienda?"

"Exactly. Although when I went to camp, the counselors weren't trained killers with guns." Megan sipped her coffee. "I wonder how many implants you'd have to stick in a human head before we stop having such a vital need to take comfort in the arms of fellow primates?"

Before Heather could answer, Altschuler came through the door with an excited gleam in his eye. "Where's Nick?" he asked.

Megan shrugged. "He was in the living room with you," she said. "Maybe he went to the bathroom."

"I'll look," said Altschuler and left the room once again.

He returned with Hall in tow a few minutes later. "I think I've found a way to solve Nick's little problem," he announced when they were all together.

Hall's face lit up. "Fantastic. But I thought you said any tinkering with my implants could be dangerous."

"I did. But I've been researching and thinking about possible underlying causes of your condition. I've come to believe there must be some frequency range for which the Internet works but your psionic power doesn't. I'm sure I can write some fairly simple iterative software I can send to your implants. Programming them to modify frequencies every few seconds. You just have to keep surfing the web and reading minds while I do. I'm convinced we'll find settings that will allow the Internet to work, but will cure you of your ESP. Once we do, I can nail them down, and modify your software so your implants can't ever accept further changes to these settings. That way, nothing on earth can ever bring it back."

"How long will it take for you to prepare on your end?" asked Hall excitedly.

"A few hours."

"*Outstanding.* And this will give me time to film my bit for the press conference. If this works, Alex, I owe you a dinner."

Altschuler laughed. "Well, with that as motivation, how can I miss?"

Alex Altschuler excused himself to lie down on a bed, close his eyes, and focus on manipulating files and software with his thoughts, while the other three civilians relocated to the living room and the television.

There hadn't been a TV built in the past five years that wasn't Internet ready, and which didn't have a built-in high-definition camera for video-conferencing and for making simple YouTube videos, of the type Hall intended to make now, to be shown the next morning at the press conference. The better TVs both filmed and received in 3-D, and the one in the safe house was no exception.

The only problem was that Hall had no idea how to proceed. They discussed it for almost forty minutes, out of earshot of their bodyguards. In the end, they concluded there was no way to prove in a video format that Hall could manipulate the Internet with his mind.

Sure, if he were giving a live demonstration, it would be easy. Have several well-trusted journalists send a text message to an address in his brain while he was standing blindfolded in front of them, and be amazed as he read the message back to them. Or ask him to go to random URLs and read off from the pages he found there while they checked his accuracy on their own computers. There were dozens of compelling demonstrations that quickly came to mind.

But video was canned, and could be faked. Megan could write a text, show it to the camera, and then Hall could repeat it a moment later while blindfolded. But viewers couldn't know for sure Megan hadn't told Hall the contents of the message beforehand.

Their most creative idea involved Hall blindfolded, with several thick ski caps also over his head, in the same video shot as Megan rolling three dice. She would then enter the random results of the dice roll into her cell phone, also in front of the camera, and hit send. Moments later Hall would read off the numbers. She could repeat this several times. Since there was no way for Megan to know what numbers the dice would land on, there was no opportunity for collusion.

There were only three little problems with this idea. One, video editing techniques had become so seamless the entire shot could have been faked. Two, there was no way to know someone wasn't watching off-site and communicating the numbers to Hall through a hidden transmitter in his ear. And three, talented magicians could pull off feats even more impressive than this.

In the end, Hall introduced himself, recounted his last conscious minutes on board the *Explorer,* and described his internal Internet capabilities. He detailed the system's ability to bypass ears and eyes, and therefore cure deafness and blindness, and to allow surfing with thoughts alone. He waxed poetic about what it was like to be able to instantly harness the greatest repository of information the world had ever known. Then he worked with Megan to provide several demonstrations, before finally acknowledging that he was aware his demonstrations were not conclusive, and could have been faked. He promised, however, that as soon as his responsibilities to help those investigating the *Explorer* tragedy were discharged, he would demonstrate the capabilities of his implants conclusively to any number of famous reporters, in person, until not a smidgen of doubt remained.

Once his piece was ready, he sent it off to Fyfe in New York. It was off the cuff, unrehearsed, and the production values were amateurish, but Megan insisted its very lack of polish lent it a certain authenticity and appeal.

If lack of polish truly was a positive thing, thought Hall, it would be an extraordinarily appealing video, indeed.

49

Alex Altschuler was ready with his software even before Hall had finished his video presentation. With his most important job completed, Hall sat on the couch with his eyes closed while Altschuler retreated to the bedroom once again.

Eric Trout and Tyrone Tienda wandered through the area twice each, but were paid to protect, not to ask questions, so they didn't comment on the odd behavior of the people they were protecting: one asleep in a bedroom in the middle of the afternoon, one apparently asleep on the couch, and two women on another couch studying the sleeping figure with almost giddy anticipation.

Heather and Megan would have liked to continue their discussion and get to know each other even better, but neither was about to risk missing the outcome of this experiment.

Less than an hour later Hall's eyes shot open and he jumped to his feet. "It *worked!*" he shouted, his expression both triumphant and stunned, and a moment later he looked to be on the verge of tears.

He hugged Heather, kissed and hugged Megan, and when Altschuler vaulted into the room a short time later, Hall gave the scrawny scientist a bear hug that might have lasted ten full seconds, lifting him off the ground and spinning in circles.

"Thank you, Alex!" he said exultantly.

"You're very welcome," said Altschuler when Hall let him go. "But next time, you really need to buy me that dinner you promised *before* I let you hug me like that."

Hall laughed.

Megan's eyes became moist. "I am *so* happy for you, Nick," she said softly.

Heather didn't doubt it. She was also certain Megan was happy for *herself* as well, having no idea how any woman could handle being romantically involved with a man who could read her every thought.

Hall closed his eyes and let out a long breath. "This is *awesome*," he announced. "No more endless chatter. No more vicious, ugly thoughts from kids and parents and bosses and employees. No more disturbing sexual fantasies."

Heather had been told what Nick was going through, but as the newest member of the group, it hadn't really sunk it. "You really picked up stuff like that all the time?" she said.

"Yes. I learned to deal with it—for the most part. Suppress it and ignore it. Turn it into white noise and desensitize myself to it. But if I was around even a moderate-sized group of people, and focused on individual thoughts for even a short time, I was drowned in this type of ugliness. And some thoughts couldn't be ignored no matter what I did. The more wicked, caustic, hateful thoughts seemed to be stronger than the rest and could break through the noise." Hall shuddered just from the memory. "But thanks to the genius of *this* man," he added, slapping Altschuler heartily on the back, "the long nightmare has ended."

Heather Zambrana caught Alex's eye and nodded approvingly.

"Now I just have to find a way to prove I'm ESP free to a certain colonel," said Hall. "And all of us live happily ever after. Especially me," he said, smiling broadly at Megan.

"I don't want to bring you down," said Altschuler, "but you need to be sure Girdler doesn't manage to kill you *before* you're able to share the good news."

"You do have a point," said Hall. "And it is harder to come up with a convincing demonstration when you're dead."

Heather smiled, impressed that Hall could use gallows humor when his was the neck that was *in* said gallows. But after what he had been through, maybe it was either that or go insane.

Two hours later, Hall and Altschuler insisted on preparing dinner, using Internet recipes they conjured up in their heads to match the food they found in the refrigerator and freezer. In another hour, all six residents of the safe house were dining on tomato basil soup,

Caesar salad, and lemon chicken. Trout and Tienda, who had spelled each other while they caught a few hours of sleep, took their food back to their stations on the inner perimeter of the house, while the four civilians ate at the kitchen table.

After dinner the group returned to the living room.

Heather couldn't believe how well everything was coming together. Historic events were occurring at a rapid-fire pace. Not only did these represent monumental leaps forward for humanity, and not only were they amazing to be a part of, but they also gave her and Alex even more in common than they had before. As they began to pick up and reinforce each other's mutual signals of interest, by nine at night they found themselves so close together on the couch they were nearly touching. Even so, Alex still acted like Heather had a force field around her. And she was too shy to break the physical ice further.

When Alex got up to use the bathroom, Heather had a quick verbal exchange with Megan and then returned to her place on the couch. When the bespectacled scientist reseated himself, Megan walked over to them and shook her head. "I'm afraid I have some bad news," she said. "I spoke with Trout. It looks like you two will have to share a room tonight. " She turned to Heather. "Do you have any problem with that, Heather?"

Heather shook her head. "None at all," she replied.

"But I don't understand," said the smartest person among them— at least in some ways. "There are plenty of rooms. Why would we—"

"*Really*, Alex?" interrupted Megan. "Heather here says she doesn't have a problem sharing a room with you tonight. Are you sure you want to ask questions?"

Altschuler gritted his teeth and looked like he wanted to slap his palm against his forehead. "Right," he said with a stupid smile. "If we're short of rooms, we're short of rooms. You know, if we have to make that sacrifice, I'm certainly willing to do my part."

"Well played, Alex," said Hall with a grin.

The conversation continued, and soon Altschuler had his arm around Heather and she had her head on his chest, both of them content as could be.

The group was discussing their favorite movies twenty minutes later when Eric Trout rushed into the room and over to a window. "I just got an alert from Tanya," he said, speaking once again of the PDA that serviced the home's TVs, computers, and security system. "Do you hear that?"

Now that he mentioned it, Heather realized she did hear something—several sirens, very faint in the distance. Everyone joined Trout by the window. The sirens grew louder, and soon the unmistakable flashing lights of several police cars could also be seen in the night sky.

"Are they coming here?" asked Altschuler, a hint of panic creeping into his voice.

Trout put in an immediate call to Ed Cowan and described what was happening, but within minutes it became clear the cars were not headed in their direction, after all, to the relief of the group.

A short time later Cowan called back and had a brief conversation with Trout.

"Cowan did some digging through police channels," explained the bodyguard. "Some woman was getting brutally beaten in her house. Apparently, by some guy her husband hired to kill her. And to do it slowly so she would suffer."

Megan shuddered. "And I thought *my* parents' divorce was bitter," she whispered with a mixture of sadness and revulsion. "Talk about hating your wife."

"Were they able to save her?" asked Heather.

"They were," replied Trout. "They caught the bastard who was doing it before he finished. The woman will need a few nights in the hospital, but she should pull through."

"Thank God," said Heather.

Hall shook his head. "Humanity," he said sadly. "Sometimes it's really hard to be a fan."

"That's for sure," said Megan. After a long silence, she added, "But as horrible as this is, we should try not to let it bring us down right now."

Everyone nodded their agreement with this sentiment.

"I know," said Megan a few seconds later with a sly smile. "Why don't we adjourn to our respective rooms and find some positive way to reaffirm *our* humanity."

Altschuler turned away from Megan and gazed deeply into Heather's eyes. "Now *that*," he said, having learned from his previous mistake, "is the best idea I've heard in a long time."

50

Alex Altschuler had never been happier in his life. He and Heather had made love several times during the night and early morning, and had chatted like teens at a slumber party when their bodies weren't otherwise preoccupied. They had only managed a few hours sleep, but Altschuler was giddy in mind and body, and Heather Zambrana seemed to radiate happiness beside him.

The press conference was scheduled for ten in the morning, New York time, which meant seven o'clock in California. They had set the alarm for six, but at five-thirty they were wide awake and decided to get a jump on the day, since Altschuler was sure he wouldn't be able to make love again for many hours—maybe never.

They both took quick showers, and were on their way to the kitchen to surprise the rest of the house's inhabitants by making a pancake breakfast, when they heard a pained shriek. "*Nooo!*" bellowed a voice that sounded like it might be Nick Hall's, coming from a nearby bedroom.

They rushed to his room and Altschuler rapped on the door. "Nick, are you okay in there?"

There was no answer.

"Nick. If you don't answer, I'm coming in."

When they still didn't get an answer, Altschuler turned the handle and he and Heather stepped into the room.

Hall was sitting in the bed, wearing a pair of light blue pajama bottoms with no shirt, with a stunned look on his face, as though he were in a coma. He was holding a piece of notebook paper, with writing scrawled all over it.

He glanced up at them as they entered, but didn't move. The piece of paper dropped from his hand and fell to the bed.

"Nick?" said Heather, an anxious look on her face. "What's going on? Where's Megan?"

Hall caught Altschuler's eye. "Read it," he said, as though he were in agony, making the smallest gesture with his head toward the fallen piece of paper. "Go ahead, Alex. Read it out loud."

Altschuler glanced at Heather, only then realizing they were holding hands. He removed his hand from hers and retrieved the paper from the bed. He walked to a point midway between Heather and Hall and began reading.

"*Dearest Nick,*

In the short time you've been in my life, I've come to care about you more than any man I've ever known. After we made love last night (well, to the limits of what's possible with an injured Neanderthal) I had the irresistible urge to tell you I loved you. How psycho is that? I'm scared, Nick. I've never felt this way before. I've fallen for you too hard, too fast.

Did I mention I'm scared? Funny, people have been trying to capture or kill me for days now, but my feelings for you scare me more than any of that.

I'm so happy for you that your psionic curse has been lifted. Soon you'll have your life back. You'll be famous beyond famous, and since you won't be a pariah, you can have any woman you want. I know you said you didn't love Alicia anymore, but I suspect that was just sour grapes, because you knew you couldn't have a relationship with her anyway in your previous condition."

Who in the world was Alicia? thought Altschuler. And what did Megan mean by *injured Neanderthal?* He had begun to think he really knew Nick Hall, but apparently not. Now wouldn't be a great time to ask him these questions, he decided, so he continued reading:

"*This isn't your fault, Nick. You've been incredible. Fun. Smart. Heroic. Everything I could possibly ask for. But this is becoming too real, too fast. You know how I feel about marriage. My parents once loved each other passionately, and that ended in nothing but bitterness and hatred. And I won't even mention the incident nearby we heard about last night. So maybe humans aren't meant to marry.*

But when I'm with you, I don't believe this anymore. You're like a mind-altering drug. One that I fear may be very bad for my health.

Besides, being the girl a celebrity dated before his fame, who just happened to be in the right place at the right time, before being tossed aside for something better, just isn't my style.

So I'm leaving. I need time to get away from your zone of charisma. Time to think. And you need time as well.

Don't worry, I'll check in with Ed Cowan every few days. I've taken some of your poker winnings so I can stay off the grid until he tells me it's safe to stick my head up again. Maybe one day I'll be able to call you and see how you're doing. But I suspect this will be too painful to do for some time to come.

Good luck, Nick. You're a wonderful man, and I wish you nothing but the best. I know I'll be reading and seeing all about you in the days ahead.

With fondest memories,
Megan."

Altschuler looked up from the letter. Heather's eyes had teared up, and Hall still looked like he had been hit by a train.

Altschuler could only imagine what Hall must be feeling. How would he feel if Heather walked out of his life, just when they had made such a great connection? How would he feel knowing the reason for it wasn't something he had done, but simply because she had fallen for him *too* hard. What a brutal irony. What a bitter pill *that* would be to swallow.

Suddenly, as Altschuler looked on, Hall's expression went from utterly despondent to furious in the blink of an eye. He jumped up off the bed. "Wait here," he said as he raced by them to the door, still shirtless.

Altschuler and Heather ignored Hall's instructions and rushed after him.

Hall marched straight for Eric Trout, who had manned the graveyard shift while his partner slept, and was due to be spelled shortly. "Anything interesting happen last night or this morning?" asked Hall in a venomous tone.

Trout was taken aback. "No. We still seem to be locked down tight."

"*Really?*" thundered Hall. "Are you *that* incompetent? Do you know that Megan Emerson isn't in this so-called safe house anymore? *Do you know that?*" he shouted.

From the look on Trout's face, it was obvious that he didn't. "That's impossible."

"I'm fucking positive!" shouted Hall. "So how is that *you* don't know that? Weren't you and your partner watching the doors? Watching your video? How could you let her just waltz out of here?"

Trout's lip curled up into a snarl, and he looked about ready to crush Hall's windpipe, but managed to control himself. He was being paid to protect these people, not kill them.

"Tanya," he said to his tablet computer with barely contained fury. "Did Megan Emerson leave the premises?" He shot Hall a contemptuous look, as though he was sure Hall was about to be proven wrong and shown to be a hotheaded jackass.

"Yes. Megan Emerson left at three thirteen this morning," replied a soothing, unflappable computer voice.

"*What?*" barked Trout, horrified. "Why wasn't I alerted?"

"Megan Emerson was listed as a resident. I've been programmed to ignore the comings and goings of residents."

"God dammit!" screamed Trout. "What kind of fucked up . . ."

Trout paused and visibly tried to get a grip on himself. He turned to Hall, his eyes still burning. "I apologize, Nick. This is idiotic programming, which I'll fix. This shouldn't have happened without me knowing it. But I can't be everywhere at once," he continued, anger seeping into his tone despite his best efforts. "So if Megan decided she wanted to wait until I couldn't see her and slip out, there's nothing I can do about it. At the end of the day, I can only protect people who *want* to be protected. If she's suicidal enough to leave here, she takes her chances. Where the *fuck* did she go, anyway?"

Hall's demeanor had changed again, and now he looked like a whipped puppy. "I don't know," he whispered. "She just left. She plans to stay off the grid and check in with Cowan every few days."

Hall turned and walked away without another word, and Altschuler and Heather followed him back into his bedroom, where he sat on the bed once more.

"Nick," said Heather, "are you going to be okay?"

"I don't know," he said woodenly, but it was clear he was devastated.

Altschuler stared at what now appeared to be the shell of a man, and decided he needed to play the heavy. Not that he wanted to kick a man when he was down, but too much was going on, and they owed it to Nick—and themselves—to deliver a dose of reality.

"I feel horrible for you, Nick," he began. "But the timing here isn't great. Cameron's press conference is less than an hour away. After that, all hell breaks loose. Not to mention powerful people are still trying to kill you, at least until you can prove your ESP is gone. Again, I can't tell you how much I feel for you, Nick. But I worry about your ability to weather this storm if you can't shake this off. It's like going into a hot zone with an impaired immune system."

Heather lowered her eyes, but nodded her agreement.

Hall opened his mouth to speak but shut it once again. He stared at Altschuler and then Heather for several seconds. Finally, his right hand balled up into an unconscious fist and he rose from the bed.

"You're right!" he said. "You're absolutely right. No more moping around. I don't have the luxury. And do you know what else? I'm going to get her back! As soon as I convince Girdler I'm clean. I don't care what it takes. I'm going to convince her that I don't care about Alicia, and I don't care about fame, and I don't care about any girls I might meet in the future. I won't stop until she reconsiders. She thinks *she's* stubborn. Well, she ain't seen nothing yet."

Altschuler studied the steely gleam in Hall's eye and the resolve in his expression, and a faint smile came over his face. There were no guarantees in life, he thought. Maybe Nick Hall would fail to get Megan back, after all. But Alex Altschuler would be the last man on earth to bet against him.

51

Theia Labs had conducted corporate-sponsored press conferences before, but never in New York. Cameron Fyfe was unable to score a large conference hall in a luxury hotel on short notice, and unsure if he wanted to anyway. The conference ended up being held in a fairly small room at the Hudson Hotel, a lesser known facility that had sprouted up almost a mile from Times Square, with maybe fifteen journalists in attendance. He had intimated to each that they were being given an exclusive on a press conference they would never forget, but after seeing the limited audience and unimpressive setting, the majority began to wonder if they had been misled.

The press conference wasn't nearly important enough, or so the world thought, to appear live on any of the many hundreds of available television channels. But it was being videotaped, and could be accessed live on the web.

When the conference began, there were only five or six TVs tuned in to the web broadcast, including one in the living room of a tract home outside of Sacramento, California. By the time the conference ended, alerted by frantically texted messages from the few attendees, there were thousands.

At ten o'clock exactly, Fyfe came out onto a raised podium, just to the side of an eight-foot-tall screen that looked like a large picture window behind him. He introduced himself as the interim CEO of Theia Labs and then, without any further preamble, he launched deep into the heart of the matter.

He began by narrating actual footage of the attack on the *Explorer*, explaining it had been taken from the computer of Theia Labs' former CEO, Kelvin Gray, who was now dead—fatally shot several days earlier in a fracas that had ensued when he was confronted about his crimes.

This opening got the attention of the crowd like nothing ever had in any of their collective experiences. The footage was taken from a helicopter and zoomed in on an oceangoing vessel, almost lost amid an endless, tranquil sea of greenish-blue. As the helicopter got closer, those aboard the *Explorer* could be seen sprawled out around the deck, in haphazard poses of unconsciousness. Four other large helicopters were swooping in from the other direction, flying low, and soon the unconscious victims were being loaded into the helos like cordwood; presumably to be transferred to another oceangoing vessel within flying distance.

Fyfe calmly and methodically explained why these people had been kidnapped and killed, and showed evidence of who was responsible, and why. Gray had actually made some video entries, discussing the progress of the experimentation, and Fyfe showed a few minutes of these, just to be certain everyone recognized that Gray was behind this, and seriously deranged.

Fyfe explained that even as he spoke, hundreds of gigabytes of video and text taken from Gray's computer, giving clear evidence of his heinous crimes, were being made available to the press, public, and criminal authorities. The evidence would make it clear that Gray was responsible, along with a mysterious man named John Delamater, and that the hundreds of Theia employees and consultants working on projects based on these barbaric experiments had no knowledge of them.

As planned, Fyfe eloquently expressed, on behalf of the company, his remorse and outrage, and made it clear the families of the victims would be well-compensated for their tragic losses, although he was well aware that nothing could compensate for what had been so ruthlessly taken away from them. He then expressed the intent of Theia's management to move forward and put this behind the company through philanthropy and improving human lives.

While he made it clear that nothing could erase the horrific nature of the crime, Theia believed they were now on the verge of a cure for blindness and deafness. He showed a video presentation with a complex, 3-D animation of how implants, connected to electronic retinas and ear drums, could provide a sensory experience indistinguishable from the real thing.

He played another video demonstrating how thought-powered web surfing could be done in conjunction with the auditory and visual capabilities, and that this too had been perfected, although at a tragic cost in human lives. Society would have to judge if these inventions, paid for with the blood of innocents, would be used, but Fyfe said he hoped that, ultimately, society would not turn its back on such breathtaking advances because of the way they were obtained. That if they were used to benefit society, at least the men and women of the *Explorer* would not have given their lives for nothing. His oration on these points was nothing short of brilliant.

Fyfe went on to explain that a single member of the *Explorer* expedition was still alive, heaping yet another impossible, shocking revelation on top of the others, and serving it to the small audience whose faces had never lost their stunned expressions since the first minutes of his presentation. He then played the video Nick Hall had made, the cherry on top of his sundae of revelations.

Fyfe explained that there had been recent threats to Hall's life, so he had gone off the grid, and that no one, including Fyfe himself, knew where he was. When these threats were resolved, he assured his audience, Nick Hall would spend as much time with authorities as they would like, and would demonstrate the functioning of his implants as he had promised on his video.

Fyfe finished by cautioning that the future of this technology would depend on world opinion and on the regulatory authorities of each sovereign nation, so that even if the technologies had progressed to this point through legitimate means, it could still take several years of testing before they were released to patients or the general public.

In the hands of someone less skilled, the information Fyfe disclosed might have taken much longer to reveal. But Fyfe knew that he needed to convey it in an hour or less for it to go viral around the world. In an age of ever-shortening attention spans, Fyfe managed to pack a punch the size of an asteroid into every last minute of his presentation.

He ended the conference at exactly eleven a.m., said he would not be taking any questions, and left before anyone knew what was happening.

Even so, had he not thought ahead and made sure two Cowan-hired men were present to run interference, he would have been swarmed by the small group of journalists before he could get *near* an exit. As it was, he slid safely into a car waiting for him outside of the hotel, was driven to a nearby helipad, and in less than an hour was boarding the private jet he had chartered to fly him to California.

52

The fallout from the conference was everything the civilians in the Sacramento safe house thought it would be. Within five hours, over four hundred million people around the world had viewed all or part of it. The initial speculation was that it was a hoax, especially since Nick Hall was conveniently unavailable for corroboration.

But as investigators, journalists, and citizens poured over the hundreds of hours of video and thousands of pages of additional evidence Fyfe had downloaded to public sites, many were now convinced it was all true, and the world was abuzz with visions of a technological and medical revolution beyond all others.

There were debates, both on television and online, about the ethics of using the results of illegal experimentation, but the sentiment was hugely in favor of doing so, as had been obvious since Fyfe had asked Altschuler if he would suppress the absolute cure for cancer just because Hitler had discovered it. Of course the answer was no.

Debates raged on, centering principally on the addictive potential of the technology, and asking the question, at what point do we stop being human? Many had also seized upon other key controversies: porn, lack of privacy, anything said near someone else potentially recorded for all eternity, and so on.

Hall's photo was downloaded millions of times, and Hall sightings were reported in dozens of countries, with citizens of each hoping to spot him with all the fervor of kids trying to find the golden ticket in a Willy Wonka contest.

And this was just the tip of the iceberg, since many had yet to learn of the story and many still believed it to be a hoax. When the story was absolutely proven out, things would really start popping.

Every last Theia Labs employee was visited by the media and hounded for interviews. The press breathlessly reported that the one man they most wanted to interview, Alex Altschuler, Gray's second-in-command, was nowhere to be found, despite their best efforts.

But the employees they did reach reported that they hadn't been aware Kelvin Gray was dead, and that while Theia was working in this general technological realm, they didn't know anything about these breakthroughs, and were just as shocked as everyone else.

Most Theia employees confessed they had thought Kelvin Gray to be a model CEO; handsome, brilliant, a great orator, and a kind and generous man. But as difficult as it was to believe he had committed such atrocities, the evidence was compelling.

Almost six hours after the press conference had ended, Fyfe called Altschuler to let him know that he had landed in California and should arrive at the safe house within an hour or two with Ed Cowan. He said he was looking forward to seeing them all, but especially to meeting the man of the hour, the newly famous Nick Hall.

Hall still wasn't himself. And Megan's absence was deeply felt by Altschuler and Heather as well, who had both gained quite an affection for her in the short time they had known her. But they were so high from their newfound relationship that even if their mood were dampened by half, they would still be euphoric.

Right after Fyfe's call, the group of three civilians returned to the TV vigil they had been maintaining since the press conference many hours earlier, surfing news channels and Internet reaction to the conference. Hall and Altschuler were both using their internal Internet connections as well, and if they found something truly noteworthy they would throw it up on the television for all to see.

They were watching a news program, which was reporting that a pentagon source had confirmed the authenticity of the *Explorer* footage Fyfe had shown, when Alex Altschuler gasped.

"Holy shit!" he said to his two companions. "You need to see this."

Moments later it was up on the main TV. It was an online teaser for an article scheduled to run on the front page of the *Iowa Gazette* the next morning. It was entitled, "ESP: Did Theia Labs Leave Something Out?"

Hall's mouth fell open. "But how could they possibly suspect?" he said.

"You're not going to love the answer," said Altschuler, gesturing to the screen.

Hall and Heather read the short article in silence.

The writer, Janet Hollinger, described how she had received an e-mail addressed to her and over forty other journalists the previous Thursday. The message had indicated it was from someone named Nick Hall, who had no memory, could surf the web with this thoughts, and was desperately reaching out to anyone he could, believing his life was in imminent danger. Oh, and it had also contained one other minor detail.

Hall had claimed to be able to read minds!

The teaser displayed Hall's entire message, in full, and was basically identical to the one he had sent to the police and government types, the contents of which he had read from the mind of Justin Girdler. But Girdler had not been aware Hall had also sent the message to a second batch of addressees.

Janet Hollinger went on to explain how she got hundreds of hoax e-mails each year, but happened to read this one since it was even more creative and farfetched than most. She suspected spam filters had prevented it from being seen by many of her colleagues, and any others who did read it had certainly also thought it was a hoax. How else could it have been seen at the time? Alerted by her, a number of other journalists were confirming that they had now found the message in their spam folders or deleted message archives as well.

When Janet Hollinger had seen a video of the recent press conference, she had remembered the e-mail. Her paper had then conducted a quick investigation, which the expanded story the next morning would describe in greater detail.

But the gist of the investigations was this: the warehouse mentioned in the e-mail was the same one recently disclosed by Theia Labs in the mountain of evidence they had released. The same one videoed several times by Kelvin Gray. And it had been the site of a devastating fire very soon after Hall's e-mail had been sent. They had also learned that several people had been questioned about the warehouse by members of a mysterious government agency.

The e-mail message could still be a hoax, but given it had correctly disclosed the nature of Hall's implants, and the location of the warehouse, days before Fyfe's revelations, it looked for all the world to be legitimate.

So could it be that Hall's implants also gave him ESP? The ability not only to surf the *web*, but to surf the *thoughts* of other people?

Hall hadn't lied about anything else in his desperation e-mail message, the reporter pointed out, so why lie about this? And how else could he have escaped from Kelvin Gray?

The story ended by suggesting that if the message was completely accurate, Cameron Fyfe had quite a bit more explaining to do, and finally, that the expanded report would be available the next morning for anyone who purchased the print or online version of the newspaper. There was little doubt that for one day, the *Iowa Gazette* would have more readers than the *New York Times*, *USA Today*, and the *Wall Street Journal* combined.

"Wow, Nick," said Heather. "You don't remember writing any of that, do you?"

Hall shook his head no.

"You sure kept yourself busy in that warehouse," said Altschuler. "I'll bet it took some major effort for you to find the e-mail addresses of that many journalists."

Heather turned toward Hall. "How big of a problem is this?" she asked. "I mean, you can't read minds anymore. You could for a while and now you can't. End of story."

"I wish it were that easy," said Altschuler.

"It'll be okay," said Hall, but Altschuler wondered if he was trying to convince *himself* of this as much as he was trying to convince his companions. "We can walk this back," he continued. "It adds to our headaches, but it isn't the end of the world. I'll just say my mind had undergone repeated traumas, and I must have hallucinated the ESP thing. That this part wasn't true. And that when others get the implants, they'll see that they don't magically get any voodoo ESP."

"*Voodoo* ESP?" said Heather, raising her eyebrows.

"Well, you know, I'm just trying to make it sound ridiculous. Anyway, there will always be those who believe the ESP I mentioned in the e-mail is real. But when people start getting implants and see they can't read minds, this report will become an unimportant and discredited footnote of the history of this era."

They continued to discuss this and other topics, and to monitor the never-ending barrage of coverage generated by the press conference. It would all be wild enough if they weren't involved, but since they were at the very epicenter of the quake, it was *crazy*. The word *surreal* didn't even begin to do it justice. Especially for Nick Hall, whose photo was prominently displayed in the corner of every major television channel, and who was being talked about, and dissected, on each one.

Fifteen minutes after they had read the *Iowa Gazette* story, Hall was responding to a question Heather had posed to him, when her eyes fell shut. Alex Altschuler noticed this unusual turn of events even before Hall. "Heather?" he said in alarm. "Are you okay?"

But even as he said this, Heather Zambrana toppled over to become an inert lump on the couch.

"What the hell!" said Hall, reaching for her to check for a pulse.

But before he could find it, *his* eyes fell shut as well, and a second later he toppled to the floor.

The video footage Fyfe had shown of the unconscious bodies on the Scripps *Explorer* flashed into Altschuler's mind, but only for an instant, before he, too, slipped to the floor, and into the waiting arms of absolute darkness.

53

Altschuler realized his internal Internet connection was down the moment he began regaining consciousness. Hall had mentioned Girdler had used an electronic device to suppress the WiFi in Hall's vicinity, and no doubt this tactic was being repeated. Like Hall before him, he was struck by how dependent he had become, already, on a capability he had had for less than two days.

He still felt groggy, and his thoughts were swimming in molasses, but he gradually became aware that he was sitting on the beige carpeted floor of the panic room they had toured earlier, against the wall, his hands behind him and handcuffed together. Heather was beside him, to his right, and Hall was situated on the other side of her, all three handcuffed in the same manner.

Altschuler tried to resituate his hands behind him and realized he was also somehow attached to Heather, who was no doubt attached to Hall in turn, a paper chain of unwieldy humanity. Cameron Fyfe had just finished injecting Hall at the end of the short line with an unknown drug, and since Heather and Hall were both now stirring, it must have been a reviving agent.

Cameron Fyfe seated himself on the steel workbench against one side wall, several yards to the left and several feet above the row of prisoners sitting on the floor against the wall. His legs dangled down, not quite reaching the floor, as he set the semi-automatic and dart gun he had confiscated from Hall beside him. Weapons that had recently been the property of Colonel Justin Girdler.

A sense of dread came over Altschuler more palpable than any he had ever experienced. He couldn't die now! Not on the eve of being an integral part of an unparalleled technological revolution. And not when he had just found comfort and happiness in Heather Zambrana's arms.

It wasn't fair.

And yet he knew in his heart that the cosmos could be cruelly ironic, and that his pending death was a certainty.

"How long have we been out?" whispered Altschuler, his tongue still thick. He noticed the time posted on the sleek bank of silver-edged monitors affixed to the opposite wall even as he asked this. It hadn't been long. An hour at most.

He looked around the room. "Where's Ed Cowan?" he added, his mind finally beginning to clear.

Fyfe ignored him.

"Cowan was here already," answered Hall, sounding a little drunk as his faculties gradually returned. "He helped drag us in here. They killed Trout and Tienda, who were also knocked out. Cowan is disposing of the bodies. He'll be back in an hour or two."

Fyfe raised his eyebrows. "Very good, Nick," he said. "I was wondering if you were going to continue pretending you couldn't read minds."

"What's the point? You know I can."

"You can still read minds?" mumbled Heather drunkenly.

When no one answered, she turned to Fyfe, "You killed our bodyguards?" Her words were still slurred but getting better. "Why?"

"Tell her, Nick," said Fyfe.

"Because now that I'm a celebrity, they know too much. They know who I am, that I was here, and that Fyfe was well aware I was here."

"Exactly," said Fyfe, turning back to Heather. "When I burn this place to the ground, and all of your remains are identified by dental records and your skeletons, I can't have any loose ends. Trout and Tienda were loose ends."

"Why are we in this room?" asked Altschuler.

Fyfe shrugged. "I always feel safer in here. And having your remains found in a panic room adds something to the worldwide story this will become. Don't you think?"

Heather's full faculties had finally returned and she stared at Fyfe in horror. "What's all this about? Have you lost your mind?"

Fyfe shook his head in amusement. "You two really didn't tell her, did you?" he said, and then with a shrug added, "I guess it makes sense. No sense staking your futures on her acting abilities."

Heather turned to the two men beside her on the floor. "What's this all about?" she demanded, panic growing.

Once again, everyone ignored her, which her flushed face made abundantly clear was infuriating to her.

"Why haven't you killed us already?" asked Altschuler.

"Tell him, Nick," said Fyfe.

Hall shook his head. "I'm not going to be your mind reading puppet so you can spare your own vocal cords. I can read minds, but not intent. So for the most part, it's better if you formulate your own answers. I wouldn't want any of your psychotic thinking lost in translation."

Fyfe shot Hall an icy glare that was so intense, Hall couldn't help but blink several times. "I'm willing to keep this civilized," said Fyfe calmly. "But if it becomes *uncivilized*, consider who is in a dominant position here and who isn't. Have I made myself clear?"

Hall nodded reluctantly.

Fyfe turned back to Altschuler. "Why haven't I killed you yet, Alex?" he repeated. "Because I've obviously made some mistakes. Or else you wouldn't have suspected I was John Delamater."

Even though their suspicions had now been confirmed, Altschuler had been so certain Fyfe and Delamater were different men—and on wildly different ends of the criminal spectrum—that even knowing the man in front of him was John Delamater, he still couldn't help seeing him as Cameron Fyfe.

"So before I send you to the afterlife," continued Fyfe, "I wanted to understand where I went wrong." He paused. "Do any of you know of a man named Jose Capablanca?"

Fyfe's question was met with blank stares all around.

"He was world chess champion from 1921 to 1927, and widely thought to be the most naturally talented chess player in history. He believed you could learn more by studying your defeats than studying your victories. I'm a grandmaster level player in my own right, and I happen to agree. And while I did win in the end, I stumbled a bit in the middle-game."

He leaned closer to Hall. "So tell me, Nick. Where did I go wrong? How did you know to suspect me?"

"Okay," said Hall. "I'll tell you everything you want to know. In as much detail as you'd like. But I want a quid pro quo. You have to answer our questions as well."

"Oh? And why should I do that?"

"Because you have all the time in the world, so who cares if it takes an extra hour or two to humor us? Because you know this is the easiest way to get total cooperation. And because you love chess. And we've been worthy opponents. Far more worthy than you ever expected. And you have a measure of respect for what we've been able to do. In that same vein, this is your chance to share your brilliant moves with an audience who can appreciate them. One of the only chances you'll ever have. And if a brilliant game is played in the forest, and no one is there to admire it, was it really played at all?"

Fyfe smiled, but it was more crocodilian than amused. "Very Zen, Nick. You can read my mind, so you know what arguments will be effective. But that doesn't diminish their effectiveness. You are correct. In life, as in chess, you can admire an opponent's play, even as you prepare to topple his king. Okay. You have a deal. But why don't you and Alex go first. Tell me where I went wrong?" He gestured toward Hall. "I assume it was you who first suspected."

Heather caught Altschuler's eye, curled up her lip, and glared at him angrily. He couldn't blame her. He and Nick had deduced a danger existed, and had decided to take certain risks, without consulting a woman whose life was also endangered by their decisions. Hopefully she would come to understand why they had decided not to confide in her in the short time they had left. He wasn't sure why it mattered, but the thought of her going to her death thinking he had betrayed her trust was too much for him to bear.

"It wasn't a single thing that made me suspicious," replied Hall, "but a combination. And it started with Ed Cowan. Alex trusted you and Cowan implicitly. You had been the one to bring Gray's crimes to light. And Cowan had saved Alex's life. But when you've lost your memory and everyone is trying to kill you, you learn to be very paranoid. So I vowed not to fully trust anyone whose mind I hadn't read. You were a fair distance away," continued Hall, nodding at Fyfe, "but Cowan was based in Northern California, and even rented the suite at the Homestead Inn for us. So it was curious that he never got within mind reading range of me. I read all of the mercs he hired, of course. None of them knew anything about his past or present, which I found odd. And which made me wonder how legitimate he really was. And several of his hires wondered themselves why he maintained the distance he did from the civilians he was so eager to protect."

"But what would cause you to think he knew about your ESP in the first place?"

"Actually, I didn't guess this until later. But I'll get to that. It was just strange that I never had the chance to read him. But the most suspicious behavior of all came very early on. Ed Cowan was the least paranoid bodyguard in history. I read from Alex's mind that *Alex* had been the one to push for extra precautions at the Homestead Inn. Cowan wouldn't have even posted guards next door. And even when he did, he told them he didn't expect trouble. Why? How could he be so sure the fabled John Delamater, who had shown himself to be incredibly resourceful, wouldn't pick up our trail again?"

Fyfe nodded thoughtfully. "Yes. And you realized one possibility was that he knew Delamater wasn't going to trouble you, because he was working *with* Delamater." He sighed. "A small but telling oversight we shouldn't have made. He still needed to act as though Delamater was a huge threat, to better keep up the facade. I see it now."

"So this line of reasoning led me to suspect the man he was working with was potentially John Delamater. Which meant you. You had hired Cowan and brought him into the picture in the first place. I used my implants to research you and Cowan but found almost nothing. Neither of you left even the faintest footprint. You both had a single web page with your cover identities, and that was it. A big dead end."

Hall paused. "Even more suspicious, the night the military raided our suite at the Homestead, when we conferenced with you in Heather's car, you never once asked how Heather came to be involved in the proceedings. Or what Alex and Heather were doing at the Madera facility that night. These should have been the first questions you asked. You swore us all to absolute secrecy, but you didn't seem too troubled by this development."

"I did realize this mistake afterward," admitted Fyfe.

"Right," said Altschuler. "Which I assume is why you grilled me about Heather the next day."

"Correct."

"I reasoned that you failed to bring it up when we were in Heather's car," continued Hall, "because you knew very well what they were doing. Which meant you probably had bugs in our suite at the Homestead Inn. Just speculation, but that would be my guess."

"Good guess," said Fyfe. "Go on."

"Since you knew about our planned experiment," said Altschuler, "and didn't intervene, I assume that you approved of it."

"Yes. I was just as eager as you were to confirm the success with Hall could be duplicated. And that ESP wasn't an unwanted side effect. My compliments to you and Heather."

Altschuler's jaw tightened. Even though he and Hall had guessed he had been bugged, this confirmation of it still made his skin crawl. Fyfe had been three steps ahead of them from the beginning. And even when they thought they were doing something off script, it had ended up serving his interests.

"After the call in Heather's car," said Hall, "I decided to share my suspicions with Alex. It was the perfect time, because now that he also had working implants, I didn't have to worry about any eavesdropping. We could communicate in perfect silence, and perfect secrecy, using our Internet connections. Alex even set up a PDA that mimicked each of our respective voices to read IMs we sent each other. Half the time it seemed we were having actual conversations, only ones that no ears or bugs could ever pick up."

Fyfe frowned deeply, clearly annoyed at himself for not having considered this obvious possibility for evading his surveillance.

"Once Hall had shared his concerns," said Altschuler, " I set out to find you in SEC filings. Even the most silent of investors have to be on file with the SEC, as you know, even if the filing isn't in the public domain. So you didn't have any footprint online, but if you truly were invested in a number of companies as you claim on your web page, in addition to Theia, you'd have to leave a footprint at the SEC. I was able to hack into their private files with my implants."

"And I had no footprint there either," said Fyfe, shaking his head. "I must say, I am truly impressed. I almost regret the need to kill you." Then, with his upper lip curling into a sneer, he added, "Almost."

Altschuler glared at Fyfe with an inhuman intensity. Recent events had toughened him up, hardened his spine, and he was no longer the sniveling geek, nervously cleaning his glasses, that he had been when he had first confronted Gray. As small and relatively unathletic as Altschuler was, had he not been chained to two other people, he would have found a way to break the neck of this smug bastard, no matter how many bullets were pumped into him on the way.

But chained as he was, and dealing with an unpredictable psychopath, he decided to continue to cooperate. Like Hall, he was curious to learn the exact nature of Fyfe's plan, and he didn't want to enrage the beast, which might boomerang back on Heather.

Altschuler took a deep breath and found a way to stay calm. "I had also hacked all of Gray's files," he continued. "As you also know. I searched them all for mentions of Cameron Fyfe. But I didn't find a single one. Which was impossible. Gray recorded his every impression for posterity. Hell, he had notes about me and every other employee at Theia. His thoughts. Were they bright, were they pricks, how to deal with them. Their worth to him—because everything revolved around him and how he could use people. He even had extensive notes on suppliers he dealt with. No one got a pass. *Except* Cameron Fyfe."

Altschuler raised his eyebrows. "The only way this made sense is if Gray knew Cameron Fyfe was really John Delamater. Gray's records make it clear that Delamater had access to his computer files, and wouldn't tolerate any mention of him other than his involvement in the raid on the *Explorer*. The absence of any mention of you was striking."

Fyfe nodded. "Very impressive, Alex," he said. "Well done again. Perhaps in the afterlife you can be a detective."

He slid off the steel workbench and onto his feet, and stared down at Hall from an even higher vantage point than before. "So tell me, Nick. How did you know I was aware of your ESP?"

"If you really were Delamater, then you were the one trying to kill me initially. To clean up a mess. I could blow the lid off Gray's illegal experimentation, and you couldn't have that. I can read your mind now, so I know why you changed gears and stopped trying to kill me. But I'll let you explain your reasoning to Alex and Heather later."

"And I will," said Fyfe. "But it's still your turn. How did you guess I knew?"

"I was leading to that. As I was saying, you were the Delamater trying to kill me when I escaped Gray's warehouse. So given you knew the precise details of all of my escapes, you also knew the parts I was leaving out of the story when I thought you were Cameron Fyfe. In the role of Fyfe, you were smart enough to act skeptical of my luck, to enhance your believability. And in the role of Delamater, you were smart enough to understand I must have had something else going for me to be able to escape your men. I guessed you might have come to suspect an ESP-like ability. But I became certain that you knew of my psi abilities when I was kidnapped by a colonel named Girdler. I told you I escaped before we interacted, but this wasn't true. We talked at length. Girdler told me the paramedics who worked on Megan had been murdered. I knew you had to be responsible. And that they must have revealed that I could read minds before you killed them."

"Well reasoned," said Fyfe. The hint of a cruel smile came over his face. "And I'm glad you mentioned Megan. Sorry to learn that she left you. That has to really hurt."

Hall glared at him, but remained silent.

"But just so you don't think this is a lucky break for her," continued Fyfe, "it isn't. She won't be spared. When she checks in with the man you know as Cowan, as she plans to do in a few days, we'll take care of her as well." He shrugged. "But you really have been a worthy opponent in this game, so I promise to make her death quick and painless."

"If you as much as break one of her nails!" thundered Hall, his face a mask of pure hatred, "I'll see to it that . . . that . . ."

Fyfe shook his head. "That nothing, Nick," he said, almost in bored tones. "Unless you can protect her from beyond the grave, there isn't a single thing you can do about it."

Hall's face reddened even further. "You present a very pleasant facade," he hissed between clenched teeth. "I'm just glad for the sake of my friends here they aren't able to see inside your diseased, psychopathic mind. It's like swimming in a cesspool."

"As I warned you previously, this pleasant facade can disappear in an instant. This is your last warning. I'm trying to make your last minutes on earth civilized. But I can also make them so uncivilized that you'll beg me for death," he added casually, as if chatting about the weather. He hoisted himself back onto the steel workbench and added, "But please continue."

Hall had been clenching his fists behind his back, but he now took a long, cleansing breath. "The murdered paramedics tipped me off that you were on to my secret," he said finally, and despite his level tone, his eyes continued to burn with hatred. "Which explained why you and Cowan were being so careful to stay well clear of me. But this was all supposition. Maybe an impressive string of reasoning, but Alex and I didn't have a single shred of hard evidence. This was a big problem, because if you really were Delamater, I knew you would have to kill me very soon."

"But why?" said Heather in confusion. She had largely stayed silent during the conversation, a fascinated spectator, but in this case she hadn't been able to help vocalizing what had come to her mind.

"Heather, I know how bright you are," said Fyfe. "So I'll just assume the knock-out drug has addled your mind. Hard to believe you still haven't put this together."

Altschuler opened his mouth to respond, wanting Heather to continue keeping as low a profile as possible, but Hall beat him to the punch. "He'd have to kill me because he couldn't stay out of my range forever," he explained. "And the second he was in range, the game was up."

Heather's mouth fell open and her eyes grew wide. "*Of course*," she said simply, nodding at Hall. "That's why you had to convince him Alex had cured you of your ESP. So he wouldn't have the need to kill you anymore. And so he'd feel comfortable coming within your range. So you could get hard evidence of his identity and plans directly from his mind."

"Exactly," said Hall. "And we figured this house was bugged. They couldn't get close enough to place bugs on anyone's clothing without me reading this intent. But they *could* bug places ahead of my arrival. Like the suite at the Homestead Inn. And this safe house. If Alex and my conjectures were correct, this place is crawling with them."

"So you and Alex put on a show of curing your ESP," said Heather. "For Fyfe's benefit," she added, no longer using his first name now that he had revealed himself to be a monster. "To draw him out."

Heather nodded to herself. "I *thought* it was too easy to be true. But I didn't question it, only because Alex is the smartest man I've ever known. I figured if anyone could find a way to disable your ESP, he could." Heather paused. "But how could you be sure Fyfe still wouldn't want to kill you, even if you *did* lose your mind reading ability?"

"I *couldn't* be sure. But I figured if he did still have plans to kill me, I'd be able to detect it in his mind while he was still miles away from here."

"So how did you know Nick was faking?" Altschuler asked Fyfe. "And how did you knock us out?"

"Is it my turn already?" said Fyfe mockingly.

"You know we've told you every last mistake you made in great detail," said Hall. "We've lived up to our part of the bargain."

"I thought I was a psychopath. What does a bargain mean to me?"

"You are," said Hall. "And if it suited you to ignore your word, this wouldn't trouble you. But we both know you have nothing better to do anyway until your partner returns, and you bore easily."

"Very true," said Fyfe. "So I guess I *will* take my turn in this inquisition, after all."

54

"I'll answer Alex's second question first," said Fyfe. "I had my men install a remote controlled system for gassing this house just before you arrived. When dealing with a mind reader, you need remote ways to incapacitate. Just in case."

Altschuler nodded. So Fyfe was careful and brilliant at planning ahead. Not surprising in someone so accomplished at chess. "And my first question?" prompted Altschuler. "How did you know we were faking? That Nick could still read minds?

"I wasn't sure. Your acting was good. But not great. And now that I think about it, not letting your girlfriend here in on it did add to the authenticity. But regardless, I did have some suspicions. The effortless way you did it just seemed *too* easy. And too convenient. But for you to be planning a ruse like this meant that you had figured out almost everything. And I'll admit, I couldn't see how this could be. Even so, I'm very cautious. Just because Nick's loss of ESP was too good to be true didn't meant that it wasn't true. It just meant I needed to be sure."

Hall was shaking his head and wore an expression of utter disgust, and Altschuler guessed he had read how Fyfe had confirmed his suspicions, and that it had made him sick.

Fyfe smiled and tapped the top of his head with an index finger. "This was a very challenging chess problem. How could I learn if Nick's ability was really gone or not, without giving away that he was being tested? And without getting within range of him if it *was* still intact? May not sound all that challenging, but trust me, it took me an hour to come up with a solution."

Altschuler was fascinated despite himself. And also stumped. Fyfe could see this in his face and it added to his already heightened sense of superiority.

"In the end, it was simple. I called a ruthless killer that an associate of mine, a Russian named Vasily, had worked with in the past."

"The same Vasily you murdered recently?" whispered Hall.

"Are you actually trying to make me feel *guilty?* Vasily was also a ruthless killer, so don't pretend to be outraged. As you can see in my mind, I liked Vasily. It was just that I was about to be an international celebrity of sorts, under the name of Cameron Fyfe, and it would have been bad to have someone alive who knew this face belonged to John Delamater as well. But where was I?"

"You contacted a killer," said Altschuler.

"Right. He was only an hour away from Sacramento. I checked records for homes within five miles of here, looking for any that were owned by a woman living alone. When I found one, by the name of April Underwood, I contacted this killer-for-hire using the name Bill Underwood. I told him Vasily had sent me, and offered to pay him a small fortune to slowly beat the woman to death. I told him she was my wife." Fyfe raised his eyebrows. "But I'm sure you're way ahead of me by now."

Altschuler and Heather now looked just as sick as Nick Hall had, as the horror of what Fyfe had done to a random, innocent woman, just to conduct a test, hit home. Fyfe seemed to revel in their revulsion.

"The rest is history," said Fyfe. "Our boy Nick here read their minds, despite this happening after his ESP was, supposedly, eliminated. I figured the thoughts of a woman getting slowly beaten to death would reach him if anything could. And being the good Samaritan he is, he sent an e-mail tip to the local police, specific enough to be believed. I was monitoring their computers to see if such a message came in. If his loss of ESP was a ruse, he must have been aware this house was bugged, so I knew he wouldn't *call* the tip in, because his knowledge of this faraway beating was proof he could still read minds."

Fyfe turned toward Hall and gave him a condescending shake of the head. "I bet you had visions of becoming *Batman*, didn't you, Nick? Fighting crime in a six-to-ten-mile radius with your bat senses."

Altschuler glanced at Heather and could tell she was about to explode and say something that would draw Fyfe's ire. He had to find a way to change the subject quickly. "How do you know Nick's range?" he blurted out.

For the first time, Fyfe looked at Altschuler as if he were stupid. "He discussed it with you at the Homestead, remember? In the suite that was bugged. Remember?"

"Right," said Altschuler quickly. "Of course."

Heather had settled down to some degree, but she looked at Fyfe as though he were a particularly disgusting breed of cockroach. "And it didn't bother you in the least," she said, her voice dripping with contempt, "that if Nick really *had* lost his ESP, an innocent woman would have been beaten to death?"

Fyfe shrugged. "Blame Nick. If he couldn't read minds so perfectly, I wouldn't have had to take my test to such an extreme. Besides, the police did catch the killer I hired, which will end up saving lives down the road. So I should probably get a medal for this."

Heather glared at Fyfe with absolute contempt, but wisely remained silent.

"So was it worth it?" said Altschuler. "All the murders, all the schemes? You were already a rich man. How much more money did you need?"

Fyfe laughed. Whether in the persona of John Delamater or Cameron Fyfe, the man rarely smiled, and almost never laughed. But he did now. And there was something very chilling about it. "Come on, Nick," he said. "How much longer are you going to wait. Tell them already."

"Tell us what?" said Altschuler, and from Hall's expression, he was suddenly unsure he really wanted to know.

Hall locked his eyes on Altschuler's and shook his head woodenly. "He didn't do it for the money," he said. "We thought it was about greed and power. That he was a brilliant, psychopathic businessman run amok. But I'm afraid the truth is even worse than we thought," he added, his tone as grim as his face. "*Far* worse."

55

Fyfe gazed down at his helpless, handcuffed prisoners and realized he was enjoying himself. He hadn't faced off against anyone who was close to his equal, which included his recently deceased partner, Kelvin Gray, for a long, long time. These three had done well. Forced him to make better moves to win than were typically needed, including the move to verify Hall still had ESP, of which he was very proud.

But they would never understand him. *Could* never understand him. Their brainwashed worldview wouldn't allow it. They thought he was a psychopath, but he was more compassionate and more pious than any of them.

His parents had arrived in the US in 1985. They were heroes. And ultimately martyrs. Leaving the land they loved, Saudi Arabia, to come to the Great Satan was a sacrifice no one should be asked to make. But they made it proudly.

They were brilliant, and true believers in the Koran. And they took the long view. They would try to gather intelligence for others to use in the war against the West, a war the West was too arrogant to even know it was in until September 11 of 2001.

And they taught their sons well. Taught them to love Allah and hate the decadent West. Taught them to be pious. And taught them to be patient, for the Koran said, "Be patient in adversity; for, verily, Allah will not let the reward of the righteous be wasted."

And their parents planned to be more patient than any other devout Muslims in history. They devoted their lives, not to their own glory, but to assuring the glory of their sons decades in the future. They devoted their lives to honing human weapons capable of striking at the heart of the West. Teaching their sons through love and patience the serenity that was the Koran, and the false deity of secularism that was the soulless American way of life.

He was given the putrid American name of John Delamater, but his parents made sure he loved and respected his real name, Hassan Ahmed Abdullah, and that of his older brother, Rashid. And his parents had made every sacrifice for them. They had disappeared when he and his brother were in college. He had later learned through sources in Saudi Arabia that they had believed the US authorities were closing in on them, so rather than put him and Rashid at risk of discovery, they had martyred themselves in Jerusalem, strapping bombs to their chests and blowing up a school bus, ensuring the soulless children within would never grow up to become the enemies of Allah.

His parents were without equal. No sons had ever had more devoted parents, and he knew that even now they were both in the special place in heaven reserved for martyrs.

His father had always told Hassan and his brother that they would be the most potent weapons ever unleashed, because they were born in the US. In the belly of the beast. They could speak like a native. Pretend to believe in the decadence of the society, all the while using this to sharpen their hatred. They could blend in and bend the rules ruthlessly to get ahead, to gather resources around them until they could come up with a way to destroy the West.

Their parents had taught them the concept of Taqiyya, or concealment, which, taken broadly, specified that until that great day that Islam was ascendant in the world, they had the right to proclaim one thing and do another. It was the ultimate ends-justify-the-means provision. If Hassan had to pretend to love America while secretly despising it, this was fully acceptable. Whatever he had to do to defeat the infidel was acceptable; adapt to Western styles, cheat and steal from infidels, ignore his obligation to prayer for long periods of time when he might be discovered. Allah was a forgiving God, and would understand transgressions that were in service to a greater cause.

Hassan never doubted his destiny. He was a chess prodigy, and his brilliance in chess extended to every area of thought. So he bided his time. Became wealthy so he could pursue his goals, whenever he found the right project.

He wasn't interested in anything that had been tried before. Bombs—conventional, nuclear, or dirty—did not interest him. Destroying buildings did not. He was determined to deliver to the West nothing less than a Sampson-smash blow. To fundamentally shift the game in favor of Islam and sharia law forever. And he was just a handful of years from doing just that. Even his brother was now fully on board, having once thought his plans were far too ambitious.

And Hall had been right. The man they knew as Fyfe had played a brilliant game, and he would enjoy sharing this with the three Westerners before he burned them alive.

"What are you waiting for, Nick?" said Fyfe, finally breaking the extended silence that had fallen over the panic room. "Tell them."

A weary frown came over Hall's face. "The short version," he said, his voice lifeless, "is that Fyfe, or Delamater if you prefer, is really an American-born jihadist named Hassan Ahmed Abdullah. The ultimate sleeper agent. Along with his brother, Rashid. Who also goes by the very American name of Ed Cowan."

Altschuler blanched. "You have to be *shitting* me," he said.

"If only," replied Hall miserably.

"I don't understand," said Heather. "What does any of this have to do with *jihad?*"

"Do you see, Nick," said the man they had known as Cameron Fyfe. "Even now, it's impossible for you Westerners to see it. Even when it is staring you in the face."

"See what?" said Altschuler in confusion.

"Before I tell you," replied Fyfe, "I will explain the superiority of my ideology. I know I'm wasting my breath on infidels with little time to live, and who are incapable of understanding. But I will do so anyway. As an exercise in patience. You Westerners automatically think the true believers of the word of Allah are barbaric. Luddites who want to turn the world back many hundreds of years. And this is anathema to you. But this is only because you worship the false god of technology. But what has technology led to? Weapons of mass destruction. Addiction. The loss of human connection. Man is moving too fast. He has no time to revel in the world Allah has created.

To pray. To contemplate. Instead, he is moving ever-faster on an ever-shortening treadmill. Your attention span is gone. No matter how much technology you have, all you crave is the next advance. The next toy. Your lives have become hollow, superficial, meaningless, and unfulfilling."

Fyfe paused. From the expressions on the faces of his prisoners, he could sense they were actually conceding the truth of some of what he was saying. This surprised him greatly.

"You're like a sprinter who will sprint forward forever," he continued, "just for the exhilaration of the sprint. Sprint until your heart explodes or you hit a mine—because you can't stop. And you don't have any real idea where you're going. True believers shun modern technology. Because we don't want to poison our true natures with secular toys. The human psyche isn't built for these so-called advances, even as you crave them. Consider experiences like playing a game of chess on the beach, or walking in the woods with a friend, discussing philosophy. Contrast this with rushing around like headless chickens juggling multiple electronic gadgets at once. Multitasking far beyond the human ability to multitask. Are you happier under *this* scenario, or more stressed out? Is technology truly indispensable, truly the source of happiness? Or is getting back to your human, spiritual roots the key?"

Given the oratorical skills Fyfe had demonstrated at the press conference, Altschuler wasn't surprised he could be so persuasive, even in defending the indefensible. "You do make some good points," he acknowledged. "When put in this way, a return to a simpler life does sound alluring. But you're also romanticizing these times. Before technology, man had a short, brutish existence. Ravaged by lack of access to clean water, by disease, and by a complete lack of sanitation. Surrounded by an ever-growing accumulation of human waste. Days were filled with heavy burdens, boredom, and drudgery."

"I'm not suggesting we set the clock back to zero," said Fyfe.

He opened his mouth to offer additional arguments but then closed it again. He could debate this for hours. But what was the point?

"It's time to change the subject," said Fyfe. "I've wasted too much time on this already."

"So will you now tell us what we've been missing?" said Heather. Fyfe sighed. "Just remember that you asked for this," he said. "And that you were too blind to see it."

He paused. "Consider the implant technology. And surfing the web with your thoughts. You've managed to see every possible problem with this but the most obvious. You see issues with privacy and with addiction. And naturally, the decadent Western mindset sees everything through the prism of pornography and sex." He shook his head in contempt and disbelief. "But do you know what you don't think twice about? Letting someone stick a device in your *brain!* One that can hit visual and auditory neurons. Not to mention other vital real estate. Even after you learned I'm a jihadist, you still couldn't see it."

Fyfe noted that Hall's expression didn't change. The mind reader knew full well what he was getting at. But Hall's two companions suddenly looked ill as the obvious finally hit them like a kick to the gut.

"I'll be the CEO of the company that will have the *monopoly* on implants," continued Fyfe. "Not everyone in the West will want them immediately. But enough will. The rich and powerful will get them first. It'll be too big of a disadvantage for them to be left out. But soon the masses will follow suit. Before long, the technology will be hungrily adopted by all the peoples of the world." He raised his eyebrows. "With the exception of devout Muslims, of course."

His features hardened and a chilling intensity came over him. "And *I'll* control the product and its production," he whispered. "Think about it! Millions and billions of Westerners willingly sticking something in their *heads.* Something that *I* control. If you can implant a power cell that runs on glucose, why can't you implant one that can be triggered to release trace amounts of botulism? A toxin so potent that a single kilogram could kill every man, woman, and child on earth."

He let this chilling thought hang for a moment and then continued. "But this would be crass and inelegant. The possibilities to wreak havoc are endless. I'll have backdoor access to the brains of massive numbers of people. You think the Internet has unleashed some bad computer viruses? Wait until you see what *I* can unleash. Inside your brains. I can send instructions to the system to blind everyone who has implants. Or instead of having the implants stimulate neurons in the visual cortex, I can have them hit the pain centers of the brain on my command. Or even worse," he added with a malicious gleam in his eye. "I can have them hit the pleasure centers."

Fyfe could tell from the puzzled expressions of his male guests that only Heather, who looked properly horrified, realized the full implications of this last.

"Heather," he said. "Why don't you tell your friends about the Olds and Milner experiments. I can tell by your reaction you're familiar with them."

Heather swallowed hard, but didn't reply.

"Don't be shy," he said, gesturing toward Heather with his right hand. "Please. Enlighten your friends."

When she didn't immediately begin, he shot her a look of such pure, distilled menace that her breath caught in her throat. "I *won't* ask you again," he said.

Heather scowled but did as he asked. "In the 1950s," she began, "James Olds and Peter Milner implanted electrodes in rats. In the nucleus accumbens. Which has also been called the pleasure center of the brain. This region plays a role in sexual arousal and the *high* people get from certain drugs. In later versions of this experiment, rats could cause this region to be stimulated by pressing down on a lever." She shuddered involuntarily. "Turns out the rats would repeatedly hit the lever, as many as seven hundred times an hour, ignoring food and water. Until they died from exhaustion."

Fyfe smiled humorlessly. "A perfect metaphor for the West, wouldn't you say? Only *your* lever brings technology. When will you get enough? Fewer and fewer of you read anymore. More and more engage in an endless orgy of promiscuity and sexual deviation. The four of you in this house were on the eve of a technological revolution, and yet you copulated last night, out of wedlock, like worthless, filthy animals in heat. Pushing the orgasm lever as often as you could. Your society is already soulless, mindless, and purposeless. No time for reflection into the mind of Allah. You *already* want to activate your lever over and over, ignoring all else, until your deaths." He shrugged. "So why not allow my technology to activate your pleasure centers more directly? Give you what you want."

Altschuler looked as though he was choking back vomit. "You're right," he said after several hard swallows. "We missed the obvious. We looked only at the dangers of the technology itself. We didn't consider the greater danger of others actively trying to turn it into a weapon."

"And now it's too late," said Fyfe. "As of this morning, the train has left the station. But I intend to be patient. Not show my hand. Westerners won't view the implants as blasphemous. They won't see they're making themselves impure. At the same time, my fellow true believers will shun this technology as they shun other false gods. Meanwhile, I'll be worshiped by the West, *as a god,* for giving them the toys they crave. I'll funnel the billions I earn back into other jihadist causes. And then, when implants are as pervasive as cell phones, I'll bring the West to its knees with a single blow."

Fyfe enjoyed the looks of total horror on the faces of his guests. Hall had been right. It was good to share, after all.

"As should be obvious," he continued, "Kelvin Gray didn't come up with the idea for this project. I did. I was lucky to find a brilliant psychopath like Gray I could convince to perfect the technology, while I played the role of muscle, hiring an army of mercenaries. And I was able to plant these seeds in such a way that Gray thought the idea was his. I set him on the slippery slope and let gravity take care of the rest. He was blind to my end game."

"What *was* your original end game?" said Altschuler.

"Nick, you've been quiet for a while," said Fyfe. "Why don't you tell him."

Hall didn't respond for several seconds, as though the question didn't quite register, but he finally nodded. "His plan was to wait for Gray to perfect the technology in his human guinea pigs," he said.

"Then, knowing they had already tripped all the landmines—not caring how many people died in the process—they would conduct FDA trials with all the care in the world. Zeroing in on the perfect recipe on the first try. Flying through the trials with an immaculate safety record. When it became approved, Kelvin Gray would at some point have an accident, and Fyfe, being the majority shareholder, would vote himself CEO."

"So what caused you to change this plan?" Heather asked Fyfe.

This time Fyfe decided to answer for himself. "When Nick escaped, we had no idea the implants were working for web surfing. He lied to Gray and said they had failed. And we had no idea about his ESP. Which I have no interest in, by the way, since this is blasphemous and would be just as destructive to Muslims as Westerners." He shook his head. "But even when I discovered his implants were working, I still wanted to stick with the original plan. I didn't want to create the controversy I've now created. I wanted to avoid any hint of taint. Even if it took an extra year or two to get the technology out."

"Again," said Heather. "What changed?"

"What changed is that Nick was too good. Too elusive. I became unsure that I could kill him. And if he regained his memory, he could ruin everything. But I realized I could lure him in if I sacrificed Gray a bit earlier than planned. So I played the whistleblower and hero with Alex, and set Gray up. I played both ends against the middle. As Delamater, I warned Kelvin Gray there was a man named Ed Cowan working with Alex, but that I had him in my sights. My brother, of course, was never in the sights of John Delamater. He faked a few injuries, made up a story about using martial arts to defeat Delamater's man, and knocked on Gray's door. He shot Gray in such a way that Alex was sure to buy everything—especially that I was one of the good guys."

Altschuler nodded. "And you counted on me to realize we could contact Nick Hall through a backdoor Gray had set up."

"Exactly. If you hadn't suggested it, I would have. With Gray still alive, there was no way we could lure Nick in, regardless of an ability to message him. Not when he could read minds. But with Gray sacrificed and you pure as the driven snow, I knew Nick would read your mind and trust you implicitly. Read for himself that you were on the side of the angels. Working to right the wrongs committed by your boss. Then he would have no fear of coming in. Once he did, and was actually under my control, as Cameron Fyfe, I figured he could help us legitimize the press conference. Demonstrate the technology. Add to the story."

"And then you could kill me at your leisure," said Hall in disgust.

"I only wish I could have used you as my pawn for a longer period of time, but your mind reading was a real problem."

"You were going to promote Alex to CEO at first," said Heather. "Was that garbage from the beginning?"

"No. I wanted to stay out of the limelight as long as possible. Especially during the fallout over Gray's experiments. I'd wait a few years until the company's reputation had improved, let Alex weather that storm, and then see to it *he* had the accident I had planned for Gray."

Fyfe paused. "But the emergence of this colonel who kidnapped Nick, and tried to kidnap Alex, was unexpected. And I really didn't want this kind of variable in the equation if Alex became CEO. So I decided to take the CEO role from the start." He shrugged. "This wasn't the way I planned it. I wanted the *Explorer* crew forever thought to be at the bottom of the ocean, and for the world never to know about Gray's experiments. But this way does have some advantages. I'm now seen as a whistleblower and hero. Nick did a great job of demonstrating the appeal of the technology. And the sympathy we'll get when it's discovered that Nick has been killed will be a big positive as well."

"Without Nick," said Altschuler. "Everyone will think his video was a hoax."

"Let them. They'll see otherwise soon enough."

Fyfe glanced at his watch. He had planned to wait to kill them until his brother had returned. But he had waited long enough already, and it was time to begin preparing the house to burn.

"Checking your watch?" said Hall with a sneer. "What's the matter, *asshole?* Wondering why your brother isn't back yet?"

Fyfe met Hall's withering stare. What was *that* supposed to mean? Was Hall just showing off his mind reading abilities further? Or did Hall really know something that *he* didn't?

"Well, I have some bad news for you, *Hassan*," spat Hall, emphasizing his name bitterly. "I'm afraid that your brother's been a bit delayed."

56

Fyfe raised his gun and pointed it at Hall's forehead, ignoring the two weapons he had confiscated that were sitting on the workbench beside him. "Are you trying to be cute, or do you actually know something?"

Fyfe paused in thought for a moment and then pointed his gun at Heather instead. "If you haven't convinced me you know something in three seconds, I take out Heather's kneecap," he said.

Hall read that he had decided threatening to maim Heather was a better strategy than threatening to kill *him*, since he had promised to end Hall's life anyway.

Nick Hall smiled pleasantly. "No need to threaten," he said. "I'm more than happy to tell you what I know. Your brother was captured. By Megan Emerson. About thirty minutes ago. She had a few . . . preparations . . . to make, but she'll be calling in a few minutes to arrange for a trade."

"Impossible! She could never find him. And even if she did, she could never capture him. Besides, she's long gone. You've chosen a poor bluff."

Hall shook his head. "I may not be a grandmaster at chess," he said, "but you've done a great job teaching me to be paranoid this past week. I knew I was in over my head. You see, you're very good. So good, I knew it would be dangerous to underestimate you. I couldn't see how you could turn the tables like you have, but I still thought it would be good to have one last ace in the hole." He raised his eyebrows. "Just in case."

Hall almost smiled from the shocked expressions on the faces of his two friends, who were just as confused as Fyfe.

"Turns out I can't read Megan Emerson. I don't know why. Everyone wonders how she can stand being in a romantic relationship with a mind reader. Well, now you know. She isn't. But while I can't read her mind, we *are* able to communicate telepathically. That's how I was able to escape Girdler. So it occurred to me it might be nice to have her as a fail-safe. She can be very effective. And she's saved my ass before."

Hall could tell Fyfe's mind was racing, trying to assimilate this new information. "So her letter to you was faked?" he said.

"That's right. We discussed our plan at length telepathically. Yet another way to have a discussion without fear of eavesdroppers. We decided she would take the guns she confiscated from Girdler's man and leave. Buy a cheap car with my poker winnings and stay within our telepathic range. Just in case Alex and I had miscalculated. But we had never told Alex or Heather about our telepathy. Until we felt entirely safe, Megan and I decided to keep this to ourselves. And we wanted their reaction when they thought she had left me to be as genuine as possible."

"I'll be damned," mumbled Altschuler. "And that's why you had me read the letter out loud. And why you confronted Trout about failing to stop her. Just to be positive you would get the attention of those listening to the bugs. So Fyfe would think she was long gone and not factor her in."

"Exactly," said Hall. He had tried to force himself to cry but hadn't quite succeeded. He had no idea how certain actors could cry on command, but this was a very impressive feat.

"So Megan didn't sneak out on me," continued Hall. "I *helped* her leave. I read the security password from Trout's mind, and used this and my Internet connection to reprogram Tanya. Trout was furious the PDA didn't alert him that Megan was leaving. I thought the way I confronted him on this was great theater, if I do say so myself. Although, to be fair, Trout didn't know it was an act."

"Well played," said Fyfe. "But there is no way that waif of an untrained civilian captured Rashid," he insisted. "You're still bluffing."

Hall found it odd to think of Ed Cowan as a man named Rashid. His name was *Ed,* and he came across as the consummate American. And if Hall had been told the name Cameron Fyfe was an alias, he would have believed the man's real name was John Delamater long before he believed it was Hassan Ahmed Abdullah. Which was entirely the point, he realized.

"Without my help, you'd be right," said Hall. "But it was easy for me to direct Megan to your brother once he got within range. I knew from reading him he was going to fill up his gas tank. So I had her wait until then. She pretended to fill up as well, spotted him, and acted excited to see him. I read his mind. He was excited to see her too. It saved him the trouble of hunting her down and killing her later. He wasn't the slightest bit suspicious."

Hall shook his head condescendingly. "You'd think he might have considered just how coincidental it was to run into her. But he didn't, not even for a moment. She asked him to get in the used car she'd just bought so she could drive behind the station, where it was more private. She said she wanted to show him something very important. Then, when I assured her his guard was down, she shot him with a tranquilizer dart. As simple as that."

Fyfe pulled out his phone, intent on calling his brother to verify what Hall was saying.

"He won't answer," said Hall. "But that's okay. Megan is dialing your number now. To discuss the terms of a trade."

The instant Hall said this, Fyfe's phone vibrated and indicated an incoming call, from his brother's phone. He answered.

"Hello, Hassan," said Megan Emerson. "Nick tells me you're expecting my call."

Without saying another word, Fyfe lifted one of the guns beside him on the steel workbench, pointed it at Nick Hall, and pulled the trigger.

57

"What have you done?" screamed Megan Emerson into the phone.

"You weren't in telepathic contact with your boyfriend when I pulled the trigger, were you?" asked Fyfe mockingly. "Because that would be cheating."

"You killed him?" said Megan, unable to keep the hysteria from her voice.

"No. I didn't kill him. I used a dart. Just like I understand you did on Rashid. I was told you were calling to trade for my brother. Do you really think I'd let you stay in contact with someone who can read my mind during negotiations? Seems like an unfair advantage, don't you think?"

"Let me talk to Alex!" she demanded.

"I'm putting you on speaker," said Fyfe.

"Alex, is he telling the truth? Is Nick okay?"

"Yes," said Altschuler. "So far." He couldn't help but admire Fyfe's move. His quick calculation to take Hall out of play was impressive.

"Call me back in five minutes," said Fyfe, and then ended the call.

The phone vibrated immediately, but Fyfe ignored it. Instead, he pulled a roll of gray duct tape from a drawer under the workbench and wrapped multiple layers of tape around Heather's and Altschuler's heads and mouths, until even a scream would have no chance of escaping.

When he was done, he said, "Megan Emerson is impressive when she's getting advice. Let's see how she does when she's on her own."

Fyfe's phone vibrated again, on cue, and this time he answered, putting it on speaker for the entertainment of his guests.

"What the hell is going on?" demanded Megan.

"I was taping your friends' mouths shut," explained Fyfe. "They're a little too chatty for my taste." He paused. "So you claim to have my brother. Can you prove it to me?"

"The proof is on this phone," she replied. "Saved as a video file named *Cowan*. Have Tanya access it and put it on the monitors behind you."

Fyfe told Tanya to comply, and seconds later the video began playing on the panic room monitors. It began with a close-up view of the front seats of a four-door sedan. Cowan had been propped up in the passenger's seat and looked to be taking a nap.

The camera panned over to the floor of the driver's seat. A deep, rectangular casserole dish had been placed on the carpet, six inches in from the brake and gas pedals. A pool of clear liquid filled the dish to about three inches in height. In the center of this pool, a blue candle, about the size of a tall can of soda, was being held in place by a heavy glass candleholder, which was fully submerged. A small, orange flame danced innocently at the top of the candle. One end of a wet cotton blanket, tied to the steering wheel, was hanging about a foot above the candle, with the other end resting on Cowan's lap.

Finally, the camera panned to the back seat, where four large, plastic bottles of Kingsford lighter fluid, for barbequing, were lying on the floor.

The video ended, and began to repeat in a continuous loop.

"Did you see it?" said Megan.

"I saw it," snapped Fyfe.

"Nick was relaying the highlights of your conversation to me," she said, and Altschuler realized this must be why Hall had seemed to check out of the discussion periodically for extended periods. "And I learned you were planning to burn my friends alive. So I thought I'd return the favor."

Megan paused to let this sink in. "Your brother is still in my car. I've drenched him and the blanket in lighter fluid. These things aren't all that precise, but the candle I bought is *supposed* to burn down about an inch every thirty minutes. Which means that in an hour or so, it will have burned low enough for the flame to make contact with the pool of lighter fluid it's sitting in. When it does, flames will shoot up and hit the blanket. If my calculations are correct, your brother's entire body should be on fire about four seconds after that. Give or take a few."

After another brief pause, she continued. "I have to admit I'm new at this. I had to Google, *delayed reaction fire*, to get ideas—using your brother's phone, by the way. A few of the results involved kitchen timers, but I liked the simplicity of this one. Would you like me to send you a link to the YouTube video?"

"You're very proud of yourself, aren't you?" hissed Fyfe.

"Yes. Yes I am. So here's the deal. I want to be able to see Alex, Heather, and Nick, alive and well, in front of the living room window. I'll be there in about ten minutes."

"Where are you?"

"The more important question is, where is your brother? Where did I leave my car? Could be at the back of a huge parking lot. Maybe behind an abandoned church. Could be anywhere. Once I lit the candle, I took a cab back to your brother's car, which I'm driving now. I'll come to the front door. Let me in. Once I confirm that my friends are okay and we're driving away, I'll call you with your brother's location."

"A trade of three for one. That hardly seems fair."

"What hardly seems fair to me is that a psychopathic butcher asshole was planning to kill my three innocent friends in the first place. I'll be there in ten minutes. You can choose to kill me when I arrive, of course. But just know that if you do, your brother will become a bonfire long before you have any hope of finding him."

Fyfe nodded. "I'll see you in ten minutes."

58

The man who would bring the West to its knees unlocked the cuffs that linked each of his prisoners, one to the other. "Get up!" he ordered Heather.

With her hands still cuffed behind her back, and her mouth taped firmly shut, this wasn't easy, but she managed. Once she was on her feet, Fyfe had her turn around so he could unlock her cuffs. He then handed her keys and instructed her to free Altschuler, while he held a gun on both of them.

Altschuler grunted several attempted words at Fyfe, who raised his eyebrows in mild amusement. "What's that, Alex?" he taunted. "I'm having a little trouble understanding you."

Altschuler ceased his efforts at communication. He was trying to ask what Fyfe's real plans were, but what did it matter? He knew the gist. Megan was walking into an ambush, despite how impressively creative her plan had been.

If Fyfe were to actually make the trade, to let them leave, his grand plan was over. He thought he now had the ultimate winning hand in the *Clash of Civilizations*, and he wasn't about to give it up. Not for his brother. Not for anything.

If Fyfe's brother had to be sacrificed, even burned alive, Altschuler was certain the man could accept that. In a religion that glorified martyrs, he might even be happy that his brother would secure a premium position in the afterlife through this sacrifice.

Megan was thinking like a Westerner, and believing Fyfe would as well. And Fyfe had taken advantage of her inexperience, brilliantly isolating her from Hall by rendering him unconscious, and making sure he and Heather were unable to shout a warning to her either. She had done remarkably well since Hall had stumbled upon her, but her Western thinking and feelings for Nick Hall were blinding her to the obvious.

And there was nothing Altschuler could do about it.

Fyfe instructed Altschuler and Heather to drag Hall's unconscious body out of the panic room and to the front of the house. Even dragging him, and with two of them, it was backbreaking work. Lifting Hall up and seating him against the windowsill, with his face pressed awkwardly against the window, was harder still, but they finally managed.

While they struggled, Fyfe had Tanya unbolt both locks on the front door, and display the perimeter camera feeds on the television.

Fyfe's phone vibrated once again.

"I don't see Heather," snapped Megan when he picked it up.

Fyfe motioned for Heather to get closer to the window.

"And how do I know Nick is still alive?"

"You should be able to see his breath against the window," said Fyfe.

Fifteen seconds passed. "I'm coming in," said Megan, obviously satisfied that the three prisoners were still alive.

Several additional minutes passed. Finally, the camera feed on the television showed Megan carefully approaching the front door. She was alone, as promised.

The handle turned, and the door swung slowly inward. Megan stepped inside. She tried to put on a brave front, but Altschuler thought she looked as skittish as a rabbit; not that he could blame her.

Fyfe, his gun raised, quickly worked his way around her and closed the door. "Megan Emerson," he said. "Welcome back."

Megan walked over to the three prisoners and inspected Hall carefully. "Help me bring Nick to the car," she said to Alex and Heather.

Fyfe's upper lip curled into a scowl. "You aren't going *anywhere*," he hissed.

Even though this had been utterly predictable, Altschuler's heart dropped into his stomach.

"Pull a double cross and your brother burns," snapped Megan. She tried to sound in control of the situation, but her hands were shaking. "You know better than that."

"I do love my brother," said Fyfe softly. "But I love Allah more. I'm willing to sacrifice my brother for the cause, just as he would be willing to sacrifice himself."

Megan searched Fyfe's face for any hint of a bluff and found only icy resolve. There was absolutely no doubt that Fyfe would let his brother be burned alive without batting an eye.

The last of Megan's brave exterior melted away and her eyes began to fill with tears. "I knew you might be psycho enough to pull something like this," she said, thoroughly defeated. "But I had to take the chance." She glared at Fyfe hatefully as a single tear slid down her face. "But at least I'll die knowing I took your brother with me."

"I don't think so. I think you'll tell me where he is."

"You can *think* whatever the hell you want. But unless you let us leave here, your brother fries."

Fyfe laughed. "You really do think you're tough. But you've led a sheltered life. So here's what we're going to do. I'm going to start by carving out your right eye with a knife. But I'll leave your left eye alone, so you can see me kill your three friends in the most painful of ways. I can't go as slow as I'd like, because Rashid's candle *is* burning down, but it will be slow enough. They will suffer terribly. They will scream, and in the end, beg for me to kill them."

He paused to let this sink in. "Or," he continued, "you can tell me where my brother is. Right now. In which case I promise to give you all quick and painless deaths."

"You can go fuck yourself!" spat Megan.

Altschuler could barely breathe. He considered attacking Fyfe, but he was too far away, and Fyfe would have plenty of time to turn and shoot him. But what did it matter? At least he would force him to end his life quickly. He tensed his muscles and planned out an approach in his head. His only chance was stealth. If Fyfe was preoccupied with Megan, maybe he could get close enough to lunge at Fyfe without him realizing it.

"Suit yourself," said Fyfe, removing a switchblade knife from his pocket. "This is going to hurt you a lot more than it's going to hurt me," he added, herding her toward the wall.

Altschuler willed himself to be silent and invisible and crept away from the window.

He managed four catlike steps before Fyfe heard him and turned, his gun drawn and his finger on the trigger. Altschuler closed his eyes.

But instead of the expected bullet to a kneecap or other vital part of his body, he heard a spitting sound coming from the back of the room.

"I don't know, Fyfe," said a deep voice, coming from the same direction. "This might hurt you more than you think."

Altschuler opened his eyes and took in the scene. Behind him, a man was holding a silenced gun. In front of him, Cameron Fyfe was lying on the floor in a large pool of his own blood, which continued to pour from a gaping hole in the back of his head. The front door was splattered with so much blood it looked like a Jackson Pollock painting.

Heather sank to the ground while Megan fought back vomit.

As Altschuler took in the scene, the man who had spoken came into the room, his gun still held in front of him.

Altschuler hastily pulled enough tape from the bottom of his mouth to partially free his lower lip. "Who are you?" he said, his words garbled.

"I'm Colonel Justin Girdler," the man said as he walked by Altschuler to the window. He grabbed the unconscious Hall by his shirt, and lowered him to the floor.

"So nice to see you again, Nick," he said.

59

"Get away from him!" demanded Altschuler, his words still garbled by the tape over most of his mouth. "I can cure his ESP."

Girdler shook his head. "Believe it or not, that's the last thing I want."

"It's okay, Alex," said Megan. "The colonel is on our side now." She thought about this for a moment. "Well, sort of."

Heather had joined Altschuler near the center of the room, and he took her hand in his.

"I'll tell you what," said Girdler to the two of them. "Let's get that tape off you both, brew up some coffee, and have a little talk in the kitchen. Nick will be okay. He'll be awake in a few hours. I know. The darts Fyfe used were from *my* gun."

Ten minutes later the four of them were at the kitchen table once again, cups of steaming coffee in front of them. When they were all situated, Altschuler studied the colonel, watching carefully for any signs of treachery. "So you don't plan to kill Nick anymore?"

"No," said Girdler simply.

Heather had been watching him intently as well. "Good choice," she said. "Because we wouldn't want to have to hurt you."

Girdler laughed. "I'll say this for Nick, he can turn people who don't know him into loyal friends in no time. I found myself liking him as well."

"Thank you, by the way, for saving our lives," said Heather. "But where did you *come* from? I'm guessing there is some explanation other than your arrival being the luckiest bit of good timing in history."

"You're right," said Girdler. "Good timing had nothing to do with it. You owe it all to Megan here."

Heather faced her new friend, who was taking a sip of coffee. "Okay, Megan. How did you pull this off?"

"I'm glad you asked," replied Megan with a smile. "Because I'm dying to tell you. I was in telepathic contact with Nick when the three of you were watching coverage of the press conference. Just before I lost my connection with him, he managed to think the words, *sleep drug*. After that it was radio silence. I was totally panicked at that point. I thought about rushing back to the house, guns blazing, to save him. But there were problems with this strategy. I didn't know if only Nick had been knocked out, or if everyone had. And if the two bodyguards were behind this and still conscious, this could end very badly. Besides, I'm just a graphic designer. The guns blazing thing really isn't my strength."

"Didn't you only have one real gun, anyway?" said Heather with a smile.

"Yeah. There was that, too. So it would have been, *gun* blazing. So I decided to wait until Nick awoke, so he could feed me telepathic intel and give me instructions. Having him on the inside, guiding me, was the only way I was going to be able to help him. We never told you this, but that's really how Nick and I managed to escape the colonel."

Girdler winced. "And I've been trying so hard to forget that ever happened," he said in amusement. "Thanks for bringing it up again."

"You have to admit it was effective," said Megan.

"Exceedingly effective," said Girdler.

"Even so," continued Megan, "it occurred to me I could use an ally. Someone who knew what he was doing. Not a graphic designer pretending to be a Navy Seal. And that's when it hit me. Nick had told me telepathically about the breaking story on his ESP. The *Iowa Gazette* story. I realized this might change everything with the colonel."

Altschuler pursed his lips in thought, and began to nod seconds later. "Good thinking," he said in admiration. "Because you realized the genie was out of the bottle anyway. That this story was so credible, even without Nick Hall in the picture going forward, people would take it seriously. The ESP arms race the colonel feared was going to happen no matter what."

"Right!" said Megan excitedly. "Given that, I thought it was worth asking the colonel if this would cause him to have a change of heart. Nick thought highly of him. So if he told me he'd consider sparing Nick, I decided I would trust him. Besides, I knew he was by far the best chance for us to survive."

"How did you get ahold of him so quickly?" asked Heather.

"Along with the car, I had bought a disposable cell phone," replied Megan. She turned to Girdler and rolled her eyes. "You know, to replace the one your men took from me."

"Yeah. Sorry about that."

"Anyhow," she continued, an amused smile on her face, "I called the pentagon, told them I was Megan Emerson, and demanded to speak with Justin Girdler of PsyOps. They told me there was no one there by that name. I gave them my number and told them if he didn't call me within five minutes, I wouldn't be responsible for the loss of life."

Girdler nodded approvingly at Megan. "That was more than enough to do the trick," he said.

"Really?" said Heather.

"Yes. Our computers flagged her call immediately and brought it to my attention. They knew I had a keen interest in Megan Emerson. I called her back right away. I'd already seen the Internet story about Nick's ESP and reached the same conclusions she had."

"I thought he'd still be close by," said Megan. "And he was. So he was able to helicopter out to meet me in record time. He arrived even before Fyfe revived anyone."

"Must be nice to be able to get a helicopter on short notice," said Heather.

"It *can* come in handy," admitted Girdler.

"The colonel planned everything," said Megan. "Thank God for that. If you want to plan a deception, you can't do better than having the head of PsyOps on your side. So *I* didn't capture Cowan. He did. With mind reading intel from Nick, which I passed along. Colonel

Girdler came up with the idea for the candle." She beamed. "You have to admit—*that* was pretty cool."

Heather grinned. "Cool in a demented, horrific, Rube-Goldberg-device sort of way, for sure. But given I was handcuffed in a panic room with a madman at the time, I have to admit I was a big admirer."

"Me too," said Altschuler.

"It wasn't real," said Girdler. "We bought the containers of lighter fluid, but the casserole dish was filled with water. And the blanket and Cowan were soaked in water as well. Once we filmed the scene, I had a colleague helicopter in from Edwards Air Force Base and take Cowan to an interrogation facility."

A half smile played across Girdler's face. "So the burning alive thing was just stagecraft," he said. "The *real* key to all of this was getting Fyfe out of the panic room. Before he killed anyone. Inside, there was no way we could touch him. Not if we wanted any of the innocent hostages to survive."

"Speaking on behalf of the innocent hostages," said Heather, "I'm glad this was a consideration."

"So you presented a credible hostage exchange scenario and lured him out," said Altschuler. "Knowing that he wouldn't feel the least bit nervous going head to head against Megan." He shook his head. "I knew the bastard would never let us walk. I thought Megan was being naive."

"She knew he'd never let you walk as well," said Girdler. "She was being naive on *purpose*. To make sure Fyfe was comfortable walking into our trap. And we have Nick Hall to thank for helping me get the drop on Fyfe, by the way."

"Really?" said Heather. "You do know he was unconscious at the time, right?"

"Saving the day while out cold *is* pretty impressive," said Megan with a grin. "But it was obviously his ability to plan ahead that did it. If I was going to be a fail-safe, Nick figured I might need a way back in. In case the, ah . . . *waste* . . . hit the fan. So he reprogrammed Tanya. To ignore me leaving. And, if she ever detected me *returning*, to immediately unlock the back door and ignore any breach there."

Altschuler laughed. "This has to be the cleverest group of people I've ever known," he said. "How brilliant is *that?* So that's why you came in the *front* door like you did. I thought you were crazy."

"Sure enough," said Megan, "as soon as Tanya's cameras saw me approach the front door, she unlocked the back door as programmed, allowing the colonel to slip right in. While Fyfe was preoccupied at the front of the house, convinced he had the upper hand and that I was a fool, I got the last laugh."

"Incredible!" said Altschuler in admiration.

The room fell quiet as each member of the group reflected on how flawlessly Megan and the colonel had carried out their plan. Only sips of coffee broke the perfect silence.

"I have an idea," said Girdler. "The three of you have had quite a traumatic day. Why don't you shower, get into fresh clothes, and we can reconvene when Nick is awake."

"That sounds great," said Heather. "I guess you really do have a knack for planning."

60

Hall's eyes fluttered open. After a short while, he realized he was on the couch in the living room of the Sacramento safe house. A splattering of dried blood was on the front door and a trail of blood ran across the carpet, as though a recently deceased body had been dragged through.

Hall seized on the first mind he came to, belonging to Alex Altschuler, and quickly read what had happened, learning that his assessment had been correct.

Fyfe was dead!

They had outmaneuvered a grandmaster. They had stopped a man who was, without question, the most dangerous threat the West had ever encountered. Hall was ecstatic.

His mood was elevated even further when Megan, realizing he was awake, threw herself into his arms. They kissed, even knowing they were putting on a show, and then she sat down beside him, beaming. Heather and Alex, seated on the couch across from them, were smiling from ear to ear. Even the colonel, seated in a chair to the left of the couches, was in high spirits.

"Welcome back, Nick," said Megan, uttering the first words spoken since he had come to. "Did you already use your ESP to learn what happened?"

Hall nodded. "I did." When he had regained consciousness in the panic room, Megan had let him know telepathically that she was now working with Girdler, and described their plan. And while he had expected to be able to witness it unfold himself, he was thrilled to read how flawlessly it had gone. "What happened is that you saved my sorry ass. Again! You know what, Megan? I have an almost ir-resistible urge to tell you that I love you. How psycho is that?" he added playfully, but in such a way that he knew Megan would realize this hadn't been said entirely in jest.

"Hey," she complained, recognizing this exact line from the fake letter she had written. "That's plagiarism. That was some of my best work."

Hall laughed. If he could read her mind, he suspected that some of the letter was truer than she would like to admit. But what he had said to Alex was true also. He was never going to let this one get away. Never. Even *pretending* that she had left him had been a brutal blow to his psyche.

Hall turned to the colonel. "Thanks for helping Megan on this one," he said. "And especially for not killing me."

Hall could read that as upset as Girdler was by the *Iowa Gazette* story, he was also happy that the story was effectively a last-second pardon for Hall. At least now the colonel felt like he was on the right side of things, *helping* innocent people rather than trying to kill them. Now all he had to do was avert a possible global catastrophe. Hall also read that the group had filled Girdler in on Alex's recent implant surgery while they were waiting for him to regain consciousness, so the colonel knew that ESP and cybersurfing were not two sides of the same coin.

Hall took Megan's hand in his and turned to face her. "And thanks to you for being smart enough to see how that ESP story might have changed things after we were knocked out."

"About that," said Girdler before Megan could respond. He blew out a long breath. "You know what I'm about to say to you, Nick, but for the benefit of everyone else, I'll still say it. Even though I don't want to kill you, I'm afraid I also can't let you be cured of ESP. The arms race is about to begin. The e-mail you sent to reporters, in conjunction with the flood of information Fyfe released about Gray's experiments and the implants, is just too credible for the world to ignore. This arms race will be well under the radar, but numerous countries will mount programs. They'll start by copying the placement of the implants Theia uses in their clinical trials, and begin tinkering from there. Trying to find the recipe for ESP. With horrible consequences if they do, as we've all discussed."

He leaned in closer to Hall. "So what we have to do now is find an antidote. Which means we need your ESP to be working, so we'll know if we've succeeded. We'll assume someone will eventually find the recipe to unleash ESP, and we'll dedicate ourselves to finding a way to block it. A simple formula we can share with the world. So even if someone does crack the code on the weapon of mass destruction that mind reading represents, we'll have already discovered the shield."

"With Megan being a big part of this effort, correct?" said Hall.

"I don't know if you cheated on that or not, but that's right."

From Megan's expression, it was clear this was a new one on her.

"Because she's immune," whispered Heather, having figured it out. "That's why she's so important."

"Yes," said Girdler. "She's naturally resistant. There will be others in this category as well, but she'll be the only one in the inner sanctum. But she, and these others, will be the key. We have to discover why they're immune. Study their genes, their DNA. Test them. Study the nature of their resistance. Hopefully it's something simple. But we can't rest until we find it. And when we do, if there's ever any evidence that ESP is out of the bag, we can give it freely to the world."

"Until then," said Heather, "just how secret is this program going to be?"

Girdler frowned. "You know the old joke that goes, 'It's so secret, if I told you, I'd have to kill you?' Well, in this case, it really isn't so much of a joke. Please keep that in mind. The five of us in this room, and my second-in-command, Major Mike Campbell, will be the only ones to ever know about this. I'd hate to kill someone over being a leak, but I will." He gestured toward Hall. "Nick?"

"I'm afraid he's serious," confirmed Hall. He smiled at the colonel. "But the good news, Colonel, is that I'm reading their minds as well—everyone's but Megan's—and they *will* keep this secret."

"I'm sure they will," said Girdler. He paused for a moment and then changed the subject. "It looks like Alex will be the new CEO of Theia Labs now that Fyfe is gone."

The colonel turned to Altschuler and raised his eyebrows. "You'll be a multi-billionaire, Alex. One who secretly knows about top secret government research. More than that, since you are one of only six in the know, and a genius, we'd love to tap you as a consultant from time to time. You can be like Bruce Wayne. Mild-mannered billionaire CEO in the daytime—"

"Yeah," interrupted Hall, cringing. "Please don't go there. Fyfe made a reference to Batman earlier today that kind of pissed us all off."

"Really?" said Girdler. "Two Batman references in a row?" He looked puzzled. "And what could piss anyone off about Batman, anyway?"

Seeing the expressions around the room, he decided to move on. "Okay, forget that I said that. But we would greatly appreciate your intellectual input, Alex. I think you know how important this is."

"You've got it," said Altschuler.

The colonel nodded his thanks. "Nick and Megan, I'm afraid you're going to have to come work with me and Mike Campbell on a more full-time basis. I wish I could give you a choice in the matter, but I can't. There's only one acceptable answer in this case, and that is, 'I'd love to cooperate with you, Colonel."

Hall glanced at Megan. "I'd love to cooperate with you, Colonel," they both said in unison.

"Outstanding," said Girdler. "So here's the way I see things going forward. We get out of here. Mike Campbell is on his way and will burn this place to the ground with Fyfe in it. We'll also plant two corpses and change Nick's and Megan's dental records to match them, so it looks like they were caught in the blaze as well. Everyone but the five of us and Major Campbell need to believe this is true, including my boss, General Sobol. When Alex learns of the tragic loss of Nick Hall and Cameron Fyfe—and there's no need for anyone to ever know Fyfe's true identity, or his purpose, by the way—he assumes the CEO position. Even before this, he needs to cast doubt on the ESP story as best he can." Girdler sighed. "Good luck with *that*, Alex. Not an easy assignment."

"Thanks," grumbled Altschuler.

"Alex, I'll also want you, as CEO, to work with me to begin talks in Congress on how best to police the web surfing technology. Fyfe's plans were pretty damn scary. I'm convinced there's no way to stop the implants from happening. And I'm not convinced we would want to if we could. But we do need triple redundancy safeguards at every level of software and production. And a series of nested Firewalls will need to be designed to be just as foolproof and secure as this. We need to be absolutely certain that nothing like Fyfe had planned could ever happen."

"Amen to that," said Altschuler. "I would be honored to lead this charge."

Girdler smiled. "Fantastic. I have to admit, it's going to be fun secretly working with you when you're the mightiest business titan in the world." He paused. "But back to our plans for Nick and Megan. We'll need to change Nick's appearance and set up a facility in a desert somewhere for them. Isolated for more than ten miles so Nick won't hear voices—unless we want him to. We'll bring in support personnel that Nick can't read. We can just line up candidates and Nick can tell us which ones he can't read. We'll hire them."

"Are you going to at least pretend to conduct an interview?" asked Heather with a grin.

"Of course," said Girdler, returning the smile. "Pretending is one of the very best things I do."

Then, serious once again, he continued. "We'll get everything up and running within a few weeks. And then we'll get to work. We'll learn everything we can about Nick's abilities and how to block them. Nick, you know I'm doing this to stop ESP, not to use it, but there may be the odd time I need you for an interrogation. I'll try to keep this to the bare minimum."

Hall read that Girdler was sincere in this regard. If a terrorist knew the location of a nuke that was about to detonate, Girdler reserved the right to have Hall invade his mind for the information. Hall had no problem with this. In fact, given what he had come to know about the Abdullah brothers, he couldn't wait to get in range of a man who had called himself Ed Cowan. "I understand," said Nick.

"Thank you," said Girdler. "Megan, you won't be engaged full-time in these experiments, so we'll give you a change of identity. You can still be the owner of a graphic design firm, just a different firm, under a different name, which you can locate in offices next to Nick. I'll make sure you get as much graphic design work from the US military as you can handle. If you're one-tenth as impressive a graphic designer as you are a fugitive, then we'll be in great hands."

"Sounds good," said Megan, looking like a kid on Christmas morning. "Thanks."

"But regardless," continued Girdler, "the two of you will have to spend a lot of time together. In close quarters. A *lot* of time." An amused smile came over his face. "Is that going to be a problem?"

Hall realized he was still holding Megan's hand. He looked across at the opposite couch and noticed that Heather and Alex were holding hands as well. Megan had told him she thought there must be something in the water, and it was hard not to agree. Something that had turned four adults into giddy seventh graders. Holding hands? *Who did that anymore?*

And even though he wasn't trying to pry, he couldn't help but read that Heather and Alex were crazy for each other, and not on the superficial level on which Hall had once operated, but on the level he believed he had finally achieved with Megan.

No, spending time with Megan Emerson was not going to be a problem. The only problem would be his time away from her. "No. I think I can tolerate her for a little while," he said with an impish smile. "You know, Neanderthal that she is."

"*Really?*" said Girdler. "*That's* the way to a woman's heart? Calling her a Neanderthal? That must be where I've been going wrong with women all these years."

"Well, there is a back-story involved," said Hall sheepishly.

"Good. You'll have plenty of time to tell me all about it in the months and years ahead. But for now, let's go figure out a way to safeguard the world from psionic monsters like you. Shall we?"

From the Author: *Thanks for reading MIND'S EYE!* As always, if you enjoyed this novel, I would be grateful for your help spreading the word. Please consider writing a sentence or two about the book on your favorite retail site, or on your Facebook page, so that others will know what's in store for them. When I published my first tech-nothriller, *WIRED*, I expected that only a handful of people would ever read it. But when a word-of-mouth explosion led to the novel going viral, I gained firsthand knowledge of how much the world has changed. I discovered that in today's world, readers, rather than just New York City publishers, have the power to determine a novel's fate. Without a doubt, any success I have achieved in the writing realm is entirely due to the help and support of my readers, and I will never forget this.

If you would like to write to me, my e-mail address is doug@san.rr.com. Also, if you would like to stay current on my activities, please feel free to Friend me on Facebook at Douglas E. Richards Author.

Also by Douglas E. Richards
WIRED (Technothriller/Science-fiction)
AMPED (The WIRED Sequel)
THE CURE (Technothriller/Science-fiction)
MIND'S EYE (Technothiller/Science-fiction)

Middle Grade/YA (Enjoyed by kids and adults alike)
THE PROMETHEUS PROJECT SERIES (Science Fiction Thrillers)

Book 1: *TRAPPED*
Book 2: *CAPTURED*
Book 3: *STRANDED*

THE DEVIL'S SWORD (Mainstream Thriller)
ETHAN PRITCHER, BODY SWITCHER
OUT OF THIS WORLD (Science Fiction/Fantasy)

ABOUT THE AUTHOR

Douglas E. Richards has been widely praised for his ability to weave action, suspense, and science into riveting novels that straddle the thriller and science fiction genres. He is the *New York Times* and *USA Today* bestselling author of *WIRED, AMPED, THE CURE,* and *MIND'S EYE.* He has also written six middle grade/young adult novels widely acclaimed for their appeal to boys, girls, and adults alike. A former biotech executive, Richards earned a BS in microbiology from the Ohio State University, a master's degree in genetic engineering from the University of Wisconsin (where he engineered mutant viruses now named after him), and an MBA from the University of Chicago.

In recognition of his work, Richards was selected to be a "special guest" at San Diego Comic-Con International, along with such icons as Stan Lee and Ray Bradbury. He has written numerous feature articles for the award-winning magazine, *National Geographic KIDS*—some having appeared in a dozen languages in as many as sixteen countries—as well as essays for the BBC, The Australian Broadcasting Corporation, Earth & Sky, Today's Parent, and many others.

The author currently lives in San Diego, California, with his wife, two children, and two dogs.